I'm Spartacus

DAVID ORD

Book Publishing.com

Editing, design, typesetting and publishing by UK Book Publishing

www.ukbookpublishing.com

ISBN: 978-1-917329-39-2

Eleven years of Thatcher,
Eleven years of hell,
Eleven years of heartache,
And dispare aswell,
Eleven years of cutbacks
mines factories even a town,
For eleven years Thatcher
had kept the working class down,
Thatcher, Thatcher, Thatcher,
dictator from the right,
You got rid of the enemy within us,
those who weren't a Thatcherite,
Thatcher, Thatcher, Thatcher,
oh what a terrifying name,
You led our poor into poverty,
You should have hung your head in shame.

Prelude

It was a balmy, mid-July morning at Easington Colliery. A couple of smartly dressed, elderly men strolled at leisure alongside their two young grandsons through well-manicured grounds of a cemetery, with each of the young lads holding onto almost identical red and white flowery wreaths. One of these chaps was Tom Gilroy, a bald-headed guy with a wide neck that tallied a frame which was plump, not unhealthy plump, but nevertheless it was still plump. Tom's grandson Robert was no older than eight, and flourished a hale and hearty freckled face that was married to a mop of radiant red hair and piercing blue eyes. The other elderly gentleman was Jack Gilroy, Tom's junior sibling, who stood notably taller to that of his brother while possessing a full head of silver hair that fitted a distinguished, well-trimmed goatee beard. Young Steve, Jack's grandson, was a little older than the other boy, perhaps ten, and was a rather gangly-looking kid who exhibited a healthy body of hair which shone black, complementing violet-coloured eyes that were highlighted by thick, jet eyelashes.

Pausing... wreaths were laid at the foot of a freshly embedded headstone showing, Irene Gilroy, born 23/03/1939 died 11/06/2023... aged eighty-four. Stepping back a pace, both men were stood in deep thought when Tom whispered, "A' carn't believe it's over a year since she left us."

Jack squeezed his brother's shoulder, comforting, "A' nar, young'n, it's absolutely flown ower."

Tom nodded towards the headstone, asking, "Well, what do ya think of it then?"

Jack slowly ran his eyes over the gravestone, puffing. "It's grand enough alright, but it still doesn't seem to do Ma any justice, it doesn't show any evidence or nowt about what she stood for, let alone what she had achieved in her life."

"What headstone ever did," uttered Tom amidst a deep sigh.

Robert pointed out, "What's that picture on Nanna's headstone, Grandad?"

"That's a Sunderland Football Club crest," laughed Tom.

"No, not that one, Grandad, that other one."

Tom rubbed the boy's head. "Orr that!? That's a coal miners' safety lamp, that is, son."

"What's coal miners?" came next from the youngster.

Tom sighed, drawn-out. "I'll tell ya what coal miners are, sorry lad, what they were, they were a once proud, salt of the earth breed of men, who worked damned hard in the bowels of the earth digging out coal to keep the likes of all our power stations producing electricity, and sometimes they even worked seven miles or more out underneath the North Sea, just like me and your Uncle Jack used to do."

"Wow!" enthused the lad. "Did you not get wet, Grandad?"

Casting a grin he tittered, "Sometimes a' did, Robert, sometimes a' did."

Jack smiled widely, adding, "Aye but if we did manage to get wet, I made damn sure we got paid an extra ninety pence a shift wet money though."

Steve looked up at Jack, hesitantly asking, "So, why aren't there anymore coal miners left now for, Granda?"

"'Coss an evil owld bugger called Maggie Thatcher decided to thraw them all onto the scrapheap of life, that's why, bonnie lad."

Robert squinted inquisitively at Jack, questioning, "Was she eviller than what Darth Vader and Voldemort were, Uncle Jack?"

"Who, Maggie Thatcher!? Why aye! She was ten times worse than what them two were! She had ya poor Granda and me out on strike for a whole year, that one did."

Robert puckered, confused. "What... is a strike?"

"A' know what one is," broke in Steve all enthusiastic.

Jack ruffled Robert's hair, explaining, "A strike is when ya down tools and stop working, son, when ya're in a dispute over wage rises, or other things like better working conditions and that." He blew deep, continuing, "But way back in 1984, well, it was a different kettle of fish altogether that was, ya see we were fighting for our pure existence then, fighting to keep our pits open so we could preserve our humble way of life."

Steve looked at the headstone, saying, "Grandma Lucy said Nanna helped feed all the striking miners and their families during that strike; did she, Granda?"

"She did that, lad," chuckled Jack, "she helped feed all of Easington's miners and their families throughout the entirety of the strike."

Tom eyed Jack, asking, "How's the drilling business gan'n, young'n?"

"It's ticking ower nicely, how's the farm macking out?"

"Great, the lads are more or less running the place on their own, I've taken a well-earned step back since Pat had her mini stroke." Tom smiled at his brother, asking, "Are ya still putting up with Hoss and Billy at work then?"

"Why aye!" Jack grinned broadly, cackling, "Nowt's changed there, a's still mollycoddling the owld buggers, just like a've done all me life!"

"Ya going to have to fetch the family down to the farm, Jack, the Peak District's so lovely at this time of the year."

"A' might just do that, young'n, Lucy's always bending me ear about us popping down, but it's finding the time and getting them all together, what with our Irene running her own radio station, and our Tom and Julie both solicitors." Puffing his cheeks, he added, "A' suppose our Jack could had the fort at work till a' got back, like, but then again he's got no interest at becoming a gaffer, all he wants to do is drill all day, pull the birds, and gan abroad on holidays with his mates, the bugger's got no inkling of responsibilities whatsoever, loopy as a judge on the sherry so that one is."

Tom snorted. "A' wonder where he gets that from then?"

"God... nars!" moaned Jack, shrugging his shoulders in bewilderment. "It baffles me, Lucy says it's because he's the youngest and he unexpectedly came along late in our lives."

The four were sat at a bench when Robert looked to his grandfather, asking, "Tell me about this strike thing, Grandad, what did Nanna actually do again? And what did you and Uncle Jack get up to?"

"Yeah! Tell us, Uncle Tom!" urged wide-eyed young Steve.

Handing around apples, Tom glanced mischievously at Jack to be met by an even wickeder beam. "Gan on then!" whooped Jack. "It's your story!"

Eyeing the boys, Tom sighed lengthily, saying, "Well, it all started a long time ago–"

"Aye, but it wasn't in a galaxy far, far away though," broke in Jack, much to Tom's annoyance, "it was just down the bottom of the street there."

Tom side eyed his brother, moaning, "Are ya ganna let is tell this story or what!?"

Jack bit into an apple, spluttering, "Aye, by all means carry on... but ya canit start a story off like that, man... grumpy!" .....

I'm Spartacus

CHAPTER ONE, MAY, "H-H-HELEN OF TROY WAS!"

In the East Durham pit village of Easington Colliery, at number two Cuba Street, Irene Gilroy mopped her brow before sliding a chop board full of finely sliced onions into a large, cream coloured enamel crock to join chicken breasts, mushrooms, and other appetising ingredients. After placing the dish into her oven, she fidgeted a cooker dial prior to dragging her feet from out of an olive-hued kitchen. Entering into an emerald sitting room, she paused at a flowery chimney breast to examine her face through a slightly misted-up wall mirror, which hung a little off centre between a plastic framed print of a lustful Spanish senorita, and a lopsided portrait of Pope John Paul II. At the heart of the mantelpiece, a traditional carriage clock whispered away time by the graciousness of soft ticking and was flanked by an assortment of family photographs, including a recent framed photo showing Irene standing proud between Jack and Tom, her two grown up sons. At one end of a stone hearth an authentic miners' lamp faced a horseshoe-shaped companion set where a selection of brass tools dangled, consisting of a short poker, a slightly singed hearth brush, mini shovel, toasting fork, and a set of grippy coal tongs. At the other side of the fireside, a miniature statuette of a pitman was on show alongside an impressive brass sculpture of a rearing Mustang stallion, that burnished to a streak-free sheen. A set of mahogany wall lights were unlit inside an attached alcove where a trio of ornamental brass plates dressed a wall with each salver exhibiting eye-catching etchings of ancient sailing galleons. Aside these shiny platters hung a special photograph showing a headshot of Thomas Garside, Irene's once-handsome elder brother, who, at the age of only twenty, had been tragically killed in a horrific pit explosion at Easington Colliery, along with another eighty of his fellow coal miners, and an additional two members of a miners' rescue team.

After a quick wipe of the mirror, Irene stepped closer to inspect faint lines which had recently crept across her forehead, and not for the first time she was convincing herself that these furrows were growing deeper by the day. Oblivious to Irene, was how her warm, azure eyes set off soft Celtic freckles, and a mass of auburn hair which fell in a slight whorl to rest just above her waistline. Fidgeting with her blouse, she thought that, even though she had kept her figure trim over the years, she somehow felt much older than forty-five, and this was mainly down to the anguish of nursing her husband through a long, but devastatingly losing battle with throat cancer. Blowing a sigh, Irene glanced at a trio of her wedding day photographs, thinking how it would be four years this July since her husband Robert had passed away; yes, July 3rd, 1980, was a date that was forever rooted within her thoughts.

Puffing out her cheeks, she slumped herself into her favourite armchair, and it didn't take long for her to lose herself amidst the soporific flames of the fire. Reflections of happy times long gone brought about a pensive smile before reality kicked in and she yawned drawn-out while idly contemplating changing the décor from green to magnolia, or perhaps terracotta. Within an instant, all thoughts of decorating were cast aside, as for some strange reason it had slipped her mind what her two sons had wanted ironing for their ritual Friday night out; grinning slightly, it came back: black trousers and a white dress shirt for Tom, denim dungarees and a yellow tee-shirt for Jack. Her beam stretched ever so slightly as she reflected on how her two lads were as different as chalk and cheese; even the manner in which they were born differed, as Tom came into the world without any fuss whatsoever, Jack on the other hand, well, he had allegedly managed to gnaw the midwife on both thumbs as he arrived kicking and screaming with all guns blazing.

Tom, at twenty-seven, was the eldest of Irene's two sons, and she would be the first to admit he could be a little grumpy at times, but generally he was a very sensible, well-mannered young man who, despite his blushing coyness around the opposite sex, was quite popular within the community. Chuckling to herself, she deliberated how his crooked, boxer-like nose, chiselled chin, and receding red hair were all attributes he had inherited from her side of the family, yes, a true Garside was Tom, for he stood just over six feet parading strapping shoulders, and eyes that were honest blue. Widening her smile she thought how her eldest somehow resembled Great-uncle Victor, an illustrious actor from the silver screen who participated in an unforgettable fight scene with John Wayne in that classic film, 'The Quiet Man'. Whether or not Victor McLaglen was actually related to the Garsides was undoubtably questionable, but, truth, Garside truth, or pure fabrication, it made no difference to Irene, for it was her father himself who had regaled her all her life with a combination of hilarious and heroic yarns regarding Great-uncle Victor's escapades, and this was more than good enough to convince her that Great-uncle Victor was indeed a Garside.

If Tom had the Garsides' hereditary features bestowed upon him, then Jack boasted the Gilroys' genes for sure, for at twenty-four he towered six feet-three and was blessed with a dark complexion and a lean, yet muscular physique. His lengthy black hair shone healthily, topping off strong facial features including a distinctive Kirk Douglas dimpled chin, high cheekbones, and hazel coloured puppy dog eyes that were marble clear and enhanced within long, inky eyelashes. Despite his Hollywood handsomeness, Jack was a renowned brawler who was without doubt the alpha male within the village, yet still, he boasted another reputation, that of a womaniser, for unlike his brother, he was so at ease around the ladies, and with him possessing a certain kind of brashness that went hand in hand with his film star looks, he found it ever so natural to flirt with eager females.

While she would never admit it, Irene sometimes wished Tom would carry some of Jack's poise, but then again, she often wanted Jack to adopt more of Tom's principles too. With both her sons coal miners, who were currently on strike, Irene was ever so proud of them, but at the same time it was always at the back of her mind that the longer Thatcher allowed this dispute to linger, the more chance it had of turning nasty, and if doing so, it would only be a matter of time before Jack's rebellious, devil-may-care attitude would land him in serious trouble, and worse still, he would probably drag Tom down with him too.

Irene glanced from her window onto a murky May morning. Lighting up a cigarette, she inhaled deeply as she switched on her television set to be faced by Leon Brittan, who was in the midst of mouthing off a scathing attack on Arthur Scargill and his fellow miners, who had struck without a ballot in response to a list of pit closures sought by the current British Coal president Ian MacGregor. Promptly, she aimed a TV remote, grousing, "It's ower early to be listening to that bugger!" then, pressing a red button, the dodgy Home Secretary faded into darkness. Standing, she was on poking the fire when the sound of Mick, her spoilt Jack Russell terrier, was heard scurrying across the kitchen canvas prior to him popping his head warily around the side of a sitting room door. Irene took one look at him, scorning,

"Where've you been!? Ya better not have been rolling in that cow muck again mind!?" and the thought of yet another dreadful bath sent the canine cowering to a shiver as he ogled back and forth between Irene, and the sanctuary of the back of a settee. "Don't you dare, Mick!" she ordered, but, as Mick had so often done in the past, his choice was to bolt to the refuge of a gap between a wall, and the rear of the sofa. Irene snuffled at the nauseating smell. "Ya stink to high heaven! You just wait and see, ya going straight in that bath after I've banked the fire up!" Leaving the house, she blew sharply as she stooped to one side, retrieving a rusty hand shovel from a doorstep before scurrying a yard to face a coalhouse where she tugged open a weather-beaten door to be taken aback at the sight of several plastic bags that were huge, and each filled to the brim with coils and coils of cut up copper wiring. "Where the hell's all this come from!?" she whinged, as she struggled to drag a weighty bag to one side, and after just about managing to scrape up a half-filled shovel of coal, she shook her head with a prolonged sigh, moaning, "Wait 'till a' see that bloody Jack!"

The pit gates were the main entrance of three to the coal mine at Easington Colliery, and this ingress was barricaded end to end with a concoction of upturned pit tubs, a couple of lengths of Heras fencing, rusty girders, a length of metal spiked fencing, railway rails, and additional fragments of heavy scrap metal and other weighty stuff. To the rear of the obstruction, a traditional picket line fire burned to a glow inside an oxidized drum which was warped, and almost ready to implode upon itself. Directly behind the pyre stood a makeshift cabin that was erected more than a tad skewed with the words 'the Alamo' painted across its frontage. Adjacent to this shelter, Jack Gilroy's old Ford flatbed buffed to navy-blue and chrome and was loaded to three-quarters capacity with numerous sacks of coal, whilst at the crown of a slight incline stretched a drawn-out wooden building that was stained oily black and home to all of the colliery's trade union offices.

Under the density of an overcast morning, Jack and Tom Gilroy exited the Alamo cabin to stand by a fire when Tom nudged his brother with a smile as he pointed out a cocky robin warbling gaily whilst proudly brandishing his handsome breast. Curling up the lapel on his donkey jacket, he moaned, "It's still as card as Thatcher's tits out here mind, Jack..." Tom's accent wasn't that of a typical Newcastle Geordie, or indeed the dialect of a Mackem from the nearby town of Sunderland, it was its own unique East Durham pitmatic twang. He continued, "... and it looks like it's ganna rain again."

"Tell is about it," agreed Jack, juddering up a shiver, "it's supposed to be May, and it's frigging freezing!" Jack turned his collar to the wind as he looked eastwards across the pit yard in the direction of a scattering of coal heaps that slightly hindered a backdrop dominated by the North Sea, which today stirred white topped and angry grey. Standing fidgety he checked his watch, raising, "A' wonder what's keeping them two?"

"God nars, but it's ganna have to be the last run, if Cunningsy–" Tom side-eyed attention to the truck– "sees all of them bags of coal in the back of that thing he's ganna have a right dicky fit!"

"Fuck him!" snapped Jack. "It's got nowt to do with him what's in the back of my truck; besides, half the colliery's nicking coal, it's not just us tha nars!"

"Aye but they're only tacking a bag or two at a time ta keep their homes warm, there's a canny difference ta what we're doing."

"There's no difference whatsoever."

"Jack, man, there is a difference! For a kick off they're not pinching a grit truck full every day to sell. I'm telling ya now, if the union finds out what we're doing we'll be in front of that committee quicker than shit off a stick–"

"Ballicks committee!" interrupted Jack, blowing a defiant sigh. "They're nowt but a bunch of crinkly ard farts, if they think a'm ganna stand around here bored shitless for six hours a' day for a measly couple of quid, well, they've got another thing coming."

"Another thing coming!?" repeated Tom in slight sarcasm before asking, "Why's that, like!? Everyone gets paid the same when they're on picket duty!"

"Picket duty my arse! If a' can get coal I'm getting it, simple as!" retorted Jack, much to his brother's annoyance.

"Any...way," stretched from Tom as he picked up a shovel to cast coal into the heart of the fire, "what if security finds out what's gan'n on, we'll lose our jobs for sure."

"Security!?" Jack hastily jigged to one side in avoidance of the billowing smoke. "Ya having a giraffe, aren't ya!? They're worse than us, them lot are, they're nowt but a bunch of thieving little toerags!" Offering a cigarette, he mellowed saying, "Give ower worrying, man, everything'll be fine."

"Something'll gan rang," groaned Tom, angling the shovel against the cabin, "you mark my words it will, it always does." After lighting up, he presented a flame. "And we'll have to get rid of all that copper wire an'all, if it ever gets out it was us who nicked that cable last night, God nars what'll happen, probably's jail."

"I've already told ya twice that'll be gone by Sunday, I'm weighing it in then."

"Why mack sure ya do!" Squinting beyond towering pitheads that mothered over the rooftops like a couple of mechanical parents, Tom inhaled deep on his cig uttering, "Here they are now."

"It's about bloody time an'll!" Jack drew long on his own cig. "They've been gone frigging yonks!"

In the distance, Hoss and Billy Ward struggled to push a rickety old bicycle that was overloaded with several sacks of coal. Hoss was at the front steering as he leant against the hefty bags in an attempt to counterbalance the weight; at the same time Billy laboured, pushing on a saddle while straddling a wobblily back wheel that juddered out protest by means of a sequence of rhythmical squeaks.

Hoss stood six feet-four, tipping the scales at well over eighteen stones, and even though he was a little chubby he was an extremely powerful man with a natural strength that was renowned throughout Easington Colliery. His hair was mousy coloured and swept back in no specific style to rest above a neck that was healthily thick, tallying enormous shoulders and huge arms that were naturally strong, and not gym enhanced. Aged twenty-seven, Hoss' real name was Martin Breester, but ever since his teenage days he had assumed the nickname of Hoss, because of his uncanny resemblance to Dan Blocker, an actor who took the part of Eric 'Hoss' Cartwright in a popular cowboy series called 'Bonanza'.

Hoss and Tom Gilroy's friendship stretched way back to the pram; but truth be known he was more like a family member to the Gilroys than an actual friend as Irene had taken him under her maternal wing ever since his own mother had sadly passed away when Hoss had not long started at the infants school.

Aged twenty-four, Billy Ward was Jack Gilroy's lifelong pal. He was quite a puny-looking redhead brandishing a heavily freckled face and a slightly turned up nose, his lips were rounded, complementing brown eyes that simply cried out honesty. Due to an abusive, and often violent upbringing he had suffered as a child, Billy was left with a stammer that could be intense at times, but despite his so-called speech impediment, he maintained a very dry, witty sense of humour. Unlike Jack, Billy was never sporty, as it was reading which partook most of his spare time, and with every word Billy read, the information he absorbed stayed with him, resulting in him becoming a likable, if occasionally annoying, encyclopaedia on legs. He was married to Marie, and they were blessed with two small girls, Kelly aged four, and Alisia who had just turned two, and with very little income coming into the household, they were more than struggling financially.

Hoss and Billy grappled to force the bicycle through an endless concave of thick industrial slurry before they eventually joined a meandering pathway which zigzagged them up a steepish incline and back towards the pit gates until their arduous journey ended with them leaning the heavily loaded bike up against the side of Jack's truck. Hoss looked to Tom, and in a deep, robust voice he said, "That'll have to be the last run for the day, that bike's just about buggered; besides that, security's on doing their rounds again."

Tom joined them, asking, "How many guards is there, like?"

"At least... half a d-d-dozen..." broke in Billy, slightly out of breath, "...and two of them have dogs an'all... right v-v-vicious looking things they are t-t-too."

"What, the dogs or the guards?" joked Tom, climbing up into the rear of the pickup.

"B-B-Both!" laughed Billy, retrieving a hand shovel from between the sacks to rest it against a back wheel of the truck.

"Aye," sighed Hoss, "and that horrible Nazi-looking fucker who got poor Loll James the sack is with them an'll." Picking up the bags with ease, he handed them up one at a time saying, "They reckon his name's Robert Hardy, apparently, he's from somewhere up Newcastle way."

Jack joined them at the side of the pickup. Scratching the back of his head, he eyed his big friend saying, "I've done some enquiries myself, Hoss, and ya right, that's exactly what his name is, Robert fucking Hardy, and believe you me I'm ganna have the bastard first chance a' get." After lobbing the hand shovel into the back of the truck, Jack looked around the group, griping, "Fancy getting a canny ard man like Loll the sack ower one measly bag of coal, the fucking tosser, and to add insult to injury the twat's a Newcastle United fan too!" Passing up a canvas tarpaulin he looked to his brother, instructing, "Mack sure that sheet's tied down properly this time, will ya?"

"Are ya taking the piss or what!?" barked Tom, glaring at Jack with daggers.

Handing up the old boneshaker, Jack sniggered, "Nar a's not, besides, ya canit tack the piss out of shite."

Tom snatched away the bicycle. "Divan't start! I'm telling ya, mind!"

"Or aye! What's wrong with thuw like, due on again or what?"

"I'm not ganna tell ya again, Jack! Pack the fucker in or I'm ganna wrap that shovel rit 'round ya lug!"

"Chill out, man! I'm anly having a bit fun for Christ's sakes!"

"That's the trouble with thuw," carped Tom, unfolding the sheeting, "ya always having a bit of fun, ya want ta graw up a bit you do, ya think ya so—"

"The pair of yas want ta graw up if ya ask me," interrupted Hoss, "yas are always at each other's throats, I've niver narn two brothers like yas!" After eying disapproval at the brothers, he slowly turned to stride towards the cabin, and as he was passing Jack, he paused in stride to cheekily flick him on the back of his head, whispering, "Give ower winding him up, Jack, he's owlder than you."

Billy joined Jack, asking, "Lend is a t-t-tab, young'n?" just as the union office window creaked open and Alan Cunnings popped his head out.

"Jack! Jack! Get ya arse in here, a want to see ya a minute!"

"Aye two ticks, Alan!" he yelled, handing Billy a cigarette.

"Never mind two ticks! Now! And fetch your young'n with ya!" Alan clashed the window shut prior to crossing a room where he slumped himself into a hoary armchair positioned behind a wonky desk that faltered slightly, despite a couple of coasters wedged to balance beneath one of the legs. The room was dingy and reeked of staleness, with walls decked top to bottom in appalling wood panelling which did anything but match up with a yellow and blue diamond patterned canvas. A small table stood under one of three windows, housing a kettle, a fresh bottle of milk, a three-quarter empty jar of coffee, and an open box of teabags that stood alongside a plastic container which had **Shugar** misspelt across its lid in black felt pen.

Alan Cunnings was the NUM (National Union of Mineworkers) lodge secretary at Easington Colliery. Aged in his mid-forties, he was tall and gangly and proudly sported a thick, black coloured Mexican-style moustache which drew attention to warm eyes of brown, and an ashen complexion, and though Alan was indeed pale skinned, shadowy blotches had started to form under his eyes – whether this was due to lack of sleep, or perhaps the pressure of the strike, God only knows, but one thing was for certain, these puffy splotches weren't there at the start of the dispute. Most of the men at Easington Colliery looked up to Alan, not only for his Socialist beliefs, or even for the way he locked horns with management while defending his members; it was mainly down to his uprightness, and the virtues he displayed at being an all-round good guy. Easing himself further into his chair, he rested his size elevens upon the desktop just as Tom and Jack drifted into the office, where Tom sat across the desk while Jack parked his backside onto a stone-cold radiator asking, "What's tha after, Alan?"

"I'll tell ya what a's after, Jack, yas haven't heard owt about a hundred-metre electric feed cable gan'n missing sometime during the night, have yas?"

"Nor!" he answered, shaking his head all mystified. "Has one gone missing like?"

"Why aye one's gone missing! That's why I'm asking ya for!" Alan leant over the desktop staring Tom directly in the eye. "Have you heard owt?"

Tom shook his head in denial, gulping, "Nor, I've never heard nowt, how do ya nar one's gone missing like?"

"How!? I'll tell ya how! Because they found the remains of a fucker burnt out behind the allotments early this morning with all the copper core stripped away, that's how, and–"

"Howld on here," broke in Jack indignantly, "ya not trying to blame us for this, are ya?"

"No, I'm not trying to blame ya's at all, I'm just asking if ya's have heard owt?"

"Why we haven't!" snapped Jack, crossing his arms all defensive. "And it sounds to me like ya are trying to blame us an'll!"

"Well, a's not, I'm just–"

Clearing his throat, Tom cut Alan short, asking, "Have ya asked them who were on picket duty last night if they've heard owt? Seeing as that's when it allegedly went missing."

Alan sighed. "Nor not yet, who was on duty like?"

Tom rhymed off, "Davy Bennett, Peter Hall, Micky Gray, Ger Pye, Stephen Gillan, and Nobby, at least a' think it was Nobby, a' could be wrang mind ya, it may well have been Bob English not Nobby, anyway it was one or the other."

"It'll have nowt to do with them," muttered Jack.

"A' nar that," groaned Alan, "but some buggers took it, a' mean the bloody thing didn't just graw a set of legs ower night and decide to tack itsell for a walk down to the allotments and set fire to itsell! Did it!? Thousands of pounds them bloody things cost!"

"How much!?" frowned Jack, astounded.

Alan's eyes rolled to Jack, repeating, "Thousands of pounds! The police are involved and everything, it's like a scene from 'Murder She Wrote', down them allotments, the law's all ower the bloody place. They wadn't even let poor Hoss' dad gan down to his pigeon loft this morning to let his birds out..."

Jack couldn't stop himself from bursting out giggling, even Tom struggled to conceal his laughter.

Alan shook his head continuing, "... hey! It's not funny, lads! Joe's got pigeons away next weekend and he canit even get them up for exercise!"

Still chuckling, Jack looked at Alan, mumbling, "Thuw wants to give ower worrying about cables gan'n missing thuw does, it's not your job to worry about owt like that, it's managements, you watch, ya'll be giving ya sell a blinking heart attack one of these days."

"Tell is about it! I've got enough on me plate with this bloody strike, niver mind worrying about all this shit. And to top things off a' think I've got Amnesia."

"Amnesia?" frowned Tom, befuddled.

"Aye..." Alan paused for a while thinking up the right words. "... tha nars, when all ya hair and that drops out due to anxiety. Well, I'm telling ya now, mine's coming out by the handfuls, it's dropping out like there's ne tomorrow."

"That's Alopecia" sniggered Jack, "not Amnesia, ya daft bugger, and ya haven't got that, ya just gan'n bald, that's all."

"Aye whatever, Jack, but I'm telling yas now, all this stress is affecting me health, a' can hear me heart pounding me chist on a night when a's trying to gan to sleep, not to mention me ulcers, they're absolutely bubbling them buggers are. You just wait and see, one of these days I'm ganna gan off in a right ard pop, and will anyone be bothered, will they heckers like!"

Jack sniggered, "Ya getting as bad as Lemsip, thuw is lately."

Alan's eyes narrowed. "What's tha mean by that, like!?"

"Why, man, tha's always complaining about some sort of illness, ya just like what he is."

"Aye but Lemsip's ailments are all in his head, Jack, mine's not, mine's genuine."

"Aye whatever!" sighed Jack, unconvinced, before he scrutinized Alan. "Having said that like, ya do look a little bit peaky." He turned to Tom. "Think he looks a bit under the weather, young'n?"

Tom squinted. "Aye ya're a bit pasty like, Alan, are ya feeling all right?"

"Why a's not now, am a'!" Alan sat monitoring his own pulse by means of a finger on his wrist. "Me hearts gan'n like a tanner watch here, a' bet me blood pressure's rit up through the roof again."

Tom eased. "It might be just the run of the mill thieves that's took that cable tha nars, Alan, it might have nowt to do with anyone we nar."

"Aye," concurred Jack, "there's some right dodgy bastards kicking about out there on a night-time, I'll tell ya!"

"That's true!" grumped Alan just as the phone started ringing. "Morning, Easington Colliery NUM, Alan Cunnings speaking... hello Irene... two ticks, pet lamb, I'll ask him now... no, it's no bother whatsoever, he's standing right in front of me as we speak." Smiling broadly, Alan covered up the mouthpiece on the phone, whispering, "It's ya Ma, Jack, she wants to know where ya yeller tee-shirt is 'coss she can't find it to iron for ya for the night, apparently it's not on the ironing pile where she left it."

Jack raised his jumper. "Tell her I've got it on, ask her if she'll do me purple one instead, please?"

Alan spoke back into the phone, "He's wearing it, Irene, and he wants to know if you could iron his purple shirt instead... right... right... right I'll tell him." Once again, he faced Jack muttering, "She says ya shouldn't be wearing that shirt, Jack, it's not ironed, and she'll be the place's talk."

He laughed. "Aye right owe. Orr! Ask her what's for tea, Alan?"

"Irene, your Jack wants to know what's for tea?... Ooh! That sounds blum'n lovely that does, a' can smell it from here...

right... right, I'll tell him that." He cast a grin towards Jack. "It's chicken casserole, Jack, and she said ya have to tell Hoss to come round 'coss she's made plenty." Alan spoke with Irene for quite some time, and on the odd occasion he would laugh aloud while glancing carefree between the brothers before ending the conversation with a sigh, saying, "That's lads for ya, Irene, trouble with a capital T so they are, don't you go worrying ya bit sell, I'll definitely ask them about that alright... bye now... bye-bye... " Blushing slightly his tone lowered to an embarrassing whisper as he added, "... and me too."

"What's she said now!?" hooted Jack.

Alan laughed sharply. "Nowt really," his facial expression slowly transformed into an accusing scowl with eyes shifting rapidly between the two, "she just wants yas to get rid of all these bags of copper wire which have mysteriously appeared in her coalhouse owernight, that's all..." Jack and Tom sat gobsmacked. "... well, come on then, what have yas got to say for ya sells?" Still the two were muted as Alan's glower rested solely upon Jack with him asking, "What's wrong with thuw, lad, cat caught ya tongue, has it?"

"Nor! Desperate times, desperate measures."

"Desperate times my arse! Don't you dare come that with me, Jack Gilroy!"

"Here!" snapped Jack. "If we can mack a bob or two we're gan'n tee, anyway, we're robbing the rich to give to the poor," he winked hidden at Tom, continuing, "and me and our kid's the poor."

Addressing Tom, for some reason Alan's attitude mellowed, "Do ya nar something, a' knew gobshite there was capable of nicking that cable, but I never thowt in a million years that you would ever have owt to do with stuff like this mind, Tom."

Tom heaved a sigh. "Sorry, Alan, but our youngn's right, desperate times, but you have my word it won't happen again."

"Nor it'll not happen again!" he barked, purple faced. "You bet your bottom lip it won't!" After a few lengthy sighs he calmed himself down saying, "Look, lads, a' turn a blind eye to most things gan'n off around here, and by the way that includes the little coal business ya's are running, but–"

Jack cut Alan short sarcastically asking, "What do ya mean, the little coal business we're running? What–"

"Jack! Shut half ya gob!" intervened Tom.

Alan carped, "You know exactly what a' mean, Jack, proper little coal merchants ya's have turned out to be, and like a' said, a' don't mind that, but taking electric cables, well, that's a different kettle of fish all together, that is. Do ya nar something, if ya's had gone and got ya sells caught nicking one of those things ya'd have ended up doing a tidy stretch inside Durham jail."

"Aye right owe, we get the jest!" moaned Jack who was now becoming bored with the ticking off they were receiving.

"Good, a' hope yas do, and not a word to anyone about all this mind, 'coss if this shit ever gets out a' won't be able help yas, not one little bit will a'."

"We won't say owt," sighed Tom.

Glaring at Jack, Alan placed a finger to his own mouth ordering, "And you keep that zipped!"

"Divant worry, I'm not as daft as a' look, a' might look it but a's not."

"Jack, man!" moaned Alan, fumbling open a fresh packet of cigarettes. "Thuw's owt but daft," he lit up, continuing, "if anyone's got the gift of the gab thuw has, lad, a' sometimes think tha's been dipped in the bloody Shannon, sell pegs back to the Gypsies thuw could." He drew long and deep on his cig. "Go on then, fuck off back on the gates." As the brothers were turning to leave, Alan coughed slightly. "Look, lads, this strike's ganna be ower and done with one way or t'uther, but the way things are vanishing from around here a' doubt if we're ganna have a pit left ta gan back to."

"We've promised ya, it's the last," pledged Tom.

Jack furthered, "We dinit mack a habit of nicking cables tha nars."

"A' hope yas dinit! Or, afore a' forget," quickly scrummaging through a desk drawer he handed over a brown envelope to Tom, muttering, "give this to ya Ma when yas gan up the club, tell her there's three hundred quid in there for the kitchen fund, it was donated last night by the Mechanics Union." He smiled sharply at Tom before squinting accusingly at Jack. "And Tom, please mack sure Errol Flynn here doesn't get his thieving little paws on it."

Jack narrowed his eyes, frowning. "Errol who?"

"Errol Flynn! Tha nars, Robin Hood! Funnily enough, he was a protecter of the people, just like thuw is, Jack."

"A protecter of the what?" asked Jack who was now stood totally flummoxed.

"A protecter of the people," repeated Alan before explaining, "tha nars, robbing the rich to give to the poor."

"What... ever," stretched Jack as they left the office. Alan shouted after them, "And mack sure yas don't misplace that envelope mind!"

"What envelope's that!?" yelled Jack from out of sight.

"Fuck off, Jack!" Sauntering to the window, Alan looked on in awe as the brothers joined the other two at the pit gates where Jack started fooling around fun boxing with Hoss. Alan puckered a grin, whispering, "Jack by name, Jack by bloody nature that one is, the bugger's frightened of nowt, not man nor bloody beast." After a bit of a sigh, he dragged his feet across the room to pause in front of a lengthy wall mirror where he examined underneath his eyes before running his hand over his hair, double checking that nothing had fallen out.

Up at Easington Colliery Club, known locally as simply 'The Club', an appetising aroma of cooking vegetables drifted from a temporary kitchen which was set up in a room located to the rear of a rather impressive hall branded 'The Singing End'. This kitchen was run by an assembly of women volunteers who were committed to the task of not only feeding the striking miners, but also their families too, and at the helm of these dedicated volunteers stood Sue Temple and Irene Gilroy.

Aged in her early thirties, Sue Temple was a happily married mother of two boys. She was tall and slender, exhibiting thick rimmed, tinted spectacles, which indicated both integrity and intelligence, as well as drawing attention to high cheekbones and a head of dark hair styled to just above shoulder length. Holding militant left-wing views, Sue was an active member of the Labour Party, who was held in the highest esteem throughout the community, not least for the enthusiasm that she displayed whilst representing the populace on both Parish and County councils alike.

The makeshift kitchen comprised a pair of donated old cookers, a stainless-steel double sink, and a couple of wooden worktops which ran parallel across opposing walls for almost the full length of the constricted room before one ended in front of a mustard-coloured timeworn fridge, while a bulky chest freezer hummed to an unhealthy high pitch at the end of the other. Balancing a huge dish, Sue hunkered to carefully slide the container into one of the ovens, saying, "Keep an eye on that mince please, Debbie?"

"Aye, ne bother," replied Debbie Millison, a tall, attractive girl aged in her early twenties who flaunted fashionable black lace ribbons throughout her highlighted hair. Large plastic earrings dangled to cheek to match up with plastic bangles running her arm, giving her the appearance of a pop star fresh in from America known as 'Madonna'. Debbie stood peeling potatoes alongside Jean Brown, a plump woman aged in her mid-to-late thirties who brandished a stout, jolly face topped by a mass of frizzy black hair.

On a separate workbench, sisters Bev and Tracy James prepared vegetables. Bev, aged twenty- three, was bubbly and of average height, possessing lengthy auburn hair which harmonized bulbous lips and eyes of emerald green. Although Tracy was two years Bev's junior, she towered way taller, and like her sister she too was a brunette who had inherited full lips and beautiful Irish eyes.

Irene stood at a cooker inspecting pans of simmering vegetables as Sue firstly divided, then rolled up, sticky dumplings before placing them onto a large tray lined in waxy baking paper. Looking to Bev, Sue smiled, asking, "Put some music on pet-lamb?" At once Bev leaned over a punnet of vegetables to switch on a radio and a fast beating Duran Duran track blasted loud.

"Turn that down a bit, love!" grumbled Irene. "Ya'll waken up them poor buggers buried ower in the graveyard so ya will."

Sue smiled at Irene from over her spectacles. "Ya showing your age now mind, Irene."

"What do ya mean?"

"Why, asking for the music to be turned down, it's one of the first signs you're getting old that is."

"I am getting old, creaky old."

"Give ower!" hooted Jean. "What with that fantastic figure of yours, you're absolutely gorgeous, man, Irene. Look at this ..." Jean ran her hands up and down her generous curves in a racy way as she danced along to the music. "... this is what having six kids does to ya, I'm every shape a woman shouldn't be."

"Get away," laughed Sue, "ya still looking good."

"I'm feeling good, and a' can still shift this ard heap of mine." The whole cluster broke out laughing, encouraging Jean to keep on dancing.

"Go on, Jean!" whooped Sue. "Give it some jip, girl!"

"God a' couldn't have that many kids." whispered Debbie, turning away. Looking at Irene she blew her cheeks. "One's enough for me like."

"Get... away!" stretched Irene. "You and your Peter will surely have more kids, ya'll probably's end up in the same boat as Jean here, and ya wouldn't swap them for the world, just like she wouldn't."

"Just like she wouldn't what, Irene?" asked Jean puffing a tired sigh as she slowed her salsa movements down to an almost standstill.

"Swap your kids for the world!" laughed Irene.

Now out of breath, Jean managed to chuff, "Too true a' wadn't... not for ... all the tea in China ... would a'."

Irene turned to Debbie, "Anyway who the hell's this playing?"

"It's Duran Duran, they're canny good, aren't they?"

"A' wadn't gan that far, flowerpots, a' mean they're not exactly The Beatles, are they?"

"A' think they're great!" enthused Bev. "That Simon Le Bon's frigging gorgeous."

"Think so!?" questioned Tracy. "A' think Nick Rhodes is miles better looking than him."

Irene's eyes shifted from sister to sister with Bev persisting, "Is he heckers like! He's ower girlie Nick Rhodes is, he wears far too much makeup for my liking!" Tracy shook her head. "They're supposed to wear makeup! They're New Romantics, man!"

"They're New what!?" broke in Irene, now totally baffled.

"New Romantics, Irene," put in Sue, "it's a phase the kids are currently going through, girls having thick mascara-clad eyes with lots of hair, while the boys have even more hair and lots more mascara. They're a canny complicated bunch the New Romantics are."

"Why they divant sound very romantic to me," sighed Irene, "in fact they sound rather frightening."

Tracy nudged her sister, uttering, "A' bet that Nick Rhodes' mad in bed though."

"A' bet he is," she replied, "but a' bet Simon Le Bon's better."

"What are you two gan'n on about now?" asked Sue with an inquisitive grin.

"Who'd be the best shag between Simon Le Bon and Nick Rhodes," sniggered Bev brazenly.

"Eee! Bev James!" heaved Irene at once. "It's a good job ya Mam's not stood behind ya listening to ya talking like that!"

"Well, I'd rather shag that Shakin' Stevens me like," tittered Jean, "he can't half move them hips of his, he's just like Elvis was."

"Now a' do like Shakin' Stevens," chuckled Irene, "but a' like his music, not his hip movements."

Bev looked at Irene with a wicked grimace asking, "How'y then, Irene, if ya had the chance to shag any pop star in the whole wide world, who would it be?"

"Me!?" Irene stood all of a fluster. "None! A' wadn't be able to look Father O'Conner in the eye at mass on Sunday mornings."

Bev turned to Sue. "What about you then, Sue?"

Spoon in hand, Sue stood in thought for a second or two. "Why, a' wouldn't exactly say I would shag him, but that George Michael's a bit of alright."

"Which one's George Michael again?" enquired Irene.

"Him from Wham, Irene," put in Debbie, "they sang, Club Tropicana'."

"They sang what?" frowned Irene, lost. "Never heard of it".

"He is gorgeous looking mind," said Sue smiling broadly, "he's all tanned and has a gorgeous head of hair and a set of the loveliest white teeth a've ever seen."

"Orr a' think I've got ya now!" mumbled Irene. "Is that him who dances around with them white socks, and them white short, really short, shorts on?"

"Aye that's him!" enthused Tracy. "He is canny good looking, isn't he?"

Irene blew unsure, mumbling, "Yeah, he's a handsome enough young lad all right, but a' think he's got one or two issues, a' can't quite put my finger on it mind, but there's something sadly wrong with the poor lad, a' mean..." checking over her shoulder Irene's tone lowered to almost a whisper, "...them blum'n shorts are outrageous, they ride right the way up his jacksee..." All the girls burst out tittering. "... Why they do!" she defended red faced.

Bev turned to Debbie, asking, "Who would you like to shag then, Debbie?"

"Apart from Jack Gilroy, that is," mumbled Tracy just that little bit too loud.

"Hey! I heard that!" snapped Irene. "Debbie's a happily married woman I'll have you know and leave our Jack out of it if yas don't mind, he's a coal miner not a blinking pop star thank you very much!"

"He is very sexy though, Irene," sighed Bev, "he's the pip of Matt Dillion."

"No way..." argued Tracy, and once again Irene's eyes shifted back and forth with Tracy continuing, "...he's more like Rob Lowe but with bigger muscles, but we all fancy a crack at your Jack, Irene."

"Too right we do," prattled Bev, "he's a dish."

"I'm bloody sure he is," muttered Sue in deep thought before blowing, "he's got that sexy, sort of David Essex twinkle about him, come to think of it, a' wadn't mind a roll in the hay with your Jack mesell, Irene."

"Will ya's give ower!" moaned Irene pretending to be all offended while inside she was bursting with pride. "Our Jack's a good Catholic lad."

"He's drop dead gorgeous," purred Tracy rather wickedly, "isn't he, Debbie?"

"I'll go and put some serving tables out," responded Debbie who was trying her utmost to stop herself from blushing. Making her way to the doorway she cast a scathing glower as she barged past Tracy. Irene immediately picked up on this, and for a split-second, awkward questions ran through her mind before she swiftly dismissed them. Heaving a sigh, Irene struggled to lift a weighty pan of potatoes from cooker to sink where she carefully strained away steamy water before adding milk and a good knob of butter ahead of mashing them to perfection.

"How'y then, lasses!" encouraged Sue, clapping her hands. "Chop-chop, it's nearly time to get this lot out!"

It was almost midday at the pit gates at Easington Colliery, threatening rain clouds had blown over to be replaced by an endless lid of blue, yet still, a bit of a chilliness cut the air. Jack, Tom, Hoss and Billy stood smoking around a fire drum when Hoss gazed out to sea with a look of study sketched across his face. Facing Tom, he narrowed his eyes before hesitantly asking, "Do ya nar when the tide comes in down the beach, Tom?"

"Aye, what about it?"

"Why," he drew on his cigarette, "when it comes in at our side of the sea, does it like gan out at the other side, tha nars like in Norway and that?"

Tom scratched the back of his head in thought before "God nars, Hoss" came back amidst an unsure sigh.

"It must do," jumped in Jack, "the watter's got to come from somewhere."

"A' think ya'll find the m-m-moon controls the tides, Jack," said Billy, "that's how ya get huge Spring tides w-w-when it's at its closest p-p-point to the earth."

"Aye a' think ya might be right there, Billy," agreed Tom, "a' heard that somewhere me sell."

"Is he shite right!" argued Jack, drawing deep on his cigarette.

"How do you nar?" muttered Hoss. Looking at Jack with a frown he raised, "Ya not exactly Richard Attenborough tha nars!"

Jack narrowed his eyes, puckering, "Hoss, ya've got something on ya chin, marra." Instantly the big man ran his hand over his chin in response to Jack's words when Jack chuckled, "Not that one, man! The other one!!"

"Fuck off, ya cheeky twat!" retorted Hoss, nudging Jack friendly, yet still his brute strength staggered his friend backwards a pace or two.

Billy now addressed Hoss, correcting, "It's, D-D-David Attenborough who's the naturalist, Hoss, not Richard, Richard's the actor in their family, he was in T-T-Ten Rillington Place, and Brighton R-R-Rock."

Hoss smirked. "Why whichever of them it is gob shite's nen of them, 'coss he canit act, and he nars nowt about what effects the tides neither."

"Why a' nar it's got fuck all to do with the moon, Hoss!" responded Jack.

Tom pried, "How d'ya mack that owt like, Jack?"

"'Coss it just doesn't!" he argued on. "'Coss the tides still come in and out through the daytime as well as what they do on a night."

"So," tittered Tom, "what's that got to do with it?"

Jack flicked his cigarette butt into the fire, then scanning the sky he said, "Why look, the moon's not there is it? It only comes out on a night-time."

Tom snickered, "Don't talk so baldy headed! It's still in the sky, ya just canit see it, ya daft bugger!"

"Your Tom's right," said Hoss as he too cast his cigarette end into the fire, "at least a' think he is."

"Hello, is there anyone there!?" floated a hidden voice from beyond the barricade, abruptly interrupting the lunar tide debate and sending Hoss all a fluster as he rushed towards the barrier.

"Halt! Who goes there!?" bellowed the big man peering through gaps. "Friend or foe!? Friend or foe!?"

"I'm Jim Foster, the postman!" came back in a high-pitched, almost feminine voice.

"Ya who, a' mean ya what!?"

"I'm the postman!"

"What's tha after!?"

"I've a letter here to deliver for a mister, Alan... Cunnings."

Hoss looked over his shoulder to the lads in search for some kind of guidance. Jack shook his head in response before Hoss scratched the back of his neck shouting, "Why ya canit come in here!"

"Why not, for like!?"

"Why not, for like! Because it's a picket line, that's why not for like! Ya canit just cross a picket line willy-nilly tha nars!" Unawares to Hoss, behind him the lads were now bent double trying to hold in their laughter.

The postman pleaded, "But I have to deliver it! It's my first week on the job!"

"A' divan't give a monkey's armpit!" bellowed Hoss. "Ya still not coming in here. A' tell ya what to do though, ya can either bring the letter back when the strike's all finished with, or ya can thraw the thing ower the top of the barricade and I'll give it to Alan next time a' see him."

"Will you make sure he gets it like?"

"Why, aye!"

"Promise!?"

"Aye a' promise!" snapped Hoss. "Fa fuck's sake man!"

"What's your name?" asked the postman.

"My name?"

"Yes, your name?"

"It's Hoss, why me real name's Martin Breester, but everyone calls is Hoss."

"Here you are then, it's coming over now." A brown envelope was drifting over the top of the barricade when a sudden waft caught hold of it and the thing glided into the heart of the fire where it instantly burst into flames. "Did you get it, Martin?"

"Aye," shouted Hoss before whispering, "sort of."

"Thank you," said the relieved postman, "ta tar for now, and good luck with the strike."

Hoss joined the lads as they stood gazing down in disbelief at the engulfed envelope. Tom raised his eyes at Hoss, and with a shake of his head said, "Ya should've let him in, Hoss, it's against the law to interfere with the Royal Mail."

Hoss defended, "It's alright saying that, but he might not have been a postman, might he."

"Why who could he h-h-have been like?" asked Billy.

"Why a scab!"

"A scab?" frowned Tom. "Wearing a postman's uniform!"

"Aye, tha nars, like in disguise and that!" explained Hoss.

Billy poked the fire, muttering, "Do ya nar something, Hoss, they h-h-hung Dick Turpin for interfering with the p-p-post."

Hoss upheld, "Aye, but he was a proper highwayman, wasn't he? A' mean the bugger had a cape, a mask and all that other shite!"

Jack looked to his big friend, chuckling, "Hoss, ya'd baffle Interpol at times thuw wad, marra."

At the Colliery Club, the ambience in the singing end was above vibrant as families, friends, and work colleagues sat conversing while eating meals around scattered tables. The elevated stage area was taken up entirely by an assemblage of elderly women volunteers who were busy preparing Friday's weekly food parcels for the miners and their families. These packages consisted of tinned peas, tinned beans, tinned tomatoes, tinned beans, spaghetti hoops, tinned beans, loose teabags, tinned beans, tinned meat, tinned beans, and on the odd occasion a packet of fishfingers or fishcakes was thrown in to enhance the taste of: tinned beans.

All these provisions were bestowed by local shopkeepers, and their generosity was indebted throughout the whole of the tight-knit community. At the back of the room, Tony the Vicar aided a couple of union officials as they emptied out collection buckets onto a tabletop ahead of painstakingly arranging the coinage into several columns starting from half pennies and rising up through the currency to end with new one-pound coins, and a few notes.

At first glance, Tony the Vicar's appearance was that of a comical clergyman you may find in some rib-tickling sketch on television, as he was tall, pear-shaped, and almost certain to be found dishevelled with tunics soiled in egg stains, soup stains, or whatever stains he had eaten that day, or indeed previous days. His appointment as the Vicar at Easington Colliery didn't go down too well with the plastic snobs amongst his congregation who were forever plotting his demise, but despite their constant backstabbing, Tony was, well, simply adored by the majority of his flock, even if he was constantly on the cadge for the odd cigarette, or continually abstaining from paying his turn at the bar when out socialising in the company of others.

Four lengthy tables stretched nose to tail down the centre of the room; on the first table a variety of cutlery was presented inside large Tupperware containers placed alongside stacks of different patterned dinner plates. Sue was at the head of the servers heaping dollops of potatoes onto eager plates; next came Jean, smiling, her usual friendliness whilst spooning out helpings of steamy mushy peas. Tracy and Bev James were at the centre of the chain serving out portions of cabbage and carrots ahead of Irene who rested a single dumpling onto each individual plate; last, but not least, Debbie was positioned at the end dowsing meals with a rich mince and onion gravy. Today was a lot more hectic than usual as the senior school had broken up a day early due to a half term break and the additional children had created a lingering queue which stretched the full length of the hall before doubling back as far as the lobby doors. Wiping her brow, Debbie puffed her cheeks to a sharp sigh before whispering, "Where's all these come from, Irene? It's never-ending this is."

"God nars, just soldier on, flowerpots," she uttered from out of the corner of her mouth, "but gan canny with that mince, there's not much left." Irene's eyes followed Debbie's gaze as Jack and the lads entered the hall to join the queue, and the manner in which Debbie fidgeted with both her hair and clothing, once again sent all sorts of uneasy questions swamping Irene's mind. After a while, Jack was first to be served, closely followed by Hoss, Billy, and finally Tom. Inching the line, Jack battered his puppy dogs at Bev and Tracy and was rewarded with heaped amounts of veg compared to Hoss's lesser portions. Proceeding further, Hoss was becoming restless until he came to Irene where he smiled hugely as she slipped him an additional dumpling. Approaching Debbie, Jack winked impishly, sending her to a bit of a fluster with her hands shaking slightly as she flooded his plate with extra mince. An additional wink was then cast from Jack as he swaggered away plate in hand in search of an empty table, leaving Hoss presenting Debbie with his own plate whilst beaming all optimistic; but his grimace went unheeded, and a reduced serving of mince was given out.

Settling at a table, Hoss brandished a face like thunder as he gawked at Jack's overloaded plate. He grumbled, "It's not fair this like! Look at the size of your dinner compared to mine; ya've got twice as much as me!"

"He's got twice as much as all of us, Hoss," put in Tom, as Billy and himself joined them at the table.

"Stop twisting, man, ya's are like a couple of ard biddies," said Jack with a straight face, "it's not my fault I'm irresistible." He cracked a smile saying, "Here ya soft sod," ahead of him exchanging plates with Hoss.

"Cheers, marra!" gushed the big man. "Can a' have that extra dumpling back what Ma put on that plate please?" His smile extended further as he watched Jack scrape a dumpling from plate to plate. As Hoss ate, people on neighbouring tables couldn't help but look on as he relentlessly wolfed his food while humming along to some made up composition he was creating with each mouthful, and it wasn't long before he was scraping his plate clean.

"There's nowt left," moaned Tom snatching away Hoss' fork, "ya ganna tack the pattern off the thing afore long." Tom shook his head with a sigh as his friend reluctantly rested his knife prior to shuffling himself into the back of his chair.

"A b-b-bulldozer couldn't have shifted that as quick as w-w-what thuw did there mind, Hoss," chuckled Billy between mouthfuls of mash, "ya didn't even come up f-f-for air."

"He couldn't have enjoyed it, shovelling it in like that," voiced Tom, "he didn't have a chance to taste owt!"

"A' bloody did though! And it was frigging lovely!" responded Hoss who was now running a finger around his plate, sucking what remains of gravy there was into his mouth.

Tom leaned over the table, whispering, "Will ya give ower, people's watching ya for Christ's sake."

"Let the buggers watch!" intervened Jack aloud. "And leave him alone!"

Hoss looked over his shoulder at the dwindling queue; facing back to the lads he licked his lips, gushing, "A' wonder if we can gan for seconds, like we used to do at school?"

"Don't even think about it," muttered Tom.

Holding onto collection buckets, two elderly miners staggered into the hall via an opened exit door situated at the rear of the room. The taller of the two limped slightly while brandishing a burst lip and a swollen eye. The smaller had his coat all ripped with blood trickling down his face from a cut high on his forehead. Irene noticed them. Removing her apron she said, "Hand them dumplings out, Debbie." Quickly leaving the serving tables, she approached the stricken men, ushering them into a backroom. "What the hell's happened to you two?" she asked, aiding them into a couple of chairs.

"We got jumped on," said Salty Watson, a bald man aged in his late fifties who was small in stature yet brandished a huge, almost round beer belly, "a bunch of lads set about us."

"Set about yas? Where at like?"

"In Durham city centre," broke in John Hunt, a lanky chap whom God had blessed with a full head of silvery hair and a rather handsome moustache, "we were collecting at our usual spot just off Market Square when they came up to us saying we were Commy... please excuse the French, Irene... bastards! And that we should all be flogged back to work."

Irene stretched, "The cheeky, so and so's!" Clicking open a first aid box she started cleaning blood away from Salty's face and forehead. "How many of them was there like, Salty?"

"About fower a' think, it was hard to tell, but we had no chance, there was only us two, and they were all fit young lads around the same age as your Jack and Tom. Mind you, twenty years ago we'd have–"

"Twenty years ago, we'd have what?" broke in John. "We'd have still done nowt!"

"Here speak for ya sell, thuw!" snapped the little chap.

Prodding Salty's cut, Irene grumbled, "Fancy picking on two owld men, the rotten buggers!"

"Steady on with the owld, Irene!" joshed John. "I'm anly sixty-one, and a'm gan'n out on a date I'll have you know."

"On a date!?" she queried light-heartedly. "Where at like?"

"Why here."

"What the kitchen!?"

He broke into a smile. "Nor, ya daft bat, the Friday night disco the night."

Switching her attentions to John, Irene laughed, "Or aye! Why if this lip doesn't gan down there'll be no snogging going on, anyway; who's the lucky lady, anyone a' nar?"

"Aye, Mary..." John's grimace slowly broke into a brazen smirk, "... Robson."

"What, the Black Widow!?" she raised all shocked. "You want to keep as far away as possible from her, John Hunt, she's like a praying mantis that one is, every husband she's ever had drank themselves into an early grave."

"That's exactly what I told him, Irene!" agreed Salty with purpose. "But will he listen, will he heckers like! He thinks he's still a twenty odd year ard man, the daft owld bugger."

Irene once again focused her attention back to Salty's injuries as Jack and Hoss entered the room just ahead of Sue. The instant Jack eyed the men an avenging rage burned from deep down inside of him. "What's gone on here!?" he asked.

"We got jumped on, Jack," said Salty, rubbing his injured head.

At once Irene slapped the back of Salty's hand, ordering, "Give ower touching it, man! I've just sterilised the blum'n thing!"

"Sorry, Irene," he responded, now rubbing the sting from his hand.

"Yas got jumped on!?" fumed Sue. "Where at like!?"

"In Durham city centre just off Market Square," responded Salty, "they noticed the **coal not dole** stickers on our collection buckets and they set about us."

"A' think they were National Front supporters," raised John.

"How do ya mack that owt like?" asked Hoss. "Were they like, Skinheeds and that?"

John sighed lengthily. "Nar they weren't, Hoss, they were just normal run of the mill lads, in fact they were all well-dressed in nice shirts and suits, but as they were knocking us about the biggest one of them said, tell your Comrades when you get back to the shithole where ya's crawled from that you have just bumped into the NF, he also said that if he ever caught us cadging money in Durham City again he would give us a right good kicking like."

"Did he now! We'll see about that," seethed Jack just as Billy and Tom entered the room.

"What's happened to you two?" asked Tom all concerned.

Salty lifted his eyes pitiful. "We got jumped on, Tom, they gave us a right going over, I've lost me cap and God nars where me spectacles ended up at, a' think they may have went into the River Wear!"

"Did yas nar who it w-w-was like, Salty?" asked Billy.

"It was National Front supporters, that's who it was, Billy," huffed Irene as she delicately covered Salty's cut on his forehead with an overlarge Elastoplast. "Disgraceful it is, young lads picking on owld men."

"Div a' not get a lasta-plaster like, Irene?" asked John in a mannerism of a rather pathetic schoolboy.

"No, a' don't think so, John, a' can't put a one on ya lip, but a' tell ya what though, ya ganna have a right owld shiner in the morn."

Sue looked to Tom. "Something needs to be done about this, Tom, it's not on this, like."

"Something will be done, Sue; you mark my words it will!" he replied in the manner of a promise to trigger a look of apprehension shooting Irene's face.

Jack nodded agreement, fuming, "Aye will it." He faced his mother. "We'll not be long, Ma, we're just ganna pop out for a bit, or afore a' forget, there's three hundred quid in the truck for ya, Alan sent it up, I'll fetch it in when we get back."

She ordered, "Don't you's go planning anything stupid mind!"

"As if," jested Jack with a reassuring smile ahead of them leaving the room. "A mean it mind, Jack!" she shouted after them before she turned to concentrate once again on John's injuries.

Hoss returned to pop his head around the doorway, and after an attention-seeking cough he asked, "When we get back is there any chance of seconds, Ma?"

Irene smiled warmly. "If there's owt gan'n spare there is, son," her words bringing about a beam from the big man as he left.

"Your Tom's just like ya Great-uncle Victor mind, Irene," whispered John, "he's got a right radge on him."

"That he has," she answered, blowing a motherly sigh, "but it's t'uther one I'm more worried about."

John chuckled. "Ya've got a good right to be, he's as hard as nanny-goats' knees your Jack is."

"Are ya finished with the first aid box, Irene?" asked Sue.

"Yeah, remind is on in the morning to get some small and medium-sized Elastoplasts, Sue, there's nen left, 'a haven't the foggiest where they've all gone to, like, seen as we've never had one single casualty yet." She tapped the top of her head, adding, "touch wood".

Storing away the first aid box, Sue smiled back and forth between Salty and John, asking, "Are you two lads hungry?"

"Aye am a'!" enthused John.

"I'm bloody starved!" jumped in Salty. "A' could eat a scabby hoss."

"We haven't got one of them, but will mince and dumplings do yas?"

"Ooh aye please, Sue!" gushed Salty.

"Right then, two mince and dumpling dinners coming up." Heading towards the door, Sue glanced back over her shoulder with a grin, asking, "Salt and pepper?"

"Yes please," responded John.

Salty answered, "Just pepper for me please, Sue, a's not allowed salt since a' had me last heart attack."

John scorned, "Tha wasn't allowed salt after tha last but one heart attack, man, Salty, but that's niver stopped ya before... has it!?"

The Friday night discotheque at Easington Colliery Club was in full swing with a darkened 'Singing End' crammed to the rafters with youth. Up on a raised stage a disco flashed various coloured lights that blinked from colour to colour in sequence to the beat of the music. Directly in front of this light display, a raised wooden floor heaved to a mixture of dancing couples, and clusters of girls who bopped in circles around handbags as testosterone-fuelled lads stood in the wings of the dancefloor looking on with peacock enthusiasm. To one side of the room a queue had formed at a bar, keeping a half-dozen diligent barmaids busy, while at the back of the hall, Jack and the lads stood chatting with pints in hand.

Jack's mullet hairstyle was gelled to its usual perfection as he posed in a purple Lacoste tee-shirt, faded denim dungarees, and white Adidas trainers. Hoss wore a grey polo shirt, loose-fitting jeans and his treasured blue suede winklepicker boots. Billy was clad in his usual cream top, brown trousers, and tan brogues that were in desperate need of a polish, while Tom donned a white dress shirt, modern black trousers, and glossy black patent leather shoes.

Hoss nudged Jack, drawing his attention to an attractive girl dancing in front of the disco lights and each time a dazzling white light illuminated up the dance floor, her flowing lace dress became transparent. "Seen her!?" gasped Hoss delighted. "Look, she's got ne bra on!"

"Too right!" gushed Jack. "Look at them titties, they're bouncing around like two puppies playing in a bag!" Jack elbowed Billy slightly. "Seen that?" Not taking his eyes away from the girl, Billy bobbed confirmation into his pint glass as Jack prodded Tom. "Seen her, young'n!?"

"Aye," rolled uninterested from Tom ahead of him, nodding awareness as Debbie Millison and Bev James weaved their way through the crowded room heading in their direction. "Here's trouble," moaned Tom drawing on his cigarette, "you need to kick her into touch, Jack, and the sooner the better if you ask me."

"Well, I'm not asking you am a', so keep ya neb out of my business if ya don't mind; besides, I'm only having a bit a' fun." Jack inhaled deeply on his cigarette, sarcastically suggesting, "Ya wanna try it one day, tha never nars ya might enjoy it."

"Be a bit of fun if Peter finds out about yas."

"Or aye, and what's he ganna de like?"

"Probably's nowt," replied Tom unconcerned. Looking around the lads, he raised his glass. "Same again then?"

"Aye p-p-please," returned Billy.

"Aye," agreed Hoss, adding, "get is a bag of crisps an'll please?"

"What, another one!?" Shaking his head, Tom turned to walk off in the direction of the bar.

"Salt and vinegar, marra!" shouted Hoss after Tom, before he faced Jack with a smile, asking, "What ya's arguing about now?"

"Nowt really, he's just being arsey about Debbs again."

"He's only looking after your best interests, Jack; besides, it'll break Peter's heart if he ever finds out about the pair of yas, not to mention what it'll do to Ma."

"I'd better mack sure they don't find out, then, hadn't a'!" sighed Jack ahead of him drinking off the remainder of his pint. "Anyway, what a' do is my business, it's got fuck all to do with him, you, or anyone else."

"Alright!" retorted Hoss. "Keep ya heed, the price of wood's gan'n up! Anyway, what's wrang with ya? Ya've been edgy all night."

"Why, man, it's our young'n," grumbled Jack, "he canit de nowt wrang, he should have entered into the Priesthood like Ma wanted him to, every bugger and his dog thinks the sun shines out of his arse, even me Nanna thinks butter wadn't melt in his mouth, yet she can barely acknowledge me at times."

"That's 'coss he's nice, Jack."

"And I'm not, like!?"

"Aye ya nice enough alright, ya've got a heart of gold, but ya let that cock of yours rule ya brain, why sometimes ya do, sorry, most times ya do."

"Aye d-d-do ya," voiced Billy, stumping out his cigarette, "and ya want to keep well away f-f-from that Debbie Millison an'll, she's f-f-forbidden fruit, Jack, she's just like that, H-H-Helen of Troy was!"

Debbie and Bev approached the lads. Debbie looked stunning in an off-the-shoulder brown leopard print mini dress split by a russet belt dangling loosely across her slender hips, tan coloured elf like boots set off lengthy bronzed legs, while her highlighted hair was back combed to harmonise with thick mascara-clad eyes. Bev was dressed in fashionable turquoise shorts and a matching top, and was looking rather attractive herself with her lengthy hair also backcombed and eyes mascara-thickened. Glass in hand, Bev stood to one side, talking with Hoss and Billy, while Debbie paused in front of Jack; snuggling up to him she looked into his eyes purring, "I love you, Jack Gilroy."

"Don't start all that again!" he snapped, stumping his cigarette. "It's every time ya out on the lash ya gan all Jekyll and Hyde on is, I've told ya a thousand times ya married with a kid, man, Debbs!"

"I'll leave him, a' don't love him, a' love you."

"Will a give ower talking like that!?"

"Talking like what!?"

"Like all that slopy shite and that!" said Jack. "You knew right from the start how we stood."

"So, what ya trying to say is, after nearly four months ya still have no feelings for is at all, I'm only a bit of fun on the side for ya, is that what ya saying?"

"Aye, that's exactly what a'm saying."

"Well, it's gone beyond that, I'm afraid, Jack." She tried to hug him, but he was having none of it and he pulled away, grabbing his arm she tugged him back into her. "Don't you dare pull away from me!"

"Not in here, Debbs, people will talk!"

"So! A' couldn't care less! Let them talk!"

"Well, a' could care less." Noticing she was unsteady on her feet he looked her up and down, asking, "Are you pissed?"

"No, I'm not actually, why, I've had a few but I'm not exactly pissed." She tenderly stroked his hand, "Are ya coming back to mine tonight? Peter's away working all weekend down his brothers and the bairn's stopping around his Mam's till Monday morning."

"We'll see." He looked around, making sure no one was watching before pecking a kiss on her shoulder, whispering, "Ya looking good mind, Debbs."

"It's all for you, Jack, it has been for ages." 'Borderline' by Madonna blasted from the disco; at once Debbie rested her drink, instructing, "Watch that, I'm going for a dance." Taking Bev by the hand, she smiled, saying, "How'y, Bev, it's dance time!"

Bev just about managed to set down her own glass before she was dragged away in the direction of the dance floor, and with every step Debbie took she made sure all her vital bits were swaying in all the right directions, knowing fine well that Jack would be watching.

Billy looked on open mouthed, whispering, "The f-f-face that launched a th-th-thousand ships."

Jack slowly turned to face Billy, snapping, "What's thuw gan'n on about now!? Bloody Helen of Troy! A thousand frigging ships!?"

"Nowt! A' was just th-th-thinking out aloud, marra."

Drinks in hand, Tom returned from the bar with a packet of crisps dangling from out the corner of his mouth. Passing around the pints, he handed the crisp packet over to Hoss, saying, "There's no salt and vinegar, Hoss, so a' got ya cheese and onion."

"Cheers, marra, nee bother!" Hoss ripped open the seal and the crisps were almost gone in a matter of seconds.

"Giss a crisp, Hoss?" jumped in Jack in jest.

Tilting his head back, Hoss shook the remains from the packet into his mouth. "Ya ower late, there's nen left," came back amidst a shower of wetted crumbs. Jack shook his head with a smile as he watched his big friend suck his fingers clean. Lighting up a cigarette, Hoss turned to Jack, asking, "Are ya stopping out the night or gan'n yerm?"

"Stopping out probably's, and yes you can have me bed afore ya ask."

"Champion!" He turned to Tom. "We'll pop to the fishy on the way down yerm and get Ma a fishcake, should we?"

"Aye we can do, Hoss." Lighting up a cigarette, Tom faced Billy, asking, "Fairsey's later on, marra?"

"Nar, not th-th-the night for me, Tom," he answered with an air of disappointment.

Jack took in his best friend's grimace, approaching Billy, he stealthily slipped him a crumpled up five-pound note and for a split-second Billy stood speechless. Jack winked hidden before turning away to scan the packed dancefloor.

Alan entered the hall to stand at the doorway. After searching the room, he eventually spotted the lads, and it took a while for him to thread his way through the crowd ahead of him joining them, where he took Tom to one side. "It's all set for the morning, Tom, half nine at yours."

"Good, are we taking your car, my car, or our kid's pick up?"

"Nor, best take mine," he said prior to asking, "are yas all up for it then?"

"Aye are we." Tom drew on his cigarette. "We're more than up for it, our youngn's still frigging livid; having said that Billy's a bit worried like, but dinit fret, he'll be alright."

"A' bit of fear never hurt anyone," said Alan with a reassuring smile, "without fear there would be no courage."

Alan and Tom joined the others where Alan exchanged nods of recognition. After talking for a good ten minutes or so, Alan poked his ear with a twisted face, whinging, "How the hell yas can listen to this is beyond me! It's not music this, it's just a frigging loud noise."

"That's 'coss yar an owld fart, man, Alan," chortled Jack.

"Ya could be right there, Jack," he chuckled before he caught his eye on Debbie returning from the dance floor. Noticing a snifter placed next to Jack's pint, Alan narrowed his eyes, raising, "Mack sure ya don't sleep in, in the morning, Jack, it's half nine at yours." Shifting his concentration back to the advancing Debbie he shook his head, adding, "If ya catch me drift that is?" then with a sharp smile he looked around saying, "Well... I'm off back into the bar to catch ard Jarpy afore he gans yerm," and as quickly as Alan had joined them, he was gone.

Debbie stood in front of Jack with her back turned away to him, slowly she placed her hands behind her and started caressing up and down the inside of his thighs before tantalisingly stroking his crotch, and this time Jack never attempted to pull away; instead, he feathered a kiss on the nape of her neck, sending her shivering all goosepimply.

Somewhat tiddly, Tom, Hoss and Billy staggered from Fairsey's fish shop with each clutching wrapped up fish suppers and Hoss undertaking his Friday night ritual of ordering an open bag of chips and batter for him to eat on his journey. After briefly talking amongst themselves, Billy said his goodnights then cut away in a different direction from the other two, to start his uphill trek home to a private housing estate dubbed 'Canada'.

Crossing over Bede Street, Hoss and Tom entered a housing estate branded as 'South', where all the streets started with the letter 'B', and ran in uniform rows from West to East, before ending at Station Road, 'south', a lengthy street which unfolded from North to South along the entire bottom of the estate, with each house number rising in even digits only. Walking down the back of Beaty Street, Hoss offered Tom a chip, but he refused with a shake of his head. Hoss side eyed Tom, asking, "How long do ya reckon this strike's ganna gan on for, young'n?"

"God nars, Hoss, but it's dragging its feet a bit, we've been out for nearly seven weeks now and there's been no progress whatsoever."

"Bloody hell, has it been that long already! It's flown over, hasn't it?"

Tom moaned, "It has that, young'n, it would have all been done and dusted by now if them scabby bastards down Nottingham, Leicestershire, and South Derbyshire had come out with us, fucking scabs!"

"They're nowt but a bunch of spineless lowlife the lot of them," groused Hoss, "a' hate them with a passion." Once again, he offered his friend a chip, but yet again Tom refused in silence. Walking further they passed by a small club called The Officials, which was nicknamed 'The Leathercap', and it was in this social establishment where the colliery undermanagers, overmans, deputies, engineers and others of their ilk mingled. Hoss smiled at Tom, reminiscing, "Can you remember in 1974 when we were only seventeen and we caused a three-day working week?"

"Aye, good old days them were, marra," tittered Tom, "the dispute only lasted about seven weeks before the Tories caved in and got booted out of office."

Hoss hiccupped. "Aye, but we weren't dealing with the likes of Thatcher in them days though, young'n." Again he hiccupped. "A' don't think she even wants this strike to end, she'll not budge a frigging inch."

"She'll never budge, Hoss, she's after revenge for what we did to Ted Heath, she'd rather burn bars of gold than give in to the likes of Scargill she wad. Hitler in drag that fucker is."

"The bugger's as bad as Hitler!" moaned the big man as he munched on chips and bits of crispy batter that reeked of pungent vinegar. "She's got the same horrible, beady little eyes as what he had; ya can tell she's evil just by looking at the twat."

"Can't argue with you there, marra," agreed Tom with a smile as they arched a sharp corner where the lit-up pit shafts came into view, and beyond these towers there was nothing but the darkness of night, then Norway.

Hoss finished eating his chips; crumpling up a greasy newspaper, he tossed it into an overflowing refuge bin before presenting a packet of cigarettes, uttering, "A' think Billy's struggling with his mortgage tha nars, Tom."

"How do ya mack that out, like?" Tom scratched his Zippo lighter to a flicker, and the whiff of paraffin fumes was strong; after lighting up, he presented the flame, asking, "Has he said owt, like?"

Hoss uttered, "Nar... nowt." Leaning forward he swayed unsteadily as he followed the flame. "But me Da said he saw him and Marie coming out the Building Society the other day–" inspecting the tip of his cigarette he wet one side, then drew deeply a few times, saying, "and he said they looked all at sea, as if they were ganna cry or something."

Sighing prolonged, Tom pinged the lighter shut, mumbling, "Oh, dear me, that's not good! A' knew there was something up with him, but he's never said nowt, not one single thing."

"Why he wadn't, wad he! Tha nars what he's like, he's always kept his problems to his sell, Billy has. Can ya remember when we were youngn's when he kept all that bullying to himself, that went on for yonks till your Jack caught wind of it and nipped it in the bud."

"I'll have a word with our Jack in the morn, see what we can do for him."

Chatting nonstop they cut across a miniature stretch of grassland to step over a stubby stone wall which ran from a lamppost up to the side of a brick bus shelter. Crossing a main road, their pace picked up notably in avoidance of approaching headlights before they strolled down a short alleyway which ended in a sharp right, bringing them to the top of another colliery housing estate called 'East', which like South, paraded identical streets of houses running from West to East, but this time the streets ended at a drawn-out concrete blockade that stretched along the entire bottom of the estate, and was dubbed 'The Pit Wall'. All the street names of the estate in East started with the letter C, apart from Office Street, and Station Road (east), and this time all the houses along Station Road rose in odd numbers only, but similar to that of Station Road (south) the road unfolded from North to South to stretch along the entire top of the vast domain before it ended at an alleyway adjacent 'The Station Hotel', an enormous, old fashioned public house which the locals had named 'The Trust'.

Talking amongst themselves, they half staggered along Station Road going by Charles Street, Chandler, and Castle Street before they turned into Cuba Street, where they entered into the warmth of the second from the top house to be greeted by Mick who was almost turning himself inside out as he wagged his tail welcomely. Irene sat crouched, drifting in and out of the Friday night movie; propping herself up, she looked over her shoulder, gushing, "Where's our Jack at!?"

At the Millison abode, at number nine Chandler Street, Marvin Gaye set the mood for Jack and Debbie as they lay face to face across a comfortable fawn-coloured settee. Not uttering one single word, Debbie stood and straightened out her dress before she left the sitting room to enter a kitchen. Jack sat upright, and he had just lit up a cigarette when Debbie returned holding a glass of water and wearing nothing but a wicked smile. Not taking her eyes from his, her beam extended into lust as she removed the cigarette from out his mouth, after puffing once she stumped it, then taking Jack by the hand she led him up a wooden staircase to where a bedroom awaited.

NEXT MORNING

The aroma of spitting bacon filled the house at number two Cuba Street. Hoss, Tom, Billy and Jack were sat in the sitting room chatting while in the background a kids' cartoon sounded from a television. Mick jumped from Jack's lap to toddle through a set of open doors to stand by Irene who was stood way above contentment at her cooker, making breakfast butties for her two sons and their friends. She shouted through, "So, where did ya end up last night then, Jack?"

"Down Sizzlers playing cards," he returned, winking around the lads.

"Did you win!?"

He sniggered, "Or aye, a' was well up towards the end."

"You shouldn't take money off your friends, it's not nice, especially with yas all out on strike." Irene made up a stack of sandwiches. Placing them onto individual plates, she shouted through, "What do you want on your bacon butty, Tom?"

"Tomato sauce please, Ma."

"Jack?"

"Chop, brown sauce please."

"Billy, what do you want on yours, love?"

"R-R-Red sauce please, Mrs Gilroy."

Irene broke into a smirk. "What do you want on your bacon sandwiches, Hoss?"

"Just an egg and a couple of sausages, please, Ma," responded the big man, his words sending her grin widening just as a knocking at the door rattled ahead of Alan entering into the sitting room.

"Who's that come in!?" yelled Irene through.

"It's only me," replied Alan, sitting on the sofa between Hoss and Jack.

Smiling slight she hollered, "Would only me like a bacon butty?"

"Why a' wadn't say no, Irene, thanks."

"Dead crispy with red sauce?" she asked.

"Yeah please," he returned just as Mick trotted into the room to jump onto his lap where he started to lick around his mouth and face.

"A' dinit nar why our Mick always seems to mack a fuss ower you for, Alan?" baited Tom, winking hidden at Jack. "He never does that with anyone else coming to the house."

"That's 'coss he's a good boy!" encouraged Alan speaking in a put-on, childlike voice as he messed about encouraging the hyped-up canine to lick even more around his mouth and face.

"Do ya nar, our Mick's been licking his arse all morning!" said Jack straight-faced. "A' think he might need worming again."

Spring had fashioned up a delightful Saturday over Durham City, the sky was clear as the morning sun radiated a pleasant, balmy warmth. The ancient cathedral stood momentous in all its historical grandeur, while the cobbled streets below thrived with both shoppers and traders alike. At a busy Market Square, Salty

Watson and John Hunt paced back and forth, rattling collection buckets while shouting, 'Support the miners! Victory to the miners!' and the response from the public was overwhelming with many donating into plastic buckets covered in **Coal not Dole** stickers. At one side of the square two automobiles were parked abreast with their engines running. Inside one of these vehicles, Alan was perched at the driver's seat alongside Hoss, who yawned, slumped, while Billy found himself sandwiched in the rear between Jack and Tom. Ralph Ward, Billy's elder brother, was sat smoking a cigarette behind the steering wheel in the other car. Tom scanned the Market Square, ending with him focusing on an imposing bronze statue of a cavalier perched upright upon a majestic-looking horse. Stretching a sigh, he looked around the lads, asking, "A' wonder who the hell he was? He must have been canny important to have a statue like that built of him."

"He was important, Tom," voiced Billy, "h-h-he was the third Marquis o-o-of Londonderry, his name was Charles W-W-William Vane Tempest Stewart, he died way back in 1854, and the statue w-w-was created by an Italian artist called Monti, who sculptured it exactly d-d-double real life s-s-size, it was e-e-erected in 1861, at least a' think it was 1861 ... yes it was, 'coss it was unveiled the s-s-same year as the American c-c-civil war b-b-broke out; anyway, that's Charles William Vane T-T-Tempest Stewart sat up there on that g-g-gallower. Mind you he was a bit of a t-t-twat like, he allegedly turned his troops o-o-on the striking miners, or something along those l-l-lines."

"Given half the chance that's what Thatcher would do to us, set the troops on us," moaned Tom before he laughed sharply and sarcastically ahead of saying, "it's a good job they're not building a statue of her, isn't it?"

"Not yet they're not, but they will do one day," put in Alan, "that's what the Tories like to do, erect statues of themselves."

Alan looked at Billy, questioning, "How do ya nar all this shit like, Billy?"

"A' don't know, a' j-j-just do."

"A' tell ya what," chipped in Jack, "we should come back the night and pull that fucking thing down and weigh it in for scrap, a' bet there's a tidy bit bronze there like."

Shaking his head, Alan sighed, "A' think you've got enough shit to weigh in ower the weekend, don't you, Jack?"

"Aye up there's away!" raised Hoss as he eyed Salty and John scurrying across a set of steps at the market square with a quartet of young men following in close pursuit. To the astonishment of shocked bystanders, they weaved in and out of market stalls prior to racing by a couple of shops before disappearing down a narrow, dead ended alleyway.

"I'm n-n-not cut out f-f-for all this shit like," heaved Billy all panicky.

"You'll be fine," encouraged Jack with a reassuring grimace before suggesting, "don't forget, lads, that big fucker's mine!" The four hastily exited the vehicle, and much to Alan's annoyance, they slammed the doors heavily behind them.

"Watch me fucking doors!"

"S-S-Sorry, Alan!" returned Billy.

Running the length of a narrow alley, Salty and John came to a stop in front of a brick gable end. Smiling nonchalantly, they slowly pivoted to face their pursuers.

"That was a bit silly running into a dead end, wasn't it?" said one of the young men who was broad shouldered, sporting short, cropped hair and a badly pockmarked face.

John shrugged his shoulders carefree. "A' divant nar, you tell me, was it?"

Wearing an evil smirk, the largest of the foursome stepped forward with clenched fists. "Yes it was, and what did I say would happen if I caught you's cadging money here again!?"

"A' canit quite remember," laughed Salty equally unperturbed, "would you like to run it past us again?"

"Who the fuck are you laughing at, ya silly old twat?" snarled another one of the young men who was a little plump, while brandishing a distinctive, horseshoe-shaped scar which ran above and to the outside of his top lip.

"How the hell does he nar what he's laughing at," broke in John, "there's nen of yas got labels on, we don't even know if yas are humans or animals yet, ya ugly fuckers look a bit like monkeys in suits to me, like!"

The smallest of the four was rather puny looking, showing thin shoulders, and fine, almost feminine features. Narrowing his eyes, he gritted his teeth, threatening, "Now, now, what have we got here then, a couple of old commie comedians or what!? Do you two know how much shit you two are actually in?"

"We haven't the foggiest," chuckled Salty, shaking his head carefree as he looked beyond the tetrad, "but a' nar one thing, yas are in a canny bit deeper shit than what we are." Following Salty's gaze a look of dread overcame the men as they encountered Hoss, Jack, Tom and Billy standing behind them with fists clenched at the ready.

"Like bullying old men, do yas?" growled Tom, stepping forward.

Jack's eagerness got the better of him, and without warning he barged past his brother to grab the largest of the strangers by his throat, clattering him up against a doorway shutter, then, with breakneck speed, he head butted the man, breaking his nose and sending blood splattering in all directions. Ignoring screams for him to stop, Jack set about punching the man continuously in his face until he fell to the floor; standing back a pace, he kicked the guy in his midriff, and he lay whimpering with Jack crouched over him, yelling, "Listen carefully, you arrogant fuck! You lot go near any of our lads again and we'll be back! Do ya understand!?"

A nod was given in answer. "Good! 'Coss if we have to come back through here again, ya'll get ten times worse than this, is that clear enough!?" Again, a bob of the head was returned before Jack once more put the boot in, but this time it was to his head and the man lay limp.

All rights and wrongs were long gone from Tom's conscience as he seized the pockmarked guy, forcing him into a headlock before he started uppercutting him repeatedly around his head and face until the man fell screaming to the ground where he instinctively rolled himself up into a protective ball. Tom straddled him, and seizing him by his throat he snarled, "Keep away from our lads or yar fucking dead! Understand!?"

The petrified man just about managed to nod before Tom once again jabbed him around his face.

Hoss scrunched his massive hands into fists as he slowly advanced towards his adversary, the traumatised man's heart pounded his chest as his blemished lip trembled uncontrollably. Ignoring the stranger's pleas for mercy, Hoss stepped one pace nearer to within striking distance, and after a quick sidestep to the right he set himself before letting loose with an almighty hook which landed with a sickening thud on the side of the man's temple, instantly buckling his legs and sending him crashing to the floor in a lifeless heap.

The smallest of the bunch tried to scurry away, but Billy managed to trip his legs from beneath him and he staggered three or four paces before sprawling facedown. Billy set about kicking him around his head and body until Tom barked, "Right! Time to go!"

Walking through the alleyway, Salty shook his head in amazement as he looked down at the stricken men. Nudging John, he laughed aloud, mocking, "If that's the master race I've shit better."

"Too right ya have," chuckled John, "mind you, that Jack's a handy bugger, isn't he?"

"Aye is he," laughed Salty, "he's just like his Ma's great-uncle Victor was."

On a fine, sunny Sunday morning, Jack's pickup truck was parked at an angle half on and off a kerb, at the side of a grimy scrapyard located in the midst of a neglected industrial estate on the outskirts of Hartlepool. Wearing old clothes, Hoss and Billy sat talking in the rear of the cabin, while Tom was up front in the passenger seat getting himself all agitated with a tuning dial as he tried in vain to find any kind of radio station. "Is there fuck all works in this thing!" he moaned walloping the radio.

Sporting rigger boots, combat trousers, and an old grey hoody which hung under a worn-out leather jacket, Jack emerged from the scrapyard gates. Strolling by two graffiti-smeared factory units, he joined the others inside the vehicle saying, "There's a fucking dog in there would eat ya alive given half a chance, it's got a heed on it," he stretched out his arms gushing, "this fucking big!"

"How big!?" enthused Hoss.

Once again Jack widened his arms and was just about to repeat his words when it dawned on him that Hoss was taking the piss. He snapped, "...fuck off, Hoss!" his words sending all into rapturous laugher before he slowly joined them with a half-smile of his own. "All right, funny fuckers!" he said removing a huge wad from inside his jacker pocket. Counting out a variety of notes it totted three hundred and fifty pounds. Turning to face Billy, Jack coughed slightly, asking, "How much is your monthly mortgage repayments, Billy?"

"My mortgage repayments!?" frowned Billy, totally bemused. "Ninety f-f-five quid a month, w-w-why?"

Jack shuffled out exactly one hundred and ninety pounds, and with a warm smile he handed over the money saying, "There ya gan, there's two months repayments there."

A' can't take all th-th-this!"

Tom broke in, "Yes you are taking it, Billy, end of."

"You need it more than us, Billy," voiced Hoss with a heartfelt grimace, "ya married with kids."

Sniffing away tears, Billy looked around his friends. "Thanks, lads, a' d-d-don't even nar what to s-s-say."

"Ya don't have to say owt," beamed Jack. Taking out a twenty pound note he presented it around, saying, "This is for next week's diesel money, which leaves us thirty-five quid each." Jack's smile widened as he handed everyone their share of the money.

"B-B-But I've already got my share here!" said Billy, holding up notes.

"Nor that's for your mortgage, the other thirty-five's for you," explained Jack prior to him brandishing yet another bundle of cash, "and there's another sixty-five quid each from this week's coal." They all sat elated until the sound of heavy barking intensified. "How'y!" hooted Jack. "Let's get the fuck out of here afore that thing gets loose and decides to eat one of me tyres." Driving away, Jack delicately pressed a button on the radio and Boy George joined them in the cab, singing a tale concerning a rather naughty chameleon who liked to change his colours. Looking to Tom, he smiled mischievously, goading, "You've been fucking about with the radio again, haven't ya?"

"Aye, it's fucking useless!" responded Tom. "It wants binning! And don't start neither."

Wearing a cheeky grin, Jack fleetingly glanced over his shoulder, chortling, "A' see he's still on his periods then!"

"Fuck off!" snapped Tom. "And keep ya eyes ..." Flustered, he pointed a finger beyond the windscreen. "... peeled on the road ahead there!"

Knowing this bickering would prolong for the whole of the journey home, Hoss deliberately changed the subject by asking, "What's Ma making for Sunday's dinner, Jack?"

"A'm not too sure, roast lamb a' think," he answered, shifting up a gear.

The big man tooted, "Lovely jubilee, it's me favourite, that is! She macks the best mint sauce gan'n."

Jack side eyed Tom, tittering, "Girly, girly," before he handed his brother a cigarette, and that was enough to set the two laughing aloud. Heading home, they talked nonstop as they drove through Hartlepool town centre before travelling northwards along a coastal road taking them past Crimdon Dene, a delightful little parkland that housed a developing caravan site and a spectacular, multi-arched railway viaduct. Beneath this overpass, a tarmac footpath followed the route of a meandering stream through the heart of leafy fields and woodlands before ending at a sweeping beach dotted in lofty sand dunes. Driving further, they chugged through Blackhall Colliery, a small, pit-less mining village, before descending another steep gradient where they came across Castle Eden Dene, which like Crimdon, exhibited a rather lengthy, multi-arched railway viaduct. Jack's truck struggled slightly, so he dropped down a gear to scramble up a drawn-out incline which brought them up into another pit village named Horden Colliery. Exiting Horden, they came to Grants Houses, a small estate known locally as 'No Man's Land', as it wasn't a part of Horden, or indeed Easington, but still most of the residents classed themselves as Easington people anyway. In the distance, Sizzler and Lemsip were arguing by the roadside with Lemsip stooped, desperately retrieving coal that had strewed across the road, while Sizzler was leant over a broken bicycle. Jack noticed them; nudging Tom, he grinned broadly, chuckling, "Look at the clip of these two numpties, Bud and Lou in disguise these two fuckers are."

"Bloody hell! Look at them," chuckled Tom, "they're warking around like one a' clock half struck."

Hoss propped himself forward between the two front seats, pointing, "Aye up! Lemsip's limping again!"

"He's been l-l-limping ever since he l-l-learned how to walk," put in Billy, picking up a newspaper.

Sizzler, aged twenty-three, was a short, stocky, dark-haired young man, who was so laid back, despite him bearing an awful facial disfigurement which he had unfortunately obtained as a child due to a freak accident with a faulty electric blanket.

Lemsip was a tall twenty-four-year-old possessing a mop of blond curly hair, which funnily enough harmonised with his lankiness and a pallid complexion. After years of endless mollycoddling from his widowed mother, Lemsip had developed into a fully-fledged hypochondriac, hence the nickname Lemsip.

Jack rolled down the window as he slowed to a stop. "Aye, aye, what are you two ladies up to then?"

"The back wheel's buckled," said Sizzler, flinging the misshapen wheel to the ground.

Lemsip looked up at Jack, whimpering, "Look what Sizzler's done to me ankle, Jack, he's ran is ower!" Rolling down his sock he unveiled a slight graze on his ankle. "Look at it! It's a frigging git gash!"

"Shut up, man, Lemsip!" chuckled Jack. "I've had bigger scratches on me cock-end, ya soft sod. Get in the back, and mack sharp in case the law's about." After slipping back overs a couple of times, Lemsip eventually managed to scramble his way up into the back of the truck before Sizzler started handing up sacks of coal. Jack shook his head. "Will yas hurry up, a' haven't got all day, and thraw that bike in an'll!"

"It's ne good, Jack, it's well and truly buggered," returned Sizzler.

"That's nowt, it'll gan on our scrap heap," he said as he wing mirrored Sizzler hand up the last of the sacks and the kaput bicycle before pulling himself up to join Lemsip. "Hang onto ya hats, ladies!" he yelled, grinding the pick-up into gear ahead of it juddering away.

Turning a page on his newspaper, Billy presented a clipping to Hoss showing Rock Hudson looking extremely poorly. "Seen the state of, R-R-Rock Hudson, Hoss, he looks frigging awful."

Hoss looked at the photo. "Fucking hell! A' never thowt I'd see the day I'd be better looking than Rock Hudson, mind!"

"He must have c-c-cancer or something," said Billy, "he looks dreadful, look at his face, it's all drawn-in, the poor s-s-sod's just a b-b-bag a' bones."

"A' like Rock Hudson," chipped in Tom, "he's as funny as owt with that Doris Day."

"Aye is he," agreed Billy, "especially in, P-P-Pillow Talk, and Send Me No F-F-Flowers."

"I liked them in Move Over Darling, too," broke in Jack, checking his side mirrors.

Billy corrected, "He wasn't in that p-p-picture, Jack, that w-w-was Doris Day and James Garner, it wasn't Rock H-H-Hudson."

Jack knew Billy would be right, so he didn't attempt to argue his case; instead "it was still a good film though!" came out.

"Aye was it," agreed Tom.

"Rock Hudson plays the part of a hypochondriac in that Send Me No Flowers, doesn't he?" laughed Hoss. "He's a bit like what Lemsip is."

Billy chuckled, "Can ya r-r-remember last N-N-November, when we went f-f-fishing up Scotland and L-L-Lemsip's Ma ran his gloves through his coat s-s-sleeves on string, like w-w-what the infants and juniors kids' Ma's d-d-do?"

"Aye!" laughed Jack. "And the silly sod still managed to lose one! And he got rang off his Ma when he got yerm!"

Tom shook his head, reminiscing, "Best of all though, was not last year, but the year 'afore, when we all went to Blackpool for the weekend on that jolly boys' outing, and his Ma packed him a hot water bottle inside his suitcase?"

"Aye that was f-f-funny as fuck that was!" laughed Billy.

Jack sniggered, "Too right it was!"

Hoss joined in with the laughter, scoffing, "It was a cracker, wasn't it? But best of all though, was when Lemsip asked the landlady in the hotel to fill the fucker up with hot watter afore he went to bed, she didn't nar whether to stick or frigging twist!"

ALMOST ONE WEEK LATER

Down at Eden allotments, a noisy cockerel beat its wings, greeting in a brand-new day as men of young and old rose early from their beds with several of the exhibition growers already busy at work sprucing up their leek trenches. One or two of these leek men scanned around making sure the coast was clear prior to surreptitiously measuring out hush-hush feeds in preparation of pouring the stenchy stuff into cut up ten-inch plastic tubes that were embedded at a slight angle between each of the nurturing leeks. A few of the traditional growers used secret liquid formulas which were more often than not passed down from generation to generation, with some feeding their leeks with a nutritious concoction based around pigs' blood and heaven knows what other additives, but most fed the things on stale beer slops collected from numerous pubs and clubs that ran the length and breadth of Easington. Up in the blue, individual flocks of pigeons circled the skies above their own specific lofts to a diversity of shouts, or whistles, coming from separate pigeon men, who, not too dissimilar to the leek men, possessed cloak-and-dagger tendencies, especially when in the presence of fellow flyers.

Regular, run of the mill gardeners were also busy at their plots, either hoeing or weeding around young brassica plants or churning over fresh ground to a spade's depth in preparation for Brussels sprouts and other winter veg to be planted out at a later date, and with each shovel turned animated blackbirds looked on from off the tops of cabins, greenhouses, or high fencing in anticipation at a banquet of juicy worms. Overlooking smouldering fires, a few of the elderly horticulturists were happy enough just to lean against garden forks or spades as they gossiped endlessly over rickety fences, whilst to their annoyance from somewhere within the allotment estate, loud music sounded irritable from a radio, but despite this audible distraction all was dandy in and around the allotments of Eden on this sunny Saturday morning.

Breathing deeply, Joe Breester, Hoss' father, leant onto a sweeping brush, struggling to catch his breath. Scrutinizing his pigeon loft, he thought how the place was still in good nick despite it needing a bit of a revamp, perhaps a lick of interior paint would do the trick, but it would have to wait now, wait until the racing season was over and done with. The loft was expertly constructed from out of the finest tung and groove lumber, and it stretched for a good ten metres in length, by just under three and a half metres in width while separated into three specific sections. The end unit was caged off in chicken wire and housed forty of his young birds that were content to roost on perches or even laze in straw-lined wooden boxes. The midsection was where Joe kept a couple dozen pairs of his finest breading stock birds, and finally the last sector contained sixty of his primed racing pigeons, with each pigeon nestled inside its own individual wooden punnet the size of a large shoe box.

Joe was only sixty-two but looked and felt decades older due to his ill-health. With each breath taken, agony riddled his drawn-out face as pneumoconiosis (a coal miners' nightmare) slowly ate away at his already ebbing lungs. A once proud, powerful man, Joe hated how he had faded to a former shadow of himself, he loathed the fact he had no strength and very little energy left to even carry out his customary daily routine; he also held a sadness that he had just about given up the will to fight; but worst by far for him was, he detested the fact that with each day passing he was slowly losing what dignity he had struggled to retain.

Hoss carried a couple of bags of pigeon feed from the allotment gateway along a grassy pathway before resting the sacks down at the foot of their colourful pigeon loft, which his father and himself had meticulously painted in red and white stripes, influenced by the colours of Sunderland AFC, their beloved football team. Joe was soldiering on, trying his best to sweep out the loft when a bout of endless coughing overcame him. Hearing his father fighting for his breath, Hoss rushed inside where he took away the broom before aiding the old man outside to a veranda where he gently lowered him into a dog-eared rocking chair, saying, "Just sit there and catch ya breath, Da, I'll finish cleaning the loft out after I've stocked the feed up."

"Cheers, son... yar a good'n." Once again Joe started coughing. His hands shook noticeably as he pulled out a handkerchief to wipe away black mucus from around his mouth.

"Giss a look at that," said Hoss, practically snatching the hankie away from his father's clasp, "how long's this been like this for?"

"It's just... started ... today," lied the old man.

"You need to go back to the doctors, Da; it's getting worse, this is."

Joe breathed deeply, trying to catch his breath. "It's a... waste of time... son, there's... nowt they can do... so just leave it... please."

"Where's ya inhalers?"

For some unknown reason Joe flashed an impish grin. "A' left... the buggers... down yerm, they divant even... work, man."

"If they didn't work, they wouldn't have given ya them in the first place, Da, you bide there, I'll not be long."

"Where... ya gan'n?"

"Down yerm to fetch ya inhalers up, and don't you dare budge, a' mean it, mind, Da, just stay put till a' get back." Hoss quickly left the allotment unawares that his father was once again overcome by another bout of endless coughing.

Billy scraped the remains of porridge around a bowl before carefully spooning it into Alisia's gaping mouth, and like a normal two-year-old toddler she instantly spat it back out then proceeded to pick up handfuls of the stuff, plastering it everywhere. "Alisia, please don't do that, sweetie," moaned Billy, who funnily enough showed no signs of a stutter when speaking to his children. After wiping her hands and face, he plucked bits of breakfast from out of his daughter's hair before lifting the child from a highchair to settle her onto a settee. Strolling to the foot of the stairs he wiped himself down, shouting, "Kelly! Kelly! Do you want a chucky egg and some soldiers putting on flowerpots!?"

"Yesim's, Daddy," she replied sweetly from an upstairs landing before carefully stepping down a couple of runners, dragging Pippy, her fluffy toy pooch, by an already ripped ear.

"Right then, boiled eggs it is," he murmured to himself before ordering, "be careful on them stairs, love."

"Daddy I'm four, not two you know," came back in the manner of a typical four-year-old little girl; "anyway, I'm going back to my bedroom to play for a bit more."

Billy crossed a room where everything seemed to be coloured in various shades of browns and beiges. Against one wall, a cooker and fridge-freezer matched in identical two-tone colours of brown and gold, while a pine table and benches were positioned under a window, harmonising with a grand looking Welsh dresser that set off a corner with a fine collection of china teapots on display.

A wall cupboard and a separated cubbyhole housed a stainless-steel sink and automatic washer to finish off a small kitchen area. Underfoot, a recently fitted brown and beige shag pile ran the room to flow beneath a stone archway that separated two stone firesides creating one large open plan area, where once it was two separate rooms. Cork effect wall tiles surrounded a kitchen end inglenook, while modern cream wallpaper covered walls at a lounge fireplace where a mahogany coffee table stood central at the front of a brown three-piece suite. To one side of a lounge fireplace, a state-of-the-art Amstrad Hi-Fi stack was on display inside an alcove, alongside an ultramodern television set which was silver in colour and purposely placed below another window that was draped with fashionable cream and russet curtains.

The backdoor sounded to a slam ahead of Marie Ward entering the room holding a jar of 'Mellow Birds' coffee. Looking around the room, she removed her coat, moaning, "Have ya not hoovered yet?"

"Nor, not y-y-yet, I've just finished feeding our Alisia." Searching through a wall cupboard he rattled out a small saucepan and a couple of eggcups which were chipped but still managed to resemble miniature swans, even if one of the holders had somehow become decapitated. "Do ya want a boiled e-e-egg putting on, love?"

"No, tar ..." Standing five-feet-four, Marie was an ashen looking twenty-five-year-old woman possessing shortish dark hair and a prominent hooked nose. Although she was quite slender, she held a pear-shaped figure as her hips and protruding backside outdid the rest of her frame. "... Don't forget I've got to go for an interview up at the Colliery Club the safta about that barmaid's job, ya'll have to watch the bairns till a' get back, so don't be making any plans with ya mates."

"A' won't, are ya sure ya w-w-want to wait on, love? Ya've never d-d-done it afore."

"I have no other choice, have ah! Besides, it canit be all that hard if Loraine Ply can manage it, and God nars we more than need the money."

Billy stretched a sigh, saying, "It's up t-t-to you, pet." After filling a pan of water to half full, he placed it onto a cooker ring just as the door once again slammed ahead of Tony Ward, Billy's favourite nephew, entering the room. Billy welcomed, "Hello s-s-son!"

"All right!" replied Tony, a strong looking eighteen-year-old lad who sported a slightly pockmarked face. "A' thought you were up Tow Law picketing?"

"Nor, it's c-c-cancelled, do ya want a light boiled e-e-egg putting on?"

"No thanks," he said, parking himself next to Alisia. The instant Billy's back was turned, Tony's eyes floated to Marie with eyebrows raised; shaking her head she shrugged her shoulders wide-eyed in return before Billy swivelled, holding a couple of eggs.

"I'll make us a coffee?" she hastily said just as a scratching at the front door sounded.

"Will someone let the d-d-dog in?" raised Billy as he carefully placed slices of bread under a smoky grill.

Marie opened up, and Beauty, their faithful Jack Russell terrier bitch, swaggered herself into the room. Instantly, Tony sat up bolt right with fear as Beauty took one look at him, and with raised hackles she set off growling her customary warning at him before she turned away and started eating bits of porridge that had dropped to the carpet. "No need to hoover n-n-now, love!" joked Billy.

Picking up her knitting, Irene had just settled into the comfort of her favourite chair awaiting Roy Plomley to introduce his guest on Desert Island Discs when a faint knocking at her door set Mick away barking nonstop in his usual flighty manner. Irene stood, ordering, "Shut up, ya daft bugger!" Opening up, she faced Peter Millison, a tall, fair haired, slightly plump young man who was stood in an obvious distraught state. "Hello, son," she greeted politely, "if you're looking for the lads, I'm afraid they're not in, they're down the allotment."

"It's you I've come to see, Mrs Gilroy, not them," he muttered, his stare not leaving the ground.

Irene took in the state Peter was in, and she had more than an inkling at why he was standing at her front door. After side eyeing in both directions seeking out nosey curtain twitchers, she muttered, "How'y in, son." Ushering him from the doorstep, then through a lobby way and into the sitting room, she smiled. "Sit ya sell down, do you want a cuppa?"

"No, tar, a' canit stay long." His bloodshot eyes slowly lifted to Irene. "This is hard for me to say, Mrs Gilroy, a' don't even know where to start so a' might as well just get to the point." After composing himself by means of a couple of prolonged sighs he breathed deeply. "Jack's been sleeping with Debbie, and it has to stop."

Irene closed her eyes, puffing her cheeks, she exhaled, "Is it not just idle gossip, Peter? Ya know what they're like 'round here, tell the hinging of a man so they can."

Shaking his head, Peter took out a handkerchief, blowing. "It's not gossip, Mrs Gilroy, a' wished it was, a' confronted Debbie this morning and she admitted everything, apparently, it's been going on for months now, and she says she loves him." An awkward respite of silence lingered briefly, a hush that wasn't natural yet spoke more than any able philosophers' words could ever do.

Sitting alongside Peter, she muttered, "Leave it with me, love, a' promise ya now, he will never go near your Debbie again."

"Thank you, Mrs Gilroy, and I'm sorry it had to come down to this but a' didn't know which way to turn, a' know what Jack would have done if I'd confronted him h–"

"Here," she interrupted, "you've got nowt to be sorry about, son, and don't you go worrying ya bit sell about him neither, 'coss I'm telling ya now he wouldn't dare say boo to ya, never mind lay a finger on ya, not after I've finished with the bugger, you just concentrate on Debbie and leave Jack to me."

"Thank you." Standing, he wiped his blond fringe from his face. "You're a good woman, and once again I'm sorry a' had to come to you, Mrs Gilroy."

Showing Peter from the house, she leaned against the doorframe with her arms folded. "You did the right thing, love. Bye now, and try and get things sorted with your Debbie; anybody can make mistakes, ya know, Peter, there's nen of us perfect."

"I know that," he replied, puffing a weighty sigh, "but 'a think it's gone beyond mistakes, a' really think she wants out."

"You try ya best with her, son, yas have a bit bairn there to think about, and above everything else he's got ta come first." Irene looked on as Peter dragged his feet away in the gait of a broken man. Once again eying left, then right, she gently closed the door before she sniffed teary eyed as her emotions overwhelmed her.

At the Gilroys' croft, local birdlife chirped back and forth while in the background a boisterous rooster wafted its wings while croaking raucously over his cluster of broody hens. Jack had finished mucking out a stable as Mowgli, his trusty nine-year old Clydesdale cross, ran friskily inside an acre and a half of lush green paddock. Jack had inherited Mowgli from his late father, and he simply adored the huge stallion as it held so many memories of treasured times spent with his father before he fell ill with his cancer; he also found it relaxing tendering to all the black steed's needs; but above all, he relished the tranquillity of hacking him around a picturesque five-mile trail which took him across the cliff tops at Easington before descending onto an undulating bridlepath that channelled him through Hawthorn Dene and then back again.

Jack forced a wheelbarrow overloaded with horse manure from out of a stable ahead of pushing the stinky load through a gateway which directed him into an extensive concrete yard containing a substantial scrapheap, a sizable mound of coal, a large pile of chopped logs, and an even greater stockpile of uncut timber. To one side of the yard an old horse box trailer stood rusted alongside a couple of timber-clad sheds. Opposite, a green-coloured brick workshop that was attached to the back of a spacious breezeblock cabin which provided all the home comforts that Tom and Jack required, including a dog-eared leather three-seater settee that was black in colour to match with a single chair; a hoary old rocky chair stood between a gas burning stove and an antique log burning stove that was so unusual it may well have been salvaged from the Alamo, or perhaps some far-flung Alaskan log cabin. A secure metal lockup was positioned at the far end of the enclosure, and it was in here where the brothers stashed away anything of value, the likes of copper, brass, lead, a pair of petrol chainsaws, a strimmer, a couple of diesel-run generators, a powerful rotavator, a petrol driven post-bradawl, and a fine collection of hand and power tools.

Jack pushed the barrow for the entirety of the compound before he came to yet another access which ushered him into the allotment side of the smallholding that was divided into three sections of which two were virtually identical in size, approximately twenty-five metres in length, by ten metres in width. The first of these sectors was planted out with twenty or more rows of sprouting potatoes and a couple of rows of swedes, parsnips and beetroot. The opposing bed was filled with a variation of young brassica plants including sprouts, cabbages, cauliflowers, kale and broccoli. Strings of climbing peas were also planted out in this fertile stretch of the plot alongside a couple of bamboo wigwams filled with rising runner beans; to one side of these wigwams grew dwarf beans, sweetcorn, carrots, onions, shallots, and a huddle of healthy rhubarb tucked away in a corner next to a perimeter fence.

The final section of allotment was considerably larger than the previous two, comprising an active chickencoop where a quadruplet of hens roamed content on a strip of lush grass. Three extensive hand-built greenhouses ran side by side with two flourishing with a hotchpotch of sapling tomatoes, chillies, peppers, and cucumbers, while the other was taken up with an assortment of developing carnations, chrysanthemums and dahlias. Two huge polytunnels stretched identical for over fifteen metres with each polytunnel enveloping three, one-metre-high by one-metre-wide trenches which ran parallel for the entire length of these tunnels. It was here, in these fecund beds, that Tom kept his giant show onions and exhibition leeks, of which several varieties had descended directly from his father's highly sought-after strains. Jack forced the wheelbarrow up a wooden ramp to tip the contents onto a muckheap ahead of joining Tom in one of the polytunnels. "What they like then?" he asked, slightly concerned.

Lifting a flag on one of the leeks, Tom pointed out tiny spots of discolouration. "Here, look at this, they've got a bit of a virus but it's nothing to worry about, Cumberlands are noted for it."

"It's not thrip though, is it?" asked Jack, inspecting the plants.

"Nor, it's not thrip, it's just the way the Cumberlands are, it'll grow owt eventually, the rest are standing champion." Tom showed Jack a healthier looking strain of leek. "Here, look at these Betty-Blacks and Yorkshire Giants, they're ticking over quite nicely." The distinct smell of Jeyes fluid disinfectant was strong as the brothers entered into a second polytunnel where Tom beamed as he pointed to yet another variety of leek that stood almost twice the size of the previous ones and flourished in a deeper, healthier green. "Look at these, young'n, they're absolutely thriving, these are."

"That's Dad's strains for ya," sighed Jack, "nowt but the best."

"Aye," agreed Tom all proud. "If a' can stop them from going ower the top a' think a' might be onto a winner with these; there's a long way to gan yet, like, but I have to say they're looking canny." Tom tapped the top of his head, adding, "touch wood".

"They are standing canny, mind," praised Jack, "so's the onions too, they're a lot bigger than what last year's were at this time." Walking away, he asked, "Are ya ganna be long finishing?"

"Nar, not really, I've just got to spray the leeks, and that should be it for the day."

"What ya spraying them for, a' thought you said they didn't have thrip?"

"They haven't, it's just precautionary, just in case."

"Righty owe then, I'll gan and lock the yard up." Leaving the polytunnel Jack glanced back over his shoulder. "Remind is on when we get yerm to phone the farrier, Mowgli needs his feet trimming again."

A rather irate Irene paced back and forth across the sitting room for what seemed like an eternity before Jack's truck rumbled to a stop outside of the house. Standing at the fireside, her hands shook as she picked up a packet of cigarettes ahead of Jack and Tom entering the room with Jack whistling merrily away. The instant Tom eyed his mother he knew for sure that something was amiss. Jack, well, he just kept on whistling. "Happy are ya, whistling away to ya bit sell?" she asked in a direct tone as she fumbled to light up a cigarette. Now it dawned on Jack all was not well.

"Aye, why," he returned with a confused frown.

"Why!? 'Coss Peter Millison isn't that happy, that's why."

"What ya on about, Peter Millison isn't that happy, what's that got to do with me?"

Irene stood eye to eye with Jack. "Apparently everything, seen as you've been sleeping with Debbie behind his back, you horrible rat!"

"Nor a' have not!"

Jack's words hadn't left his mouth when Irene slapped him hard across his face, shouting, "Don't you dare stand there telling me bare face lies, you horrible, good for nothing snake ..."

Tom slumped himself into a chair. Picking up a newspaper he held it close to his face in an attempt to hide his discomfiture.

Irene became tearful, saying, "...the poor lad's just been to me door, man! He's distraught, absolutely heartbroken so he is!"

"He'll be more than heartbroken when a' get me hands of him! I'll ring his neck!"

Irene pointed in Jack's face, threatening, "You'll do no such thing! I'm telling ya now, you so much as lay one finger on that poor lad, and you'll be out that door within the blink of an eye." Jack stood in silence as Irene belittled, "He's more of a man that what you could ever be! Do ya know that!"

"Or aye, is that right?" his words prompting Tom to rattle his newspaper signifying for his brother to keep his mouth shut.

"Yes, it is right! And do you know why, Jack, it's not because he's tougher or stronger than you, it's because he has responsibilities, responsibilities of fetching a family up, and that's something you'll never be able to do, not in a month of Sundays could ya, and do ya know why! 'Coss ya canit even fend for ya sell never mind fend for a family, that's why!"

"Aye a' can!"

"Can ya heckers like! Ya dinit even nar how many sugars ya tack in ya tea and coffee, man! Useless ya are, absolutely useless, and that's why he's more of a man than what you are, or ever could be." Jack stood, lost for words. Tossing her cigarette into the fire, Irene's eyes filled, and she continued, "You end it with that Debbie, mind, Jack, and a' mean this instant, do you understand?" He nodded in response as she wiped away tears. "Good, and don't you dare lift a finger to poor Peter neither, he's the innocent party in all this shit, not Debbie, and certainly not you, I'm ashamed of ya! Absolutely ashamed! Ya've got the morals of a blinking alley cat thuw has, lad!" Irene turned to Tom. Snatching the newspaper from his face, she groaned, "Did you know owt about this?" Now it was Tom who was stumped into silence. "Too right ya did, and that macks thuw just as bad as that daft bugger." Leaving the room, she shouted for Mick and after a minute or two, she re-entered, buttoning up her coat with Mick wagging his tail as he trailed behind on a leash. "I'm going up our Leat's, if yas want owt to eat yas nar where the cooker is." Gawking at Jack she sighed prolonged, saying, "Tha nars, Jack, there's plenty of single lasses out there for ya ta gan at without ya gan'n with the married ones." Walking away she left the house to the sound of the front door slamming.

Shaking his head, Tom sighed prolonged. "What did a' tell ya! But would ya listen!? Would ya heckers like!" Frowning deep, he looked on as his brother pulled open the front door. "Where you gan'n?"

"To the fish shop," answered Jack, "a'm frigging starving, do want owt fetching back or are ya ganna sit there moping around like a little girl?"

"Aye, get is fish fritter and chips and a couple of bread buns, and Jack, tack heed of what Ma says, end this shit with Debbie, mind."

"A' nar that, man! Anyway, it's all for the best it's come out, 'coss a' was starting to get bored with her." He left and the door creaked to a close.

CHAPTER TWO, JUNE, "R-R-ROURKE'S DRIFT!"

It was a fine June morning even if it hadn't quite broke daylight, yet still the crack of dawn had fashioned up an exquisite amber skyline over Easington Colliery, with a notably brighter orange radiating above the distant horizon of the North Sea. Birdlife stirred in the shadows of hedgerows that surrounded the Colliery Club carpark with clusters of bickering blackbirds ceasing ongoing feuds to participate in an orchestrated performance of the dawn chorus with a sprightly thrush leading as conductor, and a warbling wren flourishing on first violin. A cream and purple coloured rattletrap of a bus was parked opposite the club vestibule as queuing pickets grasped suitcases, eagerly awaiting to board. At the rear of this boneshaker...

PYEGIL'S
EXECUTIVE COUCHES
EASINGTON COLLIERY
CO. DURHAM.
TEL-271212

...had been painstakingly hand painted onto the boot by a gifted, if not slightly dyslexic engraver. At the front of the bus,

Tony the Vicar was donned in his ceremonial apparel splashing Holy Water here, there, and everywhere, as he attempted to bless the coach along with each individual picket who risked his watery gauntlet to board – these included Jack, Tom, Hoss, and Billy. Settling into seats, Jack and the lads claimed the whole back seats with Lemsip and Sizzler seated in the next row down on the lefthand side. Across the aisle, Joe Whitlewith was enjoying a smoke whilst sat alongside Ger Wilson.

Joe Whitlewith was aged in his early thirties and was an up-and-coming union man who was well liked by the men at Easington Colliery, especially by the younger generation. Boasting a lean physique, he bordered six feet, exhibiting a blemish-free complexion which was topped with a head of healthy, well-groomed hair.

Aged in his mid-twenties, Gerald Wilson was known simply as Ger, and he was Jack and Tom Gilroy's full cousin. Ger was an athletic-looking young man who had an uncanny resemblance to a certain Charlie George, a seventies iconic footballer who used to play upfront for the once mighty Arsenal. Although Ger was jaunty, he was very intelligent, and a bright future lay ahead of him as he was acclaimed to be, not only the topmost electrical engineer at Easington Colliery, but also throughout the whole of the County Durham coalfield.

Excitement filled the bus, especially amongst the younger lads, as this was the first time that they had actually picketed beyond the Northeast, and their destination for the next five days was to be Bold Colliery, a small pit village located on the outskirts of St Helens, West Lancashire. The bus hadn't long pulled away from the carpark when Jack yelled, "Are we there yet!?" – his jaunty comment triggering laughter amongst the pickets, but not so much the aloof driver. Sniggering aloud, Jack looked around the rest, saying, "By that driver's a right miserable twat, isn't he?

If the bugger smiled it would crack his frigging face!" Looking at Joe he enquired, "So where exactly are we picketing at, Joe?"

"Bold Colliery, St Helens," replied Joe, relighting a cigarette.

Jack puckered a frown, saying, "Never heard of St Helens."

Tom raised, "I have, it's got a canny rugby league team."

"It was also the f-f-first football team B-B-Bert Trautmann played for, St Helens T-T-Town," added Billy.

"Who the fuck's Bert Trautmann?" asked Hoss.

"He was a German prisoner of w-w-war during the Second W-w-world War who was incarcerated at a p-p-prisoner of war camp o-o-on the outskirts of St Helens. They used to sneak him out the compound o-o-on weekends s-s-so he could play in g-g-goal for them, and a-a-after the war had ended, he stayed here in England m-m-marrying a local lass, he was that g-g-good of a keeper h-h-he signed from St Helens to Man City where he b-b-broke his neck in the 1956 FA Cup final, and even though his neck was b-b-broken he still played out the whole of the m-m-match. He ended up a grit l-l-legend and that, and w-w-when he retired the Man City fans burnt the g-g-goal posts so n-n-no other keeper could stand between the same set of sticks."

"I've heard that story somewhere before," said Tom.

"A' think I have too," voiced Jack. Pulling out a pack of playing cards he grinned huge, "Anyone for jack doubles? We'll put the rubs in see who partners who."

"How much ya p-p-playing for like?" broke in Billy. "Just fivepences, Billy, double in the woods though!" Shuffling the deck, Jack smiled around. "How'y, it'll pass the time away till we get there." They all decided to chance their hand in the card game including Joe, Ger, Lemsip and Sizzler.

After a gruelling stint of firstly cooking, then serving meals to an ever-increasing number of miners and their families, Bev and Tracy dragged their feet across the Colliery Club singing end to join Jean, Jenny Black, and Jill Giles who were sat at the back of the hall drinking tea as they waited with bated breath for Irene and Sue to return from a County Council meeting with news regarding further funding for the kitchen. "I'm absolutely shattered," moaned Bev as she lit up a cigarette.

"Ya've got a good right to be, yas have never stopped, every one of yas are absolute treasures," praised Jenny Black, Irene's sister's sister-in-law, who was a slender lady aged in her mid-fifties possessing dark features including jet-black hair, and the friendliest, hazel-coloured eyes that were as honest as a day's long.

"Arr tar very much, Jenny, that's nice," beamed Bev all proud. "That's so nice of ya."

"It's never been as busy as this before," sighed Tracy. "Honestly, we've been rushed off our feet all day, a' don't know where they've all come from, we must have fed at least six hundred people the day."

"Aye and the rest," put in Jean. "I'm sweating like bulls' lugs here." Sniffing under her armpits, she twisted her face, saying, "It's straight in the bath for me when a' get yerm, Jim'll have ta mack the bairns their teas, a' canit be arsed."

"Is Jim not away picketing like, Jean?" asked Jill Giles, a slightly plump, middle-aged lady who was of average height showing mousy-coloured hair and marble-blue eyes.

"Nor, he's on coal duty this week, Jill," answered Jean before sighing. "A' hope he drops a couple of bags off 'round ours, we're right on the bottom, I've niver narn us not to have coal afore."

Bev checked her watch. "A' wonder how long Irene and Sue are ganna be? A' hope they've getting that grant."

"Why we'll be up a certain creek without a paddle if they haven't," sighed Jenny, "it's vital for the upkeep of the place, the union's monies are dwindling away to next to nothing now." Nodding towards the doorway she broke into a grin, enthusing,

"Aye! Aye! Look what the cat's dragged in!" All eyes glued as Sue and Irene rushed the room to join the rest of the group.

"Well?" asked Jean raising her eyes up at Sue.

"Well, what, Jean?" she answered, removing her coat and sitting.

"How did the meeting go!? Did we get it!?"

"Well–" Sue lit up a cigarette– "with this Government's new legislations coming into effect, it's apparently illegal for Durham County council, or indeed any other councils, to hand monies directly to the mining communities–"

"So, we're not getting nowt then!?" interrupted Bev, looking around the group with disappointment. "Why that's just great, that is! Bloody Thatcher's thowt of everything again, as blinking usual!"

"Hold on a minute, Bev," said Irene in a soft, calm tone as she too sat. "Let Sue finish talking, flowerpots."

"Right." Sue beamed around the cluster. "To put you all out ya misery, we've got all the funding we were asking for, in fact we've managed to get a bit extra."

"How?" asked a relieved Jenny. "'A' thought you said Thatcher had put a stop to all direct fundings from councils."

Sue flicked cigarette ash into a brimming ashtray. "She has, but we've worked out a way to get around it."

"You mean *you've* found a way around it!" gushed Irene, lighting up a cigarette.

"Why it wasn't just me, Irene, to be fair other councillors were involved in it too; anyway, what we've had to do to get round this new law was to involve a third party."

"A third party?" frowned Tracy. "Like who?"

"Like the Salvation Army," beamed Sue.

"What, the Sally Bash!?" chirped Tracy. "'A' loves them, me!"

Somewhat stumped, Jenny looked to Sue. "How come the Salvation Army's got involved like?"

"Because Sue asked them to, Jenny," put in Irene, "let her finish her story and it will all become clear." Irene looked to Sue with a nod of her head. "Carry on, flowerpots."

"Right then, ladies!" Once again, Sue smiled at the table. "What we've done is, Durham County council have donated to the Salvation Army all the monies that we were going to hand out in grants to our various community kitchens, then, the Salvation Army has returned all the monies back to each of the individual kitchens in the form of charity aid, and guess what, Thatcher can't do a single thing about it, absolutely zilch."

Irene started clapping. "'A' thinks this young lady here merits a round of applause, don't you!?" and to Sue's embarrassment all the girls applauded.

"Please don't," requested Sue, "and like a' said previous, it wasn't just me; other councillors and officials were involved in it too."

Jill looked to Irene. "Changing the subject, ladies, have we got any more volunteers yet? It's getting all too much for just us few, we're knacked."

"Yes," sighed Irene. "Liz Ord, Denise Simson, and Ellen Marr are starting this Thursday."

"We need more than just them three," moaned Jean, "we're absolutely worn-out, man, Irene, we need a break to recharge the old batteries."

Irene sympathised, "'A' nar yas do, love, I've got a few more irons in the fire, I'll pop round and see them later on the safta."

Looking absolutely petrified, Debbie Millison gingerly entered the hall. At once the girls sat in an awkward silence as she passed on her way into the kitchen. Irene stood to follow Debbie into the room. Debbie mumbled, "I haven't come looking for trouble, Irene, a' didn't expect ya's still been here, I've just come to collect a few things then I'll be out of your hair for good."

"Things? Like what things?"

"Nothing much, just me cardigan, apron and a pair of boat shoes."

"How are ya doing?" sympathized Irene with a friendly grimace. Debbie shrugged her shoulders in reply before tears filled her eyes. Irene hugged her saying, "Leave your stuff where it is, sweetheart, we desperately need you here."

"A' can't," she sniffed, "a' can't face Jack when he comes in."

"Yes, you can; anyway, we'll cross that bridge when we come to it, and like a' said you're needed here, Debbie."

Debbie nodded, sniffing. "Okay then." She even managed to force a slight smile before tears once again overwhelmed her. She sobbed, "A' didn't mean to fall in love with your Jack ya know, Irene, it just happened, a' can't help the way a' feel."

"Debbie, love, our Jack doesn't love you; he never did, and he never will, he's not capable of falling in love, not with you, nor anyone else come to think of it, and even if he did a' would have put a stop to it the instant a' found out; you have your Peter and that canny little bairn to think about, forget Jack, you have to move on, sweetheart."

"I'm trying to," she said, wiping her eyes on her sleeve.

"Good!" chirped Irene, handing over a handkerchief. "Now, pull ya sell together and get in there and join in with the meeting, they've all missed you, and I have too." After Irene had left the room, Debbie was stood at a mirror, drying her eyes when hoots of elation echoed ahead of Bev and Tracy dashing into the kitchen to hug her.

Bold Welfare Hall stood grand within manicured grounds. At one side of the Art Deco structure a tarmac road wound down to a football pitch and changing rooms, while a display of well-kept shrubs and lawns stretched along the entire frontage of the building. Purple and yellow striped wallpaper greeted at a corridor to continue up a flight of stairs and into a huge first floor dancehall.

At the heart of this hall, Jack and the lads had laid down their claims to sleeping quarters by means of sleeping bags, blankets, pillows and other forms of slumber material. The odour of tobacco smoke was strong and had just about overcome the mustiness of the room as pickets sat around scattered tables listening to an elderly, bald-headed union official finishing off a lengthy prep talk at why the Easington pickets were invited down to Lancashire, and what was required of them on the picket line. "Reet then, any questions?" addressed the official in a strong Lancashire accent. Jack hesitated before he gingerly raised his hand to speak. The man beamed at Jack. "Go on then, cock, ask t'way, lad."

"Why a' was just wondering like," said Jack warily.

"Aye, wondering what? Come on, don't be shy, spit it out." Sensing Jack's nervousness, the man encouraged Jack with a reassuring smile. "Nowt te worry about here, kidda, tha's amongst nowt but friends."

"Why, a' was just wondering like." Clearing his throat, Jack rattled a string of coughs, then grinning his usual impishness, he blurted, "Where does all the fanny get te on a night?"

Within an instant, the man's expression descended into a deep frown. "If tha means local lasses, they get over te Cherry Tree pub 'cross t'road, there's one of those fandangle disco things on the-neet, but please don't go upsetting locals, 'tis scabs and coppers tha's down here te sort, not locals."

Jack pledged, "Divant worry about that, we'll sort them all right."

Ogling Jack, the man scowled. "I hope tha's not going te be handful, lad?"

"Who me!" gushed Jack pointing at his own chest. "Why not likely, I'm a good Catholic lad so I am," and once again he cast a grimace that was way above brazen.

"Aye, sure tha is," mumbled the man before asking, "reet, any more questions before I get off home for tea?"

Hoss slowly raised his hand. "Is there a fish shop nearby?"

"Aye just up t'road, cock, three hundred yards past Cherry Tree pub on left-hand side." He beamed wide, adding, "Makes lovely Lancashire Hotpot pies too I tell thee, award winning so they are, lad, award winning."

Hoss grinned ear to ear, nudging Tom, he lit up a cigarette and with an enthusiastic tone he said, "Never had an award-winning Lancashire Hotpot pie afore, have you, Tom?"

Tom's response was to shake his head with a sharp smile, replying, "A' canit say a' have, young'n."

The theme music to Coronation Street sounded at number two Cuba Street just as Irene rushed into the sitting room holding a couple of meals. Handing a plate over to Alan, she cast a quick smile, asking, "What have a' missed?"

"Nowt much, love, a' think that Mike Baldwin's trying to home in with that Deirdre Barlow, or... Bill Webster's put an offer in for Elsie Tanner's house an'all."

"He hasn't!?" she enthused.

"He has, honestly."

Irene pointed the television remote, increasing the volume by means of a couple of green-coloured bars showing on the screen. "How much has he offered for it, like? Did he say?"

"Aye, eleven and a half grand."

"Eleven and a half thousand!? He's got a right nerve that Bill Webster has, far too cheap that is! Well, that's it then, I'm afraid that's the last we'll ever see of Elsie Tanner, a' can't see her coming back from Portugal now, not for love nor money, she's been out there since just after Christmas." She looked at Alan, raising, "There's plenty of pie left in the oven if you fancy some more, love?"

"A' will later." His eyes ran over a plate filled with a mouthwatering wedge of homemade steak and onion pie, mushy peas, and chunky chips he asked, "It looks bloody lovely this does.

So, what am I doing the night then, Irene, a'm a' staying, going, staying, going or what?"

"Staying!" came back all fidgety. "But you will have to be up early in the morning, just in case somebody sees ya leaving the house."

"Irene, love, we're not exactly having an affair tha nars! You're single, I'm single, and it's been over eight months now, do ya not think it's about time we let people know about us, especially the lads?"

"No, not yet!" she answered all of a fluster. "When the time's right I'll tell them."

"And when's that ganna be, like?"

She sighed. "A' don't know yet! Anyway, eat ya supper 'afore it gans card."

Settling to a grin she watched Alan cutting into his pie. He returned a beam and after tasting the crispy pastry and tender filling his face lit up further. "Is it all right?" she asked.

"Alright! It's above alright this is, love, it's blum'n lovely so it is."

"Oh a' forgot!" Resting her meal on the arm of her chair she quickly left the room to return holding a couple of slices of buttered bread. "Here," she said, handing over the slices prior to leaning over and pecking a kiss on his lips. "How's the strike going love?"

"A' haven't a clue, I'm just a local union secretary who's deliberately kept in the dark I am."

"Kept in the dark from who?"

"From the National Executive, Irene, that's who."

"Why pity about the buggers, then!" she snapped just as Mick entered into the room to park himself at Alan's feet with its tail wagging nonstop as it looked up all bright-eyed in anticipation of titbits.

The Cherry Tree public house stood huge and whitewashed just off a main road at the heart of Bold Colliery. The pub had a lengthy single-storey extension built onto the rear, and it was here where a disco bounced to a jampacked room compromising both local and Easington revellers. The darkened room was narrow but drawn-out, to the front of a raised dancefloor, a neon disco flickered colours as an attentive disc jockey sifted his way through aluminium boxes, picking out a selection of records to arrange in order of play. At the heart of a crammed dancefloor, Lemsip and Sizzler were up dancing with no one in particular, while Joe Whitlewith and Ger Wilson sat at a table laughing and joking as they tried their utmost to cop off with a couple of the local girls.

Togged out in their best attire, Tom, Hoss, and Billy stood at the bar area looking on as Jack danced with a tall girl aged in her early twenties who flaunted a beautiful head of long blonde hair that was crimped in soft wisps. A red, backless minidress hugged her figure to perfection while matching coloured stilettos set off long, shapely legs.

Oozing confidence, Jack just knew he looked good as he posed in a pale blue designer tee-shirt which ran with faded loose-fitting jeans and suede, sandy coloured elflike boots. Jack smooched closer to rest his hands onto the girl's hips, breaking away she gazed up into his eyes as she feathered her head onto his shoulder whispering, "What aftershave are you wearing, Jack? It's absolutely gorgeous."

"Kouros," he returned, nibbling tenderly on her lobe, "and it's not aftershave, it's cologne."

"What's the difference, like?"

"About five quid a bottle love," he returned with a cheeky grin. Pressing himself up against her, he whispered all kinds of sweet nothings into her ear and after tender grimaces were traded, she once again wrapped her arms around his neck.

Raising his pint to his mouth, Tom looked on at his brother's cavorting for as long as he could take, then turning away he found himself face to face across a bar counter with an attractive looking barmaid. "Four pints of lager please, pet," he said, raising his glass.

Pulling the drinks, for some reason the barmaid took an instant liking to Tom, and even though he came across a tad rough and rugged, she was taken in by his blue eyes and honest face; she also found it a refreshing change that he, unlike most punters, wasn't trying to smooth talk his way into her knickers every five minutes or so. She beamed in a friendly way. "I take it you are not into dancing, then?"

"Pardon?" managed Tom leaning his ear closer.

"You, you don't like to dance?" she repeated, resting a couple of filled pints onto a counter.

"Nor, it's not my forte, love, I'm afraid it's more dominoes than dancing for me. Get ya sell a drink by the way."

"Thank you very much, I'll have a half of lager if that's okay?" After pulling the rest of the drinks she turned away to operate a till and uncharacteristically of Tom, he found himself checking her over, noticing how she wasn't that tall, he more than liked how her dark hair was styled modern with blue highlights feathering at the side of her slightly rounded face. Tom was on guessing her age and was going to come up with somewhere in the region of the mid-twenties when the barmaid unexpectantly turned and instantly he started blushing like a naughty schoolboy who had just been caught out looking up his teacher's skirt.

"You weren't ogling at my bum by any chance, were you?" she asked stern faced.

Tom was lost for words, but after coughing nervously, he managed, "No, em, a'... no way, a' certainly was not... how much do I owe ya?"

"Three-fifteen," she sighed, uninterested, with her hand outstretched palm showing.

Fumbling coinage, Tom was on handing over the exact amount of money when she broke into a brazen grin, saying, "I had you going there, didn't I?" Relieved, but still embarrassed, he managed a sharp, coy smile before picking up the drinks and turning to stand alongside Hoss and Billy.

"What was that all about?" asked Hoss, receiving his pint. "Has she tried to shortchange ya or something?"

"No, we were just having a bit craic on that's all."

"Are ya alright, Tom?" asked Billy. "Ya l-l-look a' bit f-f-flushed like."

"Aye I'm fine." He handed Billy over his drink. "It's just a bit warm in here that's all." Swilling a huge gulp Tom couldn't help himself as he clandestinely glanced over his shoulder at the barmaid as she served other punters, but unknown to him, she had detected his every gaze.

Billy checked his watch. "A' wonder what time that f-f-fish shop sh-sh-shuts?"

"God nars," mumbled Tom, his thoughts lost elsewhere.

"A' hope it's still open," moaned Hoss with a tint of apprehension, "a'm frigging starving here!"

"Me too," chipped in Billy, "a's canny h-h-hungry like."

Hoss scanned the dance floor, uttering, "Looks like Jack's in again." Handing around cigarettes, he added, "No doubt he'll not be coming back with us to sleep on that wooden Welfare floor the night."

They all stood observing Jack who was now engrossed in a full-blown snog with the blonde beauty.

Lighting up, Hoss smiled. "Mind you, ya've got to tack your hat off to him, he's the best I've ever narn at pulling the birds."

Tom half groaned. "That's 'coss it's his favourite hobby, man, Hoss, he's a right fanny rat! He's got mare neck than a frigging giraffe, our young'n has!"

"A'm sure he has," laughed Billy, "he'd get in where g-g-gas wadn't." Billy drew deep

on his cigarette. "Charm the knickers from a n-n-nun's arse thy Jack could, the lucky s-s-sod."

Tom's eyes followed the barmaid as she came from behind the counter. Rushing between tables, it was a good five minutes before she returned with a mountain of empty glasses stacked one inside of the other and balanced over one shoulder. Passing Tom, she grinned ever so slightly before she pressed a button to activate an automatic glass cleaner sending brushes spinning like a mini carwash, and within no time whatsoever all the glasses were steam cleaned to shine and returned back onto wooden shelves. "Let it go, Thomas," he whispered beneath his breath.

The barmaid sighed lengthily as she stood at the end of the bar to light up a cigarette before she leant against the counter observing Jack as he philandered with the girl. "Bit of a Don Juan your friend is, isn't he?" she said, grinning at Tom.

"Or he's more than that, love, he's Don Juan and two that one is, and he's not exactly me friend..." She frowned confused before Tom chuckled, "... I'm afraid to say he's me brother, why, I'm not exactly afraid to say it, though sometimes he can be a bit of an embarrassment, a' suppose."

She puckered her brow. "Orr got you, well at least I think I've got you." Pulling a pint, she stood it on the counter. "There you go, that's on the house."

"Tar very much, that's very kind of ya, em, what's your name if I may ask?"

"Pat," she beamed affably, "Pat Turner."

"Well thank you very much, Pat Turner, I'm Tom Gilroy, Thomas if a' divant like ya, but you can call is Tom. So... do you like working here then?"

"No, not particularly..." She couldn't stop herself from laughing inside her mind as she thought how his shyness was so obvious; she continued, "... but it's money I suppose, and with me being a poor little student, well you know."

"Student eh, so what are you studying for then?"

"To be a nurse," she spoke with a hint of proudness. "I'm in my final year, thank God."

"Nurse eh! Well good for you, girl," praised Tom who was way above impressed.

Hoss interrupted the conversation: "Are we gan'n to the fish shop soon, Tom? It's getting on a bit now and it might be–"

"I'm afraid he's not going to the fish shop tonight," interrupted Pat, "he's walking me home, that's if he wants to... that is?"

Tom nodded, mustering, "Yes of course." He stood perplexed for an eternity of a few seconds thinking, 'this sort of thing doesn't happen to him; this is Jack's department not his'.

Slowly breaking into a grin, he turned to Hoss, breathing, "I'm ganna give the fish shop a miss the night, Hoss, I'm seeing this young lady safely back home."

Pat and Tom exchanged smiles before she swivelled to walk away in the direction of an office. Hoss grinned wide at Tom before he nudged Billy, and they were all giggling around each other when Jack approached hand in hand with his conquest. Looking to his brother, he asked, "Did ya get is a pint in, Tom?"

"Aye it's on the bar there," he said, nodding towards a filled glass.

"Champion!" After downing half his drink, Jack licked froth from his lips, saying, "By, it's red hot on that dancefloor." Grinning briefly, he drew attention to the girl. "This is Donna by the way–"

"It's Diane actually," she interrupted, raising her eyes while flicking her locks to one side, "not Donna."

Jack smiled all apologetic, saying, "Sorry my mistake, love, this adorable creature here is Diane..." smiles were giving out, received, then returned, "... isn't she delectable?"

"A' thowt ya said sh-sh-she was D-D-Donna, s-s-sorry D-D-Diane," joked Billy.

"Alright funny fucker!" snapped Jack.

Buttoning up her jacket, Pat emerged from behind the bar. Standing next to Tom she grinned. "Are you right then, Tom?"

"Aye a's ready, love." He smiled at the group, saying, "Catch yas later on then."

Jack stood gobsmacked, his eyes following Pat as she linked his brother before they walked off to exit the room through a set of double doors. Frowning, he queried, "Have a' missed out on something here?"

"Aye, your youngn's managed to pull the barmaid," said Hoss with a huge grin.

"A' think it w-w-was more the b-b-barmaid p-p-pulling him," added Billy, smiling colossal.

Lemsip and Sizzler approached to stand next to the lads. Lemsip lit up a cigarette, glancing sheepishly at the girl he then faced Jack, whispering, "Jack, do is a favour, marra?"

"What favour's that, Lemsip?"

"Why, do ya see them two lasses sitting ower there?"

"Which lasses? Sitting ower where?" asked Jack, squinting the darkened room.

Lemsip pointed over to a couple of girls who were sat smoking at a table. "Them two ower there, man."

Again, Jack narrowed his eyes. "Which two, man, Lemsip!?"

He whooped, "Them two sitting in the corner, man! One's got a blue top on, the other one's wearing a purple dress."

"Or aye, got ya now, what about them?"

Lemsip smiled uncertain, and with a lowered tone he asked, "Why, will ya gan ower and ask them, if me and Sizzler can walk them home, like later on like!" Lemsip's expression almost touched desperation as Jack rolled his eyes in disbelief at his friend's weird suggestion.

Arm in arm, Pat and Tom ambled down a main road for a good quarter of a mile. Talking nonstop, they entered, then exited, a couple of shadowy underpasses, and after arching a drawn out bend they strolled by a crescent of flats which ushered them into a concrete shopping precinct that housed the usual: VG mini market, Butcher's Shop, Chinese Takeaway, Greengrocers, Fish and chip shop, Laundrette, Off Licence, Bakery, and of course a Ladbrokes Betting Shop. Walking further, they passed by a gable end that was scarred in multicoloured graffiti before they entered into a housing estate to be met by row upon row of terraced houses which ran front to front across narrow cobbled streets. Tom glanced up at the smoky rooftops and was thinking how this estate somehow epitomised his own domain when from out of the blue, he started quivering.

"Are you alright?" asked Pat, rubbing warmth into his arm.

"Aye, someone's just warked ower me grave," he responded jokingly.

Sauntering further, Pat slowed her step to stop under an amber blush of a lamppost, looking Tom in the eye she gently tugged him into her, and they kissed passionately before she once again linked his arm to continue on with their journey. "Not long now, it's just around this next corner here," she said before Tom was once again overcome by a bout of tremors. "Are you sure you're, okay?" she asked, narrowing her eyes.

"Aye," he replied with another quick shiver, "a' should have put a coat on, as just a' bit card, that's all." They upped the pace until reaching Pat's abode; after putting key to latch, they entered into the house where Tom sighed himself into the comfort of a candy and grey striped settee. Scrutinising the room, he was rather impressed at how the layout was all open plan and furnished with the most modernistic fittings. "You have a nice home, mind, Pat."

"Ta very much, that's down to my father's generosity, I'm afraid... Tea or coffee?"

"Tea please, no milk no sugar."

"Put the television on if you want, the remote's somewhere underneath the coffee table, at least I think it is."

"Cheers." Searching amongst magazines Tom hadn't long picked up the TV remote when he was engulfed by yet another episode of spasms but this time the shudders lingered and sweat wettened his brow.

Pat looked at him with concern. "You look terrible, Tom, do you want a couple of paracetamol?"

"Aye if ya don't mind, please, a' canit stop shaking, I'm as dizzy as a duck, here."

She entered the kitchen area; returning she handed over a strip of pills and a half-filled glass. After softly dabbing perspiration from his brow she said, "You're running a temperature, Tom, you're absolutely boiling up."

"That's funny 'coss a' feel as card as owt, a canit stop shaking."

"Come on," she said, supporting him to his feet, "you need to be in bed."

"Are ya sure? A' don't want to be a burden to ya."

"Yes, I'm sure, and you're not a burden." Resting his arm around her neck she aided him up a flight of stairs and into a bedroom where she sat him onto the edge of her bed to remove his shoes before fully opening up a window to be hit by a pleasant coolness of a night draught.

"Thanks," he mumbled, still shivering, "I'm sorry... for all the trouble."

"It's no trouble whatsoever, now get your clothes off and get into bed. I'm just going to pop downstairs and lock up."

The instant she left the room Tom coughed uncontrollably; his whole body ached as he listlessly stripped down to his briefs before he struggled to slide himself under the coldness of a bed sheet. Pat re-entered the bedroom and started to undress.

Joining him under the sheets, she whispered, "Get some sleep," as she rested her arm delicately around his impressive sixpack.

"Thanks for everything," he just about managed to burble ahead of his eyes blinking to a close.

It was a damp, early morning at Bold Colliery, a pungent aroma of dank sward filled the air with a sweetness as shrubberies at either side of a road wilted slightly due to the weight of a recent downpour. A visiting sparrowhawk had placed the local birdlife on high alert, sending flighty blackbirds shrieking warnings of its presence. Fronting hedgerows ran alongside a winding road in the direction of a set of lofty pithead wheels, before ending at a set of yellow and black striped barriers where to one side stenchy smoke drifted from within an oxidized drum. Adjacent this pyre stood a ramshackle cabin which the local pickets had constructed out of fragments of scrap wood that was then enclosed within a nailed down oily canvas, which today sheltered a quintet of elderly pickets who were content to sit and chat with hands cupped around chipped, coffee-stained mugs. To the right of the shelter a couple of hundred pickets congregated on a grass verge talking in separate groups with a cluster of the younger lads running around kicking a football, with the local pickets representing Manchester United, while the Easington lot were proud representees of Sunderland A.F.C, and with not long left to play, the current score was sixteen to nine in favour of the visiting Black Cats.

Behind a wall of transparent shields, line upon line of battle clad policemen blocked off a main entrance to a pit yard where an assemblage of police vans were parked side by side with drivers grouped in a circle laughing and joking aloud. Amid the pickets, Jack, Hoss, and Billy stood conversing amongst themselves.

Handing around cigarettes, Jack glanced to the clouds, saying, "At least the rain's eased off now."

"Aye," sighed Hoss. Drawing on his cig he looked to Jack with a glimpse of concern mumbling, "A' wonder what's happened to your Tom?"

"God nars, but if he's got any sense about him, he'll be still snuggled up nackers deep with that barmaid."

"So, what happened with you a-a-and that girl, last night then, Jack?" chirped Billy with a mischievous grimace. "Did she b-b-blow ya out, or what?"

"Why aye she blew is out! We had newhere to gan, did we, the daft cow's still living at her parents' house!"

"Ya should have invited her b-b-back to that Welfare Hall then," laughed Billy.

"A' did! But she was having nen of it, she just looked at is as if a' was away with the show folks."

"She had a good right," put in Hoss, "it was as uncomfortable as owt laying on that frigging floor, a's still aching."

"Tell is about it!" moaned Jack. "A' was laid next ta ya listening to ya snoring ya heed off all night."

"A' don't snore!" defended Hoss rather taken aback.

"Ya dinit what!?" moaned Jack in amazement, "Hoss, man, ya was really bad, ya was grunting away like a wildebeest with pneumonia!"

"Was a' heckers like!"

"Ya was l-l-like, Hoss," broke in Billy, "ya sounded like a b-b-broken-down steam t-t-train!"

Hoss was still in denial of his alleged stertor sounds when Jack groaned, "Besides all ya snoring, a' couldn't get comfortable thinking about that tart. A' thought a' was well in with her, she was cleaning me tonsils and doing all sorts of things with that tongue of hers." Jack drew deep on his cigarette. "She couldn't keep her hands off is when a' was up giving it some Fred Astaire on that dance floor, a' even did the forbidden and bought the bugger half a' lager, then what does she do! She gans and fucks off, leaving is stranded outside that pub like one a' clock half struck..." Billy and Hoss burst out laughing, Jack glared at them with a shake of his head. "...Dinit laugh, it's not even funny! And it gets worse, 'coss when a' set away walking to find that fish shop a' went the rang way, didn't ah! It was a good quarter of an hour afore a' realised and a' had ta double back on me sell and by the time a' got there this stone-faced ard boiler slammed the door straight in me face saying she was closed! A' was absolutely famished, in fact a' still is, I've never had owt to eat since me Sunday's dinner and it's now frigging–" Jack looked to Billy with a puzzling frown asking– "what day is it?"

"Tuesday!" laughed Billy.

"Is it!? Frigging hell, I've had nowt to eat for nearly two days now."

Hoss laughed aloud. "A' tell ya what mind, Jack, ya missed a canny supper, them Lancashire Hot Pot pies were frigging lovely, weren't they, Billy?"

"Aye were tha, a' could b-b-barely get through mine it w-w-was that big, how the hell you ate three of them and an extra b-b-bag of chips is beyond me, Hoss."

"Did ya!?" frowned Jack, eying Hoss with an air of disappointment.

"Did a' what?" asked Hoss.

"Eat three of them Lancashire thingmajigs?"

"Too right a' did!"

"And an extra b-b-bag of chips!" put in Billy. "Divant f-f-forget them."

Jack sulked, "Ya could have saved is one, Hoss."

"What, a chip?"

"Nor, one of them hotpot thingies!"

Hoss whooped, "Why we didn't nar ya was coming back! We must have been asleep by the time you rolled in, anyway, we thowt ya was tapped up with that bird."

"Well, a' wasn't, and ya should have saved is one just in case."

Joe Whitlewith, and a gaunt looking middle-aged man who donned a typical checked flat cap, approached the lads. Joe looked around, introducing, "Lads, this is Donald Noble, he's the union secretary here at Bold Colliery." Friendly handshakes were exchanged before Joe looked directly at Jack. "Donald needs ya's to do a favour for him, Jack, if ya's can, that is?"

"Or aye, and what favour's that like?" queried Jack.

Donald now addressed the lads. "Well, scab bus will be here soon..." With each word he spoke he blinked a nervous twitch. "... what I need is a big push from everyone te try te stop scab bus, some of my lads are armed wit metal spikes te puncture tyres, but what I need from thee is te hold coppers back, you know, protect my lot for as long as possible so we can sort tyres and disable bus."

"Aye, that'll be ne bother at all." Jack smiled.

"Where's your Tom?" asked Joe, looking around the group.

"Orr, he's just gone for a shite," bluffed Jack, "do ya want is to gan and get him for ya like?"

"Why nor, you can explain to him what we're ganna do."

"So, what exactly are we allowed to do to stop these coppers then, Donald?" enquired Hoss.

"Whatever thee wants te," answered the man who stood astounded at the sheer size of Hoss. Looking him up and down, he laughed, repeating, "Whatever thee wants te, lad," his words of encouragement sending a grin rippling across Hoss' face.

Two blasts from a police whistle sounded. Immediately the police line parted sideways like well-drilled Roman centurions allowing a quartet of hefty-built police officers to emerge from the ranks before the line shuffled back to a close again. These four officers were all members of the feared SPG, Special Patrol Groups, who were known simply as 'Snatch Squads', and the leader of this particular Snatch Squad was police sergeant

Dryden, or in the local pickets' eyes, Darth Vader, named as such because of his evil brutishness. The uniforms these policemen wore had no identification numbers showing on their lapels, and they were armed with small round shields, short truncheons, and blue coloured hard helmets which had protective visors attached. Walking at the side of the mass they lashed out at anyone who had the misfortune to venture to within striking distance before they confronted with the cluster of elderly men who were stood by the cabin doorway. Angry words were in the midst of being exchanged when from out of nowhere, Dryden jabbed the edge of his cudgel directly into the face of one of the elderly pickets, sending his Granddad mug flying as he collapsed to the ground. Fellow pickets aided their comrade back to his feet and heated protests were directed towards Dryden before a brief skirmish broke out and two of the objecting pickets were arrested and carted away to be manhandled into the back of one of the awaiting police vehicles. Instantly the atmosphere became hostile.

Witnessing this skirmish, Jack turned to Donald, asking, "Who the fuck's he!?"

He blinked. "That's Darth Vader, Jack, his real name's Dryden, he came up from Met just t'other week with t'uther three, apparently they are sent rit round country te different pit villages, they're rit mad fuckers, but he's worst by far, he's proper psycho, my advice is te stay well clear of them, especially him, they've already had twenty of our lads locked up on jumped up charges and that bastard's personally put five of my lot in hospital, all with similar head injuries, he likes te use trudgen diss Darth Vader."

"Does he now?" seethed Jack, not taking his glower from the policeman.

"Aye he diss that," blinked Donald, "we think he's military, not Met, but we can't prove it, and like I said stay well clear, he's not got stop button that one hasn't."

Jack scanned the scene. Spotting small breakages in the hedgerows he faced Donald, asking, "What's behind them hedges?"

"Nowt really, just open fields and wattery ditch, it runs full side of field, why do thee ask for?"

"A' tell ya why, Donald, 'coss that–" Jack once again cast a long, hard stare at Dryden– "twat's ganna end up face down in it, that's why."

"Good luck with that!" whooped Donald before muttering, "But personally, I would stay well clear, cock."

Three high-pitched whistles cheeped aloud, signifying for the police line to advance forward, pushing the pickets away from the roadside before a heavy timbre of a diesel engine sounded as a single decker bus, driven by a faceless driver, crept into view with all of its windows enclosed by protective meshing. 'Here We Go! Here We Go! Here We Go' chanted the pickets as they hurtled themselves crashing into the heart of the police line, forcing them backwards. The bus slowed considerably due to police and pickets grappling back and forth across the road like a colossal rugby scrum. From behind transparent shields, truncheons walloped down onto the pickets' heads, one young lad held onto his face with blood gushing from a gash above his eye before another blow landed onto the back of his head and he fell to his knees screaming in agony. Blood oozed from a ripped ear of another young picket, yet still, he persisted to shove with all his strength against the wall of shields. Individual skirmishes had broken out along the entire length of the police line, a haziness rose mist-like above the mass as truncheons still rained down on heads; in return, pickets lashed out with their fists. One picket managed to rip a helmet away from a frontline policeman, he then proceeded to punch him in his face with such intensity that the officer toppled to the ground. Seizing the upper hand, the pickets drove over the stricken policeman, trampling him unconscious, then, forcing onwards they soon had the police on the backfoot before the line eventually collapsed and the bus ground to a halt, 'Scabs! Scabs! Scabs! Scabs!' rang out as pickets swamped the bus, ripping away the meshing before windows erupted due to a bombardment of bricks and heavy lumps of concrete. Petrified scabs lay curled up on the bus aisle, even the quisling driver left his seat to join them on the floor ahead of the front windscreen shattering to a burst. Ger and Joe were amongst a handful of pickets who had managed to enter the bus via a rear exit door, they set about beating the scabs as a flood of fellow pickets joined them and soon the bus driver was demasked of his balaclava before he too received a heavy kicking. Tyres exploded to a domino of blasts, pickets and policemen wrestled on the ground with other pickets putting the boot in. At one side of the road, Dryden pulverised a man with his baton until he dropped limp to the grass. Flashing a wry smirk, he moved onto another picket where he started pounding him around the head, but oblivious to Dryden, Jack was now fighting his way through the mayhem to get to him. Lemsip was caught up in a scuffle and a truncheon thwacked his nose, sending him to one knee before another heavy blow to the back of his head laid him out cold. Sizzler hunkered to aid his friend back to his feet when he too was bludgeoned unconscious. Jack was almost upon Dryden when a policeman ran at him wielding his baton, Jack grabbed the officer's arm, twisting the bludgeon from his grasp. Seizing the copper by his throat, he punched him in the face, knocking him to the grass; as the constable tried to clamber back to his feet Jack booted him in his face, snarling, "Fuck you!" Hoss held a policeman by the scruff of his neck, clutching his other hand onto the constable's belt he lifted him from the ground, running him headfirst against a tree trunk. Moving to another policeman, he punched him in the side of his jaw, at once the officer's legs buckled, and he collapsed to the road, stunned. Drawn in by the flow of the horde, Billy had somehow found himself at the centre of the turmoil and was rolling the floor with a rather plump policeman when Hoss came to his rescue, tugging the officer away before knocking him out with an almighty uppercut. Billy smiled in gratification, but as he was rising to his feet he was bludgeoned on the back of his head, and he sank, laid out cold. Hoss lifted Billy over his shoulder then proceeded to carry him through the heart of the chaos before resting him at the relevant safety of a hedgerow.

At the other side of the road, Jack had just about reached Dryden, who was grinning fiendish as he beat a young lad's face to a pulp with his truncheon. He raised his baton to strike out again when Jack snatched hold of the cudgel, twisting it from his grasp. Tossing the baton to one side, Jack smiled roguishly, then, flicking his head he gestured for the petrified lad to leave.

Without speaking a single word, Jack and Dryden squared up to one another like a couple of manic gladiators. Jack moved quickly, grabbing hold of Dryden by his collar, but he wrestled himself free, then, using his hard helmet as a weapon, he head-butted Jack, stunning him backwards with blood dripping from a deep cut on the bridge on his nose. Regaining his senses, Jack knew he had to somehow remove Dryden's helmet; stepping forward he tried to grab hold of the headgear, but the policeman once again wriggled himself free, then, with lightning speed, he battered Jack square on in the face with his shield sending him staggering back overs with blood trickling not only from the cut on his nose, but also from an additional incision on his lip and the inside his mouth. "Not had enough yet? Cu... nt!" snarled Dryden in some insignificant Southern, Cockney-sounding accent.

"Hardly's," scoffed Jack with an untroubled grin, "you hit like a little girl."

Dryden's eyes bulged as he threw a punch, but Jack stooped before lunging at him, wrenching away his shield prior to grabbing the officer by the neck, where he ripped the visor away from him before entangling his fingers under a chin strap of the headgear. With all his might, he tugged and tugged until the strap finally parted, allowing him to yank away the helmet before lobbing it high over a hedge top. Jack laughed exaggeratedly, as for the first time he was met by Dryden's facial features at which paraded a prominent nose that leant slightly to one side, a thick tash fanned above narrow lips, and his eyes were black in colour creating a beady, emotionless stare that more than hinted of evil. Jack smiled wickedly, goading, "A' didn't realise ya was such an ugly twat!" Circling the officer, he cuffed him stinging to his face, and even though Dryden managed to land a few blows of his own, he was mainly throwing wild punches at nothing but fresh air. Jack lashed out, hitting the officer time and time again around his head and face. Dryden's eyes had swelled to slits as heavy blows pommelled his face beyond recognition, and it wasn't long before the ill-fated policeman was out on his feet. Jack's blows intensified further before he grasped the dazed policeman by his hair; after dragging him facedown through a gap in the hedgerow he booted the sergeant down a steep embankment into a dike. Joining him in the watery ditch, he started stamping viciously on the cop's head before he straddled him, pounding him repeatedly with viscid blows. Blood now poured from deep incisions around Dryden's eyes, nose and mouth as Jack proceeded to thrash him limp, then, seizing him by the scruff of the neck, he head-butted him with so much force that blood spewed from a protuberance of cartilage and gristle where once there was a nose. Rising to his feet, Jack flung the cataleptic police officer into the shallow dyke, sneering, "Yar nowt but a fucking numpty!" From out of the corner of his eye, Jack glimpsed Donald standing at the top of the embankment.

"Mary mother of Jesus! Is he dead!?" tooted Donald, removing his cap and running his hand over his head in amazement.

Jack shrugged his shoulders. "Does it matter?"

"Not really, no," he returned with a succession of blinks. "Christ almighty, I've never seen anything like that in all my life, what do they feed you lads on up there in Durham?"

"Stotty cake," joked Jack with a bold grin. Looking down at Dryden he sniggered, "he'll not be beating anybody up for a while," then after wiping blood away from his mouth he stretched out his hand asking, "giss a hand up then".

Donald grasped Jack by the hand, pulling him up the bankside. "Well done, son," he said, patting him on the back. "Joe told me, tha were top man, Jack, and by God he wasn't joking." As the two walked away, Donald laughed aloud, snorting, "He was also telling me some cock and bull story about how thee was somehow related te Victor McLaglen, tis it reet then?"

"Or aye, we're related alright, he's me Ma's great-uncle Victor." Jack scanned the area, asking, "Where is Joe by the way?"

"I'm afraid he's gone and got himself locked up with t'uther lad of yours called... Ger Wilson, at least I think 'tis lad's name."

"Fa fuck's sake!" griped Jack. "That's our Ger, he's me cousin."

"Is he!? I'll de some enquiries when we get back te Welfare, see what I can do te help, no doubt I'll have te bring solicitors back in again." Donald sighed lengthily, then blinking nonstop he said, "I'll get them out of there as quick as I possibly can, Jack, but it'll not be easy, and it could take a while."

"Try ya best, marra," said Jack, looking Donald straight in the eye, "they're both good lads them two are."

"I will, cock, don't worry thee bit sell." Donald smiled as they joined the mass who had now backed off up the road away from the police line. Donald clapped his hands, attracting attention. "Reet, lads, time te fuck off before this lot's reinforcements arrive!" The pickets walked away absolutely elated at having won a rare victory. Strolling up the road, they burst out singing to the chorus of that wonderful Welsh Hymn, 'Bread of Heaven. *'Arthur Scargill, Arthur Scargill, We'll Support You Ever More... We'll Support You Ever More, Arthur Scargill, Arthur Scargill, We'll Support You Ever More... We'll Support You Ever More...'*

Inside the union office at Easington Colliery, Alan was sat at his desk reading a document when Lawrence Young and John Wood joined him in the room. Aged only nineteen, Lawrence Young was a fresh-faced kid of average height who paraded strapping shoulders and a mop of dark hair as well as proudly showing off a sprouting moustache that was more bumfluff than actual moustache.

John Wood aged in his late twenties, was also of average height with muscular arms and upper body, who exhibited hazel eyes, and a mass of lengthy, mousy-coloured hair that hung straight, but John had no inkling of a moustache, not even the slightest hint of a one, although he did possess a rather dapper leather biker jacket which had **'METALLICA'** etched across the shoulders.

"Can we have a quick word with ya, Alan?" asked Lawrence.

"Why aye, son, sit ya sells down. Yas are up early, what's the matter, shit the bed or what?"

"Nor, we're just mooching about ta see where security is," joked John.

"What can a' do for yas then," smiled Alan all friendly as the two pulled up chairs to sit across the desk.

Lawrence lit up a cigarette, saying, "It's more what we can do for you, Alan." He exhaled smoke, ending with a singular smoke ring. "We think there's an informer amongst us, marra, and I'm sorry to say this, but it's got to be a union official."

Alan put his finger to his lips, shushing Lawrence. Standing, he crossed the room to close the door before returning to his seat. "There's someone in NACODS office, we don't want them bastards eavesdropping. So, how do ya mack that out then, Lawrence?"

"Because there's too many coincidences happening lately, that's how."

"What do you mean by coincidences?"

"Why, put it this way," broke in John, "how come every time we go picketing, and it doesn't matter whereabouts, it could be up Tow Law, Steetleys, Philadelphia, or any of the other sites, the cops are always there in mass waiting for us to arrive, and the bastards haven't got the manpower to cover all the sites like this, there's simply not enough of them, so how the hell do they know where to go to before we arrive?"

Lawrence joined in, "If it's not the bus company tipping the bastards off, then it's got to be some fucker from inside this office."

"It can't be the bus company, Lawrence," sighed Alan. "They don't even know where we're targeting until we inform them just before the bus pulls away."

"So, what does that say then?" said John lighting up a hand-rolled cigarette that drooped misshaped while seemingly sticking to his bottom lip.

Alan formed his hands into fists. "It says some twat's a snitch! That's what it's saying!"

"Any...way," stretched Lawrence, "what me and John did yesterday just to prove our point, was to drive around all the sites and guess what, there wasn't one single copper to be found until we got to—"

"Philadelphia," interrupted Alan.

"Exactly," confirmed John.

Alan muttered, "Right, lads, a' want yas to say nowt for now 'coss I've got a canny good idea who the bastard is; leave it with me and I'll figure something out. Thanks though, yas did really well."

The two smiled all proud before John relit his cigarette, asking, "Will ya let us know who it is, Alan?"

Alan laughed sarcastically sharp. "Too right a' will! Every man and his dog will get to know who the treacherous fucker is! It's worse than being a scab this is, why, not exactly worse, but it's on par with it like." Leaving his desk, he moseyed to a table to switch on an old-fashioned kettle that had a spout caked in lime resin. "Do yas want a coffee, or something?"

"No, tar, we have to gan," said John, standing. "We're in a bit of a hurry."

"Bit of a hurry? Where yas gan'n te at this time of the morning, like?" Alan checked his watch. "It's only half seven."

"To nick some coal to sell, we're fucking skint," put in Lawrence.

"Why, watch what yas are doing, and for crying out loud divant be getting ya sells caught."

"As if!" chuckled Lawrence, crossing the room.

"See yas soon then." Alan smiled. "And thanks once again, lads, ya's did really good."

"Ne bother," said John from the doorway, "see ya later."

"Aye, catch yas later." Spooning coffee into a mug, Alan sighed elongated before muttering, "You two tack care now."

"Aye, you too, Alan," said Lawrence ahead of them leaving the office.

Tom was lying half propped up in bed when Pat rushed into the room, brushing her hair and wearing a white uniform top and blue trousers. Leaning over him, she smiled, whispering, "I'm running late," and after a slight puffing up of his pillows she feathered a kiss on his cheek, asking, "how are you feeling?".

"Nowt flash still, I'm aching from top to bottom, ya'd think I'd been run ower by a double decker bus or something."

"Are you still having those dizzy bouts?"

"Aye, but only when a' sit up."

"Take two of these now," she instructed, handing Tom a sleeve of tablets, "they're just paracetamol but they'll help with your temperature, take a couple more after six hours, there's a jug of freshwater on the bedside table, try and get some rest and I'll see you when I get back, I'm only on a half day placement at St Helens hospital so I should be home around one, that's if all goes to plan that is, which it seldom does."

"Are you sure it's okay for me to stay? A' feel as if I'm putting onta ya good nature here like."

"Don't talk so daft, you're not putting on to me at all, if you pick yourself up a little, I may just make us something nice for tea, if not, you will just have to have some toast or a bowl of soup or something." Looking into Tom's eyes she leaned forward, pecking a kiss on his lips. "I'll have to go, try and get some rest... bye."

"Bye... love."

"Love?" she said, glancing over her shoulder with a huge grin. "Where's that come from?"

"Why, tha nars what a' mean, it was just a figure of speech." Forcing a slight grin, he watched her leave the room and after shuffling himself to the edge of the bed he just about had enough strength to fill a glass up.

In glorious sunshine, Sue and Irene were stood at the doorway of a Greengrocer's shop located at upper Seaside Lane, the main shopping street at Easington Colliery. Entering into the shop, they were instantly hit by a delightful waft of fresh fruit and vegetables as Jeff Jones, a stout, purple faced greengrocer, aged in his early fifties, greeted them with a grin, saying, "Morning, ladies."

"Morning, Jeff," returned Irene, "have ya got owt for us today?"

"Aye a' have actually," he replied, removing a white hat to mop his brow, "there's a dozen or so cabbages and a couple a' sacks of tatties out the back for yas, the cabbages need using up in the next few days mind."

Sue smiled. "Thank you very much, Jeff, you're a star, we'll use them in the morn, might put a shepherd's pie on, or perhaps mince and dumplings."

He laughed. "Very nice an'all, a' might just pop up there mesell!"

"Why ya more than welcome, Jeff," beamed Irene.

"Thanks, but that's more for the needy not the greedy, Irene. So, what time will John and Micky be coming down to pick the stuff up, like? I'll have young Andrew put them outside ready for them."

"Whatever's best for you?" answered Sue, friendly.

"Any time will do me, flowerpots; it makes no difference whatsoever."

Irene suggested, "Will half elevenish be okay?"

"Aye, that'll be fine," he confirmed before asking, "how many of yas are on duty up the kitchen today, then?"

"Six 'a think," responded Sue; after second thoughts she corrected herself, "no, sorry, there's seven of us, got a new starter today, young Denise Simson is joining us."

Jeff sifted oranges from a wooden punnet; handing them over to Irene he smiled sharply. "There's an orange apiece for you and the girls then."

"Thanks." Placing the fruit into her shopping bag, Irene beamed. "How's Mary keeping, Jeff?"

"Orr, she's fine, she's still waiting impatiently to be a grandma, like."

"Not be long now!" wide eyed Irene. "Give her my regards when ya see her, and your Julie too?"

"A' will do, how's the lads keeping?"

"Orr they're champion, they're away picketing somewhere for the week." Irene closed up her shopping bag, praising, "Thanks once again for your generous donations, Jeff, it's very much appreciated." Smiles were exchanged all around before the girls left the shop just as a shabby dressed young lad popped his head around the doorway.

"Any bruised fruit, Mr Jones?" he asked sheepishly.

"Aye here tha is, bonnie lad." Jeff winked as he handed the delighted kid a bunch of slightly ripe bananas and a couple of apples.

"Tar very much!" flashed the youngster before he quickly left the shop.

Irene and Sue chatted amongst themselves as they entered shop after shop for the entire length of Seaside Lane. Passing familiar faces, they traded friendly smiles alongside nods of recognition, or they simply exchanged, 'morning, hello, hiya,' or 'how ya keeping?' and on the odd occasion they would come out with, 'Eeh! How are ya doing? Haven't seen you in yonks!' or even, 'Long time no see!' was greeted. Crossing a main road, they turned into Bede Street where they knocked on the door at Fairsey's fish shop, and to the sound of a bell tinkling, Jean Fairse, a middle-aged woman who possessed dark hair that was styled man like short, unlocked the door to usher them inside where they were hit by the pungent smell of fresh fish.

"Hiya Jean, how's things?" asked Sue.

"Canit grumble a' suppose," she answered with a prolonged sigh.

Sue removed her spectacles; taking out a handkerchief she cleaned the lenses as she asked, "Have them fishcakes arrived yet?"

"Yeah, they're out the back in the freezer, seven boxes for eight quid."

"Any chance of a bit more discount?" enquired Irene.

"Sorry, Irene, but that's cost price, and that's not counting the box I've donated."

"And it's much appreciated too," mumbled Sue. Fumbling her purse, she eventually came up with the correct amount of money.

"Thanks... Jean," then stretched before, "you're a gem. I'll send the lads down to pick them up today between half eleven and twelve, if that's okay?"

"That'll be fine, Sue, just make sure they go straight into a freezer if ya not using them, they can gan off canny quick like."

The girls had a good chinwag for ten minutes or so before they said their goodbyes and left the shop to the sound of a bell once again clinking.

The aroma of fish and chips was overpowering at Bold Welfare Hall, as the lads from Easington sat around tables finger picking fish suppers from greasy newspaper wrappings. Jack scrunched up his paper; tossing it into a bin he smiled at Hoss. "Well, that's filled a gap up that has, and ya right, Hoss, those hotpots are bloody lovely."

"Told ya they were." Hoss grinned, tucking into an extra portion of chips. "The chips are nice an'll, lovely and crispy, aren't tha?"

"Aye are tha!" agreed Jack. Lighting up a cigarette he looked at Billy, saying, "Giss a look at that head then." Billy leant forward and Jack inspected a deep gash that was shaped like a fish's mouth, "It looks sore that, mind, Billy, ya might need a couple of stitches in there young'n."

Crumpling up his newspaper wrapper, he moaned, "It'll have t-t-ta wait till a' g-g-get back yerm, I'll gan to me arn d-d-doctors."

"Do ya want is to clean it up for ya?"

Billy shook his head, muttering, "Do a' heckers like! J-J-Just leave it, Jack, it's p-p-putting like hell."

Hoss sighed, "He's fine, Jack, just leave him."

"Okay then." Jack patted Billy on his back. "I'm ganna see how Lemsip and Sizzler are, I'll not be long." He left the lads to cross the room where he joined Lemsip and Sizzler who were sat smoking at a table. Jack beamed affably, asking, "How are you two mack'n out then?"

Lemsip raised his eyes. "A' thinks me nose might be broke, Jack, a' canit breathe properly." Moaning aloud, Lemsip scrunched his face in agony as he illustrated how painful it was for him to inhale through his nose.

Jack carefully inspected Lemsip's snout, saying, "It's definitely broken, marra, ya ganna have two canny shiners in the morn an'll. What's ya heed like?"

Lemsip leant forward flinching as Jack gently parted his hair revealing a weeping gash that looked inflamed and painful. "Ya ganna need that stitching up, marra, it's wide open," said Jack sympathetically.

"Ne chance!" bleated Lemsip. "It'll frigging knack!" Sighing lengthily, his eyes rose all pitiful. "A' divant think me mam'll let is gan away picketing anymore after she sees the state a's in."

Jack looked to Sizzler. "How are you, marra?"

Sizzler lifted his hand in recognition of Jack's words, then forcing a bit of a smile he uttered, "I'm fine, Jack, just a bit dizzy, that's all."

Jack beamed. "Yas did good today, we well and truly levelled them, didn't we!"

"It doesn't feel like we did," disagreed Lemsip.

"Why we did, you believe me we did," reassured Jack. "Did ya see the state we left that bus in, a' canit see that thing running scabs anywhere, why, not for a long time, anyway." He winked at the two, muttering, "Catch ya's in a bit then." Jack was on crossing the room when Donald Noble and a young thinnish man rushed their way into the hall.

Banging on a table, Donald drew attention, announcing, "Reet, lads, can I have tha attention please... gather thee stuff together, you will have te leave within the hour."

"Why?" raised a young picket with a hand rolled cigarette dangling unlit from out of the corner of his mouth. "What's gan'n on like?"

"Plod are going te raid here and run thee out of village, that's what's going on, and not only that, but bastards are also coming te arrest as many of thee as they possibly can, if tha's not gone within hour all of thee risk chance of getting lifted, including t'bus driver too, so gather thee stuff up, we've made arrangements for thee to kip at Manchester University for the neet, or if tha wants te thee can go straight back home, it's up te thee." Protests ran the room as the pickets reluctantly started packing up their belongings. Donald once again banged on a tabletop, "Before thee goes, lads, I'd just like to say how proud we are at what happened here today, for the first time since strike started, we actually claimed a victory over bastard coppers, and you believe me, we will be forever indebted te thee, it was legendary what we achieved here together, legendary, and it will be talked about for generations te come. And may I say, in such a brief period of time friendships have been forged amongst us, special friendships that will never be broken, and will hopefully last a lifetime whatever the outcome of this bloody strike is. Orr I nearly forgot, regarding Joe and Ger, we have a car on standby ready te take them back up to Durham the instant they are released from nick, so don't go worrying yourselves about them, and once again, and I mean this so sincerely, I would like to say thank you, tis been an honour and a privilege te stand shoulder to shoulder with tha's." Donald and the young man started applauding; in response the Easington pickets returned the applause.

Jack looked to Hoss and Billy, saying, "Pack mine and our young's stuff up, I'm ganna have to gan and find him, if we're not back in time just tell the driver to fuck off without us, we'll mack our arn way back yerm." Skurrying the floor, Jack pulled Donald to one side and after a brief conversation Donald handed over a set of car keys to the young lad and the two hastily left the room.

Tom was sat upright in bed, slurping soup, with pillows propped to feather behind him. Breaking up pieces of bread, he dipped them into the bowl as Pat entered the room.

"How's your soup?"

"Lovely, but a's struggling a bit?"

"Are you not feeling any better?"

"Why nor, me throat's killing is, and a's aching all ower, a' feel like a's dropping to bloody bits!"

Pat sat on the edge of the bed, after she examined his throat the muttered, "I think you may have tonsillitis, Tom, try and get some more of that soup down you."

"A' canit eat anymore, Pat, sorry and that, but a' feel sick."

"Why if you can't eat, you can't eat, there's no need to be sorry." She had just stood to take the tray away when a heavy pounding sounded at the front door. "Who the hell's that!" she moaned, resting the salver before hurrying from the room. After a brief conversation at the doorway heavy footsteps thumped the stairs before Jack popped his head around the bedroom door, wearing a cheeky grin.

"Or aye!" laughed Jack aloud. "It's alright for some lying in bed like a loppy dog all day while others are out there fighting for ya future."

Tom gulped, trying to clear mucus from his throat. Eying the gash on Jack's nose and the puffy swelling around his lips, he narrowed his eyes, asking, "What's happened to you?"

"Orr nowt really, a' had a bit of a run in with a psycho copper this morning, that's all, that's why I am here for actually, apparently due to the state I've left the bastard in we're being kicked out the village, the bus is leaving in about forty minutes."

"Kicked out of the village!? Leaving for where!?"

"For yerm! So, get ya lazy arse out of bed and dressed an–"

"He can't go anywhere," broke in Pat, entering the room, "he's not fit enough to get out of bed, never mind go traipsing halfway up the country."

"But we've got to get out of here and fast!" explained Jack. "The cops are not pissing about, flowerpots, they're ganna lift everybody an–"

She once again interrupted Jack: "Look, I'll put some time owed in at work, and when Tom's fit enough to travel, I'll bring him up there myself."

Tom gulped. "I'll be okay here, Jack, honest I'm as weak as a creaking gate, young'n."

Jack scrutinised his brother, muttering, "Ya look nowt flash like." After a lengthy sigh he continued, "Okay then, I'll gan and find this Donald gadjy and get him to send ya suitcase around for ya." He grinned impishly at Pat, joking, "He's not quite house-trained tha nars, love."

"Don't worry, I've got a collar and leash in the bottom of my wardrobe somewhere if it's needed."

Her mischievous comment caused Jack to look at her open mouthed while Tom chuckled under his breath. After a sharp sigh Jack once again faced Pat. "On that note a' suppose I'd better bugger off then! Please tack care of him, he's the anly brother I've got."

Pat reassured, "He's in good hands, I'm a nurse." Showing Jack from the bedroom they stood chatting briefly at the front doorway ahead of her locking up. Re-entering the bedroom, she was met by Tom's impish grin. She smiled, asking, "What are you smirking at?"

"Nothing, a' was just thinking."

"Thinking what?"

"Nowt really, just what it's ganna be like when our Jack tries to explain to Ma why he's come yerm without is."

"Yerm?" She frowned, mystified. "What on earth is this yerm?"

"Sorry, it means home," he explained, "yerm means home."

"Never heard of that expression ever. Will it be an issue with your Mum, with you being like, left behind down here with me?"

"Just a bit," he managed to mumble in between spluttering out a mixture of laughs and coughs, "he'll be getting questions hoyed at him from all ower the place, it'll be a bit like that Spanish Inquisition thingy!" Tom grinned widely, asking, "Ya wouldn't happen to be a Catholic by any chance, would ya?"

"I am actually," she responded with a bemused glower.

"Arr why that's a canny start a' suppose."

"You've got a lovely smile," she said softly. Sitting next to him she took hold of his hand to peck a tender kiss on his knuckles. "I really like you, Tom."

"And I do you," he said, stroking her hair away from her face, "more than you could ever imagine." He leant forward and pressed a gentle, loving kiss to her forehead.

At number two Cuba Street, Irene lay in bed wrapped in the warmth and comfort of Alan's tattooed arms. They were just about drifting off to sleep when the front door creaked, and Mick set away barking nonstop. "Shush up, ya daft bugger!" whispered Jack, closing the door gently behind him. "It's just me!"

Hearing Jack's voice Irene sat up bolt right raising, "My good God! The lads are back!" Jumping from her bed she twirled herself into a dressing gown whispering, "Stay there, Alan, and for goodness sake keep quiet." Leaving the bedroom, she rushed the stairs where she entered into the sitting room to be greeted by the soft ticking of a clock prior to Jack entering via a kitchen door.

"Sorry if a' woke ya," he said, chewing on a chicken drumstick.

"It's alright, a' was awake, what ya doing back, a' thought yas were away till Friday?"

"So did ah but we got kicked out the village."

"Kicked out the village? What for, like?"

Jack shrugged his shoulders. "A' divant nar really."

Noticing the swelling around his mouth and a gash running the bridge of his nose, she asked, "What's happened to ya face!?"

"Nowt, a' slipped ower, that's all," he answered, casting a reassuring grin.

"Slipped over my foot," she uttered as the two sat on the settee. Examining his nose, she half smiled. "At least the thing's not broken." Looking around the room, Irene frowned slightly, enquiring, "Where's our Tom at?"

Jack paused, sighing, "... He's still down Lancashire, he's poorly."

Irene quickly spouted out a trio of nervous motherly questions: "Poorly!? What do ya mean by poorly!? What's happened to him like!?"

"Settle down, man, Ma, nowts happened to him, he's just gone and got his sell tonsil-titis or something, he's stopping at a lass' house, she–"

Irene broke in, "At a lass' house!? What lass' house!?"

"A' divant nar! All a' nar is she's called Pat, and stop worrying, man, he's getting well looked after."

She then threw the obvious, "How come he's ended up at this girl's house like?"

"Why, it's a canny lang story, but basically he walked her home from a pub on Monday night and apparently he took a bad turn, and he's been in her bed ever since."

Irene calmed herself down, half smiling. "Is she nice like?"

"Aye, she seems canny enough like." Jack bit into the chicken leg, spluttering, "Apparently she's a nurse."

"Is she!?" gushed Irene who was rather impressed that Tom had managed to walk a nurse home. Her tone dropped dramatically as she looked into Jack's eyes: "Do ya think she's Catholic?"

"A' haven't the foggiest! A' forgot to ask her that one, should a' gan back down there and ask her?"

"Stop being arsy, but does she look Catholic? Or does she look like a... ya nar... a Protestant?"

"Mam, man, they all look the same." Jack peeled away the crispy skin from the drumstick, feeding it to Mick. "Protestants, Catholics, there's no difference in their appearances, for crying out loud!"

"You try telling that to Father O'Conner and see what happens, he'll clip ya rit around the back of ya lug." After pecking a kiss on Jack's cheek, Irene stood with a stretch saying, "Anyway, I've got an early start in the morning, so night, night and God bless."

"Night, night, Ma," he returned. Smiling brazen he raised his eyes to the ceiling shouting, "Night, Alan!"

"Night, Jack!" came carefree from upstairs.

Irene stood mortified. "How do you know about me and Alan?" In a state of panic, she crossed the room to stand at the mantelpiece where she fumbled to light up a cigarette before continuing: "Let alone how did ya know he was here!?"

"Ma, man, we've known about you and Alan since the day ya started seeing him, you should nar better than most they can tell the hanging of a man around here, and a' knew he was here 'coss a' can smell his blinking aftershave, it's bloody awful... besides that, his size elevens are in the hallway." He smiled warmly at his mother. "Look, Ma, not that you need it, but you've always had mine and our Tom's blessings if another man ever entered into your life, ya still young for crying out loud, even me Da wanted you to find someone after he had gone, and who better than Alan, he's a top bloke; mind you, he'll have to do something with that blinking aftershave of his like, it's canny rank."

Irene feathered a kiss on her son's brow, whispering, "Thank you, son." Stumping out her cigarette she left the room, leaving Jack to concentrate on his chicken leg with Mick sitting, shaking in anticipation of a morsel.

TWO NIGHTS LATER

Under the shadow of darkness, Jack, Hoss, and Billy were thieving coal from up on the pit heaps at Easington Colliery when the haunting screech of a barn owl startled Billy as he lay sprawled on the top of one of the gigantic coal duff mounds acting as a lookout. Below him, Hoss loaded a shovel full of duff into a homemade riddle, a device that was two-foot square in shape and constructed out of four pieces of two-by-two wood with a perforated base made from chicken wire. Jack vigorously shook away the powdery duff from the apparatus, sifting out small lumps of coal before emptying the shiny nuggets into a sack. Hoss had once again filled up the sieve when Jack looked at him, whispering, "It's tacking ages this mind, Hoss," riddling away more duff he heaved a sigh, "it'll have to be the last bag, me arms are dropping off here."

"It's the last one anyway, a' only brought six with is."

Jack carefully tipped more nuggets into the sack, asking, "What time's it?"

Flickering a torchlight onto his wrist, Hoss muttered, "Ten ta one."

"Frigging hell! We've been down here for nearly two hours now!"

Billy left his post to quickly join the others, whispering, "Security's h-h-here, there's th-th-three of them and a dog, what we g-g-ganna do, tack a b-b-bag apiece and fuck o-o-off?"

Lighting up a cigarette, Jack looked at Billy, sarcastically repeating, "Tack a bag apiece and fuck off!" his sarcasm stretched. "Don't talk sa fond, we're gan'n newhere!"

"Do ya not th-th-think it's best we just cut our l-l-losses and get out of here, Jack!?"

"Why not fucking likely! I'm not flogging me tits off filling them things up just so them bastards can keep them for themselves–"

"Mack ya minds up," broke in Hoss, all carefree. "What are we doing, are we going, staying, going, staying, or what!?"

"We're staying put, that's what we're doing!" said Jack with purpose and Hoss' response to his friend's words was to shrug his shoulders untroubled while Billy stood shaking his head.

Two average-sized security guards were more than surprised to stumble upon the lads while a much smaller officer trailed a few paces behind struggling to restrain a heated Alsatian dog that was growling and barking nonstop. "Stay where ya's are!" ordered the diminutive guard as he fidgeted to straighten a lopsided military styled cap. "Ya's are all nicked, the lot of ya's!" With the dog still straining on the leash, he advanced to within four feet of Hoss, ordering, "Empty them bags out now! Yar all coming with us!"

"Don't talk so fucking baldy headed!" replied Hoss, scratching his head untroubled. Slowly eying the guard up and down, he laughed, "Anyway, where the hell have you come from, fell off some fucker's charm bracelet or what?"

"I'll set the dog on ya's mind!"

"What, that thing?!" laughed Hoss. Stepping closer, he patted the canine, enthusing, "Who's a good boy then!" At once the thing stopped barking and started wagging its tail all friendly. Facing the tiny guard, Hoss grinned ear to ear, joking, "Shouldn't you be somewhere up Lapland helping Santy or something."

One of the other officers stepped forward. "Leave it, John, we don't get paid enough for all this shit, like."

"Too right ya's don't!" sneered Jack. "Now do ya sells a favour and fuck off afore we tack the dog off ya's."

The smaller of the guards slowly shone his torch around the lads. "I've got ya cards marked now I know ya faces, if a' catch ya's on the premises again ya'll all be nicked, you will lose ya jobs, pensions, and everything."

The lads set away laughing before the guards backed away and walked off.

"By the way," goaded Jack after them, "tell that Robert Hardy when ya see him, his fucking card's marked, 'coss I'm ganna level the twat first chance a' get!" Jack looked on with a smirk as he watched the officers depart up the side of a neighbouring mound of coal. After drawing deep on his cigarette, he handed the half-smoked cig to Billy. "Here, finish that off, young'n."

Hoss picked up a shovel, saying, "How'y then, let's get this last bag filled." It took them a good fifteen minutes or so to fill up the sack before Hoss stitched the hessian mouth together with a thin, yellow-coated copper wiring, known as 'shot wire'. Standing up a bicycle, he held the handlebars rigid while straddling his legs at either side of the front wheel as Billy struggled loading the creaky thing up with the sacks.

"Is that okay, H-H-Hoss?" he asked, resting the fifth bag at the top of the stack.

"Aye, it's not three bad."

"Leave that one," suggested Jack, looking down at the last sack. "I'll carry that and the shovel." Picking up the hefty sack, he shuffled it to comfort across his shoulders, then, nattering amongst themselves, they set off on their arduous slog home. Hoss was up front steering the old boneshaker as Billy pushed from the rear of a damaged saddle, while Jack followed a step or two behind; every now and then, Jack would stop in his stride to reshuffle the weighty sack from shoulder to shoulder before, shovel in hand, he stepped up a pace to catch up with the other two. Crossing over the Hartlepool to Sunderland railway line, they advanced through the blackness to follow a muddy trail which guided them at a side of a drawn-out farmer's field towards a single arched railway bridge that was constructed out of red brick and dubbed, 'The Second Bridge'. Trudging under the mini viaduct the path changed from mud to red ash and the lads found it considerably easier underfoot. The flattened pathway directed them past a chunk of waste land, where in the weeks leading up to 'Guy Fawkes night', scary ghost stories were spoken around campfires by adolescent Easties, as they sat guarding their precious bonfire from marauding Southies, or Cavaliers, but mainly from their main nemesis, the crafty Northies.

Strolling further, they were advancing through the murkiness when another screech from a barn owl split the night. After bypassing a string of wooden garages that backed onto rows of hallowed allotments, they came to yet another bridge which was a lot narrower than the previous and labelled 'The First Bridge', or even 'DEVILS MOUTH', for this concrete underpass was ghostly, to say the least, especially if you were a youngster, as it was common knowledge that if you and your gang were returning home in the shadowiness of nightfall and you had the misfortune to be the last child to enter into the gloom of 'DEVILS MOUTH', you stood a very good chance of not exiting out at the other side due to bloodcurdling circumstances like a fatal bite to the jugular by the dreaded Count Dracula; or, you may even be torn to shreds by the ferocious claws of a Werewolf; but the worst fate by far was to be ripped limb from limb at the mighty hands of Victor Frankenstein's hideous monster. Passing under this unearthly tunnel, a short but steep incline awaited. Hoss grit his teeth as they forced the bicycle up the cobbled slope; after bridging the peak, they turned a sharp left to be welcomed by an amber glow of the streetlights. Following the route of the pit wall, they tramped along the bottom of Office Street, Charles Street, Chandler, then Castle Street, before turning into Cuba Street where they shoved the old pushbike up a slight gradient until their journey ended at number two Cuba Street.

It was Saturday morning, and Irene had finished dusting and polishing the sitting room when she switched on a vacuum cleaner; not hearing the clatter of the front door she got a bit of a jolt as Jack breezed into the room with Mick trailing behind on a leash. "Outside now!" she ordered, switching off the contraption. "And tack them boots off!"

"Why are ya hoovering for, Ma!? Ya anly did it yesterday!" he asked as he stood at the doorway, removing his muddied boots.

"Tha nars fine well why! That lass is bringing our Tom home today and a' don't want the place looking like a tip!"

Jack removed the leash from Mick before he re-entered the room. "Ya used to do exactly the same thing when we were youngn's when the doctor was coming out on a home visit when one of us was ill, straight out with the hoover and duster ya was."

"And!?"

"And he wasn't coming out to inspect the house, and neither will that Pat be either."

"She might do, so mind ya arn business." The instant Irene restarted the hoover, Mick came tearing into the room where he started barking nonstop as he circled the noisy device, attacking it from all angles. "Give ower, ya daft bat!" she yelled at the senseless canine before facing Jack. "Will ya put him in the passageway 'till I've finished hoovering!"

Pat parked her car outside number two Cuba Street. After a bit of a chat with Tom and a reassuring kiss, they exited the vehicle to amble hand in hand through the sunshine to pass by a little girl who was singing to herself whilst chalking childlike pictures onto a wall. Tom raised a smile at Pat in anticipation, ahead of the two crossing over the threshold to be met by the aroma of home cooking. Entering into the sitting room, he offered Pat a seat on the sofa before raising, "Ma, we're home." His words went unanswered, so he yelled louder, "Ma! We are home!" After checking the kitchen, Tom returned to sit beside Pat. "She must have our Mick out for a walk, do ya want a coffee?"

"No thanks, but I'll have glass of water if you don't mind." They exchanged smiles before he left the room just as the front door creaked ahead of Jack and Hoss breezing into the room.

"Hello love!" said Jack politely.

"Hello Jack," returned Pat with a smile.

"So, ya remembered me name then?"

"Yeah." She faced Hoss. "Hello Hoss."

"Hello," he replied, holding up a hand in recognition.

"How was ya journey?" asked Jack, sitting into a chair. "Roads okay?"

"Yeah, not too bad actually, we hit some roadworks at Scotch Corner, but nothing major."

Tom entered the room, handing Pat her drink. Looking to Jack, he asked, "Alright, young'n?"

"Aye not three bad," he replied, before asking, "you okay now?"

"Aye I'm fine, still a bit weak like, but I'm getting there." Tom smiled at Hoss, asking, "Alright Hoss?"

"Why aye, I'm glad ya back, like."

"Is that ya motor out there, Pat?" asked Jack flicking his head in the direction of the window.

"Yeah, that's my baby," she said all proud.

Jack smiled, complimenting, "Nice motor the Escort Ghia, a' bet it can shift a bit."

"Too right it can!" chipped in Tom. "She almost hit a ton coming up the M1."

A knocking at the door sounded ahead of Alan entering into the sitting room with Tom welcoming, "Alright, Alan? What's tha after?"

Alan grinned coyly before he looked to Jack for support.

Jack coughed. "Alan's come for dinner, Tom, him and Ma's officially courting now."

Tom looked at Alan with an unsure squint before he couldn't hold it any longer and he slowly broke into a grin. "It's about time yas

came out, every man and his dog's narn about yas for yonks now."
His face lit up further as he introduced Alan to Pat, and the two
were exchanging friendly smiles when the front door once again
creaked ahead of Mick dashing into the room reeking of cow muck.

Irene gently closed the door behind her, shouting, "He stinks
of cow...poo... again!" Removing her coat she entered the room,
moaning, "All these years our poor Mick's been getting wrang for
rolling in cow muck and it's not even his fault, it's them bloody
cows' fault, one of them has just walked up to him and from out
of nowhere papped all ower him, right in front of me very eyes
an'll! The cheeky bloody thing!"

Tom stood to his feet. "Ma, this is Pat."

Irene smiled widely as she sat next to Pat, welcoming her
with an over-the-top hug. Looking into her eyes she enthused,
"I've been dying to meet ya, and thanks a lot for looking after
my boy." Scrutinizing Pat from top to bottom, she smiled again.
"Now look at you, yar an absolute picture so you are." Addressing
the room she committed, "Isn't she a picture!?" and agreements
were nodded in return.

"Thank you, it's a pleasure meeting you, Mrs Gilroy, you don't
look old enough to be Jack and Tom's mother."

"Keep hold of this one, son," chirped Irene, "a' like her."

"I'm glad you do," said Tom, "because we've got something
to tell ya." Tom took Pat by the hand, aiding her to her feet he
snuggled her close, and after clearing his throat with a succession
of sharp coughs he looked directly at his mother, announcing,
"Ma, a' know Pat and me haven't known each other for very long
but we are engaged to be married, I haven't bought a ring yet
because, well, you know why, with the strike and that..." Tom's
prepared speech ended abruptly as Irene stood to wipe away
tears before she rushed from the room. "...Are you okay, Ma!?"
he shouted with a bemused grimace before she returned handing
over a velvet ring box.

"This is what ya Dad gave me all those years ago, Tom, it's not the most expensive of engagement rings, but it's held nothing but love and happiness for me, and I would be honoured if Pat wore it." She faced Pat with a heart-warming smile. "It's yours for as long as you want it, pet-lamb, you can either have it for keeps, or just until our Tom gets you a better one, it's up to you, love." Tom looked to a tearful Pat as she nodded agreement, and he gently placed the ring onto her finger.

"It's beautiful, Mrs Gilroy," she said overwhelmed, "it fits perfect, and I don't need another ring ever, I'll cherish this for the rest of my life." Tom and Pat kissed softly to a round of applause.

Irene hugged Pat, purring, "Welcome to the family, love, I have always craved for a daughter to fuss over, unfortunately I was blessed with Morecambe and Wise here." Looking at her sons she stretched a smile, "Only kidding," then turning back to Pat, she looked her in the eye saying, "so, Pat, from now on you can call me Ma, but only if ya wanted that is."

"Thanks, Mrs Gilroy," sniffed Pat before correcting, "sorry, thanks, Ma."

They all took it in turns to congratulate the happy couple with a variety of words and embraces when Tom looked around the room, announcing, "By the way, Pat's Catholic."

"As if that mattered," replied Irene, flopping her hand forward in a carefree gesture while all the time she was thinking, 'thank goodness for that'.

"Do yas not think ya's are rushing into it a bit?" asked Jack direct. "Ya've only known each other for all of five minutes."

"Love can hit ya within an instant, Jack," put in Irene, "and it's as plain as the nose on ya face, even if it's all damaged like yours is, that these two are in love; besides, look at me and ya Dad, granted we had known each other for all our lives but we were married within three months off us starting courting and–"

Jack interrupted, "Aye that's 'coss ya was pre–".

"That's!" Wide eyed, Irene stopped Jack in his tracks. "'Coss a' was only seventeen and deeply in love, Jack!" She enlarged her eyes further. "That's what it was!"

"Anyway," sighed Tom, quickly changing the subject, "a' hear congratulations are in order with you and Alan too, Ma?"

"Yes." Taking Alan by the hand, she smiled. "It's in its early stages still, but yes ... yes."

"What's for dinner, Ma!?" gushed Hoss. "It smells blum'n lovely."

"Panacalty and homemade stotties," tooted Irene much to Hoss' delight. Irene looked to Jack. "Anyway, when are you going to find yourself someone nice to settle down with, bugger lugs?"

Jack flinched at the idea, replying, "On the twelfth."

"On the twelfth?" asked Irene puzzled. "On the twelfth of when?"

He chuckled, "On the twelfth of never... that's when!"

Irene returned, "Ya'll find true-love one of these days, our Jack, you mark my words you will, and it'll come when it's least expected an'll, in the meantime bath our Mick afore dinner."

"Why's it always me who has ta bath him for!?"

"Because it's your job, you're the youngest, that's why, and ya haven't found love yet like ya brother has, but don't worry ya will do one day, son."

"Aye in ya dreams!" he returned, shrugging his shoulders at the thought. "I'd rather keep bathing the dog, if it's alright with you!?"

"You just wait and see," sighed his mother, "love will catch up with ya one day, our Jack and knowing you it'll hit ya like a blum'n grit freight train when it does."

Jack had bathed the dog just as Irene finished setting the table, and the instant Alan had ended grace they all tucked into their meal. As they ate, Pat couldn't help herself looking on in amazement as Hoss set away humming while assaulting a freshly baked Stottie-Bread. Irene looked to Pat; squeezing her hand ever so slightly, she whispered, "He's a growing lad, flowerpots." Pat returned a grin as she too broke bread to dab into the delicious dish, then, from out of the blue, Pat sneezed and the whole table said, 'God bless ya!' in unison. Irene raised, "So, Pat, what do ya parents do for a living?"

"Well." Pat smiled proudly. "Father is a sheep and cattle farmer, and my mother died when I was five years old, but Jean, my stepmother, well, she's just a farmer's wife really."

Irene empathized, "Arr! You poor thing, I'll light a candle in memory of your poor mam tomorrow at mass." Changing the subject she gently rubbed Pat's arm, asking, "So, where's this farm of yours at then, flowerpots?"

"Up in the Peak District."

"Is it big?" jumped in Jack.

"Yeah, it's one of the biggest on the Downs, we have over four thousand acres."

"How many!?" raised Jack rather taken aback.

"Just over four thousand acres," repeated Pat, "mind you, just under one third is rented from the National Trust though."

Jack looked around the table, "How many sheep ya got like!?"

"Somewhere in the region of five thousand, and we have over eight hundred and fifty head of beef too, then there's Father's prized Shire horses, he only has half a dozen of those though." They all looked at her gobsmacked. Pat smiled at the table, explaining, "He likes to show his Shires at the county shows does Father."

Jack queried, "Ya haven't got any sisters by any chance, have ya?"

"Sorry," she smiled, "I'm the only child."

Jack turned to Tom. "Ne wonder ya want to marry her so quickly!" Returning to face Pat, he flashed his eyes all flirty. "I'd marry ya mesell if you ever came back on the market."

"Take no notice of our Jack, love," blew Irene, casting daggers at her youngest, "he's a bit of a rascal I'm afraid."

"I gathered that," chortled Pat.

Tom sat blushing. "I never knew ya farm was that big."

"You never asked," she returned with a carefree grin. "Anyway, does it make any difference like?"

"Nar," he said, shaking his head, "none whatsoever."

"Alright! Let the poor lass eat her meal in peace," broke in Irene, "it's not blinking, 'This Is Your Life', tha nars!"

Jack raised, "I've got a horse, Pat, it's a Clydesdale cross thoroughbred, and–"

"Jack!" interrupted Irene, knowing her youngest's words would lead further. "Pack the bugger in, enough is enough!" Jack opened his mouth to speak when Irene ordered, "Eat ya dinner!"

Smiles were cast across the table before Tom looked to Pat. "We'll go for a walk tomorrow morning if ya fancy?"

"How come he can talk at the table and ah canit like?" moaned Jack, flicking his eyes between his brother and mother.

Irene squinted. "Give it a rest, Jack; by all means have a discussion but dinit be questioning the poor lass." Turning to Pat, she beamed. "Are ya alright love?"

"Yeah, I'm fine, thank you," she answered with a broad smile of her own.

Alan looked around the table, saying, "Ya'll never guess who came to the office to see is yesterday?"

"Who?" asked Hoss, humming his way through a sausage.

"Lemsip's Ma, she came around spitting fire saying Lemsip wasn't allowed to go away picketing anymore, just local."

"Why?" frowned Tom.

Jack put in, "Orr, ya haven't heard yet, have ya? Lemsip got whacked down Bold Colliery, broken nose the lot."

"And he had to have five stitches put in his head," added Alan. "His Ma took him straight down to Hartlepool hospital in a taxi the instant he got back yerm, apparently you could hear his screams at Blackhall rocks when they were stitching him up."

Jack snapped, "Here, dinit mack fun of him, Alan! He did really well down there, he got stuck in and everything, so did Sizzler, and he got clobbered too."

"Bless them," sighed Tom, "a' like Lemsip and Sizzler, they wadn't say boo to a goose the pair of them."

"We all like them," stretched from Jack. Looking directly at Tom he blew a sigh, adding, "And by the way Billy took a canny hit on his head an'all, he needed stitches too."

"Never in the world! Is he okay?" asked Tom with concern.

Jack widened his eyes. "He is now, thank God." Spooning his stew, he continued, "And our Ger's gone and got himself locked up with Joe Whitlewith."

"Ya joking!?" blew Tom.

"A's not tha nars, apparently they never let them out of the nick till late Thursday night."

Alan voiced, "They've charged them with affray too."

"What's affray?" Irene frowned.

"It's a really serious offence, love," uttered Alan, heaving a deep, prolonged sigh, "and if they are found guilty, they could get up to life in prison."

Irene blew her cheeks. "Never! Dear God, our poor Jim and Betty must be besides themselves." Pat once again sneezed to a domino of 'God bless ya's'!

Lifting his plate to his mouth, Hoss slurped all the liquefied remains from his plate, then, smiling at Irene, he licked his lips, asking, "anymore of that Panacalty left Ma?".

She smiled. "Aye but leave a couple of sausages for our Mick."

"A' want some more, Hoss, so gan canny," said Jack.

"A' think a' might try some more too," said Alan, his words causing Hoss to leer at him narrow eyed.

Sunday had fashioned up a beautiful June morning for Tom and Pat as they strolled hand in hand across the clifftops at Easington Colliery. Tom smiled warmly as two young school kids struggled slightly to push a rusty seventies Chopper bicycle, which was loaded to capacity with a stack of sandbags that brimmed with sea coal. Ambling further, Tom exchanged good mornings with an elderly man who walked with a stoop whilst carrying a weighty plastic bag across his scrawny shoulders. Enjoying the warmth of the sunshine, Tom and Pat sauntered further before they carefully descended 'The Red Ash', a steep gradient which guided them down onto the beach itself. Although cherished by the locals, Easington beach was a far cry from a typical seaside resort that you would find on postcards as throughout the entirety of its shoreline there was not one single grain of sand to be found, only black, industrial pit waste and rocks which had accumulated over the decades due to the constant dumping of untreated slag from out of the coalmine directly into the sea.

Wandering towards a calm water's edge they came across men, women, and kids of all ages who clasped plastic buckets as they stooped, rummaging the hightide mark in search of washed-up nuggets of shiny coal. After stopping to give a young man a light on his cigarette, Tom and Pat headed northwards where they came to 'The Twelve Foots', an assembly of hefty, seaweed-covered rocks which emerged twice daily from out of the sea only to be reclaimed time after time again by incoming tides. It was here, at these rock-strewn pools, where generation after generation of kids from all the colliery estates learnt how to swim while eager eyed adults looked on from the top of these illustrious sarsens. Inching a couple of hundred yards further north, they passed under the 'Pit Pipe', a rusty conduit which usually spewed out raw slurry twenty-four-seven but was now running dry due to the current pit strike. Walking a short distance, they reached the 'Cinderella Rock', a solitary mustard coloured pillar that topped at well over forty feet in height and was shaped like a crooked witch's hat. Advancing another fifty yards or so they approached 'The Flight', a specially constructed manmade structure compromising gigantic pylons that were built entirely out of steel girders to shoulder a lengthy conveyer belt which snaked from the pit to cross over a patchwork of open fields before descending the cliffs to empty its polluted load directly into the water. Tom rested an arm on Pat's shoulder as he pointed out to sea, explaining how he worked six miles out underneath the seabed; at first, she thought he may have been pulling her leg, but looking into his eyes it soon became apparent that he wasn't, and apprehension shot her face. Taking her by the hand, they walked into 'Flight Bay', before they came to the 'Grassy Banks', a wall of high cliffs that stood steadfast while topped off in greenery. Tom paused to point out a handsome male kestrel enter a cracking in a cliff face with his freshly caught prey still seized in his talons.

After crossing a lengthy cove, they rounded a rocky headland which led them into another inlet known as 'Boaty's Bay'. Here a couple of majestic fulmars glided just above the cliff tops while below, the remains of a shipwrecked ship's boiler was laid to rest amongst seaweed-covered rocks that stretched far out to sea. Three hundred metres further out in the water, a couple of local fishermen were struggling to haul up crab pots at the side of a brightly-coloured coble boat before they cast out freshly baited pots that were attached by salty ropes to orange triangular-shaped marker flags. After crossing the length of the bay, Tom and Pat arched another peninsula which led them towards an enormous, grass-topped rock that rose stalwart from out of the water's edge and was dubbed 'The Hoss Backs'. Walking for almost ten minutes, 'Hawthorne Bay' came into view where a graffiti-covered World War Two pillar box greeted them at the mouth of Hawthorne Dene. Halfway up a cliffside, a set of caves were purposely carved into the bankside to house Irish immigrant workers who, at the turn of the century, were especially drafted to the area by the North-Eastern Railway Company to construct a spectacular multi-arched railway viaduct that spanned a gorge from way above the treetops of the dene. The back of their legs pulled to a slight burn, as Tom and Pat huffed their way up the side of a steep slope which led them past the caves and up onto the clifftops where, hand in hand, they started their journey back towards home, following a well-used pathway which ran adjacent to the main Sunderland to Hartlepool railway line.

ONE WEEK LATER

Tom entered the sitting room, holding a couple of steamy drinks. "Where do ya want ya coffee, Ma?"

Irene rested her knitting. "Just put it on the coffee table there, love." After looking into the fire, she glanced at her son. "We're running a bit short of coal again mind."

"Aye a' nar," he said as he sat. "A' think we ganna sort something out later on the night."

"Why, watch what ya's are doing, and divant be getting ya sells caught."

"Don't worry, man, Ma," he reassured, casting a slight grin, "we'll be fine."

"A' do worry though, there's men getting sacked all ower the place for getting coal." Lighting up a cigarette she coughed slightly before inhaling deeply. "Anyway where yas picketing at in the morn?"

"A'm not quite sure, a' think it's someplace down in Yorkshire."

"Yorkshire!?" Once again, she drew heavily on her cigarette. "A' thowt they were all out solid like us down there?"

"They are; anyway, it might not be in Yorkshire, but it must be canny far away 'coss we've got an early start, that's if the coppers don't stop us again that is."

"What do ya mean, if they don't stop yas?"

"Why, it seems that's all they are doing lately, everywhere we gan picketing they're pulling us over, ordering us straight back yerm. Poor Ralph Ward and his marras went all the way down to Mansfield just last week to join a rally and they were pulled over on the M1 and ordered to go back home. Apparently trying to get anywhere near Nottingham is virtually impossible these days, the cops have the place cornered off from all directions."

"Well, if yas do get through to wherever yas are ganning, watch what yas are doing, things are getting a lot more violent lately." Irene smiled warmly at her son. "Anyway, are ya looking forward to going down to Pat's next weekend?"

"Aye a'm a', apparently, I'm ganna meet her Da and stepmam."

"Why just be ya sell, son, I'm sure they'll like ya." Irene took a sip from her cup; instantly twisting her face, she asked, "Have ya put any sugar in here!?"

"Sorry, a' might have forgotten to stir it," he said as he stood.

"Sit ya sell back down." Picking up a pen, she turned it upside down to quickly swirl her drink, then, glancing at the clock she sighed. "Look at the time already, it's almost teatime, Sundays just seem to fly-by these days."

On a scorching Monday morning, Jack and the lads were dressed in shorts and tee-shirts as they sat playing cards across the backseats of the picketing bus when Alan stood from opposite the driver to waddle his way up the aisle. "Everything alright then?" he asked, smiling at the lads.

"Aye, everything's champion," grinned Hoss, "a's just about two quid up here."

Alan looked around with a huge beam. "Not be long now, we're nearly there." Slowly turning, he shifted his way back down the aisle, all the time pausing to natter briefly with a variety of individuals.

The bus left the motorway. After travelling along a winding slip road, they joined a lengthy convoy of other buses all loaded with pickets. Advancing for a further half mile or so, they drove straight ahead at three individual roundabouts before almost coming to a standstill as they stumbled upon hundreds of parked up police vehicles which stretched nose to tail for as far as the eye could see. Jack glanced from out of a window; somewhat overwhelmed, he turned to the lads gushing, "How'y tack a look at these fuckers! I've never seen so many coppers in all me life!"

Hoss joined Jack, gushing, "There's not that many cops in the whole of England!"

Everybody rushed to the windows, looking on at the police convoy, when a couple of motorcycle policeman caught Billy's eye as they stood at the side of their machines smiling welcomely whilst ushering the buses through a blockade. Billy returned a polite grin of his own before he faced the lads saying, "Bloody h-h-hell! They're n-n-not trying to stop us." He pointed out the jolly-faced officers, saying, "Look at these t-t-two here, they're waving us through with s-s-smiles on their faces, mind you, I've got to s-s-say the police down here seem f-f-friendly enough alright, they're nowt like the b-b-bastards back at yerm."

"Believe you me, they're not friendly," muttered Tom, "they're owt but."

"B-B-But they're laughing."

"Aye, laughing like hyenas, and that's what they are too, fucking hyenas!" said Jack with purpose. "A'm telling ya now, Billy, them fuckers are twats, the lot of them!"

Hoss voiced, "Jack's right, Billy, they're not friendly at all, they're owt but."

Jack nodded agreement, saying, "Too right, Hoss!" His eyes slowly ran the group, then shaking his head, he uttered, "Ya've heard the old saying, like lambs to the slaughter! Well start bleating, lads 'coss if this isn't a setup, I'll eat me hat with a stick a' celery."

"Ya haven't got a stick of celery," raised Hoss.

Billy furthered, "Ya haven't even g-g-got a h-h-hat!"

"A' nar that!" moaned Jack, "It's just a metaphor, man."

Hoss frowned. "It's just a what!?"

"Nowt, it doesn't matter, Hoss!" half snapped Jack with a look of concern sketched across his face.

Billy corrected, "Technically speaking, it's n-n-not exactly a metaphor m-m-mind, Jack."

"Whatever, Billy! Who gives a shiny shite what it is, all I'm saying is we're heading into a trap here, metaphor, or no fucking metaphor!" He turned to his brother, muttering, "A' don't like this, young'n, not one little bit do a'."

"Nor me too," agreed Tom with a prolonged sigh, "it stinks of something not right."

Inching through other police cordons the bus trudged up a steep hill where they came across yet another police blockade that was way heavier than the others. Gazing from the window Tom noticed a group of policemen who were stood on a bankside, goading the passing pickets by their now ritual waving of ten-pound notes. Another trio of policemen grinned ear to ear while exaggerating counting out thick wads of money as they stood blocking off a road sign; still laughing, these officers slowly shifted to one side of the road sign to reveal **ORGREAVE**. Looking around the lads, Tom drew attention to these arrogant coppers: "Look at these piss-taking bastards, they're waving money all ower the place!"

Jack banged on the window, giving them the old one-handed shuffle while mouthing, "Wankers! Fucking nob heads!"

Travelling a further two hundred metres or so, the bus slowed to a crawl before traffic officers shepherded them into a field to join other coaches from around the various coalfields including Yorkshire, Lancashire, Durham, Scotland, Northumberland, Wales, Kent, Nottingham, Staffordshire and Derbyshire. Coming to a stop, the bus driver announced at what time he would be returning home, he also notified everybody where this specific pick-up point was located before once again repeating at what time they were departing, emphasizing clearly that under no circumstances would he be waiting around, and anyone who found himself lagging would be left behind. The men stood and started to leave the bus in an orderly fashion, but, as Jack was about to exit, he leaned over the driver, threatening, "You leave any fucker behind, and I'll rip the front of ya face off." He looked menacingly at the driver, snarling, "Understand!?" The driver sat silent, staring straight ahead. Jack leant nose to nose, scowling, "A' said do you understand!?" and a single nod was given in return before Jack smiled sharply, if falsely, prior to him stepping from the bus to join the rest of the lads.

Lighting up a cigarette, Jack looked to a cloudless sky, uttering, "Ah, why, whatever's they've got installed for us, a' suppose it's a canny day for it." They proceeded to edge with the flow of the crowd taking them along a constricted lane which shepherded them through a small industrial estate where they passed by a fenced off scrapyard. After inching across a narrow bridge that spanned over a couple of steep railway embankments, they advanced further towards the peak of a widespread pasture, and the instant they breached the crown they looked on overawed at the sight of thousands of pickets who were sat, or stood, in separate groups scattered across the sloping meadow that tapered down towards a breach in the surrounding hedgerows where thousands, upon thousands, of battle-clad police officers blocked off the entire entrance into Orgreave coking plant. It was hard to assume the exact numbers of police officers that were on duty, but it was somewhere in the region of six to eight thousand, perhaps more, and they certainly outnumbered the pickets. Behind these pillars of blue, more than fifty mounted police officers were sat on their chargers, holding onto extra-long truncheons, while at either side of the blockade scores of police dog handlers and dozens of groups of Snatch Squads lingered menacingly in thick undergrowth that was spottled by a diversity of trees.

Scanning the scene, Billy gasped, "F-F-Fucking hell! It's like R-R-Rourke's Drift this is!"

"Too right it is!" heaved Hoss. "And this time the Zulus have all the guns and ammunition, and we've not got a' single spear between us."

Billy looked to Jack with uneasiness. "F-F-Fucking hell, Jack! There's a canny few m-m-more of them than w-w-what there is of us, mind."

Jack reassured Billy with a carefree smile, joking, "If ya that nervous about the numbers, Billy, stop counting the fuckers."

"Look, lads, we need to stick together," suggested Tom, "and watch each other's backs at all times, I've got a bad feeling about this." Mingling with other pickets, they slowly trundled the hilly meadow before picking out a spot to sit which was less than a hundred metres away from the thick blue mass. Lighting up a cig, Tom was scanning the scene when Alan walked straight by them, heading in the direction of the police line.

"Huw, where's thuw gan'n!?" bellowed Hoss.

Alan turned. "Looking for you lot! Are we not going further down to the front, get a good spot for the push?"

"Don't talk so fucking baldy-headed," said Jack, "get ya arse back here."

Alan joined them, asking, "What's the matter, like?"

Hoss looked at Alan with a shake of his head. "Alan... not being funny or nowt, but when was the last time you were on a picket line, like actually picketing, like?"

"Nineteen seventy-two! Redcar Steelworks, why?"

"Why!?" repeated Hoss. "'Coss things are a little bit different these days, in seventy-two the cops were happy enough just to arrest ya then provide ya with cups of tea all day; these fuckers are not happy unless they've beaten ya half to death, that's why."

"Just stay close," put in Jack, "'coss believe you me thing's a' ganna kick off big style."

Alan opened his mouth to speak but Tom intervened, "Do what our young'n says, Alan." Tom looked around the group, raising, "Have ya noticed there's only two ways out of here? Either..." he nodded towards the mass of policemen, "...we manage to smash our way through them fuckers..." then glancing back over his shoulder he sighed lengthily, "... or more likely than not, we run back ower that narrow bridge we've just come ower."

"Why that's not that far away, that," laughed Alan as he sat cross legged, "even ah can run that far, why, if push comes to shove a' suppose a' could."

Tom blew a sigh, saying, "That's the trouble, Alan, so can every fucker else! And that bridge is ower narrow to take thousands of panicky pickets scampering across it at the same time, people's ganna get trampled, especially if them bastards start charging at us on horseback."

From behind a line of shields, high-pitched toots sounded from a police whistle, creating a hive of activity. A red-faced police inspector shouted out instructions through a megaphone whilst walking at the side of hundreds of policemen who marched in perfect step, making them appear more military than actual police. Hundreds of extra officers, especially drafted in from the Met, joined their colleagues at the centre of the cordon as other reinforcements merged at the flanks to create a tactical formation that was set up for one thing only: entrapment. Jeered up police dogs barked nonstop, some frothing at the mouth as more dog handlers joined their fellow colleagues in the undergrowth. One handler yanked hard on a leash as he grappled to control his canine after it had stumbled upon a brace of tetchy pheasants. Another series of whistles shrilled before groups of SPG dashed from behind the ranks to stand at various positions within the shrub, blocking off all potential escape routes, whilst mounted officers pulled down visors on their helmets as their horses stomped the ground, ears pricked, ready for action.

In the distance a lengthy fleet of police vehicles advanced towards the plant, transporting even more police officers to the vicinity. Within an instant the atmosphere had turned electric; pickets rose to their feet assembling into one massive mass to stand twenty metres or so back from the first line of oblong-shaped shields. Some pickets pulled their shirts back on over their heads, others flicked cigarette ends away, some even licked their lips which had dried in anticipation of what lay ahead. To the rear of the pickets a jingling to '*I'm Popeye the Sailor Man*' chimed from *Rock on Tommy*, a typical mobile ice-cream van, as it tottered down a narrow lane to park up at its usual stopping spot at the far side of the bridge. "He's bit early int'ee!?" pitched a Yorkshire accent. "Someone run t'up there get me ninety-nine wit monkeys' blood on."

"Does tha want thousands and ones te, cock?" chipped in another Yorkshire accent.

"Neah, tee fattening, wife got me on t' diet again."

The rumble of heavy engines put a stop to the comical banter as a convoy of empty wagons rattled towards the coking plant. The pickets started chanting, '*The Miner's United Will Never Be Defeated...The Miner's United Will Never Be Defeated...*'. Individual shouts of encouragement rang out before they linked arms to slowly advance towards the shields.

"This is it, lads!" encouraged Jack. "Let's give them some fucking shit!"

"Try and stay together!" shouted Tom. "If we get separated, don't forget, make ya way straight back to that bridge as quickly as you can!"

Billy gulped, "Try and stick t-t-together though!"

Hoss grit his teeth. "Come on, ya bastards!"

"Thatcher's boot boys!" screamed Alan.

"Here We Go, Here We Go, Here We Go! Here We Go, Here We Go, Here We go -o!" resonated from the pickets, and after a brief shillyshally, they bolted the last few paces to clatter head on into the heart of the police line. The lads had somehow ended up at the forefront of the turmoil with faces pressed up against shields, more pickets joined in with the surge forcing the police line backwards until they were joined by extra officers, and by pure numbers alone, they overpowered the pickets, driving them backwards. Truncheons repeatedly battered heads; in return, pickets lashed out with their fists. Protective police shields were ripped away from one or two officers with an occasional police helmet shooting high into the air as the pickets tried to force their way through a transparent wall of shields and eager cudgels. One picket was unconscious but remained upright as the intensity from the pickets pushing from the rear prevented him from going to ground. After three toots sounded, the flanks moved inwards at either side, trapping the pickets. Immediately, SPG officers snatched away individuals, dragging them through the ranks, where out of sight from the media, and additional prying eyes, they were bounced from policeman to policeman down a chain, receiving numerous blows to the head and body from both fists and truncheons before they were manhandled headfirst into awaiting vans. After the convoy of haulage wagons had vanished into the plant, the shoving eased to a stop and the pickets backed off. A short spurt from mounted officers scattered

the pickets in all directions before the horsemen returned to be applauded by fellow officers rattling truncheons against shields in appreciation, while to the front of them wounded pickets were left on the ground motionless with blood oozing from head injuries.

Leaving the field, Jack and the lads walked the short distance into Orgreave village to join a queue outside a pie shop. Jack looked at Tom, saying, "Get me a pasty and two sausage rolls, young'n, I'll gan and get us a drink apiece from that other shop down the road." He looked around, asking, "What do yas want?"

"Get me a ginger beer please, Jack," said Hoss.

"I'll have a c-c-can of ginger beer t-t-too," instructed Billy.

"I'll have a can a' shandy, Jack." Alan smiled. Handing over a ten pound note, he added, "And get is twenty Regal King Size an'all please, Jack? I'll pay for the drinks, and the food as well."

Facing Tom, Jack smiled. "What kind of pop do you want, young'n?"

"Owt, a's not that bothered, but divant get is any of that frigging Quatro, it tastes like gnats' piss."

Returning to the pasture, the lads enjoyed their snacks, and as it was the hottest day of the year, Jack lay shirtless, topping up his tan in the warmth of the morning sun before another timbre of heavy engines sounded. The lads jumped to their feet with Jack quickly pulling on his shirt. Once again, the pickets amalgamated into one gigantic cluster before *Here We Go, Here We Go, Here We Go-o!* resonated ahead of them, smashing into the centre of the police line. Walloping truncheons split heads, yet still the pickets surged forward forcing the police line onto their backfoot, extra police quickly shouldered at the rear of their colleagues, nevertheless the iron-willed pickets pressed onward. The police flanks gradually closed in from each side, entrapping the pickets, resulting in skirmishes breaking out everywhere. Two officers grabbed Billy and were trying to drag him away when Jack and Hoss yanked him back before Jack managed to trip one of the coppers and put the boot in with Tom and Alan joining in, sending the officer to curl up in a protective ball. Hoss threw the other policeman to the ground; as he rose to one knee, he booted him in his face and the copper flopped backwards in a heap. Buoyed on by its handler, a police dog snarled ferociously as it tore into a picket's leg when from out of nowhere, fellow pickets came rushing to his defence by kicking the canine in its side before they turned on the officer, beating him limp. The dazed dog stood wandering around confused before it ran off, cowering. By this time, the now-filled haulage wagons had passed almost unnoticed. One policeman lashed a picket to the floor, then set about thrashing him senseless, while at the flanks Snatch Squads dragged away individuals repeatedly beating them around their heads before they were thrown battered and bruised into vans. Panicking pickets scattered into the undergrowth only to be savaged by enthusiastic police dogs or flattened semiconscious by out-of-control Snatch Squads. Two policemen hauled a young lad away with his face covered in blood; after running a gauntlet of cudgels he was then bundled half-conscious into an awaiting van.

Tom was now confronted by a SPG constable, the policeman swung his baton, cutting him deep above his eye, once again he lashed out, but this time Tom bobbed to grab him around his midriff, and with all the power he had in his legs he forced the cop back over onto the ground. Tom quickly straddled him, ripping away his helmet before headbutting him, then standing back a pace he set about booting him in his head and stomach, leaving the officer lying on his side, groaning in agony. Pivoting, Tom noticed Billy and Alan were struggling with a couple of burly SPG officers, so he ran behind one of these cops to lunge a drop kick into the small of his back, jolting him forward to the ground before he set about beating him as Alan and Billy wrestled the other officer to ground. Stepping back a pace, Alan kicked the cop in his chest and face, and the officer lay with blood gushing from his nose and mouth.

Fists clenched, Jack faced an officer; after a brief skirmish the cop dropped to the ground with blood pouring from out of his mouth. Jack proceeded to stamp viciously on the policeman's head before he went to the aid of a fellow picket. To one side of Jack, Hoss held a policeman in a headlock, repeatedly pounding him with almighty uppercuts until his legs buckled and the ill-fated cop sank in a heap.

Scuffles were taking place all over the shop, and the pickets were giving as good as they were receiving, when from out of nowhere a string of five high-pitched whistles sounded; instantly, the police line shuffled open, allowing horses to gallop directly into the pickets, followed by numerous groups of SPG officers who were rattling truncheons to a rhythm against their rounded shields. Panic was now everywhere, mounted police resolutely mowed down pickets before lashing them with their extended batons. A youngish woman with short hair, who must have been some kind of reporter, or perhaps a photographer, was stood at the side of a hedgerow when a mounted policeman galloped towards her, wielding his baton he swung at her head but fortunately for the lady he missed his target. Another horse trampled over a defenceless lad dressed only in shorts and a red top; rising to his feet he staggered around confused with blood pouring from a gash above his eye when a policeman set about bludgeoning him senseless, and the beating only ceased when the cop's truncheon snapped, and the flummoxed lad was then dragged away to an awaiting van. Hundreds of bricks, and other missiles, rained down on the police line and officers were dropping like flies. A mounted policeman was sent crashing from his horse as a half brick found its target, immediately a group of pickets set about putting the boot in before they scattered away in different directions. Another Mounty directed his horse over an elderly picket, as the stunned man tried to stand back to his feet; he tumbled back over, screaming high-pitched as he clasped both hands around a snapped ankle which had a reddening bone protruding through the skin with his foot drooping to an unnatural limpness while facing back over, instead of frontwards. In the scrub, police dog handlers were stood under a grand oak tree trying to coax down three young Yorkshire pickets who had climbed almost to the top of the thing, but all they got from the trio was, "Fuck off, thee daft cunts! Come up and get us, plod, see what happens tee thee when tha hasn't got thee dogs, get some fist tha's will!"

Mounted policemen were now scattering the main body of pickets up towards the crown of the pasture with SPG officers following in their wake eagerly beating mainly elderly, or already injured pickets, who had the misfortune to lag. After pounding these stragglers to a pulp, they didn't attempt to make one single arrest, they simply left the wounded where they fell before quickly moving onto others.

The lads had managed to cross over the railway bridge, but like Tom had predicted, the bridge was far too narrow, and mayhem had broken out as desperate pickets tried to cross; unfortunately for some men they went to ground to be unintentionally trampled by fearful pickets fleeing the onslaught. Due to the sheer weight of the mass, wooden fencing at either side of the bridge creaked to a collapse, sending yelping men plummeting down a steep embankment to be lost under razor-sharp brambles which towered way above head height before they eventually staggered from out of the other side with scratched faces and clothing torn to shreds. After regaining their wits, these injured pickets scampered away up the middle of the railway tracks, fleeing as far as they possibly could from the ongoing carnage.

At the far side of the bridge a group of pickets had dragged an old car from out of a scrapyard into the middle of the road where they set it afire as another group of pickets loitered from behind metal fencing casting half bricks; lumps of wood, pieces of metal, or anything else they could lay their hands on at the advancing policemen. Back at the field side of the bridge, some pickets took the decision to jump down the embankment rather than face the wrath of the Snatch Squads, with almost all of them ending up badly injured as they tumbled from out of the thicket. Jack and the lads joined others in lobing stones at SPG officers, slowing them down in their advancement for just enough time to allow the last of the pickets to cross over the bridge, but to their horror, mounted cops kept on galloping their chargers across the bridge, hunting up the fleeing pickets who were now heading towards the village of Orgreave itself. Jack removed his shirt, dabbing blood away from Tom's injured eye. "Ya okay, kid?"

"I'm fine," he replied, breaking into a brotherly grin.

Jack handed him his shirt. "Keep that ower ya eye, it'll help stem the blood," then, standing over Alan, who was bent with his head between legs trying to catch his breath, Jack asked, "Ya alright down there, Alan?"

"A'm a'... heckers like! A's ower ard for all this shit... a' canit pow here, me back legs have just about buckled!"

Jack patted Alan on his back, saying, "Breathe slow and deep."

Alan stood upright, moaning, "Will ya give ower patting is on me back! Tha's not wind'n a bit babby tha nars!"

Jack looked Alan in the eye. "We ganna have ta get away, Alan, we're sitting ducks here." He faced Billy and Hoss. "You two okay?" They nodded in answer, with Billy visibly shaking and in a state of shock. Jack hugged Billy by the shoulders asking, "Are ya sure ya okay, Billy?"

As if he was in some sort of a traumatic trance, Billy scanned the pasture, pointing out hundreds of shoes that were scattered everywhere. "Look a-a-at all of them shoes!" He looked into Jack's eyes, almost pleading, "J-J-Just get us out of here, p-p-please, Jack!"

"Fucking Jesus!" moaned Hoss, eying a mounted policeman who was forcing his horse sideways, trapping a young woman up against a wall as she desperately clung onto a pram.

Tom and Hoss ran to the mounted officer with Tom screaming, "You evil bastard!"

"Fuck you!" screamed the policeman, swiping his baton at Tom, just missing his head.

"A' tell tha what," growled Tom, "jump down from that gallower and tack a walk with me up that alleyway and see what happens to ya, ya can even keep ya baton, ya useless twat."

"Move on!" ordered the officer.

"Fuck you!" barked Tom, trying to drag the copper from off his charge. Again, the cop swung his truncheon, but he missed his target, and he set the horse to trot in pursuit of other pickets.

Hoss turned to the woman asking, "Are ya all right, pet?"

"Yeah," she replied, heaving a lengthy sigh.

Joining them, Tom looked at the young lady with concern, saying, "He was way out of order there, is the bairn okay?"

"What bairn?" she answered with a confused grimace.

Tom raised, "What do ya mean what bairn? The one in the pram, who do ya think."

Leaning over, she pulled back a sheet uncovering a sandbag filled with coal. Breaking into a smirk she tittered, "There's ne littlun i'n't pram, just bag a' coal nicked from plant."

Tom groused, "Bloody hell, missus! Ya could have gotten us locked up there, fa crying out loud, man!"

"Sorry," she replied with a mischievous grimace.

Shaking their heads, Tom and Hoss looked on as the woman toddled off, pushing the pram down a short, cobbled street, to enter into a house gate.

The lads set off, retreating further into the village when Jack pointed out a battle-clad SPG officer who was pulverising a hapless young lad whilst using his shield to pin him down on top of a car bonnet. Immediately they ran over, dragging the cop from off the petrified youth. Hoss seized the officer by the throat; after entangling his fingers through a chin strap, he dragged the cop face down into an alleyway where he set about thrashing him. Ripping away the helmet, he repeatedly punched the cop around the face with heavy blows, breaking his nose and smashing teeth. The officer muffled for mercy, but Hoss kept on pounding him until his legs gave way completely and he slid lifeless to the floor. Kneeling over him, Hoss was still hammering away at his face and was ready to strike out again when Jack intervened, "Ya wasting ya time, young'n, he'll not feel owt." Reluctantly the big man stood back, and they quickly fled the scene, leaving the copper unconscious with blood streaming from his mouth. Re-joining the other three, they had just about entered into the heart of the village when the clumping of heavy hooves rang out from behind.

"Fucking hell!" yelled Alan, looking back over his shoulder. "Run!!!"

Mounted policemen hunted after them for more than a hundred metres before the lads managed to slip into a narrow side street in avoidance of the pursuing officers. Catching his breath, Alan heaved deeply, looking around, he shook his head, huffing, "This isn't right this, cops kicking the shit out of ordinary working men!"

"That's Thatcher's Britain for ya!" raised Tom.

Jack sniggered, "To be fair, we've giving them as good as what we've getting."

"Aye we may have," returned Alan, "but there's hundreds of poor bastards back there hasn't, a' wadn't be surprised if there were deaths here today." Looking around the lads he raised, "Let's get the fuck out of here! We need to get back to that bus afore the driver decides to fuck off without us." Leaving the alleyway, they had just about turned onto another main road when scores of pickets ran past them with mounted policemen and SPG officers hunting them up. Joining the fleeing pack, Alan blew elongated, whining, "Fa crying out loud! It's never ending, this is!" Running as fast as their legs would take them, they were racing towards the waiting coaches when a mass of cops emerged from a side street blocking off the entire road ahead, while to the rear, mounted policemen and SPG officers were closing in fast.

Out of puff, Alan was now struggling to keep up; his breathing deepened, and his stride had shortened considerably. Noticing this, Jack slowed to a stop, saying, "Fuck this! Yahs can run if yas want te but I'm not, I'm sick of running from these numpties!" His words hadn't long left his mouth when from across the other side of the road an elderly woman waved them over.

Quickly, they crossed the street to join her, and wearing a warm grimace she shepherded them into her front door. The lady's smile widened as she instructed, "Go out backdoor, lads, Mrs Jepson cross t' street will let thee int her house." They hastily darted from backdoor to front door, this went on for a chain of five rows before they exited the last of the houses to be greeted by an old man who was crouched by a gable end, beckoning them with hand gestures.

As the lads joined the elderly stranger, he pointed down a cobbled street, saying, "Reet, lads, go t' end of road, turn reet at allotments then fust left, follow dirt track, t'll lead thee t'other side of field where buses are parked, a've double checked, 'tis all clear." After exchanging handshakes, the stranger smiled, saying, "Good luck," and they set off running until they made it back to the safety of the bus where a side door opened to the sound of hydraulic hissing ahead of them, stepping up into the aisle where the driver exchanged friendly nods of acknowledgement with Jack before the bus rumbled to a start to join the rear of a lengthy convoy. Leaving a field, clusters of SPG officers were stood at the roadside smiling whilst waving off the pickets with their truncheons held high in the air, a few of them even mocked the devastated pickets by rubbing their stomachs while laughing exaggeratedly, but most just smirked as once again ten-pound notes were flirted aloft.

Tom lit up a cigarette calmly saying, "Well, it's been a funny sort of day, hasn't it?"

"Aye," blew Jack carefree as he too lit up, "we've had worse days a' suppose."

"W-W-Worse days!?" questioned Billy. He lit up, continuing, "Worse frigging d-d-days! A' think we've j-j-just spent the whole of the d-d-day in the f-f-fucking Twilight Z-Z-Zone, man, Jack!"

"Orr fuck!" whooped Hoss, patting his pockets, "A've lost me frigging tabs!"

Billy shook his head, griping, "W-W-Why there's no way... w-w-we're gan'n b-b-back to look f-f-for them... Hoss!"

CHAPTER THREE, JULY, "TEN REGAL KINGSIZE, PLEASE..."

On a blistering, early July afternoon, all windows and exit doors at one side of the Colliery club singing end had been fully opened up, allowing a welcoming cross draught to circulate throughout the hall. After weeks of negotiations, Sue and Irene had managed to strike up a deal with a Sunderland abattoir, resulting in sittings of roast beef and Yorkshire puddings to be served twice monthly on every other Thursday. The lasses from the kitchen seemed in a buoyant mood, laughing amongst themselves whilst dishing out meals, and today, a fresh-face had joined the volunteers; her name was Margret Lumsden, a rather petite girl aged somewhere in her mid-twenties who flourished a mass of flaxen-hair which was naturally curly, and went hand in hand with a pallid complexion, and cerulean-coloured whirlpool eyes. After a bit of a messy divorce, Margret had moved to Easington from a neighbouring village, and she was blessed with George, her four-year-old little boy.

Sue was positioned at her usual spot at the head of the chain, greeting people with a welcoming grimace whilst heaping dollops of mashed potatoes onto eager plates; next came Bev and Tracy talking nonstop as they spooned out portions of sliced carrots and mushy peas. Margret was next in line serving helpings of savoy cabbage, that was generously donated from the allotment men, then there was a bit of a gap to Irene who rested a single slice of beef, and a solitary Yorkshire pudding onto each and every plate ahead of Debbie who was stood at the end of the line, ladling out rich, onion gravy.

In the kitchen, Denise Simson, a tall girl aged in her early twenties who displayed short hair that was cut in a latest style, was busy at a sink washing up a mound of plates. At her side stood Liz Ord, Jack and Tom Gilroy's full cousin, who was aged around her mid-thirties, boasting lengthy, raven hair, that matched perfectly with her dark, inky eyes. Although Liz was married to Brian Smith, she was still known throughout the Colliery as Liz Ord, and even though she was thin featured, she showed a slight swelling around her abdomen due to early stages of pregnancy. Towel in hand, she was busy drying a variety of crockery when Denise coughed, clearing her throat prior to asking, "How far are you on now, then, Liz?"

"Just over three and a half months," she replied with a warm grimace.

"So, what are ya wanting then, a boy or a girl?"

She smiled. "Seen as we already have two lads; I fancy a little girl this time, Denise."

"What does Brian fancy?"

"He's not that fuzzed really, he says as long as it's healthy he's not bothered what we have."

"He's right there." Denise looked to Liz, asking, "Switch that radio on please, Liz, a bit music will pass the time ower quicker?"

Grinning wide, Liz leaned over to switch on an old-fashioned radio bringing Spandau Ballet into the room singing all about, Gold. "A' like Spandau Ballet," Denise smiled, "that Tony Hadley's got a cracking voice on him." Handing over a washed plate, her grin extended. "Which singers do you like then, Liz?"

"Me, none really, I'm more into groups than singers."

"Are you? What type of groups do you like, then?" she asked, scrubbing vigorously on a pan. "Duran-Duran, Culture Club and that sort of thing?"

"No nothing like that, I'm more into Led Zeppelin, Uriah Heep, Black Sabbath, Deep Purple." She beamed widely, adding, "but a' like Free best of all."

"Well, I've only heard of one or two of them," sighed Denise, "they're not exactly my cup of tea, I'm afraid, but, like they say ower Horden Crossroads, everyone to their arn." The two exchanged smiles as they carried on with their duties.

Jack and the lads entered the hall to join the back of a lengthy queue with Jack leading the way closely followed by Hoss, Tom and Billy. Noticing Jack's presence, Irene nudged awareness to Debbie. "Do you need a break, love?"

Debbie eyed the line with a slight smile. "Nor it's alright thanks, to be honest, Irene, your Jack doesn't bother me now, I realise what I've got with Peter."

"Well good for you, girl!" chirped Irene.

Jack edged his way down the line, carrying out his customary fluttering of the eyes until he came to Margret where he winked all flirty, and much to Irene's amusement all he received was a normal portion of veg and a meaningless grin. Hoss approached Margret, and the instant she lifted her eyes to his, he smiled all coy, she beamed widely in return then proceeded to heap his plate with extra cabbage. Margret's eyes followed Hoss' every step as he inched the line to face Irene. At once Irene picked up on Margret's attentions and she broke into a beam before serving the big lad with an extra pudding and an additional slice of beef.

Settling at a table, Tom sprinkled salt onto his meal before scattering a pinch over his left shoulder. Picking up a pepper pot he looked across the table with a smirk. "A' think ya might have an admirer there, mind, Hoss."

"Eh!?" came back all mystified.

"That new starter, a' think she likes ya."

Hoss glanced back over his shoulder, checking her out. "Nar, it'll not be me she fancies." He chewed unperturbed on half a Yorkshire pudding. "She's ower nice for me, it'll be your Jack she likes not me, man."

Jack checked over his friend's filled plate. "Why, judging on all that extra cabbage thuw's got compared to my measly amount a' think our young'n might have a point there, mind, Hoss." Jack smiled mischievously, raising, "Gan and have a bit craic on with her after ya dinner."

"Why not fucking likely!" he returned, all flustered. "She's way out of my league."

"Ya haven't got a-a-a league, man, Hoss," put in Billy, "so how can she b-b-be out of ya league."

Hoss once again glimpsed over his shoulder. "She is canny nice like, pretty as a picture so she is."

Irene joined the lads, clanking down fresh salt and pepper pots. Leaning over the table top she looked Hoss directly in the eye, muttering, "That new girl's called Margret, Hoss, a' think she's took a bit of a shine to ya."

"Do ya think, see!?"

"Why aye!" Irene stretched a smile. "A' wouldn't have said so if a' didn't think she had, go over and have a bit craic on with her later on." Picking up the emptied salt and pepper pots she walked away, saying, "Don't be shy, Hoss, shy bairns get ne broth, bonnie lad."

Hoss grinned slightly as Billy looked at him, saying, "Well, a' think Cupid might h-h-have finally fired h-h-his arrow at ya, Hoss."

Once again Hoss glanced over his shoulder, but this time Margret caught his eye, and she was in the midst of casting a grin of her own when he quickly turned away to blush the table.

Sunshine lit up the union office at Easington Colliery. Alan was sat with his feet resting on the desktop while daydreaming his way through the pages of his 'Daily Mirror' when Jim Watson entered the room. "Alright, Jim?" asked Alan from over the top of the newspaper.

"Aye, canit grumble..." answered Jim, who was an immaculately dressed man sporting a black leather box jacket and a red shirt that matched with a tie that was tucked inside a high waistline of cream-coloured chinos. Aged in his early forties, Jim was a union official at Easington Colliery who held the title of G-seam representative, he was tall and thin, boasting Italian dark skin, with a crop of well-groomed ebony hair that had a slight dusting of greyness showing at the sides. On his fingers exhibited half sovereign rings while a gold chain swung from his neck to match up with a chunky bracelet that dangled loose from one wrist, while an expensive gold watch adorned the other "... Where are we picketing at in the morn, Alan?" he asked, lighting up a cigarette.

"Up Tow Law," he returned as he too lit up a cig. "We've got a seven a' clock start so, can you do is a favour and watch the office for is 'till a' get back?"

"A'm a' not in charge of the bus, like!?"

"Nar, not the morn," said Alan, drawing deeply on his cigarette. Returning his feet to floor, he rustled his paper to rest, saying, "A' think it might be best if a' showed me face, encourage the men on a bit, they seem to be down in the dumps after Orgreave and that."

"Probably's be a good idea," agreed Jim, flicking ash into an already brimming ashtray, "so, it's a seven a' clock start up Tow Law for yas then?"

"Aye, if you can get down here for say, quarter past six, I'll drop the office keys off for ya." Alan once again drew on his cigarette before he stood to approach a table where he quickly unplugged a kettle. "Not been funny or nowt, Jim, but I'll have ta gan marra, I'm in a mad rush."

"Where ya off te now?"

"Taking Irene up to Peterlee town centre to get a new cooker for the club kitchen, how's Jean keeping these days?"

"She's fine, don't forget I'm away on holiday a week come Monday mind."

"Or aye, where ya off te, again?" he asked, ushering Jim from the room.

"Spain."

"Spain!? Must be nice!" Alan locked the office door behind him, sighing. "I've never been to Spain afore, been to Skegness once or twice, but niver Spain." As the two walked side by side down a narrow corridor Alan stopped midstride. "Shit! I've left me tabs! Get ya sell away; I'll catch ya in the morn."

"What ya like!" joked Jim. "Forget ya head if it was loose."

"A' nar that, you tack care now." Alan watched Jim exit the building by means of a creaky old door. After fumbling his way through a bunch of keys, he eventually re-entered into the office where he picked up a phone; after quickly dialling, he tapped his foot as he waited impatiently for an answer. "... Benny, it's Alan, will you be able to take charge of the picketing bus for is in the morn? ... Quarter to seven... up to Steetleys... cheers, Benny, yar a star, see ya in the morn, marra, bye... bye now." Hanging up the phone, he scratched his head in frustration as he watched from the window as Jim carefully weaved his way through the barricaded pit gates. "I'll Spain him!" he hissed through gritted teeth. "The spiv bastard!" Checking his watch, he hurried his way from the office, moaning to himself, "Late again, Alan, late again!"

After enjoying their meals, Jack, Billy, and Tom left the Colliery Club vestibule to step into a glorious summer's afternoon, minus the big man, who had reluctantly subsided to a constant bombardment for him to stay behind and chance his hand at trying to get to know the new girl a little bit better. Jack's eyes shifted between Tom and Billy before they rested solely on his brother, with him saying, "I'm ganna pop down to the allotment to fill Mowgli's watter bath up. Do ya want is to watter ya leeks and onions while I'm down there?"

"Why, not likely!" responded Tom, a little irritable. "I'll do it after tea, it's ower hot to be wattering leeks at this time of the day, ya'll scorch the bloody things, anyway, a' need to pop up Ma Gars first, a' promised Pop I'd fix a washer on the kitchen tap."

"Right owe then, give her and Pop me love, and tell them I'll see them sometime ower the weekend."

Billy looked to Jack. "Are w-w-we still ganning ower the w-w-wall for some coal the night, Jack? I'm rit on the b-b-bottom again."

"Why aye, we'll meet outside mine about half eleven."

"A' need to fix that riddle first," said Tom, "the wire's come loose on the bottom again."

Jack sighed. "I'll fix it! For God's sake I've got hands tha nars! Right then, I'll have ta gan, catch yas later."

"Aye catch ya later," returned Tom.

Billy put in, "See ya the n-n-night, Jack."

Strolling Seaside Lane, why not exactly strolling, it was more of a look at me, peacock proud swagger, Jack passed a multitude of shops, all the time exchanging welcoming nods of recognition with familiar faces with most of the passing girls eying him all drooly eyed while muttering, 'hello Jack', or simply 'hiya Jack'. Smirking, he deliberately exaggerated his stride, sending a group of oncoming girls beaming to slight giggles as they too lifted their eyes somewhat abashed. Leaving Seaside Lane, he toddled Ascot Street ahead of turning into 'Sick Note Corner', where he was greeted by a red telephone box which stood isolated in front of a *Scargill Rules* graffiti-filled wall that stretched down a slight incline in the direction of the 'Colliery Offices', a rather imposing building exhibiting a stylish, slightly curved stairway which presented flights of concrete steps before ending at a set of pale blue double doors. Inside this edifice ran a maze of corridors and individual offices including a grand, oak-panelled boardroom, which housed a majestic spherical table that King Arthur himself would have been proud to park his backside at. Passing by the colliery offices, Jack was advancing towards the pit gates when Bonnie Ronnie almost jumped out from behind the barricades to stand directly in front of him. Jack smiled in a friendly fashion, saying, "How the hinging, Ronnie?"

"Not three bad, marra..." replied Bonnie Ronnie, a happy-go-lucky lad aged in his early twenties who wasn't in the slightest bonnie, in fact, to be perfectly honest, he wasn't the prettiest of sights, as his nose was huge and knobbly with a bulging warty growth plonked right on the tip that was ruddy in colour and shaped like a little arse, while his right eye was permanently bloodshot and drooped noticeably below the level of the other with both eyelids speckled in large, purple-coloured warts. Revealing a piano of buck teeth, Ronnie didn't possess the greatest of smiles neither, but that never stopped him grinning, not for one second did it, for one thing Ronnie did often was to smile. The whole of his face was festooned in bulbous blackheads and infected mattery spots, especially across his overlarge forehead, which was topped by mousy-coloured hair that was greasy and not quite long enough to cover his misshaped cauliflower ears, but, despite his appearance, not a finer young man had ever tramped the streets of Easington Colliery. "...How's ya sell, Jack?" he asked, smiling back all friendly.

"Canit grumble, marra," chirped Jack handing over a cig, "canit grumble."

Ronnie enquired, "Ya not courting yet then?"

"Why nar!"

"Nare, me neither, a' canit be arsed, especially with the strike and that."

After lighting up his own cigarette, Jack offered Ronnie a flame which danced to a slight sea breeze that blew pleasant and temperate to the face. "What's the craic then, owt happened?"

"Nor, nowt really, it's been canny quiet all morning, or sorry, that horrible security guard... I've forgotten his name now... the one who everyone hates, man, what's his name again–"

"Robert Hardy," broke in Jack with purpose in his voice.

"Aye that's the one! Anyhow, he chased Lemsip and Sizzler away from the coal heaps earlier on, he's slashed all of their bags and buckled the wheels on Sizzler's bike, he never caught them like... by he's a right nasty piece of work that bugger is, mind, Jack."

Jack inhaled deeply on his cigarette. "Tell is about it! I'm dying to get me hands on the cunt."

"Why, give him a good slap from me when ya de catch up with him, will ya?"

"A' will do," promised Jack. "I'll have ta gan, Ronnie, as in a bit of a rush, you gan canny, marra."

"Aye you too, Jack, nice seeing ya again. Tell ya Ma I'm asking after her when ya see her, will ya?"

"A' will do, marra, ne bother," he replied, before setting away walking in the direction of the first bridge. Entering into the concrete underpass, Jack smiled as adolescent flashbacks of himself dashing through Devils Mouth with the rest of his Jelly Tots gang came flooding back. Exiting the gloomy bridge, he followed an ash trail which guided him down to a string of wooden garages. Turning into a second row of three pathways, he gaited the full length of a grassy footpath before coming to a stop in front of a set of metal double gates that were topped in coils of rusty barbed wire. Unlocking a trio of separate padlocks, he forced the gates open to enter his smallholding where he crossed a yard, dragging a hosepipe until he reached an old bath which was sited next to a fence just inside Mowgli's field. Twisting a nozzle, a hissing of pressure sounded before a splattering of water filtered into a bathtub that was completely watertight thanks to dollops of brown resin smothered around a plughole and an overflow outlet. "Mowgli! How'y, son!" he shouted, and the black steed whinnied aloud, then swishing its tail it trotted towards Jack. "Hello bonnie lad," he greeted, patting the stallion on his neck.

Built in the fifties and early sixties, Peterlee was located a couple of miles southwest from Easington Colliery. Its shopping centre housed extensive concrete ramps that stretched in an arch from a first-floor landing down to ground level to be greeted by concrete fountain ponds strategically placed throughout the whole of the precinct. A varied range of outlet stores made up the two-storey centre, including a choice of banks and bakeries; a Woolworths store, a couple of furniture shops, a Halifax Building Society, Northern Electric showroom, a Ladbrokes betting shop, a police station that was adjoined onto Magistrates courts, there was also The Senate nightclub, Bradleys motor dealership, a butcher's, greengrocer's, Tates radio and television store, a brace of shoe shops, Finlays tobacco and confectionery shop, solicitors' offices, a Geordie Jeans fashion shop and an upstairs fish shop that was located across a passageway from a chic ladies boutique. Below this fashion outlet, a paved boulevard ran past a TSB bank to end at a vast Fine Fare supermarket which was attached at one side by a furniture discount store located underneath Lee House, a towering corporation building constructed out of dark brown bricks and topped by a huge clock that indicated time by means of a couple of white cursors pointing to a collection of twelve narrow oblong markers that were also white in colouring and presented in the form of a circle.

Alan held a glass door open for Irene as they entered into a Northern Electric showroom where they were greeted by an overpowering aroma of lemon air freshener. Strolling around the shop, Irene carefully deliberated over the cookers on display before a stainless steel industrial-styled stove caught her eye. After a brief discussion with Alan, she coughed slightly to attract attention; at once a young female assistant approached, and for a brief moment the fragrance of Coco Chanel overpowered the ghastliness of the citrus air freshener.

"Good afternoon, my name is Susan Thomson," she said, flicking a head of lengthy bleached blonde hair to one side whilst smiling a congenial, toothy grin. "How may I help you, madam?"

"Well," replied Irene in her usual polite manner. "I would like to buy this cooker here." She pointed out the range.

"And may I say, it's a very good choice indeed," rolled sale pitched from the young woman. "It has dual ovens with the main oven, fan assisted, and you have come on a great day too as there's a twenty percent discount starting from today."

"I'll take it then, flowerpots," said Irene at once. "Is that twenty percent off the list price shown on the tag?"

"Yes, it is actually." The girl smiled. "How would you like to pay, cash or credit?"

"Cash please, why cheque if that's okay?"

"Cheque will be fine," she said, removing the price tag from the cooker. Frowning slightly, the girl looked Irene up and down. "A' think I may know you from somewhere, you wouldn't happen be Jack Gilroy's Mam by any chance, would you?"

"I am actually," uttered Irene with a confused grin as she fussed in her handbag, retrieving a chequebook. She joked, "Mind a' hope that discount's still on? 'Coss our Jack's actions have got nowt to do with me."

"Of course it's still on." The girl smiled before waggishly adding, "Mind you, just about though."

Writing out a cheque, Irene smiled warmly, asking, "So how come you know our Jack then, love?"

"Or, it's a long story, Mrs Gilroy," sighed the girl, "but when ya see him will ya tell him Susan Thomson was asking after him?"

"A' will do, love," she grinned as she watched the young lady turn and walk away with cheque in hand. Facing Alan, Irene smiled. "She seems canny enough mind."

"Doesn't she just." Shaking his head, he frowned at Irene, asking, "You're not paying for that cooker out of your arn money, are ya?"

"Aye, a'm actually, the kitchen desperately needs a new cooker, like right now, 'coss yesterday one of them just about packed in completely on us, and there's not a cat in hell's chance we can manage with just the one cooker, no way can we, and a's not ganna ask them poor lasses to chip in, Alan, the poor souls haven't got two pennies to rub together between them."

Leaning into Irene, Alan pecked a kiss on her cheek. "You're a living saint, you are, Irene Gilroy, do ya know that?"

"Give ower!" she returned somewhat abashed. "Living Saint my foot!" Irene looked across the room. After briefly scrutinising the sales assistant, she smiled, whispering, "A' divant think that lass is from Easington, mind, Alan, 'coss I've never clapped eyes on her afore."

"Nar, me neither," agreed Alan with a frown, "she's definitely not from the Colliery; pretty as a picture so she is though."

Irene snapped, "Hey! Ya shouldn't be looking at her like that!"

"Sorry," he murmured.

"And so ya should be an'll! Ya're old enough to be her dad!"

After fiddling on for quite some time fixing up a leaky stretch of guttering, Jack soon finished undertaking all the other jobs that were required of him in and around Mowgli's stable. Enjoying the tranquillity of an afternoon stroll home, he paused to shield his eyes as he looked on in amazement as an eager eyed kestrel hovered majestic in the blue, scattering sketchy linnets and finches into the safety of a stretchy hedgerow. Approaching the first bridge he once again stopped, this time to light up a cigarette, and he had just removed his shirt to enjoy the warmth of the sun when a loud barking sounded from behind, ahead of a deep voice, ordering, "Keep pushing the fucking thing! Never mind stopping! Keep moving! Now!" Jack glanced over his shoulder, instantly recognising it was old Salty who was out of breath as he laboured to push a bicycle loaded up with hefty sacks of coal. Behind Salty, the infamous Robert Hardy held onto a keen Alsatian dog that barked frothy-mouthed. Jack hunkered behind a yellow-topped gorse bush taking in the abuse that old Salty was receiving from the brawny-looking security guard, who wasn't so tall, yet still he was a very powerfully built man with no neck, strong shoulders and a solid jawline. Weakening to a purple face, Salty stopped walking and leant over the bicycle trying to catch his breath when the guard kicked him hard on his backside. "Did I tell ya to stop, ya little twat! Now push the fucking bike!"

"I need to take my inhaler, a' canit catch me breath, man!"

Hardy pressed his face against Salty, screeching, "Fuck ya inhaler! Ya should have thought about that before ya decided to nick the coal!" After slapping Salty hard across the back of his head, he widened his eyes. "I'm not ganna tell ya again! Move, ya baldy little twat! And now!" Once again, he booted Salty, but this time it was in the back of his leg and with much more force than previous.

Salty struggled to push the old bike up a slight incline. As he was passing by Jack at the mouth of the bridge, Jack stood calmly flicking away his cigarette butt, and the instant Salty eyed him he slumped over the cycle. "Thank God it's you, Jack, this..." taking out his inhaler he puffed twice on the contraption before relief riddled his face. "...Nazi fucker's trying to kill is." Wiping

153

his brow, he pointed out bloodstained rips in his trousers. "Look what his dog's done, the evil bastard let the thing loose on is for nowt!"

Jack approached Salty, gently saying, "How many times have a' telt ya, Salty, if ya need coal just let is nar and I'll get it for ya."

"Keep out of it, he's nicked!" ordered the broad-shouldered security guard.

Totally ignoring the guard as if he wasn't even stood there, Jack smiled carefree at his old friend, but even though he was beaming, it was false, as inside Jack was way above furious and just about ready to explode. "How'y, I'll push the bike up yerm for ya," he said softly as he joined Salty.

"Right!" screamed Hardy. "It's your last chance, you either move away now, or face the consequences!"

"Consequences eh!" whispered Jack. After winking reassurance at Salty, he slowly pivoted to face the guard, and with a huge grin he stepped closer, courteously asking, "You must be the legendary Robert Hardy, are ya? Do ya nar something, I've been dying to meet you for a such a long time now," and though Jack's tone was calm and polite he was way past the point of no return.

"Move on or I'll set the dog on you!" threatened Hardy.

Speaking through gritted teeth, Jack threatened, "You let that fucking thing loose and I'll neck the fucker, then I'll slap you from arsehole to breakfast time."

"You've been warned!"

"Warned!" sneered Jack, now standing nose to nose with the guard. "I'll give ya warned, twat! Your best bet is ta turn around now and fuck off while ya still can."

Salty grinned from ear to ear, raising, "I would tack heed, mister security guard, do ya nar he's related to Victor McLaglen."

Hardy puckered his face in bewilderment at the old man's words before he turned back to face Jack, threatening, "It's you who should move on! 'Coss this little fucker's coming with me, he's nicked!" He placed his hand on the dog's collar ready to release the eager canine when from out of nowhere Jack booted the thing in its belly, and it flopped whimpering onto its side. Grabbing Hardy by the throat, Jack entangled his fingers through the guard's hair, then, with one hand he tugged him towards himself before headbutting him with so much force that it splattered his nose wide apart. Hardy fought hammer and tongs trying to wrestle himself free, but Jack tightened his grip further, then, with lightning speed, he punched Hardy in the face with numerous blows, splattering blood from both his nose and mouth. Once again, he grasped the guard by his hair, dragging him facing bent forward where he set about kicking him repeatedly, his face jolting the guard's head violently backwards with each boot. Entwining both hands in Hardy's hair, Jack forced him up against the bridge ahead of him, scuffing the side of the guard's face across the jagged concrete surface, grating away skin from one cheek. Releasing his grip, the guard slumped to his knees screaming in agony before Jack booted him hard in his face, shouting, "You useless fucking twat!" Slowly turning to face Salty, he winked impishly as he took the bicycle from him, calmly saying, "How'y then, Salty, let's be getting this thing up yerm for ya, ya owld bugger."

Inching their way under the bridge, Salty lit up a cig, saying, "A' had it all sorted tha nars, Jack, a' was ganna jump him t'uther side of this bridge here."

"Yeah, sure tha was, Salty, a' gathered that," responded Jack with a jovial smile.

"Nar, honest a' was, a' had it all planned out in me mind's eye!" Looking over his shoulder at the stricken guard, Salty's hands shook slightly as he inhaled deeply on a misshaped hand-rolled cigarette. "By tha's a right bad-tempered bugger thuw is, mind, Jack, ya just like ya ard man was."

"He got what he deserved, Salty, and it's been a lang time coming, believe you me it has, he's had more men sacked than any fucker a nar, and he's enjoyed every minute of it, it's fuckers like him that make good men like me do bad things like what I've just done."

"Good men like thuw!" chastised Salty. "Since when has thuw been a good man like!?"

"What's tha mean by that!? I'm always good, me!"

"Hadaway and shite, Jack! Yar a reet wrang'n! Ya've never even been to Sunday Mass since God nars when, and yar a grit fanny rat too! Ya fucks about with other men's wives and all sorts."

Jack defended himself: "Steady on, Salty, a' anly did that the once, and believe you, me, a' would never do it again."

"Jack, man, ya'd back scuttle a hole in the wall thuw wad, and owt ya couldn't fuck, ya'd had ta fight."

Jack grinned, chuckling, "How'y, marra! I'm sure I'm not that bad!"

"Tha is like!" Salty smiled. "And if a' was thirty odd years younger with a prostrate the size of a pea, a' think I'd be exactly the same as what thuw is, ya lucky sod!"

Forcing the bicycle up the short but steep cobblestoned incline, Jack looked at his old friend with a warm beam, asking, "Ya've never bothered with another woman since your Joan crossed ower, have ya, Salty?"

"Why... nor," he sighed, drawing deep on his cigarette. "I'd rather gan to jail than to gan through the rigmarole of falling in love again. A' still haven't getting ower how a' lost her in the first place, man, Jack, she just went to bed one night as normal, and wock up deed the next morning." They carried on with their banter as they inched their way alongside the pit wall until turning into Castle Street where Jack rested the bicycle up against a gateway at number eight before he carried the sacks to a coalhouse where he tipped them to sounds of clanking whooshes.

After refusing the offer of a coffee, Jack said his farewells and Salty smiled as he looked on as Jack strutted his way up the street.

The amalgamation of a large incoming tide, and a gentle easterly breeze, blowing in lazily from off the sea, awoke Easington to a shroud of thick sea fret that rose Hammer Horror eerie from ground level up to just below the rooftops of the terraced houses. At the Colliery Club car park, a rhythmical timbre from a bus engine fractured the early morning as pickets of all ages boarded; in amongst these was Hoss, Tom and Billy. Alan and Jack stood by Alan's vehicle talking to Benny Handy, an elderly union official who possessed stumpy legs, a big belly, and a rather large backside that was unnaturally rounded.

"Right, we'll see ya up Steetleys then, Benny," said Alan.

Benny puckered, puzzled. "Where yas gan'n te first, like?"

Alan grinned. "A' canit tell ya that, why not yet anyway, but hopefully I'll be explaining everything when a' see ya later on, and thanks again for filling in for is."

"That's ne bother, marra."

"Divant forget give us at least quarter of an hour's head start afore yas set off," said Jack.

"Right owe, son." Benny looked on with a smile as the two entered Alan's vehicle before they slowly drove from the carpark. Waddling his way to the bus, Benny blew his nose then lit up a cigarette, leaning up against the entrance door he was on talking to the driver when two young pickets skurried the carpark, joining him. "Ya nearly missed the bus there, mind, lads! What's wrang, been up all night on the nest again, or what?"

"Why nor!" returned one of the pickets ahead of them stepping onto the bus. "I've been waiting for the paper shop opening up, a's out of frigging baccy again."

"Why cut back on ya smokes a bit, lad! Cut back on ya smokes," chirped Benny with a grin before checking his watch.

Glorious sunshine lit up the heaths of West Durham. Alan dropped a gear as he slowly drove through the small village of Tow Law before he bridged a crest of a hill, bringing Banksy's open cast mine into view with not one single person in sight. Parking up, he blew fed up as he rested his head against the steering wheel, whispering, "Well, that hasn't exactly worked out ta plan."

"What's ganning on, Alan?" asked Jack, handing over a cigarette.

Alan lit up, "Divant say a word to any-fucker, mind, Jack, but we've got an informer amongst us who has to be on the union committee."

"Ya joking!?"

"A's not tha nars! A' set a trap this morning for the one who a thowt it was, and it's just gone tits up, a' would have bet me bottom lip on it being him an'll, but it's not."

"What trap?" Jack frowned, drawing deep on his cigarette.

Once again Alan puffed his cheeks. "A' told a certain union man of ours yesterday that we were picketing up here at Tow Law instead of Steetleys, and I was convinced this place would be overrun with fucking coppers, and well, look at it, so the mole isn't the one who a' thowt it was."

"Who did ya think it was, like?"

Alan hesitated for a second or two before reluctantly mumbling, "... Jim Watson, and say fuck all, Jack 'coss it's clearly not him."

"I'll not say nowt, but if ever anyone was ganna be a Judas it would be that fucker, a' wadn't trust the twat as far as a' could thraw him."

"Nor me neither, but it's clearly not him, so keep it zipped. I've wracked me brains all night, Jack, and everything just points towards him, he's even gan'n ta Spain for his holidays. How the hell can he afford that when every fucker else is on the bones of their arses? Eh?"

"That's 'coss he's got ne kids, and their lass's a gaffer up at Dewhurst clothing factory, she's on top dollar up there." Jack drew deep on his cig. "Besides, there might not even be an informer at all, for all you nar the office phone might be tapped or something."

"Fucking hell! A' never thowt of that!" gushed Alan, all relieved. "Yar an absolute star thuw is Jack Gilroy, proper little James Bond so ya are."

Jack sat straight faced before he broke into an impish grin as he pathetically tried to mimic Sean Connery: "My namesh Gilroy... Jack Gilroy." Alan shook his head, and after accomplishing a three-point turn in half a dozen attempts they sped off with Jack smiling roguishly. "Drive faster, Mish Moneypenny."

Alan snapped, "Shut up, ya silly sod! Does a' look like a Miss Moneypenny!? Yar as far gone as the crow's in May thuw is, lad."

"Aye, but a's good looking with it though," smirked Jack with a glint in his eye.

Although the plant at Steetleys was only a few miles inland from the coast, the skies were crystal clear with no hint of the heavy sea fret which had earlier engulfed Easington Colliery. A couple of rival skylarks soared high in the blue, warbling insults back and forth in competition as hyped-up blackbirds squabbled in an overgrown hedgerow that stretched the entire width of Davidson's Haulage yard. The Steetleys depot was enclosed within lofty metal fencing and consisted of a couple of workshops, a two-storey office block, numerous lockups and an immense garage that was capped by a moss-covered asbestos roof, while in the yard a fleet of over a dozen wagons were parked alongside numerous police vehicles. A narrow road ran parallel to the site, at one side of this road Easington pickets had gathered on a grass verge alongside a mass of fellow comrades from other collieries, while across the road more than a hundred and fifty police officers stood steadfast, blocking off the main entrance to the compound. The pickets had deliberately targeted Davidson's due to the firm's decision to transport imported coal from Hull docks up to Redcar Steelworks, and there was no love lost whatsoever between the pickets and firm's management, or indeed their wagon drivers.

In amongst the pickets, Hoss, Billy, and Tom were stood in a group talking alongside Sizzler and Lemsip ,when Hoss lit up a cigarette. Looking to Tom, he frowned slightly. "What time ya setting off in the morn then, young'n?"

"About six-ish, I'm meeting Pat at one of them motorway café things just on the outskirts of Middleton."

"So, you'll not be at the disco the night then?" Hoss smiled.

"Nar, a's stopping in, early night the night for me."

"I'm not turning out neither," said the big man, drawing on his cigarette, "Margret's invited is around hers for me supper."

Tom laughed sharply, joking, "Why, leave the patterns on the plate, and for God's sake divant start humming when ya scranning."

"A' divant even nar a' do that tha nars."

"Do what?" frowned Tom.

"Hum when a's eating."

"Why tha does." Taking out a packet of cigarettes, Tom looked at his best friend with a warm smile. "But not all the time like."

"I'm s-s-stopping in the night too," put in Billy. "Our lass's w-w-working behind the bar and a' canit find a babysitter for love nor m-m-money." Looking to Sizzler, Billy beamed widely. "Looks like thuw and Lemsip's g-g-got the pleasure of J-J-Jack's company the night, then."

"A' hope he doesn't cramp me style," joked Sizzler.

"What style!?" put in Lemsip all serious. "Tha hasn't got a style!"

Sizzler looked at Lemsip with daggers, retorting, "At least a' divant look like an ard fucking school mop like thuw diss!"

The resonance of heavy engines sounded from a convoy of empty wagons inching the compound before they rattled to a stop at the main entrance. Tom, Hoss and Billy scurried the road and were approaching the first wagon driver when a dark haired, burly looking police sergeant brandishing an awful 'Magnum P.I.' styled moustache, put out his hand stopping the lads in their tracks. "Where do you feckers fink you're going?" he asked in a strong Southern argot.

"To talk to the driver," said Tom.

"No, ya fecking not though! Now turn yourselves back around and feck off back across that fecking road."

"Here, w-w-we have rights, tha nars, we're allowed to talk t-t-to them!" said Billy with determination.

"You have no rights whatsoever, you just fink you have." The sergeant scowled.

"Aye we have th-th-though," argued Billy, standing his ground, "the law states six pickets c-c-can approach, and there's only th-th-three of us s-s-stood here."

"Is that r-r-right," mocked the sergeant.

"Aye it is!" jumped in Hoss. "And there's no need for that neither, ya horrible piss taking twat, why don't ya fuck off back down to Cockney land where ya belong."

"Right, you have exactly five fecking seconds to turn back around and re-join your filthy fecking comrades or you will be arrested." The sergeant turned away, and with a single hand gesture he summoned over a group of his colleagues; within an instant the officers had surrounded the lads with truncheons drawn at the ready. The sergeant poked Hoss in his chest with the end of his cudgel. "Fecking move! Now!"

"Fuck you!" growled Hoss. At once, the sergeant went to jab Hoss again, but Hoss snatched the baton away from his clasp before pushing him in the face with the flat of his hand, sending the sergeant tumbling arse over tit to the ground. Immediately fellow cops pounced on Hoss and set about lashing him around his head and body, but due to his brute strength alone he fended them off, he even managed to floor a couple of them before further reinforcements joined the confrontation and they started pulverising him with heavy blows to his head until he dropped down to one knee. Four officers were in the process of dragging him away when Tom and Billy sprang to their friend's aid, but they too were bludgeoned to the floor before all three were hauled away to be manhandled battered and bruised into the back of one of the police vehicles. Incensed pickets now surged forward, and all hell had broken out with truncheons raining down on pickets' heads as fists and kicks were thrown in retaliation. Violent skirmishes were everywhere and continued for well over ten minutes before the pickets were finally overpowered and the convoy of wagons passed through the picket line with the drivers goading the pickets by showing the proverbial finger, knowing their identities were concealed behind balaclava hats and their safety safeguarded by means of a heavy police presence and meshed up windscreens.

Alan and Jack arrived at the site and had just about parked up when Sizzler rushed to the car. Alan wound down the window with a smile. "Everything alright, Sizzler?"

"Is it fuck alright! Hoss, Billy, and your Tom's been lifted!"

"Lifted!?" exhaled Jack, quickly jumping from the vehicle. "What the fuck for!?"

"A' haven't a clue, they just went to talk to a wagon driver and next thing a' knew it had all kicked off big style and they were carted off."

"So, where are they at now then?" asked Alan as the three rushed towards where the pickets were now gathered.

"In that van there!" said Sizzler, pointing out a van where a single policeman was stood on guard.

"Arr why," sighed Alan, "there's nowt we can do for them now."

"Aye but there is though!" snapped Jack before instructing, "Alan, you go and see Oddy and Pinky, tell them to get the lads to kick off, keep those bastards on their toes for five minutes or so, then gan and start ya car up."

Alan narrowed his eyes. "What ya up te, Jack? A' don't like that look ya've got, it's full of trouble again."

Jack side eyed a perimeter fence. "A's gan'n ower that thing to free them from that van."

"Don't talk sa fucking fond!" groused Alan. "Ya'll end up getting locked up ya sell!"

Jack smiled reassurance, saying, "I'll be fine, just mack sure they cause enough of a disruption." He faced Sizzler. "You stop here, Sizzler, giss a hand up."

Shaking his head, Alan blew a sigh as he walked away, mumbling, "I'm sure he thinks this strike's just a movie he's starring in." Joining the pickets, Alan took Oddy and Pinky to one side. Oddy (David Ord) was Jack and Tom's full cousin, and was a healthy looking twenty-four-year-old who possessed red hair, sharp features, and a strong jawline, who had the resemblance of Tom Bailey, the lead singer from a pop group called the Thomson Twins. Pinky (Brian Pye), was also aged twenty-four, and was a handsome looking lad gifted with blond hair that harmonised his piercing blue eyes. Alan had just finished explaining to them what was needed when a Range Rover, driven by one of the managing directors of the firm, approached the entrance gates from inside the compound. Oddy and Pinky urged on the pickets, and an unexpected surge momentarily caught the police off-guard allowing the pickets to block off the entire entrance to the complex, causing the vehicle to stop in its tracks, and within a matter of only a few seconds, all the windows to the vehicle were smashed and punches thrown at the stunned driver.

Sizzler cupped his hands, aiding Jack up and over the fence. After scampering a short distance through the compound, he slowed to face a young constable who was guarding the van. The policeman brandished his truncheon, but Jack just smirked unimpressed ahead of a well-aimed kick to his balls, folding the cop forward before a hefty knee directed to the officer's face sent him stunned to ground. Opening up the back of the van, Jack smiled widely, joking, "Come on, ladies, playtime's over, a' canit leave yas alone for five minutes and look what happens to yas, ya soft sods." Eying their facial injuries his smile transformed into a concerned frown. "How'y, let's get the fuck out of here!" They swiftly jumped from the van and after scaling a perimeter fence, they joined Alan ahead of the car screeching away.

FOLLOWING DAY

It was a glorious summer's morning at Easington Colliery, and the only hint of greyness in the sky was a line of vapour fumes that was inconsiderately left behind by a passing aeroplane. Clutching onto snooker cues, Jack, Hoss and Billy strode by a selection of shops as they made their way up Seaside Lane en route to a huge building topped with a distinct green metal roof, which was known as the Welfare Hall, or even the Welly. Hoss and Billy both flaunted black eyes from the hiding they had received from the previous day with Hoss parading an additional gash across the bridge of his nose.

"So, what did Margret make ya for supper last night then, Hoss?" asked Jack, glancing at his big friend with a carefree grimace.

"Sausages, beans, egg and chips, and fower slices of bread and butter," he replied, licking his lips.

"Sounds bloody lovely that does," said Jack.

"It was, they were those nice Cumberland sausages too, the grit chunky ones."

Jack chuckled, "Aye, but what did ya have for afters though? That's the main question!"

"What's tha mean?"

"Ya nar exactly what a' mean, did ya stop the night or what?"

"That's nen of your business, Jack Gilroy," smirked Hoss.

"S-S-So ya did s-s-stop ower then?" put in Billy.

"It's got nowt to do with you neither, ya nosey little sod!"

After scampering a road, they strode by the rival Church of England which was constructed entirely out of red brick and crowned with a black slate roof. Billy beamed mischievously saying, "Are ya s-s-seeing her again then, Hoss?"

"Why aye, a's gan'n round the night actually, she's gan'n to the video shop to get a film in for us to watch."

Jack side eyed Hoss. "A' hope it's not one of them dodgy pornos from under the counter mind, Hoss! Or worse still, a Little House on the Prairie video or some other sloppy shit like that."

"It's nen of them actually, it's The Warriors, if ya need to know."

"Ya joking!" enthused Jack. "Apart from Kes, that's my favourite film of all time that is! A' might just come round to watch it with yas me sell."

"Like knackers ya will!"

"I'm bloody sure ya n-n-not, Jack," agreed Billy, "the l-l-last thing Hoss needs when he's trying to get a b-b-bit titty is thuw sitting there watching."

"I'm only joking, man! Besides, a's taking Tracy James out the night."

"Orr aye, and when did all this happen l-l-like?" asked Billy.

"Last night, a' walked her yerm from the colliery club disco."

"Ya jammy s-s-sod, she's absolutely gorgeous, she is," said Billy, heaving an envious sigh.

"A' suppose she's okay," stretched from Jack, "mind you I've got to say she's got a cracking pair of tits on her."

"Has she got b-b-big nipples like!?" enthused Billy.

"Aye has she! They stick out like colliery house light switches."

165

"Will you two give ower!?" broke in Hoss. "Yas are like a couple of frigging school kids."

Billy moaned, "Tha nars, I'm the anly one m-m-married out of all of us, and I'm the anly f-f-fucker not getting a sh-sh-shag!"

Chatting away, they were crossing over a junction when a car pulled up at a kerbside and a strong looking man rolled down the window. He smiled falsely, asking, "Alright, lads, can you tell me if this place is Easington Colliery?"

Billy leant into the car window and was beaming friendly around the three occupants when he noticed police uniforms folded over a back seat.

"Say a-a-again?" came from Billy.

"Is this shit-hole Easington Colliery or what?" repeated the driver in an aggressive tone.

"Nor, mate, it's Xanadu th-th-this is," came back straight faced from Billy.

The driver frowned, confused. "It's what!?"

"Xanadu," repeated Billy, before he pointed at Hoss, "and th-th-that's Olivia Newton-John ower there, she's put a b-b-bit of weight on lately like, that's p-p-purely down to her addiction to ch-ch-chocolates though." Hoss smiled goofily and the driver shook his head before winding up his window and driving away. Watching the vehicle speed off, Billy looked around the two, uttering, "M-M-Met fuckers them are."

"A' wonder why they're bringing all these cockney cunts up here for?" moaned Jack with a prolonged sigh. "There's mare Met up here than what there is local cops."

"I'm bloody sure th-th-there is," agreed Billy, "a' b-b-bet it's great being a criminal down the s-s-smoke, there's n-n-not enough coppers left down th-th-there to withhold the law. A' just canit get me head around w-w-why they're fetching them all up h-h-here for, there's no n-n-need for it, ne one's even gone back to w-w-work in Easington."

"Fuck nars," griped Hoss, rubbing his injured nose, "but there's one thing for sure, we're bound to bump into them somewhere alang the line."

At Easington Colliery Club, the smell of detergent was pungent as Sue, Irene, Tracy, and Margret were busy deep cleaning the kitchen. Wiping over one of the workbench tops, Margret looked to Irene, groaning, "Ya want to see the state of Hoss' face, Irene, it's a right mess, his eyes are all black and blue and he's got a huge gash across the bridge of his nose. It's disgraceful the way the police are treating people, they're getting away with blum'n murder, so they are."

"Tell is about it!" uttered Irene. "Our Tom's got two canny shiners his sell. God nars what Pat's poor dad's ganna think of him when he turns up down there with a face like Rocky Marciano."

"What's happened to them, like?" Sue frowned, wringing out a cloth.

Irene sighed. "Have ya not heard, like, Sue?"

"Nor, heard what, what's happened?"

Irene shook her head. "Why the lads got a blum'n good hiding off the cops when they were picketing up Steetleys yesterday."

Sue stretched, "Never!?"

"They did!" moaned Irene. "And these beatings are getting just a bit too regular for my liking, it's every day ya hear that some poor bugger's been assaulted by these so-called policemen."

"Jack seemed okay last night, mind, Irene," put in Tracy.

"Apparently he wasn't there, Tracy," said Margret, "he arrived later on and released them all from out of the back of a police van."

"Were you talking to our Jack last night like, Tracy?" enquired Irene, wringing out a cloth that reeked of bleach.

"Yeah, he walked is home from the disco."

"Ya must have taken the lang route yerm then, 'coss the bugger didn't get in till all hours of the morning, again!"

Beaming cheekily, Tracy picked up a mop, saying, "Eeh a' know, we were gobbing on for ages, we're going out again tonight."

"Or aye, where yas off te like?" asked Irene, now wiping over a cooker top.

"Just to Horden pictures."

Irene smiled warmly. "Horden pictures, eh? What's on, owt nice?"

"Aye, Trading Places," answered Tracy, squeezing a mop into a red plastic bucket.

"Trading Places?" put in Sue. "Who's in that then?"

"Em! I'm not too sure, Sue, a' think it might be Eddie Murphy and Dan Aykroyd, anyhow they reckon it's as funny as owt."

Sue winked hidden at Tracy, gushing, "A' bet it'll be owt but funny what you and Jack get up to in them double seats in the back row though! Eh!?"

"Hey!" responded Irene, taken aback. "Tracy's not that type of girl, are ya, love?"

"A' is when it comes to your Jack, Irene, given half the chance that is!" Looking around the girls she smiled sharply. "Yas'll have to go outside for a bit, 'till I've mopped up."

"What is it with you lot and our Jack!?" asked Irene, glancing around the group. "Yad think he was some sort of Errol Flynn or Cary Grant or something."

"How'y, man, Irene!" purred Sue. "Ya might be his Ma, but ya've still got eyes, he's an absolute hunk, for crying out loud."

"He is like his dad a' suppose," muttered Irene.

"Aye, they were cut from the same cloth them two were," laughed Sue.

Giggling aloud, the girls left the room to sit chit-chatting around a table. Lighting up a cigarette, Irene handed around the packet, asking, "Did yas watch Coronation Street the other night? That Mike Baldwin's a right spiv, and Deirdre Barlow, well, I'm shocked with her, absolutely shocked so I am."

"Why, what's she done now?" asked Margret. "A' missed it the other night."

Irene drew deeply on her cigarette. "She's clarting around with that Mike Baldwin again, isn't she! Yad think she'd nar better after the last fling she had with the bugger."

"Why she's got a good right to be clarting around with someone," chipped in Sue, "that Barlow's just about the most boringest ard fart that ever was."

"He is, like," sniggered Irene. Facing Margret, she smiled. "So, are you into the Street then, flowerpots?"

She beamed. "Yeah, but I'm more into Emmerdale Farm than Coronation Street though."

"Nowt wrang with a bit of the ard Emmerdale Farm, love," said Irene just as Alan rushed into the room to join them. "Hello love," she greeted with a convivial grin.

"Hi, pet." Pecking a kiss on Irene's cheek, he sat, enthusing, "I've got some good news for yas."

"Orr, aye," stretched Sue, "we haven't got eight score draws up on the pools by any chance, have we?"

"Nor, not quite, Sue," he said before grinning ear to ear as he presented a huge envelope. "But there's sixteen hundred quid in there for the kitchen fund though, it's come direct from the National Executive."

The lasses sat dumbfounded for a second or two before Tracy appeared at the kitchen doorway with mop in hand. "Did a' hear right there!?"

"Ya did that, Tracy love!" sighed Sue, removing her spectacles to wipe away tears. "A' don't know what to say, Alan, except thank you very much."

"Never mind thank you very much!" interrupted Irene, picking up the envelope. "If ya ask me, it's about bloody time they got their finger out! But still, it is very kind of them a' suppose." Looking at Alan, her beam lifted to gratification. "I'm doing mutton chops for tea the night, if ya fancy popping 'round that is?"

"Why aye," he returned, lighting up a cigarette.

Margret leant across the table, whispering, "Irene, does Hoss always hum while he's eating?"

"Only if he likes what he's eating, flowerpots," she answered, then breaking into a wide grin she repeated, "only if he likes what he's eating."

ONE WEEK LATER.

It was a scorching July morning at Easington Colliery, the North Sea slept a cobalt waveless sleep while casting a shimmering heatwave to radiate just above the level of the sea creating a bizarre optical illusion of ships seemingly hovering in the sky instead of floating on the ocean. Active birdlife was everywhere around the pit premises, particularly inside the dense shrubbery where a family of wrens chirped nonstop while fluttering from shrub to bush to join raucous blackbirds, who themselves dashed around schooling fumbling fledglings that constantly shrilled open mouthed. The lads stood on picket duty at the side of the pit gates admiring a majestic sparrowhawk as she rose then dipped before rising again in search of stray pigeons. "Ger on there!" urged Jack, flinging a stubby piece of rope across the pit yard, and after a quick dash, Beauty, Billy's bad-tempered Jack Russell bitch, beat Jack's own dog Mick, who just happened to be Beauty's son, to the old rope. Growling aloud, stumpy tails wagged enthusiastically as they tugged each other back and forth, and even though Mick was visibly a lot bigger and stronger to that of his mother, he gave way in the towing contest as he knew from past experiences how her mood could change within an instant, and she would cease the tug of war game to turn on him. Beauty retrieved the frayed rope, bringing it back to Jack to rest it at heel in anticipation of him throwing it again. "No, leave it, Beauty!" he ordered, "it's ower hot for yas!" his words sending mother and son into quivering sulks with drool dripping from panting tongues.

Hoss left the group. Sauntering to Jack's pick-up truck, he leaned into the cab, retrieving a packet of cigarettes before re-joining the others to offer them around. Lighting up, he inhaled deeply, then facing Tom he asked, "Can Pat still not get time off work to come up for the Big Meeting on Saturday like, Tom?"

Tom also lit up. "A' divant nar yet, Hoss, she's ganna giss a bell later on the night after she's finished her shift."

Jack shook his head all flustered. "A' thowt Durham big meeting was supposed to be a lad's day out only?"

Billy put in, "It's only a d-d-demonstration this year, Jack, it's not the p-p-proper gala."

"It's still the big meeting to me," argued Jack.

"Why, big meeting or demonstration, I'm gan'n with Margret this year," said Hoss prior to drawing deeply on his cigarette.

Jack moaned, "Why that's just great, that is!" Lighting up a cigarette he looked to Billy and after blowing a sarcastic sigh, he asked, "A' suppose your Marie's gan'n with you as well, is she?"

"Is she h-h-heckers like!" gushed Billy as he too inhaled deeply on his cigarette. "We hardly t-t-talk these d-d-days never mind gan out t-t-together, she spends more time w-w-with our Tony than what she d-d-does with me."

Jack shook his head, saying, "Ya want to watch that bugger, mind, Billy, he's a right devious little twat! A' wadn't trust the cunt as far as a' could thraw him."

"Nor me too," put in Tom, "he tells more fibs than Margaret Thatcher he diss, he says owt but his prayers, and he whistles them buggers."

"He wadn't even think a-a-about gan'n with our l-l-lass, man," defended Billy. "I'm his uncle! And she's h-h-his aunty, fa fuck's sake, man!"

Hoss sighed, "Just watch him, Billy, that's all we're saying, he's not as nice as what ya mack him out to be."

"Just leave it, Hoss, p-p-please!" huffed Billy, and Hoss' reaction was to raise an arm in response to his little friend's words.

Drawing on his cigarette, Jack looked around the group. "A' canit get ower you soft sods taking your lasses to the meeting, mind."

"Stop stropping, man, Jack," laughed Hoss. "Anyway, Tracy will be there, won't she?"

"Aye she may well be, but she'll not be with me, as far as I'm concerned, it's a lad's day out only, besides... I'm not seeing her anymore."

"Now there's a thing," sighed Tom, his words breaching sarcasm.

"What do ya mean by, now there's a thing!? Eh!?" asked Jack in a direct tone.

"Nowt," stretched unconcerned from his brother, "nothing at all."

"Good! You just keep ya neb out of my business, that's if ya dinit mind that is."

"A' don't mind one bit," uttered Tom, "in fact a' couldn't give two shiny shites what you get up to, especially when it comes ta ya so-called... love life."

"Do ya not mean his l-l-lust life, Tom?" laughed Billy, who was now just about over his mini strop.

"What do ya mean by that?" asked Jack eying Billy.

"Nothing, j-j-just ya've never tasted real l-l-love afore, have ya?"

Jack looked around them with a snigger. "Here! It's not my fault a' dinit gan falling in love with the first lass I've had a leg ower with! I'm not like you three numpties tha nars."

"It's a good job ya not neither," laughed Tom, "or yad be married to Brenda Buck Back, by now, she was ya first, wasn't she?"

"Hey!" moaned Jack. "There's nowt wrang with Brenda Buck Back! And I'll have yas nar her name's not Brenda Buck Back neither, it's actually, Buck Back Brenda." He drew deep on his cig. "Granted she's got a face like a pirate's flag, but she's got one hell of a body on her!"

"Jack, man! She l-l-looks like, W-W-Widow T-T-Twankey!" joked Billy.

"So, fuck!" defended Jack. "She's a cracking shag, and ya nar what they say, a bad ride's better than a good wark."

"What's that supposed to mean?" frowned Tom, totally bamboozled.

"What it means is, when we were youngn's and yas were wanking ya socks off, a' was humping the lugs off her! Bad ride for me, good walk for you three fuckers."

"Uhh!" moaned Billy, with a twisted face.

Jack snapped, "What ya uhhing at now?"

"Nowt, a' j-j-just had a vision of you kissing that B-B-Brenda Buck B-B-Back, with her having like, ne t-t-teeth and that."

Jack defended, "Here, she had teeth back then, man! Why she had one or two any how's, and who mentioned kissing, a' was fucking her not kissing her."

"Stop biting, man, Jack, we're just winding ya up," chuckled Hoss. "Margret's not even gan'n to the Gala with me, she's gan'n with the lasses from the kitchen, they've got their arn banner and everything prepared."

"Arn banner!?" twisted Jack, poking his ear. "Arn frigging banner!? Since when have they had a banner? And why!? I've never seen nen of them working down the pit flogging their guts out on a back canch or crawling up and down a coalface all shift on their hands and knees! Why the hell should them lot be allowed to carry a banner for, eh!?"

"Listen to ya!?" grumped Tom. "Do ya nar how chauvinistic that sounds!? Never mind disrespectful, those poor lasses work bloody hard in that kitchen, Jack."

"Too true they do," agreed Hoss, "there's a canny few would have starved in the colliery if it wasn't for the likes of them, and they divant even get paid neither, it's all voluntary stuff they do."

"Aye right owe, Hoss, a' nar that, man!" groaned Jack. "Anyway, what historic embroidery's ganna be etched onto this banner of theirs like?" Inhaling deeply on his cigarette, he smiled in exaggerated fashion, sniggering, "A couple of pasties? Or perhaps a pie!? Or better still a plate full of mince and dumplings, eh!?"

Tom narrowed his eyes at his brother. "A' tell tha what, Jack, if ya're so against the lasses showing a banner at this demonstration, dinit gan! In fact, dinit even gan to the kitchen for owt ta eat anymore, if that's the way ya feel."

"They reckon their banner's g-g-got something to do with women against p-p-pit closures on it," voiced Billy between puffs on his cig.

"Ballicks! Women against pit closures!" laughed Jack. "What a complete farce that shit is an'll! Anyway, I've got nowt against the lasses from the kitchen, a' nar they're deing a cracking job, a' just don't think they should be allowed to parade a banner that's all, it'll be against the whole tradition of the big meeting so it will, besides that, every time there's more than three or fower of them get together they always break out in song!"

Hoss frowned. "There's nowt rang with that."

Jack shook his head, contradicting, "Hoss, man, have ya heard them singing? They're not exactly the Nolan Sisters tha nars!"

Billy addressed Jack, saying, "They can sing if they w-w-want to, Jack, b-b-besides, it's not a b-b-big meeting this year, it's a d-d-demonstration against p-p-pit closures."

"Exactly, Billy," agreed Tom, then glaring at his brother, he voiced, "anyway, what does thuw nar about the traditions of

Durham Big Meeting, Eh? All the years ya've been gan'n tha's hardly ever made it to the racecourse to listen to the speakers, in fact ya seldom make it past the first boozer ya've managed to stagger into."

Jack responded, "Aye, and so, fuck!"

Billy added, "And ya cause trouble and g-g-get ya sell locked up nearly e-e-every year too."

"Howld on, Billy, that's not entirely down to me!" defended Jack sternly.

"Why it is, like!" jumped in Hoss. "Ya shouldn't gan round half pissed cracking every Tom, Dick and Harry out, should ya?"

"Why that's just a bit of friendly banter that is, man, Hoss!" chuckled Jack in a carefree manner. "There's no malice in it whatsoever! It's just, like, part of the Gala spirit, and what's rang with a good day out on the lash, even if it sometimes ends up with a bit of a friendly fisty cuffs... in fact that's one of the true traditions of Durham Big Meeting that is!" Jack's eyes drifted as he watched Alan weave his way through the barricaded gates to be greeted by Mick wagging its tail all welcomely while Beauty showed her teeth growling and snapping at his ankles. Drawing Alan's attention, Jack waved him over, yelling, "Huw, Alan! Here a minute! Get ya arse ower here and put these daft buggers to right on something, will ya!?"

Alan joined them, moaning, "Billy, tha wants to put that bloody thing on a leash, it's a right vicious little bugger!" Looking at Jack, he frowned, asking, "What's up, Jack?"

Jack looked around the group, sniggering, "Why it's these three stooges here! They seem to think it's a good idea that the lasses from the kitchen should be allowed to carry a banner at the Big Meeting, a've never heard nowt so ludicrous in all me life! Ridiculous it is! Absolutely ridiculous!"

"It's a demonstration this year, not a big meeting, Jack, and it's not ridiculous." Alan smiled to the delight of the other three.

"In fact, it was me who forwarded the notion for them to carry a banner in the first place."

Jack stood open mouthed, gasping, "My-giddy-aunt ya didn't!? Well, if ya ask me, a' think it's a load of ard ballicks, like!"

Wearing a grin, Alan stepped closer to Jack. "It's a good job nobody's asking you then, isn't it? But a' tell tha what though, Jack, you fetch this banner thing up with Ma and see what she has to say about it, but before ya do, just remember she's never missed a Durham Big Meeting in the whole of her life, and she doesn't just walk round all day with a half-filled can in her hand like thuw diss, she works hard in that Labour Party tent serving people hour after hour, all day long, and she's been doing that every year since she was a little girl."

Facing Tom, Alan raised an eyebrow. "When ya get five come to the office, young'n, a' need to talk to ya about a special task that needs doing tomorrow morning."

"Special task?" asked Tom.

"Aye," said Alan, walking off, "and there's a tenner in it for each of yas, if yas fancy doing it that is."

"Tenner!?" shouted Jack after Alan. "Whatever it is we'll do it!" Jack handed Tom a huge plastic container with a cap covered in a green film of mould. "While ya at the office fill this up, the dogs are desperate for a drink."

Snatching the cannister away, Tom looked at his brother, moaning, "How come it's always me who has ta fetch the water!?"

Marie Ward was sat sipping coffee, half in and out of a TV interview that was broadcasting on 'Good Morning Britain' with Michael Heseltine voicing his one-sided opinion regarding the escalating violence in, and around, the coalmining communities. Marie had just lit up a cigarette when a heavy pounding on the front door shook the whole of the downstairs windows. "Who the hell's that!?" she moaned on her way to answer the door. Opening up, she faced two men aged in their mid-thirties who were dressed in cheap suits and smelling of inexpensive aftershave. One of these men stood tall and burly with a head of greased back, brown coloured hair, the other wasn't as tall, but was quite plump, and he too boasted dark hair which was also slicked back. "Can a' help yas?" asked Marie, gripping white knuckled onto the side of the door.

The taller of the two presented his identification card, asking, "Mrs Ward?"

"Yes," she nodded.

He grinned sharply. "Mrs Ward, we are debt collectors." Checking over a document, he continued, "We are here on behalf of Reids solicitors, who themselves are representees of Chapmen's credit company, and we have called on you today to collect," he flicked a page over, "three hundred and sixty-two pounds, forty pence, you haven't got it handy by any chance, have you?"

She beamed widely. "Why not likely, or sorry, hold on a minute." After briefly closing the door, she returned, fumbling her purse. "A' just may have the forty pence, if that's any help to yas?" After tipping the purse upside down she shook it slightly, saying, "Orr bugger, there's nothing in it but cobwebs! Sorry and all that shit, like!"

The taller of the two sighed from out of his nose, saying, "Bit of a comedian I see, Mrs Ward, is Mr Ward in by any chance? Because we need this sorting today, or I'm afraid we'll be coming back to remove all of your furniture."

"No, not in at the moment he's not, he's out picketing, yas do actually know he's on strike, don't yas?"

"Yes, we are quite aware of that." The smaller guy smiled, his numerous chins wobbling slightly with each word spoken. He smiled falsely, asking, "Can we come in and discuss the matter?"

"Ya mean can yas come in and cage the joint? Can ya heckers like! A's not as green as I'm cabbage looking tha nars! So please, step away from my doorway 'coss I'm a bit busy at the moment!"

Marie went to close the door but the larger of the two smirked as he wedged his foot in the doorsill. "Move ya foot!" she ordered, wide eyed.

Handing over a sealed envelope, he looked Marie directly in the eye. "That's a walking possession order I've just served you with, Mrs Ward; if all monies owed aren't cleared within seven days, we'll be back next Thursday at nine o'clock to remove furniture." He leered emotionless as he ran his eyes over the door. "And believe you me, this flimsy thing won't stop us neither, I'll take it straight off its hinges if need be." His smirk extended into a beam as he slowly removed his foot from the doorsill. "Now you have a nice day, madame."

"Fuck you!" snapped Marie, flinging the envelope back in his face. "Now piss off!"

After the door was slammed shut, the debt collectors swaggered towards an old transit van which seemed to show more rust than the actual white paintwork.

NEXT MORNING

Up at one of the districts in Peterlee, a blue sky capped a glorious summer morning as Alan's car was parked at an outer side of a busy alleyway which ran between a hairdressing parlour and a fish shop. Donning balaclava hats, and clutching baseball bats, Jack and the lads loitered inside a metal-framed bus shelter that was constructed out of reinforced Perspex which was not quite transparent enough to see through properly. The shelter had two entrances, one at the front, and one across the opposite end of the structure to the rear, and it was sited at the roadside of a small, yet lively shopping precinct dubbed the Argus shops, named as such because of its close proximity to a popular boozer called the Argus Butterfly.

Billy was on edge as he spied through a gap in the structure as they waited for a group of four working miners who were just about due to arrive to be picked up by a scab bus. Jack joined Billy at the gap, saying, "Mind you, there's a canny few people kicking about, Billy, they must be all gan'n to work or something." He slowly turned to Hoss, asking, "What time's it, Hoss?"

Hoss checked his wrist. "Twenty-five ta eight, there's a good ten minutes or so left afore they're due to be picked up." Looking around, he patted his pockets, asking, "Anyone got a tab? A've left mine in Alan's car." But to his disappointment, not one of them had brought cigarettes with them.

Billy fidgeted with his balaclava, pulling it to a stretch. "It's ower t-t-tight this thing is! A' canit b-b-breathe properly."

"Leave it alone, man, Billy!" ordered Tom, straightening up Billy's mask. "It's not ower tight at all."

"It is l-l-like!"

Tom snapped, "It's not, man! It's fine for fuck's sake!"

Jack looked to Hoss, joking, "Huw, Hoss, ya look canny in that balaclava, mind, it suits ya down to the ground."

"Think, see?"

"Why aye, it matches all ya combat gear and everything, ya look a bit like one of those IRA fuckers!"

"Do a'!?" enthused the big man, grinning like a Cheshire cat beneath his disguise.

Tom now pressed his face against another gap, grousing, "A' wished this was all ower and done with, it's a bad tenner earned this is if ya ask me."

"Here, it was thuw who accepted the job in the first place!" grumped Jack as Billy and himself joined Tom at the opening. "If tha wasn't up to the task ya should have said no."

"Shut half ya mouth... gobshite," groused Tom to his brother, "a' never said a' wasn't up to the task."

Pulling a shopping trolley, a little old lady entered the shelter, straightening a tweed jacket she smiled around, asking, "Has the two-thirty bus to Hartlepool gone yet, lads?"

"Nor, not yet, love," politely answered Tom from beneath his mask, "why, not since we've been here it hasn't."

"It's alright, here it is now." Toddling from the shelter she looked the lads up and down, saying, "Good luck with the strike, lads, them scabs shouldn't be long coming now." Stretching out her arm, the bus hissed to a stop before she moaned her way up steps to board.

"A' carn't understand why w-w-we have to do this f-f-for in the first place!" voiced Billy. "Why can't them l-l-lot from Wearmouth sort their arn s-s-scabs out for? Why should it have to b-b-be us?"

"Tha nars why, Billy," muttered Jack. "Alan's already explained it to us, it's because their top gadgies have all got court orders served upon them, the poor buggers are not even allowed to gan picketing at their awn pit let alone do owt like this, if they got caught doing this, they'd end up serving a tidy stretch in Durham prison, man!"

"Aye and if we g-g-get caught, that's exactly what we'll b-b-be doing, an'all," moaned Billy.

Tom turned around, gushing, "Where the fuck's Hoss gone!?"

Billy glanced from out of the rear entrance of the shelter catching a glimpse of Hoss as he strode towards a tobacco and confectionery shop, still wearing his mask and clutching a bat. "A' think he's g-g-gone ower to that shop f-f-for some tabs."

Tom grumbled, "Fa fuck's sake! Is he right in the heed, or what!?"

Hoss entered into a small shop with shelves stocked with every item of household goods ranging from cleaning detergents, toilet rolls, toothpastes, up to a huge diversity of tinned foods, kids' sweets, crisps and lots of other stuff, but despite all these goods on view the shop was unoccupied except for an elderly

Pakistani lady who was one rung up a stepladder, busy stacking cigarettes to shelves from behind a counter with her back turned away. Hoss coughed slightly to gain her attention, and the instant she spun the poor woman almost fell from the ladder, as in front of her stood this masked giant with a bludgeon in his hand who was obviously going to crack open her skull prior to him robbing the shop at his leisure. She must have thought her hearing was playing tricks when, "Can a' have ten Regal King Size please, and a box of Swan vestas?" was spoken ever so politely, but even though Hoss' words were well-mannered, they did not pacify her in the slightest and her hands trembled visibly as the two exchanged money for goods. "Put the change in the charity box, love," he instructed, pointing the bat at a Save the children box, before saying, "bye now". The traumatised woman was stuck between a smile and a cry as Hoss turned, and the instant he left the shop she staggered to the entrance where she locked up before her legs gave way and she slid the door to sit uttering words of prayer in her olden Punjabi tongue.

Hoss re-joined the others at the shelter and was on opening up the cigarette packet when Tom turned from a gap. "Ya haven't time for a smoke Hoss, they're here."

Jack rushed to the space, eying a quartet of men approaching with work bags slung over their shoulders. One of these guys was tall and aged in his early twenties, wearing combat trousers and a Newcastle United football shirt, while a couple of them were aged in their early thirties sporting jeans and tee-shirts. To the front of the cluster strode a stumpy, middle-aged man dressed in grey slacks and an outdated check shirt. Picking out the younger of the quartet, Jack sneered, "Leave that Maggie fucker for me."

"We're not here to batter them, Jack," whispered Tom, "we're only here to put the frighteners on them, and that's all we're doing so keep that bat to ya sell."

"A' nar but we can still have a bit fun with them though," said Jack with a hint of mischief in his voice.

"Right then," uttered Tom, "let's fuck off round the back and when they enter the shelter me and our young'n will come in from the front entrance, while you two block off the back one, understood?" They nodded in agreement before quickly leaving the shelter by means of a rear exit ahead of the cluster of men entering the shelter laughing and joking amongst themselves. The instant Jack and Tom stepped through the front gap of the shelter the scabs' banter ceased and they scampered towards the rear exit only to be faced with Hoss and Billy standing brandishing raised bats.

Jack scrunched the younger man by his throat; clashing him up against the side of the bus stop, he sneered, "Off to work are ya, scab!?" then with the end of the bat pressed up under the terrified man's chin, he continued, "I'm going to crack ya fucking skull open, ya scabby twat!"

"Please, don't!" pleaded the man, his bottom lip trembling. "Please, mate!"

Jack growled, "I'm not ya fucking mate, scab!"

The rest of the men grouped together absolutely horrified. Tom grabbed one of them by the back of his hair, threatening, "Right! We have a situation here, scab, either you lot turn around and fuck off back yerm or we are going to batter ya heads in, do ya understand?" The man nodded in silence. "Good!" sneered Tom. "And keep away from work till the strike's finished with or we'll be back! Got it!?" Once again, the scab gestured a nod in acknowledgement of Tom's words. "And by the way, we know exactly where yas all live so I'll say it once again, just so it sinks in, stay... away... from... work... got it!?" Head bobbing notions were once again given, and Tom let go of the guy before pushing him the length of the shelter.

"You got it too, scab," threatened Jack, easing the bat on a now purple faced man.

He coughed, holding his throat, mumbling, "Yes."

Jack raised his bat. "What was that!?"

"Yes!" trembled from the scab's mouth.

"Good, because if a' had my way you lot would be levelled on the floor by now." Facing the other three, Jack once again lifted his bat. "Now fuck off afore we have a change of heart and knock the shit out of yas."

Billy raised his bludgeon, threatening, "And k-k-keep away from work!"

"Yeah," put in Hoss. "Or we'll fuck yas up big style next time."

"Go on, girt- out- of -here!" threatened Tom, hoisting his baton.

The lads looked on as the petrified scabs scampered from the shelter to scurry a road. Baton still raised, Jack stood at the entrance of the shelter, shouting, "Huw, scab, thraw that fucking scum top in the bin when ya get yerm, ya might catch dermatitis or the lurgy from it!"

Looking around the others, Tom removed his balaclava. "How'y then, let's get the fuck out of here."

"Well, that went canny, didn't it?" said Jack, pulling off his disguise. "A' really enjoyed that."

"Aye, it w-w-wasn't as bad as what a' thowt it was ganna b-b-be," agreed Billy who was relieved to be free of his mask. Hoss stood muted and was more than happy to retain his balaclava as they quickly left the shelter to make their way towards Alan's parked up vehicle.

"Are ya not taking that mask off, Hoss?" asked Tom as they strode.

"Nar, a's ganna leave it on a bit langer."

"Hoss!" snapped Tom all agitated. "Tack the frigging thing off afore someone sees ya and phones for the coppers an–"

"Leave him alone!" broke in Jack. "He can keep it on if he wants te! Ya not the fucking gaffer tha nars!"

"A' niver said a' was!" retorted Tom.

"Why, stop acting as if tha is!" snarled Jack. "Tha's always telling people what to do!"

Tom barked, "Shut the fuck up!"

"Nar, thuw shut the fuck up!" The brothers continued with their argument for the short distance to Alan's vehicle and were still going at it hammer and tongs as Alan speedily drove away.

FOLLOWING MORNING

Jack was stood at a table in the union office waiting for a kettle to boil when he caught his eye on a box filled with white armbands showing 'N.U.M. OFFICIAL' in bold red print. Removing a couple of these armbands he had just about managed to stuff them into one of his jeans pockets before Alan swanned into the room, asking, "Brewing up, Jack?"

"Aye, does tha want one, like?"

"Aye, gan on then!" he said, sitting. "Looking forward to the demonstration the morn then?"

"Aye am a'," replied Jack, parking his backside opposite. "Should still be a canny few there."

"Aye there should be, even if it's not an official big meeting there should still be a canny turn out, and dinit you be rolling around pissed at that Labour Party tent mind, ya Ma's got enough on her plate without her babysitting you all day."

"Yes, Dad," joked Jack, breaking into a smile. "Ya not ganna ground is, is tha?"

"Seriously though, Jack, ya nar how she gets herself all stressed out working in that tent, there's drunks rolling around all ower the place." Lighting up a cigarette he exhaled smoke, asking, "Are you going on with the first bus to help carry the pies and stuff?"

"Yeah, Billy's giving is a hand. She's been on baking since six this morning and she's got a grit pan of mushy peas on the go too. Does she not get paid for all this baking larky like, Alan?"

"Does she heckers like! She should do though, but she doesn't, it's all coffers for the frigging Labour Party I'm afraid! And, Jack, when ya go up yerm keep Hoss well away from them pies or there'll be nowt left for the morn."

"It's all right, she's baked a couple of extra ones for us."

"Do ya nar if she's done any extra ham and egg ones?"

"Aye, come to think of it she may well have done, she's baked over thirty plate pies already."

"Champion!" Alan stretched a smile. "Has Pat arrived up yet?"

"Nar, she's coming up later on the safta." The sound of a kettle bubbling interrupted the conversation. Jack crossed the steamy room to mast the tea exactly how he had been taught by his mother, and that was to always stir the pot anticlockwise before finishing the procedure by tapping the lid three times with the spoon. "One sugar, isn't it, Alan?"

"Nor! No sugar and just a smidgin of milk, in fact just leave it, Jack, I'll mack me arn a bit later on thanks, but switch the kettle off by the plug, the on-off button's playing up, some bright spark let the bugger boil dry the other day and the element's just about burnt out."

Jack asked, "Are you gan'n on the first bus in the morning?"

"Why nor, a's in charge of the band bus and all the others."

SATURDAY MORNING

Mother Nature had cast black clouds over Durham city. Heavy rain poured constantly throughout the morning, creating a wet and murky day, yet still, the backdrop of the Cathedral towering majestically above a fast-flowing River Wear was more than kind on the eye. The distinctive beat of brass bands filled the air, with converging streets crammed amid thousands of people who had braved the elements to descend upon the ancient city in celebration of a gala-styled demonstration in support of the miners' strike. Drenched onlookers applauded strings of brightly coloured banners along every inch of the route that started off at the famous Market Square before winding down through cobbled streets, leading up to, and beyond, the County Hotel before their journey came to an end at waterlogged fields dubbed the racecourse.

At one of a main access roads leading into the city centre, Jack and Billy looked all official wearing N.U.M. armbands as they stood ushering traffic the wrong way down a one-way system, causing a complete gridlock at the out of sight end of the road. The hiss of buses breaking to a stop sounded before Alan sprang purple-faced from the leading coach. Billy gulped as he watched Alan stomp through puddles towards them. "H-H-He made is d-d-do it, Alan!" he gasped, pointing an accusing finger at Jack. "It w-w-was all his idea."

"It's just a bit of fun afore ya start," chuckled Jack, unperturbed.

Alan ranted, "Bit of fun!" Snatching away the armbands, he growled, "Giss them things here! Where the hell have yah two getting hold of these from?"

Once again Billy aimed a finger. "He n-n-nicked them from out ya office y-y-yesterday, a' wasn't even there."

"Thanks... grass!" snapped Jack, looking twice in disbelief at his best friend.

Blowing a sigh, Alan shook his head. "Do ya nar how much commotion yahs have caused!? Yas have got the whole of Durham in a frigging gridlock! Anyway, come with me, I've got a special job for yas, a' want yas to carry a banner."

"It's not that 'women against pit closures' thing, is it?" raised Jack.

"Nor, it's definitely not that, and yas get paid twenty notes each for carrying it too."

"Champion, we'll do it then," said Jack without a second thought.

"W-W-What banner is it, like?" questioned Billy.

"It's just an extra banner we didn't know was coming here today, and the union rules state a NUM member must carry any additional banners if they haven't been approved by the banner committee beforehand." Alan's eyes drifted from Bill to Jack. "It'll be right up your street, Jack."

"Are why, sounds good to me!" laughed Jack. "As long as it's not that 'women against pit closures' shite a couldn't care less."

Alan waved the band members and all of the passengers from a convoy of five crammed buses, and it wasn't long before a stout band leader with a balding head shouted instructions to the colliery band members. Looking all prim and proper clothed in purple military-type blazers, that were styled double-breasted and decorated with gold-coloured buttons and matching epaulets, the band quickly shuffled to some sort of formation. To the rear of the main Easington banner, Sue and Jenny unfolded their own standard as the rest of the girls from the kitchen gathered in a cluster alongside their loved ones. In amongst the hundreds of followers, Hoss held Margret by the hand while Tom shielded his arm around Pat's shoulder. Jack stood thunder faced alongside Billy, who beamed brazenly as they held aloft a rainbow LGSM (Lesbians & Gays Support the Miners) banner from within a miscellany of individuals who flaunted weird kind of hairstyles that somehow harmonized with their brightly coloured, hippy styled apparel. A tiny grin briefly shot across Jack's face as he glanced hidden at two girls holding onto each other's hands in the manner of a courting couple, and daft fantasies of him copping off with the pair for a threesome stupidly ran his mind before he frowned deeply as most of the surrounding men conversed in distinctive feminine lisps. Jack side-eyed Billy, whispering, "Just one word and I'm telling ya now, this fucking thing's ganna gan stright in that river with thuw following." His shoulders shrugged in slight shock as without warning a heavy bass drum thumped three times ahead of the band blowing the start of 'Sons of the Brave', and off they went marching down a cobblestone street in the direction of the County Hotel.

Descending further, the cheering increased from all directions. "We love the gays and lesbians!" shouted one elderly lady, which to Jack's astonishment was seemingly directed towards him, and much to his horror she continued, "Thank you for all your donations! Thank you to all our gay comrades!" Inching further along the route the applauding intensified from an ever-thickening crowd before they came to a stop in front of the County Hotel where up on a raised balcony VIP guests greeted them with a variety of plastic smiles and exaggerated clapping. The band formed into a circle below the veranda and had just struck up the start of Gresford, 'the miners' hymn', when Arthur Scargill and Peter Heathfield stepped out onto the balcony to be greeted by rapturous applause. The applauding transcended into jeering and cries of Judas! Scab! and other heavier cursing as Neil Kinnock appeared briefly before he quickly turned tail to disappear back into the hotel. Finishing the heart wrenching sonata, the Easington band then marched away to the sound of a sprightlier, upbeat composition. After passing by a chain of public houses, a police station, and a rather imposing County Courts building, they descended a slight incline just as a strong wind picked up even further, causing the rain to intensify and fall at an uncomfortable angle. The parading bands quickened their step along a tarmac pathway guiding them by a boisterous fairground where neon lights flashing different colours in sequence to a rhythmical beat of blasting music. Marching further, they went by an historic cricket pavilion constructed entirely out of wood which had recently been revamped with a fresh coating of white paint, before their journey ended at the racecourse in front of a makeshift stage, and without delay everyone scampered into the shelter of various tents and pavilions.

Inside a cramped Labour Party marquee, the air filled with an aroma consisting of cigarette smoke, pies, mushy peas and freshly brewed tea and coffee. Irene and other party members were rushed off their feet serving wetted customers with food, hot drinks, and a range of other beverages. Irene handed an elderly woman a cup of tea, and a paper plate filled with a slice of pie and a healthy serving of steamy mushy peas. "There's plastic knives and forks on that table over there, love," she said, pointing to a side table. After receiving payment, the two exchanged friendly grimaces before Irene handed over change ahead of moving onto another punter just as a young lad possessing an acne face approached smiling pleasantly.

"We are nearly out of teabags, Irene, and there's not much coffee left neither," he said in a polite, soft tone.

Wiping perspiration from her brow, she half smiled, saying, "Take twenty quid from out of the kitty, George, and pop up to the Co-Op, get a tenner's worth of each, and don't forget to get a receipt." He returned a grin in response before walking off as a couple of men approached the counter. Irene sensed these strangers were intoxicated, and although she was slightly uptight, she still greeted them with a warm smile, asking, "What can I get you two lads then?"

"Two cans of lager," slurred one of the men who was dark haired and lanky while parading an untrimmed hefty bush above his top lip.

"Sorry, we don't sell alcohol here, but there's a pub just up the road that does."

"Ya don't sell alcohol!?" put in his mouthy friend, who was way shorter, with hair that was mousy and in desperate need of a good shampoo.

"It's the Labour Party tent, son, not the 'Fighting Cocks pub', we have tea, coffee, cakes, pie and peas, and cans of soft drinks–"

"Soft drinks?" interrupted the taller of the two. "What sort of shithole's this, like!?"

"Hey! Less the lip, you!" snapped Irene who though a little tense, still wouldn't take any sassiness; besides this, it was in her genes not to suffer fools gladly. "I've got tights older than you two, show a bit of respect!"

"Fuck you, misses!" growled the shorter one. Twisting his face, he leered at Irene, raising, "Who do ya think ya are? Me fucking mother!"

"Right, that's it!" snapped Irene. "I want you two to leave this instant, now get out!" The two men laughed in Irene's face before her gaze drifted beyond them as Jack and Billy entered to stand at the marquee entrance. She caught Jack's attention by nodding wide eyed at the two men before once again ordering, "Will you please leave?"

"Will we fuck!" growled the smaller. "It's pissing down out there!"

"The Labour party's a load of shite anyway," slurred the taller, "a' bet ya've never even seen a real coal miner all year till yas come here, anyway, where's ya precious leader at, eh!?"

Billy tapped the taller of the two men on his shoulder. "A' think ya better l-l-leave, mate."

The man swivelled to narrow his eyes. "Who the fuck do ya think you are you, like? Is she ya mother or what? Ya ginger little twat!"

"Nor, she's mine actually," interrupted Jack, smiling untroubled.

"Or aye, is that right, is it?" snarled the smaller guy.

Jack beamed unconcerned, asking, "Anyway what pit are yah two from then? I've never seen yas on the picket line afore."

"Dawdon Colliery," they replied almost in unison.

"Dawdon Colliery eh!" Flicking his head at his mother, Jack winked and she stood back a pace or two. He turned to face the strangers. "So, ya'll be a pair of scabs are yas?"

"What do ya mean by that like!?" snarled the taller, stepping forward to stand nose to nose with Jack. "You want to watch ya fucking mouth you do! Anyhow, which pit are you two fuckers from like?"

Jack smirked. "Me! Easington Colliery, marra, and I was there when we had to picket you lot out at the beginning of the strike."

"And a' w-w-was there too," voiced Billy.

"Shut the f-f-fuck up, ya stuttery twat!" laughed the smaller of the guys.

Jack broke in, "Hey gobshite! Stop acting the goat and let's be having yas, hit the road."

The larger of the two clenched his fists. "Hit the road? Hit the fucking road! I'll hit thuw, first!" He threw a bit of a sloppy punch, but Jack avoided it easily by stooping to one side, he then half-heartedly let loose with a soft hook rattling the man's ribcage, and he collapsed winded to the floor.

Jack turned to the other, "Do ya fancy a dance like, gobshite!?" Shaking his head, the man raised his hands as he backed away. "Come on then, up on ya feet," said Jack, aiding the stricken man up from the ground. Smiling friendly, Jack dusted him down, saying, "Now get ya sells away and keep out of bother." Still grinning he watched as the smaller man struggled to prop up his friend. Jack shook his head at the two, saying, "Have ya got something to say to Ma afore yas go?"

Looking over at Irene the two strangers gave off individual apologies before they turned and staggered towards an exit.

"The little buggers!" Jack smiled at his mother.

Irene returned a grin, saying, "That's what you are usually like when ya stagger in here year in and year out."

"Give ower! I'm not that bad!"

"Ya are l-l-like, Jack!" voiced Billy. "Ya can be canny o-o-obnoxious when ya've had a skin full." Facing Irene, he checked his money before asking, "Can a' have a c-c-coffee and some pie and p-p-peas please, Mrs Gilroy."

"Of course you can, son, would you like an extra sliver of pie free of charge?"

"Ooow aye p-p-please!"

Irene eyed her son. "What do you want then?"

"Just a coffee please, Ma."

"Do ya not want some of me pie and peas like?" she asked, slightly taken aback.

"Why nor a' had a boat load this morning didn't a'!"

"True," she sighed, turning away to carve a plate pie up into segments.

FOLLOWING THURSDAY MORNING

A huge transit van turned into a narrow alleyway to pull up outside the Wards' abode. The two debt collectors who had visited the previous week jumped from the van with the larger of the two whistling carefree as they approached the house where he started pounding heavily on the door with the side of his fist. The door opened ajar, and a nervous Marie peeped through the gap, muttering, "We still haven't managed to raise any cash yet."

"That's okay, love, we've come for your furniture," smirked the largest of the two without any hint of compassion whatsoever, "best you just let us in the house, love, or believe you me I will take this thing off its hinges."

"He's not joking," put in the smaller, smiling falsely, "today's the day, you've had plenty of time to scrape the money together." To their surprise Marie did the last thing they expected, she stood to one side allowing them entrance to the house.

Opening a separate door leading to the sitting room she gulped, "Go through there then."

The collectors entered the main room to be greeted by a carpet full of stern-faced miners including Tom, Jack, Billy and Hoss. At once, the gathering pounced on the two bailiffs, ripping their clothes from off their backs before physically bundling the stunned pair back into the street, leaving them standing as naked as a couple of new-born babies.

Billy exited the house and started goading them by dangling their van keys over a water drain before clinking them through a grate. "Whoops a d-d-daisy!" He smiled.

Marie came to the door. "See yas next time you come calling... love... now you two have a nice day!" She stood grinning ear to ear before Billy and herself entered back into the house, closing the door behind them.

Chattering away, a couple of elderly headscarfed ladies dragged wheely shopping trolleys as they wobbled to stride. Approaching the two naked collectors they slowly looked the men up and down before one of the ladies nudged her friend, saying, "Eee, a' don't know what this place is coming to lately, Betty, honstly orgies in the streets, and at this time of the morning too! Disgraceful it is, bloody disgraceful!"

The other old lady removed a handkerchief from out her coat sleeve, blowing her nose she shook her head, agreeing, "It's getting worser by the day, Freda, a' blame the blum'n council me like."

CHAPTER FOUR, AUGUST, "I'M S-S-SPARTACUS"

At Easington beach, July had relinquished glorious weather over to the safe hands of August with not a single cloud to be found. An amalgamation of a sunny day and an ebbing tide resulted in clusters of boisterous children playing in the safety of shallow pools in and around the rocky Twelve Foots. Further along the water's edge, groups of adolescent boys swam at the side of the flight while a trio of older lads knelt on a makeshift raft constructed out of a quartet of huge industrial sized drums that were strapped two together at both the front and rear of a deck constructed out of three railway sleepers joined together by ropes. Up above the beach banks a female kestrel hovered in the warm air currents, occasionally swooping with her wings folded backwards in search of prey, and after a series of plunges she finally pounced to rise with a vole, or perhaps a mouse, clutched tight in her talons.

Stripped down to just shorts and boots, Jack, Tom, Hoss and Billy sat on the grass at the top of the red ash cliffs, smoking cigarettes. Opposite stood a couple of decrepit bicycles that were propped up against numerous plastic bags that brimmed with riddled coke embers and stacked at a side of an entrance to a freshly dug out lair that they had excavated that morning. This tunnel was dug out to a metre and a half in width, by over a metre in height, and it stretched for several metres into the side of an embankment while secured by flimsy timber boards strategically placed at both the sides and roof of the burrow. Looking healthy and tanned, Jack stood to lean on his shovel; flicking his cigarette butt over a cliff top, he suggested, "How'y then, let's get the last of these bags filled afore dinner, I'm frigging starving here, and a' need a bath, I'm taking Bev James out the night."

"Why it wasn't two minutes ago tha was seeing Tracy James," moaned Hoss with a half-hearted sigh and a slight shake of his head. "Ya're as bold as brass thuw is, fancy humping two sisters one after the other."

"Aye f-f-fancy!" broke in Billy with a tint of jealousy. "They're f-f-frigging gorgeous them two are, a divant nar which one's the b-b-best out the pair of them."

"Aye they're not three bad, Billy," returned Jack. Laughing aloud, he poked Hoss, teasing, "Sorry, Hoss, but that's the way the ball bounces, marra, ya've either got it, or tha hasn't, and I'm afraid I have!" Resting his shovel, he tensed his muscles into a pose. "Do yas think a' look like a model, eh!?"

"Aye, a model frigging aeroplane," smirked Tom as he stood.

Jack beamed. "Here... a' looked in the mirror just this morning and that's the best reflection I've ever seen in the whole of my life, fantastic it was, absolutely fantastic."

Tom looked to Hoss, saying, "Remind is on to clean that mirror when we get yerm, Hoss, will ya?"

Billy laughed. "That's what that owld Witch said in S-S-Snow White and the seven d-d-dwarfs, Jack! Mirror, m-m-mirror on the wall, who's the f-f-fairest of th-th-them all."

"Well, a' think ya could be a model, Jack," voiced Hoss as he struggled to his feet, "ya've definitely got the looks, marra, especially with half ya arse hinging out of them shorts, ya grit puffta."

Jack looked back over his shoulder at the rips, chuckling, "Here you, ya shouldn't be looking at me arse... ya saucy bastard! Besides, they match with me ard rigger boots 'coss these things are totally fucked too..." He drew attention to his boots by separating a toecap from a flapped sole. "... Look at the clip of them! A' wished a' could get into them pit baths and get me ard pit beuts from out me locker."

Billy scrutinized Jack. "Ya have g-g-got something about ya like, Jack, why don't ya send a photo off t-t-to one of those m-m-model agencies–"

"Billy!" broke in Tom. "Don't encourage the daft bugger!"

"Bloody sure!" agreed Hoss. "We canit afford to let him gan wondering off willy-nilly, he's the only Dosco operator we've got for when this strike's finished with."

"A' wish the bloody thing w-w-was ower and done with, and f-f-for good too," griped Billy. "I'm sick ta death of b-b-being skint all the time."

"We're all in the same boat now, Billy," concurred Hoss with a sigh, "if ya asked me, it's about time Scargill and Thatcher got their heads together and started sorting all this shit out."

Jack sighed, "Hoss! Thatcher doesn't want the strike to end, she's lapping the bugger up, man, just like what the twat did during the Falklands war, its unconditional surrender or fucking nowt with that one."

"Aye, but we're not exactly an enemy like the Argies were though, Jack," argued Hoss.

Billy blew a sigh. "In her eyes we are, Hoss, r-r-remember what the cheeky s-s-sod said on the t-t-telly the other week, we're the enemy w-w-within."

"She's a frigging horror show," grumped Tom, picking up a shovel.

Hoss handed Billy a pick. "Get in there and start digging, Jack's got a date on the night and ya nar how lang it takes him to spruce himself up."

Pick in hand, Billy moaned, "A' wish a' had me knee pads," then whistling to the theme tune of 'The Great Escape', he crawled on all fours into the entrance to the tunnel. Clasping a shovel in one hand, and a half a dozen wooden boards in the other, Jack joined in with the whistling while following close on his little friend's heels. Tom was also in tune as he inched just behind before he stopped halfway up the channel leaving the other two to creep deeper until reaching a dead end.

With each blow from the pick, Billy found it difficult to breathe as hydrogen sulphide gas seeped into the atmosphere to fill the tunnel with an obnoxious smell of rotten eggs. Drips of sweat ran down Jack's face as he scuffed back excavated cinders from around Billy before casting shovel loads back overs to his brother who slung the stenchy stuff from out of the entrance for Hoss to painstakingly riddle out bits of embers. Within a half an hour, Billy had managed to hew out a further metre or so when his instincts kicked in, not at comfort with the surroundings he was just about to secure the roof with extra lumber when a soft sprinkling of red dust covered his head and shoulders before a loud cracking shook the whole of the tunnel ahead of tons of earth collapsing, entombing both Jack and he, but miraculously the fall stopped short of Tom. Shovel in hand Hoss rushed into the burrow, joining Tom.

"They're under all that fucker, Hoss!" spluttered Tom. "We need to get them out quickly!" Without a single thought for their own safety, they knelt alongside one another, sculling dirt away and within a matter of seconds they came across Jack's boots. Using all his might, Hoss dragged Jack from out the dirt, and thankfully he recovered quickly. After a short bout of coughing, Jack rubbed the stinging dust from out of his eyes before joining the other two as they dug frantically in search of Billy.

"Billy! Billy!" screamed Jack, but there was no response. "Billy... B... illy!!!!" They desperately dug on until Hoss came across a lifeless leg. It took all three to haul Billy out from under the fall and they had just exited from the entrance when the whole embankment subsided, wafting up a mini cloud of red dust. Tom placed Billy on his side as Jack poured water over his face while hitting his back in an effort to clear his airways, but he remained limp for what seemed like an eternity until he finally came around, spitting red phlegm. After a minute or two had passed he had recovered enough to prop himself upright with his entire body and dishevelled hair caked in thick red dust.

Billy side eyed Jack who had lost himself with emotion. "Are ya alright, J-J-Jack?"

"Aye," he gasped, and for the first time since his father had passed away, he sniffed away a tear or two. Wiping his eyes, he looked at his little friend, mumbling, "A' thowt a' lost ya for a while there mind, Billy, if it wasn't for Hoss and our young'n, God nars what the outcome of that might have been."

"A' thowt yas were both goners," voiced Hoss.

Tom gripped Jack in a tight brotherly hug. "Are ya sure ya okay, kid?"

Jack's bottom lip quivered ever so slightly as he nodded in response.

Billy scrutinized Jack who, like himself, was also smothered in red dust. Breaking into a brazen grin, he joked, "Tha doesn't look m-m-much like a m-m-model now mind, Jack, tha's more like an Apache Indian, only ya've got r-r-red hair like me."

Jack returned a warm grimace. Looking around the group, he inhaled deeply before composing himself as he struggled to his feet, saying, "Well! Fuck this for a game of soldiers! I'm afraid it's back ower the wall nicking coal from now on, and a' divant give two shiny shites whether there's coppers and extra security on duty or not!"

Irene sat at her dining table opposite Mary Morris, her long-time friend and political mentor, who just happened to be the mother of Sue Temple. Aged in her mid-sixties, Mary was a good twenty years Irene's elder, who possessed thick rimmed spectacles that were slightly tinted but didn't quite conceal deep-set creases around her eyes. Her lips had aged to a scrunched-up dryness, and the side of her mouth showed heavy wrinkles, but disregarding furrows that ran her brow, her hair still clung onto a slight trace of youthfulness whilst fashioned quite short in a loose perm. Despite her sour face, Mary was a caring Socialist and was currently the Labour Party's chairperson on Easington Parish Council, as well as serving to the best of her ability as an elected delegate on Durham County Council. She was recognised as a hard-working servant throughout the community and was renowned for never eschewing from an argument, whether it be political, or indeed street, yet still she held a heart of gold and would be the first to help out if, and when, needed. Mary was married to Jimmy, a well-liked, easy-going man who was a happily retired miner and one of Irene's late husband's oldest and best friends.

The sharp click of a kettle sounded. Irene left the table with a smile to return tray in hand loaded with a milk jug, sugar bowl, teapot, a couple of her best China cups and saucers, a freshly cleaned ashtray, teaspoon, and a half packet of her favourite shortbread biscuits. Stirring the pot anticlockwise she habitually tapped the lid three times, asking, "Biscuit, Mary?"

"No, tar," she replied, handing over a cigarette before lighting one up herself. Passing over a stylish gold-plated lighter that was slender and cylinder in shape, Mary grinned slightly, asking, "What do ya think about a weekly pie and pea supper and bingo night then, Irene? That should raise some money, and the Club will probably's let us have the singing end free of charge, why, if it's on a Monday or Wednesday night they definitely would."

"A' think it's a cracking idea," agreed Irene, inhaling deeply on her cigarette, "us two can bake the pies, and your Sue and our Jenny could steep all the peas." Pouring out two teas, she passed over a filled cup. "We could charge maybe fifty pence a ticket, young John Sterntees will print them off for us, and Mac Mayland can shout out the bingo numbers and put a bit of a disco on, he'll do that for next to nothing knowing Mac, just get him a couple of pints, and perhaps a packet of tabs as well."

"So that's sorted then." Mary smiled. "We'll fetch it up at Monday's meeting, and if all goes well it should be up and running by the following week." She inhaled short intakes of smoke, then, blowing excess clouds from out of the corner of her mouth, she asked, "You got any ideas?"

"Yeah, how's about getting some of the lasses out in the towns with collection buckets, I know the union have their own members out collecting, but if they are pitched say in Sunderland, there's nothing stopping us collecting in Durham or Hartlepool, or even both."

"Sounds good to me that does, Irene love, we can fetch that up at next week's meeting an'all, we'll have to liaise with the union first though." Sipping from her cup, Mary frowned in thought. "What about a monthly hamper draw, we could ask the Co-Op and Liptons to donate a couple of bottles of spirits and we could perhaps persuade the other shopkeepers to donate stuff too, you know, the likes of bottles of beer, chocolates, perfume or even the odd packet of biscuits, owt'll do that'll go towards making up a bit of a hamper, why, owt but beans, a' think everybody in the colliery's a bit beaned off at the moment."

Irene enthused, "That's a great idea, Mary! Do ya know, a' think we've still got loads of raffle ticket books unused from last year's Christmas hamper draw, so we won't have to pull out for them, a hamper draw should go down a treat, cracking idea that is, cracking idea."

Mary grinned slightly as she once again sipped delicately from her cup. "A' think we should ask the club committee to run a few domino cards in the bar, perhaps a one on a Friday and a Saturday night, and maybe a couple on a Sunday afternoon too, that will fetch a penny or two in for us. The grants from the County Council are due in this Friday too, they've been signed over and cheques returned from the Salvation Army."

Irene half smiled. "Aye and Alan's fighting our corner for more money from the union."

Mary looked over her cup with a face sated in thoughtfulness. "How are you and Alan making out these days?"

Irene's expression dropped, if ever so slight. "We're okay, but he's—"

"Not exactly Robert," broke in Mary.

"Why there's that an'all but no, it's not that, it's just he's engulfed with this strike and that, the poor bugger's always worrying about something or other, he canit just sit and relax for five minutes, on edge all the time so he is."

"He's got a lot of responsibilities ya know, love; he's bound ta be stressed, but he's a really good man all the same though, Irene."

"Orr a' nar that, Mary, it's just that it's been a long time since I've had a man around—" sighing pensive, she widened her eyes— "but we do get on, and the lads like him."

"Well, there you go then, enough said!" Changing the subject she asked, "Do ya think our Sue's looking, okay? A' think she's lost a bit of weight lately."

"She's fine, she's just on the go all the time, what with running the kitchen and that, the poor lass never stops, she's always the first one in through them club doors on a morning and the last bugger out."

"Why you're doing ya bit too though."

"Aye but I haven't got two kids to fend for afterwards like she has, and I don't do half as much as what she does. Ya've got a good'n there mind, Mary, she's just like what you were like in your younger days."

Drawing deeply on her cigarette, Mary muttered, "A' just hope it's all worth it in the end."

"What do you mean by that? You don't think we're going to lose this strike, do ya!?"

"Irene, love," she spoke in a deliberate tone, "if we were ever going to win this strike it would have been all ower and done with within the first few weeks of it starting."

Irene blew worried, saying, "Please don't say that, Mary, it's not worth thinking about." The door sounded to a heavy thump instantly interrupting the conversation before Jack, caked head to toe in red dust, entered into the room wearing only his socks and shorts. "Look at the clip of you!" raised Irene. "How the heck have ya getting in that state!?"

"Orr... a bag of cinders burst ower is when a' was lifting it."

"Where's our Tom?"

"Upstairs, the sly sod's jumped in the bath afore me! He nars a's gan'n out!" Looking at Mary he leered, brazenfaced, "If a' was only twenty years older, Mary–"

Smiling broadly, she interrupted, "If tha was twenty years older tha'd still be a decade or two ower young."

"By it's a bugger this age gap thing is, isn't it!?" was returned as he bent down and started tickling Mary around her ribcage.

"Give ower, ya daft bat!" she giggled, but he kept on tickling. "Will give ower! I'll wee mesell, mind!"

"Pack the bugger in, Jack!" reprimanded Irene.

"She loves it!" he teased before feathering a kiss on Mary's cheek, asking, "How's Jimmy, Aunt Mary?"

"He's... fine," she panted out of breath. Noticing the rips in Jack's shorts she chuckled, "Tha looks like that Geronimo in them blinking shorts, mind, Jack, all ya backside's hanging out and everything."

"Fa God's sake will ya go and change them bloody things!?" ordered Irene. "And put them straight in the bin when ya finished! You're an embarrassment at times you are, our Jack! Bloody embarrassment so you are!"

Once again Jack smiled sassy as he leant over Mary, whispering, "Are ya ganna help is out of these shorts then?" After pecking another kiss on her cheek, he picked up a biscuit ahead of strutting from the room.

"By he's a cheeky bugger!" giggled Mary. "He's just like his dad was, brazen bloody fond so he is."

Cup to mouth, Irene looked out of the window, mumbling, "He's that for sure, I'll give ya that, Mary, and he's been up to no-good again, bloody burst bag, my foot, he thinks I've just getting off an onion boat that sod does! A' wished he would settle his sell down a bit!"

"That'll never happen!" giggled Mary. Leaning over the table, she continued, "Do ya nar, a' think a might just try one of those biscuits, Irene."

ONE WEEK LATER

Although it was early August, this particular Thursday morning was unseasonably windy and overcast, resulting in an agitated North Sea hurling white topped breakers towards shore. At the heart of the pit yard, a dozen of Easington's miners loitered at the foot of one of the gigantic duff heaps whilst serving on coal delivery duty. Paired off, they took it in turns to fill up huge sacks before lifting the weighty things into the back of a clapped-out van. A brace of younger lads knelt, facing one another across a pitprop, pushing and pulling on an eager saw until a foot long piece plummeted from the end to be firstly split then bagged. Kenny Fishbron was ex-army, and a steadfast union official who was in charge of all coal deliveries throughout the community. Aged somewhere in his late forties, he was tall and thin with strongminded eyes, who proudly sported an old fashioned, teddy boy haircut which was heavily Brylcreemed to style showing bushy sideburns that extended down past his ears to end at either side of his jawline. His arms hinted at a misspent youth, exhibiting faded tattoos including an anchor, a skull and cross bones, a pair of mismatched daggers, and a brace of facing swallows that were shown just above a misshaped heart which was pierced by Cupid's arrow and partly covered with a diversity of bluey-black flowers that veiled a former sweetheart's name where once, in times long gone, it had been proudly on show for all the world to see.

The delivery van was soon loaded to capacity before Fat Bob, named as such because of his obese physique, rounded face and a multitude of floppy chins, wrestled his twenty stones from out of the driver's side door, asking, "Is this run for South, or up Wembley, Kenny?"

"South..." instructed Kenny, taking out a packet of loose tobacco to quickly knock up a perfectly formed cigarette, ending with him licking ever so slightly across a sticky edging of the skin. "... all the addresses are on the sheet a' give ya, start from Butler Street and work ya way back owers." 'It's nor fucking rocket science,' he thought to himself as he spoke.

Bob stretched out his arm, offering Kenny a light. "Divant forget, Kenny, when ya gan up the street a' want three Burdess' pies, two with onions, and one without."

Kenny inhaled deeply. "If there's none with onions left, do ya want is to get just three ordinary ones, or what?"

"Aye if ya don't mind, please," he said with a smile before retreating back to the van where he struggled to slide his huge frame into the driver's side door ahead of rocking the vehicle as he shuffled himself to comfort behind a steering wheel.

Pulling away, Bob steered around a multitude of potholes but with every smaller bump he hit, waves of fat juddered his chins, fat arms, and saggy man boobs. Jack's truck approached from the other direction and friendly grimaces were exchanged prior to a series of honks sounding as they passed. Parking up, Jack jumped from his truck and after saying his good mornings to all, he quickly joined Kenny, smiling. "How they're hinging, Kenny?"

"Not three bad, Jack, how's thee sell, bonnie lad?"

"Canit grumble, marra, canit grumble." Jack lit up, asking, "Ya couldn't do is a massive favour, could ya?"

Kenny relit his hand rolled cigarette. "It all depends on how massive this favour is, young man?"

"Ya couldn't get the lads to fill is ten bags of duff and a couple of bags of logs for is, could ya? Ma Gar's almost out of coal again."

"Why aye, that's ne bother." Counting out filled bags, Kenny faced the group, shouting, "Jumbo! Ashey! Tinky! Get the lads ta help ya load Jack's truck up with fifteen bags of duff, and half a dozen bags of logs, Ma Gar's about out of coal." The tercet raised their arms in reply before they started loading the hefty sacks into the back of Jack's truck. Kenny faced Jack, saying, "Say hello to Ma and Pop for me, and don't forget a' need them empty bags back we're running short again, ne fucker's bringing them back."

"That's ne bother, marra, I'll drop them off first thing in the morn, you're a fucking legend, Kenny."

Kenny looked Jack in the eye, asking, "How old's that fat Bob, Jack?"

"Mid-thirties, why?"

"Nowt really, it's just he's every shape a man shouldn't be, yad think the lazy bugger would do something about his weight, wadn't ya?"

"Aye wad ya!" laughed Jack. "A' wished a' had a pig as big as the bugger."

"Aye me too!" Drawing on his cigarette, Kenny inquired, "Where's the lads at anyway?"

"Our youngn's tendering to his leeks, Hoss is up yerm, and Billy's away picketing up Scotland."

"A' see it's all ower the news about that Bilston Glen Colliery, there's been hell on up there all week, apparently, boatloads of our lads were locked up yesterday. Alan Cunnings and a couple of other union officials from Horden and Murton have had to gan up ta Scotland this morning with a shit load of money."

"That's 'coss I'm not up there to keep them right, man, Kenny," joked Jack with a grin just as Kenny's facial expression dropped to uneasiness as he gazed beyond Jack into the distance. Jack glanced over his shoulder sighing, "Oh... shit!"

Empty sacks in hand, Peter Millison approached the heaps. Saying his good mornings to all except Jack, he handed over the bags. "Here's ya sacks back, Kenny."

"Cheers, Peter, lad, I'll get the lads to drop ya a couple more bags off for ya sometime ower the weekend."

"Thanks, marra, much appreciated."

Jack looked to Peter, chancing, "You okay Pete?" but it fell way short of what he was hoping for as Peter simply turned his back, totally blanking him before he walked away.

Kenny faced Jack with a slight shake of his head. "Ya spoilt a proper friendship there mind, young'n."

"A' nar that," breathed Jack all remorseful as he watched his former friend walk off in the direction of the pit gates, "but what can a' do, a' can't turn back time, Kenny, a' wished a' could but a' carn't."

"Never mind, bonnie lad, ya nar how the old saying goes, a standing cock's got no conscience." Kenny drew deeply on his cigarette, continuing, "Ya'll not be the first to let ya ard stump rule your brain, and ya certainly won't be the last neither, that's for sure."

After Jack's truck was loaded, he gave off a host of gratitudes and goodbyes before jumping into his cab and driving away without the slightest inkling that what lay ahead was going to change his life forever. Exiting the premises by means of a secondary access, Jack scattered a flock of dreamy seagulls to wing before doubling back on himself to head up Office Street. Passing by the barricaded entrance to the pit, he sounded his horn to be returned by friendly hand gestures prior to him entering onto a main road where he sped up the entire length of Ascot Street to turn a sharp right before parking up. Leaving his truck, he entered into Mike Baker's tobacco and confectionery shop where he bought a packet of ten cigarettes. Returning back to his truck, to his annoyance, ahead of him two cars were parked abreast with not quite enough of a gap left for him to pass. "Fuck!" he cursed, grinding the truck into reverse gear. Glancing over his shoulder, he quickly backed up and was steering around a blind gable end to enter back onto Seaside Lane when a heavy screeching of brakes split the morning ahead of a sudden jolt juddering Jack violently forward against the windscreen. Checking his rear mirror, he groaned grunts of annoyance at the sight of a black Mini Cooper embedded into the rear of his truck. Jumping from the cab he was way above road rage and more than ready to confront the other driver. Knocking on the side window, he shouted, "What the hell were you thinking!?" No answer... he pounded once again on the window, yelling, "How the hell did ya not see is!?" Still there was no response as a stench of burning rubber from heated tyres filled the air. "Have ya seen the size of the frigging thing!? It's not hard to miss for crying out loud!" Once again there was no reaction from the driver, so Jack pulled on the doorhandle; however, it was jammed stuck. Lodging a foot against the wing of the car his neck muscles bulged as he tugged with all he had until the door creaked open and he came across a young woman slumped facedown over the steering wheel. At once Jack's sarcasm came out: "What were ya doing, putting ya lipstick on through the rear mirror, or what!?"

"I carn't move, my legs are trapped, ya moron!" she responded, still doubled over the steering wheel.

Jack sighed lengthily, instructing, "Cover ya face up then," before he booted the dashboard, instantly releasing her legs prior to lifting her from the vehicle where he carefully stood her to her feet, asking, "are ya, okay?".

She snapped, "Am I okay!? What the hell were you thinking!? Do you know it's illegal to reverse onto a main road!?" She lifted her head to glare at him and the instant he looked into the violet-coloured depths of her eyes, 'Oh shit! Please no!' ran his thoughts. Transfixed by the radiance of these marble clear eyes that were enhanced by arched jet eyebrows and thick, black eyelashes that ended in a slight upward curl, a calmness he had never experienced before settled over him like a blanket. He noticed how a slight wind danced her long raven hair to one side, his eyes wandered slowly over her face taking in her high cheekbones before he settled on her voluminous, ruby red lips. Everything about this girl screamed perfection, and for the first time in his life he went all weak-kneed and smitten until, "Well!?" abruptly brought him back to reality.

"Well, what?" he managed to mumble, his thoughts still lost elsewhere.

"I need to see your insurances details that's what," and with each word spoken her eyes widened further almost hypnotising Jack... but now it was her who was scrutinizing him, and she too became captivated. Her cheeks flushed slightly as her breathing deepened, unknowingly she ran her hand up and down the side of her neck twiddling at a dainty crucifix necklace between thumb and finger. "... We need to swap... details."

He blew, "I'm afraid I haven't got mine on is at the moment." Not taking their eyes from one another they stood transfixed in a Cupid silence for what seemed like an eternity, when, from out of the blue, she leaned into him to gently wrap an arm around his neck before their lips touched to feather and they kissed a delicate 'Wuthering Heights' kiss. Breaking from the embrace, she melted into Jack's arms resting the side of her face up against his solid pecks. "Hi, I'm Jack Gilroy by the way," he whispered, stroking her hair from her face.

"Hello Jack Gilroy," once again she raised her eyes to meet his, "I am Lucy Arkinson."

"Pleased to meet ya, Lucy Arkinson. So, what are we going to do about all this then?"

"Tow it back to my dad's works yard I suppose," she answered unconcerned. "It's not that far, it's just on the outskirts of Hawthorn village and–"

"A' wasn't on about the car," broke in Jack.

"Oh... you wasn't?" Frowning slightly, her hand once again ran her neck. "So, what are you on about, then?"

He softly touched her face. "I don't know, but this can't end here, no way can it."

Lucy looked at him dreamily. "I know it can't, people never witness moments like this, it must be our destiny that we should meet."

"Yeah, that's exactly what it is, destiny," he said, holding her gaze, "but let's get your car back to ya Da's place afore a copper passes or my destiny will lie elsewhere."

It didn't take Jack long to part the automobiles before he lay on the ground facing upwards, and after a curse or two he managed to connect a rusty old bar between the two vehicles. Taking Lucy by the hand, he aided her up into his cab and after shuffling himself into the driver's seat he leant over, feathering a kiss onto her cheek. Forcing the vehicle into gear, he ever so slowly inched forward, making sure the towbar had taken up the strain of the mini. After lighting up, he offered the packet, but

Lucy refused with a shake of her head, then smiling slightly, he joked; "A' still say this was all your fault like."

She breathed, "What, the crash, or the kiss?"

"Both!" He softly caressed the back of her hand. "Seriously though, you are alright, no broken bones or owt?"

"I'm fine." Holding in her laughter she side eyed Jack with a straight face, baiting, "I suppose one day all this will be a funny story to share with our children, how their daft father tried to kill their poor mother."

"Aye will it!" After laughing aloud he chuckled, "Especially when we come to the part of the story where a' told ya a' wasn't insured!"

Her expression fell into a furrow. "What do ya mean, you wasn't insured!?"

"Sorry... but I'm not insured."

Scowling deeply, she huffed, "You're not some sought of Gypsy trying to con his way out of trouble, are you?"

"Shut up! Me a Pikey! Why, not likely, I'm just a simple coal miner who's currently on strike."

Lucy deliberated for a length of time before her frown faded to be replaced by a fully blown smile. She whooped, "Never mind! I'll just have to make up some cock and bull story to my insurance company involving a collision with a tree, or a wall or something else along those lines, it'll be a bit of a sod on my no claims bonus like, but what the heck." She raised an eyebrow rather blasé before delicately resting her head on Jack's shoulder.

Hoss' steps were unhurried as he carefully balanced a tray loaded with a steamy bowl of soup, a single tablespoon, two slices of bread, a glass filled to threequarters with gassy lemonade, and a concoction of various coloured tablets. Entering into the sitting room, he smiled at his father who was sat content on a dogeared chair watching the midday news on an outdated black and white television set. Hoss lowered the tray onto his father's lap. "There ya are, Da, mind how ya gan, that soup's piping hot." Sitting into a worn sofa that matched the rest of the old-fashioned furniture, he once again beamed at his old man. "It's pea and ham, ya favourite."

"Thanks, son... yar a good'n." Breaking a slice of bread into four, he asked, "Have ya put pepper in it?" Hoss nodded in reply just as the door creaked ahead of Margret breezing her way into the house, clutching shopping bags. "Aye...aye!" puffed Joe slightly out of breath, "If it's not Florence Nightingale herself... did ya get me tabs, pet?"

"Yeah, forty Woodbines," she answered, raising her eyes. "Do ya not fancy changing to filtered cigarettes, Joe? They're not as bad for ya chest as what them coffin nails are."

"No, tar, I've been smoking... Woodbines ever since a' was knee high to a grasshopper... and I'm not ganna change now." He slurped soup. "But thanks all... the same for the thought, though."

"Please ya self," she half moaned, shaking her head. "I'm going to have to hurry, Hoss, I'm supposed to be picking the bairn up in fifteen minutes." Rummaging through the carriers she removed a large paper bag. "Ya prescription's here, Joe, they've supplied you with an extra inhaler, you have to take it on a night-time just before bed, so don't forget." Joe may have raised an eyebrow in response to her words, but he was far too lost at what was showing on the TV. She turned to Hoss with a prolonged sigh. "Hoss, remind him on to take that new inhaler please." Hoss nodded conformation as Margret once again addressed Father, "Joe! Ya've got three inhalers to take each day now, as well as all ya other stuff, I'll put them in the medicine draw for ya."

"Cheers, bonnie lass," he said, dipping his bread into the soup until it sagged soggy.

Margret crossed the room where underfoot a threadbare carpet rested on top of a canvas flooring that smelt of slight mustiness. Opening a middle drawer of three belonging to a bulky sideboard, she emptied out the contents of the bag to join strong, morphine-based painkillers, and other medications. Grinning slightly, she eyed a multitude of framed photos arranged in a line across the sideboard top with most showing Hoss and his father surrounded by best in breed pedigree beasts from several far-flung County Shows which they had visited over the years. But it was one photograph in particular that grabbed Margret's attention, it was a happy snapshot showing Hoss as a small child standing all joyful in the middle of both his parents with all three dressed in swimwear whist holidaying at a seaside resort, perhaps Scarborough or maybe it was Whitby – no, it was definitely Scarborough as the Grand Hotel was prominent in the backdrop. More photos were on show along the entire length of another oak cabinet alongside a miner's lamp, a large crystal fruit dish which was married to a set of smaller serving bowls, and a wooden transistor radio, though ancient, still worked flawlessly. Above this sideboard hung a portrait of Hoss' mother looking ever so beautiful in her wedding gown, hanging alongside was a hoary photo displaying Joe's parents standing side by side with facial expressions reminiscent to that of feuding neighbours rather than actual husband and wife. Adjacent displayed the only photograph on show to be shot in colour, it was taken at Wembley Stadium back in 1973 boasting a victorious Sunderland football team posing in a couple of rows with Bob Stokoe, their joyous manager, up front hoisting the FA cup high above his balding head. Picking up shopping bags, Margret left the sitting room to enter into a kitchen where she loaded a few essentials into wall cupboards with one-or two doors hanging askew due to broken hinges. Resting a paper bag onto a chipped bench top, she shouted through, "There's a couple of them Burdess' pies here for ya, Hoss."

"Thanks, have they got onions in them?"

"Yeah, a' think so," she answered before sniffing the contents, confirming, "smells like they have anyway!"

"Champion!" he said as the front door juddered open ahead of Tom stepping into the sitting room. Hoss' face lit up. "All right, young'n?"

"Aye." Tom looked to Joe. "How's the birds fleeing, Joe?"

"Not too grand actually... how's ya leeks?"

"They're coming along canny," he replied, sitting aside Hoss. Tom once again glimpsed Joe. "By, that soup smells nice, Joe, Pea and Ham, is it?"

"Yeah, and ya right... it is nice." He dunked his bread, asking, "Do ya... want a dip like?"

"No, tar, thanks, you get it down ya."

Joe looked to Tom with an inquisitive smile. "Well, Thomas Gilroy... I've heard through the grapevine... that your leeks are a lot better... than just canny."

"They're not too bad a' suppose," he answered, shrugging his shoulders.

"Not too bad!" enthused Hoss. "Tack no notice of him, Da, they're absolutely massive, the best he's ever grawn."

Margret came to the kitchen doorway, asking, "Do ya want a cuppa, Tom?"

"No, tar, thank you," he replied politely. Looking around, he coughed, asking, "Yas haven't seen owt of our Jack, have yas?" They took it in turn to shake their heads before Margret turned to re-enter into the kitchen. Tom lit up a cigarette/ "Ma says he went out to get Ma Garr some coal early this morning and there's been no sign of him since."

"He's probably sold the coal and gone back for some more, man," said Hoss unconcerned. "Tha nars what he's like." Glancing at his father's meal he looked over to the kitchen door, shouting, "Margret! Do them pies need reheating like!?"

"Yeah, should a' put them in the oven for ya?"

"Aye, tar, if ya don't mind, is there any peas?"

"Aye but ya'll have to serve it yourself, 'I'm off now."

"Right owe, love, ne bother." The big man smiled.

Margret skipped from kitchen to sitting room. Pecking a quick kiss on Hoss, she leaned over feathering a kiss on Joe before smiling all around. "See yas later then." Leaving the house, she paused at the doorway, beaming. "See ya at seven tonight then, Hoss, should I get a video in for us to watch?"

He grinned in return, replying, "Yeah, that'll be nice, see ya the night, love."

"See you tonight, bye!" She left the house, gently closing the door behind her.

"Ya've got a... good'n there, mind, son," praised Joe, lifting the tray onto a wobbly side table. "Ya want to try...and hang onto her, girls like her are... as rare as hens' teeth these days." A close-up image of Margaret Thatcher appeared on the television, at once Joe struggled to his feet, switching off the set. "She's got a right set of... balls on her that Margaret bugger has."

"Who, my Margret?" frowned Hoss, lost.

"Nar, not your Margret, ya daft bat... that Margaret bloody Thatcher... if she's not a descendant from bloody Hitler... I'll suck a pint of bloody paint through... a one ended bloody straw."

Tom laughed. "Steady on, Joe, there's a canny few bloodys kicking about in that sentence."

Joe lit up a cigarette, coughing. "There's not enough bloody... bloodys in the bugger if ya ask me. 'A divant nar which one... a' hate the most, her or that frigging... Home Secretary of hers!"

"Who, Leon Brittan?" broke in Hoss.

"Aye that's the bugger! A' bet... he's a right prervert he is!"

Tom voiced, "Do ya not mean pervert, Joe?"

"What's the difference!?" snapped Joe. "Prervert... pervert, it macks ne difference he'll... be a one for sure, he's just like Enoch Powell is, and why's that daft looking bugger always... hanging around them for?"

Hoss frowned. "Which daft looking bugger? Who ya on about, Da?"

"Him with the lang bleached blond hair, man! He's always... wearing gold, he runs them marathon things for children's charities–"

"Jimmy Savile?" broke in Tom.

"That's the bugger!" raised Joe. "He follows the... Tories around like a lapdog, he's like a fly around... shit with them."

"A' quite like Jimmy Savile," said Hoss.

"Don't talk sa bloody.... fond," snapped Joe, "the bugger's... as dodgy as France!"

"He's canny good on Top of the Pops though, Da," defended Hoss.

"Top of the Pops... my arse!" Inhaling smoke, Joe coughed. "Anyway, there's never been nowt decent on there... since that daft... bugger shot John Lennon, in fact the last time a' watched Top of the... Pops, Rolf Harris was on it singing, 'Two Little Boys'."

"Was it not 'Tie Me Kangaroo Down Sport', Joe?" asked Tom. "That was Rolf Harris's biggest hit."

"Nor it was definitely 'Two Little Boys', 'coss he had... two young kiddies up on the stage with one of them... sat on his knee."

"A' like Rolf Harris." Tom smiled. "He's a canny painter tha nars."

"A' like him an'll," agreed Joe.

"Tha never nars, if ya lucky, Joe, he might be on Top of the Pops the night," put in Tom, "it'll be on ya telly at half past seven on BBC One."

Joe frowned. "Who, Rolf Harris?"

Tom laughed aloud. "Nor, not him, that Jimmy Savile, man!"

"Jimmy ballicks!" snapped the old man. "If he was in the yard... I'd draw the bloody curtains on... the bugger."

Mother nature had painted a spectacular dusk over Easington, filling the sky with quixotic shades of amber. Meals balanced on their knees, Irene and Tom sat watching, but then again not really watching, television. "What time ya setting off Saturday for Pat's then, son?"

"Early as possible, afore five a' hope."

"Why, you drive carefully, and no speeding." Irene sat thinking up motherly questions before asking the obvious, "Are you two still getting on alright?"

"Why aye, we're champion."

"Are you getting on with her dad and stepmum okay?"

"Yeah, they're both lovely."

"Good; things will be better when the strike's finished with ya know, son."

"A' know that, Ma." Clenching a remote, he switched channels to Top of the Pops just as Tears for Fears were on stage strutting their stuff.

"Turn that off, Tom!?"

"Mam... man!"

"Why turn it down a bit then!?" The sound of the door firstly opening... then after a much longer pause than usual, it closed immediately, drawing Irene's attention. "Here's bugger lugs now, well he can put his own tea out 'coss I'm not doing it!" Jack paused at the sitting room doorway. Looking him up and down, she scorned, "Where the hell have you been? Ya've been out all day and half the pigging night!?" Her scolding ceased the instant she noticed a glazed expression showing on her son's face. "What's wrong?"

He shook his head. "There's nowt wrong, Ma, a' just want you to meet somebody, this is... Lucy." Lucy entered the room looking all innocent and lovely in a knee length flowery dress, matching cardigan, and soft sandals.

"My good Lord," sighed Irene, taken aback by the stranger's beauty. Resting her plate to the carpet, she stood with arms stretched out. "Come here, you." Lucy crossed the room and within an embrace Irene knew this girl was the one for her son. "I'm Irene, or Ma."

"Pleased to meet you... Ma." She smiled.

"Put her down, man, Ma," joked Jack.

"Sorry," responded Irene, releasing her grip.

Tom rose to his feet; after a wink of approval at his brother, he opened his arms, greeting Lucy with a soft hug. "Hello Lucy, I'm Tom, the big brother."

"Hello Tom, pleased to meet you."

"The pleasure's all mine, flowerpots," he whispered to her ear as they parted.

Irene stood tearful, after composing herself she looked at Jack. "There's some toad in the hole in the oven."

"Cheers, Ma," he said, casting a grimace that overflowed with affection, and once again tears of joy filled Irene's eyes. Lucy frowned at Jack. "Or, sorry, Lucy," he said, grinning widely, "it's at the top of the stairs, first on ya right."

The instant she left the room, they sat at their usual seats and started picking at their meals as Jack lit up a cigarette.

Irene glanced at Tom with a concerned frown, whispering, "Ya didn't forget to clean that bath out after ya, did ya, son?"

"It's clean, man, Ma!" Tom nodded accusingly at Jack. "It's him who doesn't clean the bath out after him, not me."

"Aye a' do, a' always clean it out."

"Do ya heckers, like!"

"Aye a' do!" retorted Jack, whilst drawing on his cig.

"Nor, ya dinit–"

"Alright!" broke in Irene. "As lang as it's clean a's not bothered who's cleaned it out." Facing Jack, she cut into her pudding, asking, "How did you manage to meet her, son?"

"We just bumped into each other up the street, and a' literally mean bumped into each other, we had a crash."

"What, a car crash!?" she asked, concerned.

"Aye."

"Are yas okay?"

"Yeah, we're fine."

"What's the truck like?" asked Tom, munching his way through a sausage.

"It's alright, back bumper's a bit damaged but it's nowt to worry about, I'll straighten it up sometime ower the weekend."

"Don't forget to water me leeks and onions on Saturday evening, mind, Jack?"

"A' nar, stop worrying, man!"

"She's lovely, mind, son," muttered Irene, "she's the pip of a young Liz Taylor."

"That's what a' was thinking, and a' really think she could be the one, Ma."

"Freight train hit ya, did it, son?" she whispered, wearing a huge grin.

"Too right it did! Wobbly legs, the blinking lot! I actually..." He stopped himself short, saying "... it doesn't matter."

Irene encouraged, "No, come on, son, spit it out, you actually what?"

"Blushed," muttered Jack, "a' actually blushed for a brief moment when we first spoke."

"Told ya so." Irene smiled all motherly. "Anyhows she must be the one for ya, 'coss you've never brought a girl home to meet is afore." Once again resting her plate to the carpet, she rose to her feet, saying, "Watch our Mick doesn't eat that, I'll go and put yas a bit tea out, but eat it at the table, a' don't want the lass thinking we're the Clampetts."

Tom looked at Jack. "Treat this one right, kidda, she looks nice, where does she live?"

"Do ya know Smithy's ard farm at Hawthorn?"

"Aye, the one up by the Dene with all the land?"

"Aye, why she lives there, they only shifted in two weeks ago, they originate from somewhere up Washington way a' think."

"Is her family farmers, like?"

"Nor, he's a driller, he uses part of the land for a compound, the rest he rents out to a neighbouring farmer."

"What's he drill like?" asked Tom, chewing on his food.

"Bloody git big holes!" Jack laughed. "What do ya think!?"

"A' nar that, ya donk, but what for, and where?"

"All ower the place, he's got half a' dozen rigs on the go, he drills rock samples for building firms and industries like ICI and that."

"Clever man," Tom smiled.

"He is, and he's a canny bloke too, down to earth as owt, he's just like us, tha nars, like normal and that." The two brothers were exchanging smiles when Lucy entered the room. Jack shuffled along the sofa, giving her room to sit. Smiling, he drew on his cigarette, asking, "Did ya find it all right then?"

"Yeah, thanks," she said softly.

"Good, a' hope ya pulled the chain after ya, mind."

"Pulled the chain?" She frowned, puzzled.

"Yeah," sighed Jack, "like flushed the toilet!"

"Of course, I did," she whispered, blushing embarrassment as Tom sat shaking his head at his brother's words.

NEXT NIGHT

A full moon ghosted the night, casting enough moonlight for Jack to make his way from the pit premises. Pushing a bicycle laden with sacks of duff, he followed a meandering pathway taking him by silhouettes of wooden garages before he entered, then exited, the dimness of the first bridge; gritting his teeth, he struggled to force the old boneshaker up the short, cobbled incline ahead of him turning a sharp left to traipse the bottom of East estate.

Approaching Chandler Street, an unnatural flickering light immediately drew his attention, frowning slightly it suddenly dawned on him that this glow was coming from flames shooting from a housefire. Flinging his bicycle to one side, he sprinted up the street; drawing nearer, he realized it was Peter and Debbie Millison's home that was ablaze. Dashing into the yard, he kicked down a front door ahead of entering inside where he dodged scorching flames, screaming, "Debbie! Peter! Debbie... Peter!!"

"We're up here!" shrieked a distressed Debbie. Fighting his way through heated flames, he scampered up a staircase to a landing where he came across Debbie who was knelt over her unconscious husband trying to drag him from a bedroom. She sobbed, "Help him, Jack, a' carn't budge him!"

"Where's the bairn?" asked Jack in between bottomless coughs.

"He's staying at me Mam's!" she coughed, clinging onto Peter. Jack pulled her away to protests of, "No! No! No! No! Please help him first, Jack! Please, please!"

"Debbie," spoke Jack in a calm tone, "we'll have to get you out of here first, it'll be a lot quicker, but I'm promising you now, I'll come back for Peter no matter what." He removed his jumper, wrapping it around her face before aiding her down the stairs and out into the safety of the street.

A female neighbour approached to comfort Debbie with a hug. "I've phoned for the fire brigade, love, they're on their way."

Debbie looked at Jack with a dire expression, pleading, "Please, Jack! Please bring Peter out!"

"Don't worry," he reassured her before quickly re-entering into the house just as an intense fireball burst out all of the downstairs windows, startling a jumpy Debbie, and a small gathering of onlookers. After an eternity of only a few minutes,

Jack emerged through the smoke, and to Debbie's relief he had Peter slung over his shoulder in a firemen's lift. Reaching the street, he delicately lowered Peter to the floor just as an almighty waft of flames engulfed the whole frontage of the house. "Ya safe now, Peter, mate."

Peter managed to mumble, "Thanks… marra," before he rattled a sequence of deep chesty coughs.

"There's no need to thank me." Jack smiled. "I'm sure ya would have done exactly the same if the boot was on the other foot." Peter reached out, taking Jack by the hand and the two former friends exchanged affable smiles.

Debbie sat, placing Peter's head on her lap. "Thank you, Jack," she muttered through tears, "a' thought I'd lost him there." Sobbing openly, she leant forward, pecking kisses all over her husband's blackened face and forehead.

Hoss was heading home after an evening spent at Margret's house when in the distance a fire engine sped, sirens blaring with flashing red and blue lights piercing the night. Arching a corner, he stood frozen as he witnessed Tony Ward and Marie kissing passionately at the doorway of Billy's home. Parting from the embrace, they briefly stood hand in hand before entering into the house to close the door behind them. Hoss' first instinct was to go and thrash the living daylights out of Tony, but, to his better judgement, he turned and walked off in the opposite direction, cursing, "The dirty bastards!" Pausing in his stride, he once again contemplated turning back to confront them, but he had another change of mind and reluctantly sauntered away.

This particular Saturday afternoon at Easington beach banks was blessed in balmy sunshine, larks filled the sky with a song of summer trill, as skittish yellowhammers and linnets twittered back and forth through dense yellow-topped thicket which skirted a field bursting with golden corn that would willingly waltz at the slightest hint of a breeze. Nose glued to the ground, Mick ran around, constantly wagging his tail while Jack and Lucy, both dressed in shorts and tee-shirts, enjoyed the peacefulness of their stroll along the top of the cliff tops with Lucy lovingly linking Jack's upper arm. Descending onto the beach, they laughed as they witnessed school children swimming to one side of a group of enthusiastic fishermen who cast anticipated lines in search of overdue mackerel. Mick paused in stride, his head held motionless with one paw raised, then, dashing ahead he barked constantly, scattering a flock of resting kittiwakes to air before he returned all proud to heel. It was high tide, and there was no hint whatsoever of the submerged twelve foots. Further along the beach, queuing kids took it in turns to dive or backflip into the sea from off the top of the rusty pit pipe as scores of people, both young and old, rummaged at the water's edge in search of coal, with each clasping onto their own plastic buckets.

Jack picked up a stick, flinging it, and once again Mick's eagerness set him away barking nonstop; after retrieving the object he returned to rest it at Lucy's feet. Picking up the baton, she cast it for as far as she could but regrettably her aim wasn't too great, and the thing landed in the water, closely followed by the plunging dog. Every time, Mick paddled near the stick, his frantic splashing drove the thing further out to sea, and with him being the typical daft Jack Russell terrier that he was, he followed. Lucy became worried; shielding her eyes from the sun she looked on before turning to Jack. "Will he be all right, Jack? He's getting pretty far out."

"Will he heckers be all right!" griped Jack. "He's as thick as two short planks that mutt is."

"Orr stop it, he's not thick."

Jack cast a couple of uneasy glances at Lucy, saying, "Lucy, man, he's as daft as a frigging brush!"

She concentrated back on Mick who had drifted to well over thirty metres from the shore and was now struggling to keep his head above the water. "Jack!" Panic crept into her voice. "I think he may be drowning! Please go and get him!"

"Do ya nar!" moaned Jack, kicking off his training shoes. "A' shouldn't have fetched him in the first place!" Quickly stripping his tee-shirt over his head, Lucy couldn't help but sneak a peek at his tanned, muscular physique and washboard sixpack; wide eyed she blushed slightly in response before puffing a slight sigh. Entering the water, Jack shook his head in a form of a protest, then wading up to his chest, he blew his cheeks in response to the coldness before stylishly breast-stroking out to grab hold of Mick. Lucy looked on impressed as he calmly swam back to shore, holding his dog in one arm. The instant Mick left Jack's grasp he shook water from his coat ahead of running off barking out warnings at a couple of disrespectful jackdaws who had the audacity of trying to nap in his presence. Jack shivered, bleating, "It's as card as Thatcher's heart in that thing! Bloody freezing so it is!"

Lucy stood besotted, just looking into Jack's eyes; stepping into him, they kissed lengthily and as they parted, she whispered in his ear, "You're my hero, Jack Gilroy."

Jack ran his fingers through his dripping hair, chuckling, "Hero, my foot!"

"You are my hero, what with you entering into that blazing inferno last night to rescue them poor people, then today saving Mick."

Jack played it down. "Lucy, any man worth his salt would have done what a' did last night, and saving our Mick, well, it's not as if I entered into some shark infested waters, is it?"

"Well, you're still my hero." Her cheeks reddened to a blush as once again her eyes ran his torso. "Jack, if I told you something, will you promise not to freak out on me?"

"Ya not a Tory, are ya?" he joked.

"No!"

"A Newcastle fan!? 'Coss that's just as bad."

"No, I'm neither." She smiled.

"Everything's okay then, come on, spit it out, I'm all ears."

"Promise you won't freak out?"

He laughed. "A' promise a' won't! Stop being daft!"

Lucy took Jack by the hands, briefly closing her eyes she sighed lengthily, paused, then with eyes now widened to a twinkle, she breathed, "I love you."

Holding her gaze, Jack tenderly stroked the side of her face. "Good, because you're my life, Lucy, I've adored you ever since I first clapped eyes upon you in that crappy car of yours, and I always will." She stood almost hypnotised as he tenderly moved her fringe from out of her eyes. "And it would be an honour, and a privilege, to walk through life with you at my side." Again he moved her hair from her face, whispering, "My heart is yours, Lucy, and it always will be."

Tearful, she hugged his waist. "Wow! I didn't expect that response." Nuzzling him tighter, she whispered, "Mother and Father are away till Monday, and if you wanted, but only if you wanted, you could stop over for a couple of nights?"

Jack went back to being Jack. "Well, that all depends on whether or not you're trying to seduce is."

Her eyes lifted to his with her purring, "Would you mind so much if I did?"

Another cloudless sky had created a fine Monday morning over Easington. An ever-increasing flock of stray pigeons circled the pit shafts in unison as Tom, Hoss, Billy, Lemsip, Sizzler, Oddy and Pinky stood in conversation by the cabin. The timbre of a vehicle pulling up at the far side of the barricade instantly brought about Hoss' curiosity and he rushed to the blockade. Peeping through a gap, he caught a glimpse of Lucy and Jack who were sat kissing in the front seats of an old farm type Land Rover. Giggling aloud, he waved the others over and they looked on sniggering until Jack left the vehicle and they quickly retreated to stand by the cabin. Jack weaved his way through the barrier, approaching them, and they erupted into a piss-taking, if way out of tune, version of a Donny Osmond hit, *'And they called it, Puppy Love! Just because we're in our teens...'* Jack shook his head, breaking into a grin, he muttered, "Ya daft twats!" and the instant he joined them, Hoss wrestled him into a bear hug, ruffling his hair to an untidy tangle. "Watch the hair, man, Hoss!" groaned Jack.

"Who's a proper hero!?" whooped the big man, releasing Jack from his grip. "And when am I ganna meet this love of ya life!?"

Billy broke in, "Aye w-w-when are we ganna m-m-meet her?"

"Well!" laughed Jack, running a comb through his hair. "If yas come round ours about teatime the night ya might just get to meet her."

Oddy offered his hand to Jack. "Ya did well the other night, our Jack, those two would have been goners for sure."

"Cheers, cuz," said Jack as they stood shaking hands.

Oddy broke away, pretending to punch Jack in the stomach; he chuckled. "So, the mighty tree has timbered at last then, eh!?"

"Aye, a' suppose it has," he returned with a slight laugh of his own.

Oddy grinned. "Why it happens to the best of us, Jack. What's her name then?"

"Lucy," he answered, bringing a smile to his cousin's face.

"Has me Aunty Irene met her yet?"

"Aye, she loves her," returned Jack.

Pinky patted Jack on his back. "Well done the other night at Peter's, Jack."

"Cheers, Pinky," he responded just as the union office window creaked open and Alan summoned both Jack and Tom to the office. "What the fuck have we done now," groaned Jack under his breath.

Tom and Jack entered a smoke-filled room to find Alan on a phone with a look of anguish sketched across his face. He pointed to a couple of seats and the brothers sat in silence until he finished off the phone conversation with a lengthy sigh. Tom looked him in the eye, asking, "What's wrong, Alan? Ya look like ya've just seen a ghost!"

Alan puffed his cheeks; after running his hand over his head he shook as he lit up yet another cigarette, saying, "There's a scab going into work tomorrow."

"A scab!?" responded Tom. "What, here!?"

"Aye here!" Alan heaved heavily. "And it's Paul Wickson, of all people."

"What, fucking Wicky the woolyback!?" jumped in Jack. "He's a fucking psycho that twat is!" He too lit up a cig. "Isn't he due in court for throwing half a pavement slab through a police car window injuring a policewoman?"

"Not any more he's not," stretched from Alan, "his solicitors have struck up a deal with the police, if they drop all charges, he says he'll gan back to work."

"Is that lawful like, Alan?" Tom frowned. "Dropping all the charges and that?"

"Apparently it is now, and it wadn't surprise me if the Home Secretary was involved in all this, Tom."

"Good luck to them!" enthused Jack. "'Coss the fucker will never enter through them gates, I'll kill the scabby twat first!"

Tom now lit up a cigarette, asking, "The colliery manager did promise if anyone returned to work that they would have to enter through the main gates though, didn't he?"

"He did," confirmed Alan, "but is it out of his hands now?" He squinted narrow eyed, asking, "Have you got ya car, Tom?"

"Aye."

"Do is a favour, young'n, gan up ya Uncle Ref Garside's, he's got a CB radio receiver with four handsets, fetch them down to the office."

"What, now?"

"Aye, if ya don't mind, please, and Jack, will you pop up Gumpy's for is? Tell him to come straight to the office I'm calling a full committee meeting."

"Aye ne bother," answered Jack.

"Get ya sells away then, and Tom, when yas get back here a' want yas to sit in on the meeting with us." The two brothers stood honoured before hurrying from the room. Alan once again sighed prolonged, picking up the phone he dialled and impatiently waited for an answer. Hanging up, he then redialled... "Benny! Thank God ya there, ya need to come down to the office at once... I've called an emergency meeting that's why ... I'll tell ya when ya get here, but mack sharp please."

The wonderful aroma of dinner filled the air at the Colliery Club singing end, which as usual, was crammed to the rafters with people while outside the main doors a lengthy queue had formed awaiting a third sitting. Jack and the lads had finished off their meals and were standing to leave when Hoss peeled away to speak to Irene who was stood in a chain of volunteers serving food. "Can a have a quick word, Ma?"

"Of course ya can, son, but it will have to be quick, ya can see how busy we are." Quickly leaving the serving line, she took him to one side. "What's up, love?"

"Well, a' dinit nar how to say this."

She encouraged: "Just say what's on ya mind, love, but try and hurry, I haven't time to dilly about."

"Well." He puffed his cheeks. "Last Friday night when a' was on my way home from Margret's a' stumbled upon Tony Ward and Marie kissing outside Billy's house before they went hand in hand inside when Billy was stuck up Scotland picketing."

She gasped. "Was it a proper kiss, like!?"

"Aye, it was a full-blown snog."

"Dear God, what's Tony's poor parents going to say when they find out he's having a fling with his own aunty. Ya haven't told the rest of the lads yet, have ya?" Hoss shook his head. She sighed prolonged, whispering, "Good, best say nowt for now, son, it'll break poor Billy's heart."

"That's what a' thought."

Sue shouted, "Irene!"

"I'm coming, Sue!" Walking away, Irene glanced over her shoulder, saying, "Keep it shtum, Hoss, keep it shtum," before she rejoined the rest of the servers to take up her post.

At a side fire exit door, Ray Graveson, a tall, lean-framed man who was renowned throughout the northeast clubland as a fine singer entered into the hall followed by his lovely wife Margaret and an entourage of three fellow volunteers with each carrying boxes filled to the brim with groceries. Ray and Margaret were a well-respected couple who were held in the highest esteem throughout Easington and Horden as they worked tirelessly to raise both money and groceries for the striking miners. Irene waved another girl onto the serving chain ahead of her joining Ray at the back of the room where they exchanged affable smiles before they entered into the kitchen area.

FOLLOWING DAY

It was a searing August morning at Easington Colliery. Tetchy blackbirds winged raucously from bush to bush through dense shrubbery. At a North Sea backdrop, a huge oil tanker blew grey smoke as it languidly headed in the direction of the horizon whilst closer to shore, a cargo ship loaded to capacity with stacked up metal containers, trudged its way southbound en route to the nearby port of Teesside.

Outside the pit, more than a thousand pickets had gathered shoulder to shoulder, stretching from sick note corner, past the telephone box, before descending the length of Office Street to Widen Way beyond the colliery offices' steps before ending just below the blockaded pit gates.

Wearing a face sketched in determination, Alan was at the forefront of this mass, clasping a CB handset in one hand and holding a half-smoked cigarette between thumb and finger in the other. To his left grouped Jack, Tom, Hoss, Pinky, and Oddy, while to his immediate right stood Gary Gray, known locally as Urko, who was a twenty-five-year-old amateur heavyweight boxer and a real mountain of a man, flaunting humongous shoulders and looking all intimidating with his short, cropped hair, and matching black stubble. To Urko's right was his elder brother David, a good-looking lad who displayed a mullet hairstyle that was highlighted in blond tips; he also had a nickname, it was Speedy, an epithet he had inherited down from his father, due to his old man's past glories in the sport of motorcycle racing. Next to Speedy stood Fred Watson, the Grays' twenty-four-year-old brother-in-law, who was a pretty powerfully built individual himself, flaunting broad shoulders, enormous hands, and strong, stone-like facial features.

Alan spoke into the handset. "Alpha one to Alpha two, owt happening?"

"Alpha two to Alpha one, that's a negative," crackled back.

Alan clicked the radio. "Alpha one to Alpha three, confirm your situation?"

"Alpha three to Alpha one, all quiet here."

"Alpha one to Alpha four, clarify your situation please?"

"Alpha f-f-four, to A-A-Alpha one, ten four for a c-c-copy, no signs of big b-b-bear."

Alan looked to Tom, sighing, "Billy's been watching Convoy again, frigging big bear, do ya–"

"Alpha two to Alpha one," sputtered over the radio interrupting the banter, "they are here, they've just passed Liptons and are heading in your direction, there's boatloads of the fuckers!"

"That's a roger, Alpha two," answered Alan. Looking around, he shouted, "This is it, lads! They're on their way!" and within an instant the atmosphere had turned electric. A convoy of police vehicles inched Seaside Lane onto Ascot Street and was heading towards the awaiting mass when groups of extra policemen sprang from the vans, joining hundreds of their colleagues who were already stood in rank.

Surrounded by battle-clad SPG officers, chief inspector Purny, a tall, wiry man with narrow eyes, thin lips, and a large turned up nose, walked side by side with his burly sergeant who flashed a thick moustache and a snout that had obviously been broken at some point in the past as it crooked hideously to one side. They marched forward to face Alan. Purny looked Alan directly in the eye, smirking, "So, Mr Cunnings, I see Scargill's army is out in force today."

"You bet ya bottom lip it is!" replied Alan. Nodding towards the accumulated policemen, he broke into a sarcastic smirk. "See Thatcher's boot boys are up early too?"

Purny scanned the scene, saying, "I presume you lot won't disperse peacefully and let this man go about his business and go into work?"

"Ya presume right," sneered Alan.

Purny leant nose to nose with Alan, and with no emotion in his voice he grinned, threatening, "Why I am going to promise you one thing for certain, if this situation escalates into any form of violence whatsoever, you, my good sir, will be the first man to be arrested, do you understand!?"

Smiling wryly, Alan said, "Do ya worst, Purny! Bring it on!"

"Aye, do ya worst, twat!" growled Urko. "'Coss you'll be the first fucker to be levelled!"

Jack stood eyeballing the sergeant, mocking, "Hey fuck face, I'm ganna smash that fucking conk of yours back the other way, ya bent nosed bastard!" and on them words the chief inspector, sergeant and their entourage of SPG officers turned, retreating back to rejoin their colleagues.

A hive of activity sprung from the police line ending in a van reversing to the middle of the ranks before Paul Wickson was almost dragged from out of the backdoors to be surrounded by police officers. 'Scab! Scab! Scab! Scab!' chanted the pickets as they drove forward, forcing the police onto their backfoot. Truncheons battered heads but still the pickets pressed on. One officer screamed high pitched as he dropped to his knees, clutching his face with blood streaming from both his nose and his mouth. Still the pickets surged forward, leaving behind both fallen pickets and policemen. The burly police sergeant, who Alan had previously faced, grabbed him by what little hair he had until Urko came to his rescue, and with one almighty uppercut he sent the sergeant's helmet flying as the hapless cop dropped to the road before Speedy put the boot in. Jack forced a screaming cop to the floor then set about kicking him until all his screams ceased. To Jack's left, Fred Watson ran another officer headfirst into a wall and he sank to a pathway. A huge officer jabbed the end of his bludgeon directly into Oddy's eyes, but he quickly recovered to boot the cop in his nuts and as he folded forward a knee was brought up into the officer's face, sending him sprawling to the ground before Oddy quicky straddled him, pounding his face with heavy blows. Pinky leant another cop over a garden wall at Office Street and started hammering him around his head and face until he slid lifeless to the pathway. The lads had forced their way through the heart of the mayhem to get to within a few feet of Wickson, fists were flying everywhere, in return batons were splitting heads. Hoss barged a couple of SPG officers to one side, creating enough of a gap for Jack to advance to within touching distance of Wickson, when suddenly a blast of three high-pitched whistles signalled ahead of a police van speedily reversing down the street before screeching to a stop, allowing two officers to bundle Wickson into the back of the vehicle ahead of it hurtling away. The surging pickets eased off to a chorus of, '*The miners united, will never be defeated! The miners united, will never be defeated!*'

Aiding their injured comrades to their feet, cheers echoed the street due to the sight of the police convoy retreating up Seaside Lane and out of sight. At one side of the street, Sizzler lay motionless with Lemsip knelt over him, but after a few seconds he had recovered enough to scramble back to his feet with blood pouring from both a huge gash above his left eye and an additional deep laceration to the back of his head. Tom turned to Jack, hooting, "A' thowt ya had that Wickson there, mind, young'n!"

"Me too, Jack!" enthused Alan. "Ya was only inches away off nabbing the bastard!"

"A' nar!" whooped Jack. "Another surge and I'd have had the scabby twat!" Oddy joined them, parading an injured eye that had already swollen to a slit. "Canny eye ya got there, cuz," said Jack, inspecting his injury.

Oddy chuckled, "It's nowt compared to what a' did to the fucker who did it, Jack, a' twattered the cunt stupid."

Urko, Speedy and Fred joined them. "Well done, lads!" praised Alan. Smiling gratification at Urko, he cleared his throat. "Thanks a lot, Urko, ya well and truly saved my bacon there, marra."

"It was nowt." He winked untroubled. "In fact a' quite enjoyed it! Will they be coming back for more?"

"A' doubt it," stretched from Alan, "I've never seen coppers turn tail so fast in all my life."

ONE WEEK LATER

It was a fine, sunny Tuesday morning at Easington, and a few days had passed since the last of several attempts to muscle Wickson back into work had once again failed, so Tom came to a snap decision to drive down to the Peak District to visit Pat for a few days at her father's farm.

Tom's cross-Pennines journey was lengthy yet surprisingly pleasant. Leaving the greyness of a motorway, he drove through miles of winding country roads where canopies of heavy thicket and tall roadside trees constantly flickered from light to shade then back to light again. After joining a narrow road leading him up to the roof of the Dales, he drove unhurried for a few miles taking in spectacular views of rolling hills before he joined a tarmac track which guided him towards an imposing stone-built farmhouse and surrounding buildings. Sports holdall in hand, Tom stepped from his vehicle to be greeted by nonstop barking coming from a pack of Border Collies kennelled at one side of a huge barn. Drawn to the enchantment of the place, Tom briefly closed his eyes; inhaling deeply he thought how this secluded farm was a world away from Easington and the disquiet of the strike. Pat rushed from the house, and jumping onto Tom, she wrapped her legs around his waist and their lips pressed as they twirled in circles. "God, I've missed you so much, Tom!"

"And I have you too, my love."

"How long can you stay for?"

"Till next Monday or even Tuesday, if that's okay like?"

"Of course, it's okay! You, my dearest darling, can stay for as long as you want to." Taking him by the hand, they headed towards the house to be greeted at the doorway by her parents. Her father was a man aged in his early fifties, he was of average height, exhibiting a weather-beaten face, thinning black hair and leathery working man's hands. Pat's stepmother was ten years her father's junior and was rather dainty with a mass of long mousy coloured hair and a plain, yet friendly face. Handshakes were exchanged ahead of a soft welcomely hug from stepmom.

Father took hold of the holdall, and ushering Tom inside he patted him friendly on the back, asking, "How was your journey, son?"

"Not too bad actually, Mr Turner."

"Tom! How many times! For heaven's sake will you please call me John! Please, son."

Tom half smiled. "Sorry, John."

"And please call me Jenny, Tom, not Mrs Turner." Tom blushed slightly in return to her words as they walked a lengthy stone hallway to enter into an extensive, stone-clad sitting room where a welcoming fireside took up centre stage on a main wall, its tall mantelpiece filled with a variety of metal and wooden-framed photographs showing family members and Shire horses, but mainly Shire horses. An impressive Grandfather clock rested isolated in a far-off corner ticking to a dull, low tone, while three coffee coloured, leather chesterfields helped fill up a vast stone-paved floor. A huge silver-tinted television set occupied another corner of the room along with a video recorder stashed underneath, aside stood an ultra-modern stereo stack which cried out expensiveness.

Pat took hold of the holdall, saying, "I'll take this up to my room, Tom."

"I'll come with you," broke in Jenny before the two skipped away to climb an airy staircase that was carved to a slight curve from out of oak.

"I'm glad ya here, Tom." John smiled as they sat. "Bit of a busy schedule ahead of us for the next few days or so, if you fancied lending a hand?"

"Why aye, what's on the agenda, like?"

"Cutting and bailing hay, have you ever driven a tractor before?"

"No, but I'm sure I'll manage it okay," said Tom with an air of confidence, "it carn't be any harder than operating a Dinter."

"What's a Dinter?" He smiled, interested.

"It's a sturdy mining machine, John, it's about eighteen foot in length and we use it to cut away stone and coal to drive a straight girder heading, it's sort of oblong in shape, and at the front of the machine there are hundreds of cutting picks attached to rows of chains mounted onto a wide canopy."

Somewhat impressed, John raised an eyebrow. "Wow, that sounds like it's quite a dangerous bit of kit that does, son."

Tom smiled. "Only if you don't know what ya doing, John, that's why not any Tom, Dick, or Harry are allowed to operate them."

"But you operate them?"

"Of course I do, I'm the top Dinter man at the colliery, and my team are the best team throughout the whole of the pit, but we were transferred onto a Dosco just before the strike broke out, and our Jack's the Dosco operator amongst us, and he's a cracking one at that too."

"Dosco?" John frowned, intrigued. "What's a Dosco then?"

"It's a much bigger contraption than the Dinter, and it's shaped a bit like... well like an army tank really, but instead of a big gun planted at the front of the thing there's a lengthy beam attached to a rotating cutting head that's filled with picks, great machine the Dosco is, especially the MK-2A. We drive arched headings with the Dosco, not straight girders."

"Sounds to me you know your mining stuff, son; I'll give you that." Handing over a cigarette, John beamed widely, asking, "Fancy coming to see the Shires? We've had an additional member to our family since you were last here."

"That'll be great!" enthused Tom as they stood. "So, Cleopatra's had her foal at last then?"

"Yeah, a little colt, he's a beauty too."

"Everything go okay with the delivery?"

"Yeah, everything went to plan, she's a great broodmare is Cleopatra."

Heading towards the front door, Tom raised, "What ya naming him then, John?"

"Trojan." He beamed proudly.

Talking nonstop they left the house to enter, then exit, a colossal barn before coming to an open door stable where mare and foal were stood on straw bedding. Tom grinned ear to ear as he scrutinized a clumsy-looking foal that was all legs and ears. Cleopatra crossed the stable, nudging John for a pet and a polo mint as Pat and Jenny joined them with Pat linking Tom. "By the way, Mum says your boxers are groovy, Tom."

"Eeh?" He blushed.

"Take no notice of her, Tom," broke in Jenny, "she's winding ya up, love, I said they were cool, not groovy."

Pat looked to Tom. "He's a grand foal, isn't he?"

"He's a cracker all right," uttered Tom, still taken back by the boxer shorts thing.

John chipped in, "Future champion without a doubt he is, Tom." Looking at his wife, he smiled, asking, "What's for lunch, love? I'm famished and I'm sure Tom will be too, after his lengthy journey."

"Home cured ham salad with new potatoes." She smiled around, continuing, "And a side serving of my award-winning creamy coleslaw made from a recipe I managed to scoop first prize with at last year's Chatsworth County Fair."

"You did that, love," praised John, "and bloody lovely 'tis too." The group chatted away as they made their way back into the house, closing the door behind them.

Irene was stood at her sink, washing dishes, when Lucy entered the kitchen with tea towel in hand. "Here, there's no need for you to dry, Lucy, just leave it, flowerpots, I'll get it."

"No, I insist, it's the least I can do after that gorgeous meal, I've never come across Yorkshire puddings that big before, Ma."

"So, ya enjoyed them then?" asked Irene, running a dishcloth around a plate.

She smiled. "I enjoyed everything on the plate, Ma, like I always do with every meal you cook."

"Orr, tar very much." She beamed, handing over a plate.

"You will have to let me cook tea one day?"

"Do you enjoy cooking, like, love?"

"Oh yes!" she replied, drying the plate. "I love cooking, and if I do say so myself, I make a cracking Spaghetti Bolognese."

Irene frowned. "Orr, I'm not into all that fancy Chinese stuff, pet, it's traditional food or nothing for me, I'm afraid."

Frowning slightly, Lucy thought briefly about correcting Irene, but she broke into a warm smile instead as another wet plate was handed to her. A knocking at the kitchen door interrupted the moment and Irene opened up to face a middle-aged woman who was plump with beady eyes and a rounded face that was plastered in thick makeup. Irene smiled welcomely. "Hello Maude, how can I help ya?"

"I've just come to let you nar that our Mitzy's had her puppies, she had four of them in the early hours of this morning."

"Congratulations, but why come here?"

"Because your Mick's the dad."

"What, my Mick!?" blew Irene, automatically kicking into a defensive mode like she had so often done in the past whilst defending her lads when they were kids. "Don't talk so fond, our Mick wouldn't do anything like that! He's not that way inclined!"

"But, Irene, a' threw a bucket of card watter over him myself when he was fast on her, I've only come to see if you wanted the pick of the litter?"

"Why a' divant, so bugger off, ya cheeky mare!" And on that comment, the lady flashed her eyes before stomping away. Irene popped her head around the kitchen entranceway watching as the huffed neighbour toddled in the direction of the gate. She shouted, "Shut that gate after ya! And stop thrawing card watter ower our poor Mick! Do ya want him ta catch his death of cold!?" Closing the door, she faced Lucy, moaning, "Blumming brazen fond that bugger is, fancy trying to blame our poor Mick for her bitch having pups."

Jack entered into the kitchen with Mick trailing. "What's all the commotion about!?"

"That blinking Maude Bennett," snapped Irene, "she's just been to the door there trying to put the blame on our poor Mick for her Mitzy having pups."

"He probably's did line her, tha nars, Ma, he's a right horny little bugger!" Patting the dog on its head, he encouraged, "Aren't ya, son!?"

"He isn't horny at all, our Jack!" retorted Irene. "A' mean look at that innocent little face, does that look like the kind of face that would gan around the streets molesting strange bitches? Besides that, our Mick's Catholic..." Jack broke into hysterical laughter and as hard as Lucy tried to stop herself, she followed. "... Hey! Stop it, you two! He is Catholic, ask Father O'Conner!" She bent forward, stroking Mick. "Aren't ya a Catholic, my bonnie little lad, and he's far too handsome to be hanging around with that Mitzy, she's not even his type, but Trixy the Poodle up the road is though." Once again Irene leant forward, stroking Mick, enthusing, "You love Trixy the poodle, don't ya, son?"

Heavy laughter once again filled the kitchen, with Lucy joking, "God, I hope I never fall pregnant."

"Now that would be more to my liking." Irene grinned before glaring at Jack. "But don't you two go rushing into owt like that, mind, or yas'll end up like them two in that blumming cartoon film."

Jack grinned impishly. Hugging Lucy around the waist, he pecked a tender kiss on the side of her neck as he asked, "And what cartoon film's that, Ma?"

"That Lady and the bloody Tramp one, that's what film!" blew Irene before she smiled around the two love birds, asking, "Tea or coffee?"

A Motown record sounded softly as the evening sun penetrated a window, filling the Wards' sitting room with amber. Billy lay settled on a settee, reading a book when Marie entered the room already wrapping herself into a jacket. "I'm off to work, the kids are playing in their bedroom, make sure ya run them a bath before bedtime?"

"Aye, ne bother," he answered, not taking his eyes from his read, "don't f-f-forget to fetch is a couple a' b-b-bags of crisps in?"

"I'll not." Leaving the room, she exhaled, "See ya later on tonight then," ahead of a single slam of the door juddering the sitting room window slightly.

Billy rested the paperback, rising to his feet, he entered a kitchen area to switch on a kettle; after searching through a sparse pantry, he dragged his feet to the foot of the stairs, shouting, "Kelly! Is our Beauty up there?"

"Yeah, she's on my bed."

"That's okay, flowerpots, do you want some beans on toast for ya supper?"

"Yes, please, Dad!"

"Ask our Alisia if she wants some too."

"... She does! Dad, will ya put lots of butter on mine please?"

"Aye if there is any," he whispered to himself, leaving the staircase.

The children had enjoyed their evening meal, and after a quick bath they were bedded down for the night. Holding a stack of dirty clothes, Billy left the foot of the stairs to cross the room where he separated the items into a couple of piles before stuffing one lot into a front-loading washing machine ahead of settling himself horizontal onto the settee. Lighting up a cigarette, he shuffled a cushion to comfort behind his neck as the theme tune to 'Miami Vice' blasted from the television. Pointing a remote, he lowered the volume, and after a quick scratching of his ballicks, he lay entertained for a good hour or so.

Inside the men's lavatories at the Colliery Club, Hoss was washing his hands when Tony Ward entered the vicinity. Hoss glanced through a wall mirror and with every passing second, he wound himself up into an enraged state when, unintentionally, Tony pushed him over the edge by just smiling his usual brazenness saying, "Alright, Hoss?" Hoss ignored him, so he repeated, "Are ya alright, Hoss!?"

Hoss faced him with a leer, growling, "I'll be alright if you left ya uncle's wife alone."

"What ya on about?"

"You, clarting around with Marie when Billy's away picketing, that's what I'm on about!"

Tony shook his head in denial. "A' haven't the foggiest what ya on about, marra, whoever told ya that is full of shit!"

"My own eyes told me, so best skip with all ya fucking lies, and stop calling is marra 'coss I'm not ya fucking marra."

"Ya must have been mistaking." Tony frowned, and on them words Hoss gripped his huge hands around Tony's throat, clattering him up against a wall before lifting him up onto his tiptoes.

"Stop... fucking... lying... twat!" he snarled.

Tony managed to mumble, "I'm not lying, Hoss!"

"Really! So, I'm the liar then?" Tightening his grip even further, he lifted Tony from his feet before smashing him through a cubical door where he forced his head into a lavatory. Dragging him back from the cubical, he stood face to face threatening, "Go near Marie again and you're dead! Do you understand!?" Nodding slightly, Tony stood dripping as Hoss walked away, scowling. "Billy's been nowt but nice to you, ya horrible piece of shit!"

ONE WEEK LATER

Mother nature had cast a crystal sky over Easington, creating a glorious Friday morning as hundreds of pickets amalgamated shoulder to shoulder outside the pit gates. At the heart of the mass, Tom scanned the scene with concern, as it was obvious that there was something clearly amiss for there was a much greater police presence than usual. A lengthy convoy of vans stretched bumper to bumper along the entirety of Station Road east with each vehicle shepherding groups of Welsh and Lincolnshire police officers. Sections of SPG officers gathered to formation at both sides of the isolated phone box, blocking off the entire top of Office Street. In amongst these hard helmet SPG cops was Sergeant Dryden, the psychotic cop who Jack had left lifeless in a ditch down at Bold Colliery.

Unawares to the local pickets, roadblocks had been erected cordoning off all routes in and out of the village, with specific orders that no one was allowed to pass, not even public transport buses, taxis, or indeed vital workers essential to the community, the likes of doctors, nurses, pharmacists, teachers, midwifes and others of their ilk.

Tom looked to his brother. "There's something up here, mind, young'n, where's Alan at?"

"He's still inside with management," answered Jack, "why as far as a' nar he is anyway."

"He's been in there ower lang for my liking," voiced Hoss.

Tom eyed yet another convoy of police vans inching Ascot Street prior to them disappearing by means of a lefthanded turn. He lit up a cigarette, moaning, "Where's all these fuckers coming from now!?"

"F-F-Fuck nars," broke in Billy, "b-b-but there's something up!"

"Aye is tha!" agreed Hoss as he too lit up a cigarette. "They must mean business today... eh!?"

Uneasiness buzzed throughout the pickets, and it was a further twenty minutes or so before Alan appeared drawn faced at the top of the colliery office steps. Attracting the crowd's attention, Alan scrunched a frown, and after clearing his throat he raised a megaphone to his mouth, announcing, "Lads, the bastards have sneaked Wickson in through the backdoor!" At once, protesting shouts of 'Bastards! Wankers! Twats!' dominoed before the fronting windows of the building burst to a heavy shower of bricks. Throngs of pickets entered into the pit yard, smashing all the main office side windows; in amongst the turmoil, Jack and the lads had somehow become separated. Jack aided Oddy and other pickets in ripping down mesh fencing before they overturned Chief Inspector Purny's car, leaving it spinning on its roof, they then turned their attentions to more office windows where hurling bricks found their target to the sound of shattering glass. Every now and then a police photographer would briefly appear at an upper floor window of the building, clicking his camera before a combination of bricks, small fragments of metal, and lumps of debris forced the snapper to repeatedly dive for cover. Shields in hands, groups of policemen charged into the pit yard just as Billy was joined by Tom. Coupling up a firehose, Billy took aim and after mistakenly blowing a few of his fellow comrades from off the top of a wall, he drenched the advancing cops. The two friends were grinning like a couple of Cheshire cats until a police vehicle sped from the far side of the yard to park its wheels directly over the hose, cutting off the water supply. Batons raised, a cluster of Welsh policemen battered both Billy and Tom to the ground before dragging them away to be manhandled into the back of a vehicle. Wielding a truncheon, a constable chased after a lonesome picket, hunting him around a corner and out of sight, but a few seconds later the boot was on the other foot as, brick in hand, the same picket pursued the now fleeing cop. One man lay screaming on the ground with two officers lashing him about his head until his screams ceased, they quickly moved onto another picket, sending him sprawling before dragging him screaming by his ankles across bristly gravel, grating skin away from the whole of his back, then, grasping him by his hair, they set about beating him heavy handed around his arms, midriff, and head prior to marching him facing backwards towards a vehicle where they flung him into the rear. Shuffling to formation across the front of the barricaded gates, row upon row of policemen blocked off the main escape route as their colleagues regained control of the mayhem, and any picket who had the misfortune to find himself inside the pit premises was fair game to be beaten and arrested.

Deep inside the pit yard, Jack ran a corner to stumble upon Dryden; within an instant the two stood gobsmacked in reaction at the sight of each other's presence. Eying Dryden's disfigured snout, Jack broke into a cheeky smile. "So we meet again then, fuck face! A' hardly recognised ya there, what with ya new nose and that, it looks like ya've got a little cock grawn out ya face, nob head." Not returning a single word to Jack's piss taking, Dryden's eyes widened almost to a pop as he raised his truncheon, swiping it at Jack's head, but he crouched in avoidance before quickly tripping Dryden's feet from under him, sending him tumbling back overs, to the ground. Ripping his helmet away, Jack knelt over him, pounding his face with hefty blows until the cop lay limp. After rising to his feet, Jack mocked, "Welcome to God's country, twat!" before he turned and strutted away, leaving Dryden lying in a heap.

Rattling truncheons against shields, another batch of police reinforcements arrived, sending panicking pickets scattering in all directions. One young picket reached the safety of the perimeter wall and was in the process of breaching it when a couple of SPG officers hauled him back by his ankles, scraping one side of his face down the coarseness of the bricks before they pulverised him with truncheons. Another young picket was climbing to safety when a broad-shouldered SPG officer started pounding him over the back of his head until a fellow picket came to the lad's aid by activating a powder-filled fire extinguisher directly into the officer's face, temporarily blinding him for just enough time to allow the terrified lad to scamper to safety. Jack scaled the perimeter wall to straddle the top. Scanning the scene, he watched Hoss wrestle a cop into a headlock while taking a drubbing from a half a dozen baton-wielding police constables. Jack jumped from the wall and ran to drop kick one of these cops in his back, sending him sprawling face-first across a concrete floor. Hoss went to ground due to a heavy blow to his ear, with blood also streaming from a deep gash on the back of his head. To one side of Hoss, Jack was lashing out at every cop that came to within striking distance until he was pounded to his knees before additional Welsh officers truncheoned him in an out-of-control frenzy. Jack cursed, "Fucking sheep shagging twats!" ahead of a heavy blow to his temple, sending him in and out of consciousness prior to Hoss and himself being knocked from pillar to post as they were dragged away to be bundled headfirst into the back of a police vehicle.

The wonderful whiff of boiling onions filled the air at the club kitchen as a radio sounded softly in the background. Irene stood chatting alongside Sue, and they were just about halfway through peeling a huge bag of spuds when Alan dashed into the room, and by the look of his facial expression alone, Irene knew that there was something wrong. "What's happened, Alan?"

He sighed prolonged, saying, "The lads have been arrested."
Irene blinked back tears. "Ya joking!?"
"I'm not, they're locked up at Peterlee police station."
Unfastening her apron, she faced Sue, saying, "I'll have to go, Sue."
"Get ya sell away, and don't worry, they'll be alright." Watching Irene and Alan scamper away, Sue blew concern before returning back to her duties.

Up at Peterlee police station, a nauseating smell of urine drifted from a stainless-steel lavatory sited in a corner of a colossal holding cell. Surrounded by blue painted walls that were flecked with scuffed signatures such as... *Pete loves Karen, Ron was here, Tim was here, Gary & Jill forever...* Jack, Hoss, Billy and Tom sat uncomfortably on a cold cell floor alongside other incarcerated pickets and a blond haired, slender built young man who was Jim Foster, the local postman, who unfortunately was delivering letters at the colliery just as everything had erupted, and he had somehow found himself with a couple of black eyes as he too was arrested. Twinging slightly, Jack ran a finger over a seeping wound just above his left eyebrow; next to him sat Hoss exhibiting a sizable gash on the back of his head in addition to a deep laceration inside his ear which was encrusted in blood that had dried to an unhealthy black colour. Tom showed a deep incision across his nose with indications of developing black eyes, while Billy's right eye was completely closed to tally a well swollen top lip. A jangle of keys sounded prior to Chief Inspector Purny entering the cell alongside his burly sergeant and another beefy officer. Purny looked around the men. "Do you know who I am?"
"Fucking hell!" laughed Jack, then joked, "Hey, lads, there's a pig here doesn't nar who the fuck he is!"
Everyone burst out giggling. Purdy interrupted the laughter, threatening, "Right, listen very carefully, you lot, you have one

chance, and one chance alone to answer my question or all of you will be charged with affray... I want to know who turned my vehicle over in the pit yard this morning?"

Each individual shrugged their shoulders in denial before Jack slowly rose to his feet, claiming, "... I'm... Spartacus."

Tom stood. "I'm Spartacus!"

"No, I am Spartacus!" bellowed Hoss, standing.

"I'm S-S-Spartacus!" said Billy, struggling to his feet before each individual picket rose announcing that they were also Spartacus; even Jim the postman stood, and in a feminine tone he announced that he too was Spartacus.

The inspector stood furious as 'I'm Spartacus' repeated from everyone for quite some time before Dryden came to the cell door with his face battered and bruised. "You wanted to see me, guv?"

"Yes, Dryden," replied the inspector, "I need you to stay behind this evening."

"No problem, guv, will that be all, sir?"

"Yes, that will be all."

"Thank you, sir." Noticing Jack's presence, Dryden's eyes lit to a fiendish glee before he smirked wryly as he left the doorway.

Purny nodded attention towards Jack, facing his colleagues he itched the side of his nose, instructing, "It's too crammed in here, put Spartacus into a cell of his own."

The two cops handcuffed Jack's arms behind his back prior to manhandling him from out of the door, they then proceeded to bounce him from wall to wall down a dimly lit corridor that was narrow and constructed out of glossy white bricks identical to the kind you would come across on old hospital wards. Dragging him further, they kicked open a door before removing the cuffs and hurling him heavily into a restricted cell. Jack smiled up mischievously at the two, politely saying, "Nice chatting with you two gentleman."

Back at the main holding cell, Jim the postman looked at Hoss, saying, "I bet I get the sack tomorrow, Hoss."

"Why if ya do, Jim, you come straight down to the colliery, and we'll get a bus load of men up to the post office and picket the fuckers out for ya."

"Would ya do that for me, like?"

Hoss smiled. "For you, Jim, we would do owt, marra, ya one of us now."

Irene linked Alan as they approached the police station entrance where he held a door open before they entered into a reception foyer to be met by a distinct smell of pine disinfectant as a young policewoman sat writing at a desk positioned behind a transparent screen. She beamed welcomely, asking, "Can I help you, madame?"

Irene grinned. "Yes please, could you tell me if you are holding my two boys here? And if so, when are they going to be released?"

"What are their names?" queried the officer, picking up a clipboard.

"Jack and Tom Gilroy."

Checking over a list, the officer smiled, confirming, "Yes, we have them here, but they are currently helping us out with our inquiries so it may take a while."

She smiled. "That's fine, I'll take a seat if that's okay?"

Alan narrowed his eyes at the young officer, saying, "A' hope they're not getting worked over in them cells, mind?"

Smiling widely the officer shook her head in disbelief at his words before he turned away to park himself next to Irene.

"Stop being silly," whispered Irene, nudging Alan slightly, "they don't do things like that these days, man... it's 1984 for Christ's sakes."

Jack was sat in his cell when the door opened ahead of Dryden and two of his fellow officers entering. Jack looked up, grinning,

"Fucking hell! If it's not F-troop! If ya've come for a cuppa, I'm afraid a's out a' milk, mind."

Dryden faced the other two officers with a wry smile. "What did I tell you, he thinks he's a bit of a comedian this fecker does!" Slowly looking Jack up and down, his stare deepened. "Look at the state of you, you're an absolute disgrace!" Side eying his colleagues, he sneered, "Stand the cunt up and cuff him!"

The two officers cuffed Jack then yanked him to his feet. Dryden stood nose to nose before he slugged Jack in his stomach only for Jack to laugh back in his face, mocking, "If that's the best you can do, I'd pack in now, 'coss ya still hit like a fucking girl!" Once again Dryden went eye to eye, but this time Jack lunged at him, snapping a headbutt which sent the cop stumbling back overs across the full length of the confined cell. Narrowing his eyes at the sergeant, Jack suggested, "Why don't you take these cuffs off me, twat, and get rid of ya two girlfriends here so we can get down to it like proper men?"

Wiping blood from his mouth, Dryden rose back to his feet in a rage, eyes bulging, he pulled out his truncheon and with gritted teeth as he forced it under Jack's chin, growling, "It doesn't quite work that way!" Once again facing his colleagues he sighed lengthily. "Try and keep the fucker still this time!"

Grinning widely, Jack looked around all three, chuckling, "So, what are you three planning to be when yas are all grow'd up and that, then?"

Irene and Alan had been sat in conversation for a good hour, when an internal door clicked open ahead of Dryden and the two other policemen laughing their way into the oak clad reception area. Irene noticed Dryden was rubbing an injured hand. Instinctively she smiled, saying, "When ya get home put a vinegar bandage on that, it will fetch all the bruising out, son."

Dryden stopped in midstride, sneering, "You what!?"

Irene grinned, friendly, repeating, "Put a vinegar bandage on ya hand, it will bring all the bruising out."

Shaking his head, Dryden briefly leered at Irene before he turned to his colleagues, scoffing, "Honestly, vinegar bandages! I have never heard of anything so stupid in all my life! Where do these people come from!? Please!!" Chuckling away, the trio entered into a separate side door.

Irene shook her head at Alan, moaning, "Why, was there any need for that!? A' was only trying to help the poor lad out."

Taking her by the hand, Alan whispered, "Take no notice of them, Irene love, they're Met officers them three are, there's not one ounce of decency between the lot of them, I'm afraid."

She frowned. "How do you know they're Met officers, like?"

"White shirts, love! White shirts!"

Another hour and a half had dragged on before an electronic snap unbolted a different interior door and a police officer held it open as freed pickets were escorted into the room by additional officers. Irene stood greeting Tom, Hoss, and Billy. After a motherly hug, Tom softly asked, "What ya doing here, Ma?"

"I've come to get my boys." Noticing his swollen face and injured nose, she ran her hand tenderly down the side of his face. "Did they do this to you in them cells?"

"No, it was in the pit yard this morning."

Irene looked around them. "A' see yas have all suffered a beating then?" Facing back to Tom, she asked, "Where's our Jack?"

"They put him in a separate cell."

"Is he okay?"

"Yeah," stretched from Tom, "he's got a bit of a nick ower his eye but he's fine."

An automated clicking once again sounded at a door ahead of a grinning officer escorting an unsteady Jack into the room with his face swollen beyond recognition. His nose was swelled and obviously broken with eyes puffed to slits, his lips were cut and inflamed and there were now several notches showing above both eyes as well as a huge gash to the side of his head. Everyone in the room was shocked at Jack's horrific injuries, including the young policewoman. Overwrought at the condition of her son, Irene went weak; trying to gather her emotions, she approached him with tears streaming her face, then, as she attempted to hug him, he flinched. Instinctively Irene lifted his shirt, revealing deep bruises running the length at both sides of his ribs. Wiping away her tears, she whispered, "You need to go to hospital, son."

"Just get is home, Ma," he responded, mustering up some sort of a smile. "It's not as bad as it looks."

"Bastards!" cursed Tom, placing his hand delicately onto the side of his brother's face.

Looking on, Billy and Hoss shook their heads as Alan dashed to the reception desk, gushing, "So, they don't assault people in here then! Or is it only striking miners you lot are allowed to beat up!?" Still perplexed, the young officer bowed her head in silence as Alan continued, "How do a' go about making an official complaint around here?"

"Alan!" broke in Jack through gritted teeth. "Leave it, a' just want to get home."

Bananarama sounded from a radio, filling Jack's bedroom with a harmonised track regarding something about Robert De Niro talking in some kind of foreign language as Jack lay battered and bruised on top of his bed clothes, recuperating with a steamy mug of hot chocolate. The stairs thumped to a rush of light footsteps prior to the landing creaking at least twice before Lucy entered the bedroom. Looking at Jack's injuries, she sat tearfully on the edge of the bed with her head in her hands. "Hey!" sighed Jack. "Come on, love, I'm okay."

She once again scrutinised him, saying, "Jack, ya not okay! Look at the state of your face, it looks like you've been run over by a double-decker bus or something."

Jack tried to shuffle himself to some sort of comfort, saying, "It's nowt–"

"It's what!?" she interrupted. Wiping away tears, she continued, "It's police brutality at its worst, that's what this is."

"Lucy, me and the officer who did this to me had a bit of a run in not so long back, he's a right psycho."

She frowned, asking, "What do you mean, a bit of a run in?"

"Why, put it this way, I left him in a ten times worse state than this when I was picketing down Lancashire, and I'm sure our paths will cross again."

"You keep well away from him, Jack, I mean it!" she ordered directly. "And don't you dare be getting yourself locked up so he can get at you again. Let someone else do all the stupid, so called heroical stuff, instead of you."

"A' carn't do that, love," he said once again trying to rearrange his position to ease the pressure on his ribs.

"Why not!? Why carn't you!?"

"A' just can't." Jack managed to raise a reassuring grin. "Everyone sort of looks up to is and that, I'm a bit of a Zorro, but without the mask and that."

CHAPTER FIVE, SEPTEMBER, "BILLY THE KIDDER"

This particular September morning was cold and rainy at Easington, flocks of squabbling seagulls circled, camouflaged against a cathedral sky as ever darkening rain clouds drifted in from off the North Sea. Earlier that morning, a heavy police presence had once again muscled Wickson into work, resulting in dispirited pickets dispatching, almost head bowed, in silence. At the pit gates the colliery's management, safeguarded by a handful of police constables, had dismantled both the barricade and the Alamo cabin, leaving behind a solitary old fire drum as the only remaining relic left from a once spirited meeting place. Tom, Hoss, Billy, Tommy Ord, John Hutton and a fellow picket named Norman Halvey braved the elements as they stood huddled around a fire whilst on picket duty; across the cleared access police officers laughed and joked as they sat sipping hot drinks in the warmth and comfort of a couple of vans.

Hoss lit up a cigarette. "A' wonder what's for dinner the day at the kitchen?" Looking at Tom he inhaled deeply. "Did Ma say owt this morning, Tom? Any inkling?"

"Aye, a' think she said it's shepherd's pie or something, Hoss," he replied, warming his hands over the flames.

"Champion, a' love shepherd's pie, me."

Tommy Ord, who was David Ord's older brother, and Jack and Tom Gilroy's full cousin, was a twenty-eight-year-old red-head standing of average height with a stocky frame and flashing a hearty ruby-coloured moustache. Tommy lit up a cigarette; looking directly at Tom, he half smiled, asking "How's our Jack keeping, Tom?"

"He's champion now, not quite a hundred percent but he's getting stronger by the day."

"Good, 'coss that was a canny hiding he took, a' bet me aunty Irene's been aside herself, has she?"

"Too right she has," agreed Tom, "she was worried sick, anyway he's coming back picketing the morn."

Tommy grinned widely. "Great news that is."

Tom enquired, "How's me Aunt Leat?"

"She's fine," said Tommy, drawing deeply on his smoke.

"Tell her a'm asking after her." Tom smiled.

"A' will."

"Are we still on for coal the night, lads?" broke in John Hutton, a tall, twenty-seven-year-old lad flaunting a head of black wavy hair and healthy rosy cheeks. "I'm rit on the bottom again."

"Aye," agreed Billy, "I'm r-r-running short mesell, J-J-John."

"I'm not ganning..." said Norman Halvey, a man in his late twenties, or perhaps early thirties, who was small in stature, possessing an untidy mass of thinning hair that somehow married with dark, Mediterranean features, "...I've got something on."

John picked up on Norman's anxiousness. "Ya alright, Norman?"

"I'm fine," he sighed all sombre.

"Are ya sure?" put in Hoss. "Ya look as if ya've got the world on ya shoulders."

"Will ya just leave it, Hoss!" Norman rolled his eyes, snapping, "Fa fuck's sake, man, will yas give ower hoying questions at is! Look I'll have ta gan!" The group looked on in bewilderment as Norman quickly strode off with his head lowered.

"A' bet a pound to a pinch of salt he's got trouble with their lass again," muttered Tommy with a concerned sigh.

"Aye," agreed John. "To tell ya the truth it wadn't surprise me if she's fucked off and left him again."

"I'm ganna see if he's alright," said Tommy, rushing off after Norman.

Dressed in his now infamous black duffle coat, Alan exited his car to join the lads at the gates. "What's wrong with Norman?" he asked, lighting up a cigarette. "I've just passed him there and he's got a face on him like a smacked arse!"

"Trouble with their lass again a' think, Alan," sighed John.

"What, again!?" Alan turned to face Tom, asking, "Fancy a look through Durham with is, young'n?"

"Aye what's up, like?"

Alan drew deeply on his cigarette. "Urko, Speedy, Pearsy, David Carr, and Fred Watson's been arrested up at Tow Law."

"Arrested?" Tom frowned. "Up at Tow Law!? What the hell for, like!?"

Alan sighed. "God nars, there's only six of them on picket duty up there and somehow five of them's managed to get themselves lifted!" Alan cast a look of condemnation at a group of policemen sitting in the van. "Probably's their fascist colleagues kicking off again to get the arrest stats up." Flicking his head at Tom, Alan sighed lengthily, saying, "How'y then 'coss a' need ta get back as sharp as possible." After saying their farewells, the two walked away in conversation to enter Alan's car ahead of them driving away.

In the singing end at Easington Club, Sue and Irene were sat at a table emptying out the contents from collection buckets before painstakingly sorting coinage into individual rows as Liz, Bev, Tracy, and Jean were busy in the kitchen prepping food for yet another trio of sittings. A thumping on the rear fire exit door brought about Irene's attentions and she opened up to face big John Morkand and little Micky Thomson standing wearing smiles with each holding huge boxes loaded with groceries. John was a mountain of a man aged in his early forties who exhibited short black hair and a dapper moustache. Micky was a little older than John, but he was a lot shorter and slightly plump, sporting a balding head, and thick lensed spectacles.

"There's boatloads of stuff back in the van, Irene," said John, crossing the threshold into the hall. "Liptons have donated gallons of semi skimmed milk, it needs using by the morn though."

"Champion!" Irene smiled. "I'll put a rice pudding on today for afters then."

"Where do ya want these putting, Irene?" asked Micky, presenting a package as he too entered into the hall.

"Same place as usual, Micky; no, sorry, put them at the far end of the kitchen, I've left the scullery keys up yerm and it's locked up, as waiting for the cleaner to come in to open it for is."

Entering the kitchen, Micky rested his box. Grinning around the girls, he teased, "Aye-aye if it's not the Bangles, how's it going, ladies?"

Jean looked over her shoulder. "Fine, how's ya sell, Micky?"

"Why tha nars, still on the lookout for a nice little lady to settle me self-down with." He looked to Tracy with a cheeky grin, asking, "No signs of a young man in ya life yet then, Tracy?"

"Nor, not yet, Micky," she said, slowly rolling her eyes in anticipation of Micky's next question.

"There's still a bit hope for me yet then, hinny!" he laughed, running his hand over what little hair he had remaining.

Tracy snorted. "A' don't think so, Micky! Ya've got two hopes you have, no hope and frigging Bob Hope! Me Da's younger than you, man, having said that like, a few years ago when ya was thinner and ya had all ya hair and that..." Micky's face lit up slightly until she chuckled, "... ya still wouldn't have stood a cat in hell's chance."

"How many boxes is left to unload?" broke in Irene.

"About eight a' think," voiced John, "and there's another run to do after that with perhaps another ten or so boxes. Liptons have got stacks of tinned stuff to pick up and the Co-op's got a canny bit veg, and boatloads of frozen meat too."

Irene lit up a cigarette, saying, "Champion... or, while yas are out on the road will yas pop down to Fairsey's and pick up some boxes of fishcakes? There's about a dozen boxes a' think, anyway they're already paid for."

"Aye, ne-bother," said John, "any chance of a brew first, Irene, as gagging here."

"Why aye, but unload the van first," she said, drawing on her cig.

"What's it like, out?" asked Sue, entering the kitchen.

"Bit nippy, Sue," answered Micky, "we had trouble starting the van up again this morning."

Sue cast a look of angst. "Please don't be saying that, Micky, if that thing breaks down again, well, we'll be well and truly buggered 'coss there's very little money left in the coffers to fix it–"

John broke in, "Take ne notice of him, Sue, he's just pulling ya leg."

Narrowing her eyes, she shook her head, moaning, "By tha's a little bugger thuw is, Micky Thomson!"

The two buddies laughed their way from the kitchen to retrieve more parcels. After their last run had finished Irene switched on a kettle, asking, "Tea or coffee, lads?" and they both agreed on tea. Wrapping herself into a pinny, Debbie entered into the kitchen where Irene greeted her with a smile, saying, "Well, did you get one then?"

"Yeah, up Hazel Crescent," replied a delighted Debbie, "number twenty-two, it's one of the steel houses, three bedroomed, absolutely lovely so it is, it's got canny sized gardens at both the front and back and everything." Debbie faced Sue. "Will ya thank ya Mam when ya see her, please Sue, she put my case over great." Facing Irene, she added, "And will ya say thanks to your Leat an'll please, Irene, she spoke well for me too."

Irene smiled. "Ne bother, a' will do, love."

Sue grinned. "I'll also tell me Mam too, Debbie, does Peter like the house then?"

"He loves it, he's got the gardens all planned out and everything."

"Good." Sue grinned before asking, "Did them inspectors find out what the cause of the fire was, Debbie?"

"Aye, faulty wiring, the insurance company are sending out a cheque sometime in the next few weeks or so, there'll be enough money for decorating and furnishings and that."

"Are why, new home, new start," put in Jean.

"At least yas are all safe and sound," added Irene, "that's the main thing, pet-lamb."

Debbie broke into an extended smile, praising, "Yeah thanks to your Jack's heroics we are, Irene."

FOLLOWING DAY

Even if the sky was crystal, the morning was a tad crisp, not bitter cold, but nevertheless there was still a September chill in the air, and though it was broad daylight a wan outline of a half-moon was visible. At Easington pit gates, Jack and the lads stood in conversation amongst a small gathering of local pickets which the police had strategically hoarded to one side of a wall prior to a trio of meshed up police vans edging past the phone box to enter the top of Office Street. After chants of 'Scab! Scab! Scab!' a brief scuffle broke out only for the cops to quickly take control, allowing the convoy to pass unscathed through the gates. Travelling deeper into the pit yard, the vehicles slowed to a stop ahead of a group of burly SPG officers emerging from one of the vans. Then, to a barrage of vocal abuse, Wickson clambered from the rear of a vehicle and started goading the pickets by sticking up two fingers, which infuriated the men to surge forward only for four or five of them to be wrestled face down to the ground before being dragged away and manhandled into a police vehicle. At the far side of the yard another van door opened, and a quartet of police officers jumped out ahead of Noman Halvey emerging with a works bag slung over his shoulder. Jack stood in shock. "Fucking hell!" he raised in disbelief. "That's not Norman Halvey, is it!?"

"It is," confirmed Tom with a prolonged sigh, "that's the last thing we need, that is!"

"What the fuck!" put in Hoss.

"J-J-Jesus!" moaned Billy. "A' don't b-b-believe it!"

"Neither do ah," sighed Hoss, "what's Norman thinking of, he's supposed to be one of us?"

Jack looked to Hoss with purpose. "Not ne-more he's not, Hoss, and his name's not Norman neither, from now on it's Halvey the fucking scab!" Jack shaded his eyes from the sun, looking on as a set of officers escorted Halvey towards the entrance to a colossal red brick building that housed various rooms including a lamp cabin and a time office. Jack screamed, "Halvey! Ya fucking Judas bastard!" and Halvey's reaction was to smile over his shoulder while raising his hand in acknowledgement of Jack's cursing.

"Fucking scab!" yelled Tom, Hoss, and Billy in unison before the rest of the pickets pointed accusingly whilst chanting, 'Scab!

Scab! Scab! Scab!'

A good twenty minutes had passed before Alan rushed to Office Street to join the pickets. After looking around he faced Tom, asking, "Is it right then, has Norman Halvey gone in?"

Tom lit up a cigarette, answering, "Aye, they've taken him into the back of the time office, about a quarter of an hour or so ago." Tom inhaled deeply, asking, "Did management not inform ya he was gan'n back to work, like, Alan?"

"Did they heckers, like!" Alan lit up as he turned to walk off in the direction of the time office. "I'm ganna try and speak to him–"

"Dinit even think about it!" broke in Jack, grabbing Alan by the shoulder, stopping him in his tracks. "You put one foot inside that pit yard, and they'll lift ya for sure." He glanced down at Alan's feet ,noticing he was still in his slippers, and after a slight chuckle he continued, "Besides, ya canit gan round getting ya sell all locked up with just ya slippers on, what's people ganna think... eh! Ya supposed to be our leader, for crying out loud!"

"Fuck!" whooped Alan. "A' didn't realise a' was still in them."

"We'll give Norman a visit tonight, Alan," said Tom, "try and talk some sense into him–"

Jack interrupted, "Do ya not mean we should go up and put his fucking windows out! 'Coss there's ne way I'm talking to the scabby get, not now, nor ever again!"

Escorted by a couple of SPG officers, Chief Inspector Purny beamed arrogance as he approached Alan and the lads. "Well, Mr Cunnings, that's another one come to his senses, hopefully the trickle will soon turn into a flood."

Alan looked the inspector directly in the eye. "Ya do know we're fighting for our pure existence here, don't ya?"

"That's none of my business, I'm just doing my job." Purny's smile stretched as he continued, "Simply following orders."

"That's what the N-N-Nazis said at Nuremburg after the w-w-war," put in Billy.

Standing face to face with Billy, Purny frowned deeply. "You are not calling me a Nazis by any chance, are you, you stuttery little fuck?"

"Nor he's not," broke in Jack, "but I am, ya fascist twat!"

Purny grinned falsely, saying, "Well! If it's not Mr Spartacus himself, I thought you may have learnt your lesson after the last little visit you had with us up at Peterlee."

"Why, not hardly." Jack grinned unconcerned.

Purny waved over additional colleagues, and without any hint of emotion in his voice he pointed out Jack, calmly ordering, "Arrest that one."

Truncheons drawn at the ready, a couple of officers grabbed Jack. Forming fists, the lads were just about to kick off in Jack's defence when Jack looked around them. "Leave it, lads, it's ne-good all of us getting lifted, that's just what these bastards want." Once again smiling untroubled, Jack winked at Purny, asking, "So tell me, how long did ya say you have been a policeman for?" Purny smirked in answer before Jack was dragged away to be bundled into the back of a van.

NEXT NIGHT

Under the dimness of night, Billy, Hoss and Tom were on the pit premises riddling out nuggets of coal from the duff heaps when a baying fox slightly startled them. A half-moon cast just about enough light for them not to use their torches, but every now and then a drifting cloud would momentarily block out the moon's luminosity, plummeting the night into nocturnal darkness. Hoss shook nuggets of coal from the riddle into the mouth of a sack held open by Billy, and once the riddle was emptied Tom loaded another couple of shovelfuls into the wooden device. After once again repeating the monotonous procedure, Hoss looked to Tom, saying, "Tack-five." Resting the riddle, he lit up a cigarette, asking, "What time does the leek show start Saturday then, Tom?"

"I'm not too sure, young'n, all the produce has to be benched by ten though, then the judges kick us out so they can start their judging."

"Think ya'll w-w-win, like?" asked Billy, removing a half-smoked nipper from behind his ear to light up.

"A' haven't a clue." Tom also lit up. "It all depends on what the judges are looking for, a' suppose."

"Well what a've s-s-seen of ya leeks a' think ya'll w-w-walk it, marra," voiced Billy, drawing deeply on his smoke.

"Aye me too," agreed Hoss, "they're absolutely massive."

"Cheers, lads." Tom smiled. "Hope yas are right."

"When is Pat coming up, Tom?" enquired Hoss.

"She's arriving sometime Friday around teatime."

Hoss beamed. "Good, Margret will be as pleased as punch to catch up with her."

"Aye, they get on canny them two," said Tom. Looking at Billy he grinned, asking, "Is Marie going to the show?"

"Why not l-l-likely, she'll probably be w-w-waiting on behind the b-b-bar."

After finishing their smokes Tom once again loaded up the riddle for Hoss to shake out nuggets, but as Hoss attempted to empty the coal into the sack Billy wasn't concentrating and the chunks fell direct to the floor. "Fucking hell, man, Billy!" grumbled the big man, mopping his brow with his sleeve. "Watch what ya deing!"

"S-S-Sorry!"

A huge black cloud briefly swathed the ambience of a half-moon. Smoking cigarettes, Jack, Sizzler and Lemsip strode abreast one another through the lamplights of empty streets. Arching a corner, they slipped on balaclava hats before entering into Alma and the fronting Argent Street. Picking up pace, adrenalin was pumping as they advanced further until they entered into an empty yard where each of them armed themselves with broken up bricks. Standing at a gateless gateway, Jack whispered, "Not a word to anyone about this, mind, not even to Cunningsy."

"I'll not say owt," mumbled Lemsip, his face riddled with apprehension beneath his disguise.

"I'll not say fuck all," agreed Sizzler.

They set off walking almost on tiptoe as they passed by a few more houses until they crept to stoop against a wall outside Norman Halvey's abode.

"Jack, are ya sure the kids aren't in there?" muttered Sizzler.

"I'm positive," he returned, "their lass fucked off with them over to her mother's at Horden... Right, pick a window apiece, I'll put the kitchen and bathroom one's out, you two put the bedroom ones out–"

"Hold on a tick," broke in Lemsip all on edge.

"What's wrang with ya now?" hissed Jack. "Ya've been twisting ever since we set off."

"A' canit de it," gulped Lemsip in an almost apologetic tone, "sorry but a' just carn't."

"Why not!?" raised Jack. "He's a fucking scab!"

Lemsip sighed, "A' nar what he is, a' just canit de it, Jack, I'm not up to it."

"Why, gan and keep a lookout at the end of the street then," breathed Sizzler and on those words Lemsip hurried to loiter at a gable end where he scanned in both direction before raising a thumb. Taking aim, the sound of two exploding thuds broke the night quickly followed by a couple more thumps of shattering glass prior to the three scampering away to be lost in the unlit shadows of Easington's North allotments.

CHAPTER FIVE

SATURDAY

Today, hearts raced just that few beats faster for some of the menfolk in the village, as today was the most important date on the calendar – that's if they were an exclusive member of Easington Colliery's Pot Leek Society, for this particular Saturday was their eagerly awaited annual leek show, and the whole of the village had turned out dressed in their Sunday best to view the remarkable produce that was on display.

Pat linked Tom as they stepped into the Colliery Club foyer to join the backend of a lengthy queue. After inching the vestibule, they entered into the singing end to be welcomed by a variety of fragrances drifting from displays of flowers that would put to shame any manufactured scent fashioned up by *Chanel* or *Yves Saint Laurent*. Dawdling to the first table they came to an array of colourful carnations. Pat looked down at the prize cards, enthusing, "Look, Tom, you've came second!" pecking a kiss on his cheek as she whooped, "Well done, babes!"

Tom, on the other hand, wasn't too impressed at being placed runner up and a slight air of disappointment etched his face. Moving with the flow, countless colours paraded midtable from displays of dahlias and once again Pat's face lit up with excitement. "You have won this one, Tom! Look, first place!" and this time Tom managed a smile, even if ever so slight. At the far end of the table various shades of yellows, reds, pinks, oranges and whites flashed from beautifully presented chrysanthemums and once again Pat beamed widely, saying, "You've won again, Tom! Do you win everything?"

"As if," he answered with a slight smirk. On an adjoining table enormous cucumbers paraded in rows and Tom was once again presented with a red card for first place. He also claimed first prize on both stripy, and the giant marrows – the latter was so huge both Jack and he had struggled earlier that morning to manhandle the thing from the allotment to the show bench. On the tomato section of the exhibition, Pat was again rapt as a trio of red cards awaited Tom, one for a trio of yellow tomatoes, another for a troika of red tomatoes, and finally one for a gathering of smaller cherry tomatoes, which following the strict rules of the Society had to be still attached to the vine.

On a neighbouring table bunches of stumpy carrots were on parade and Tom's face once again dropped as he obtained a blue card for second place. "Never mind, love," consoled Pat, rubbing his upper arm, "you can't win them all." Impressive long carrots tapered for over a metre in length parading alongside even lengthier parsnips, with Tom winning these two categories; he also won best of the beetroot, and was placed in first spot with a cauliflower that presented a curd that was tight nipped and showing a slight arch of perfect whiteness; again he claimed a red card with a trio of veg consisting of a carrot, parsnip and another impressive cauliflower, but to his frustration he was unplaced in both the white, and red potato sections. Ascending steps which took them up one side of a raised stage, the distinct aroma of onions and leeks was pungent. On the first table, separate clusters of five shallots were on show, with just about all of them exhibited to the same shape and size whilst topped with a binding of raffia whilst expertly presented on paper plates lined in silver sand. These shallots were purposely harvested eight weeks prior to the show, allowing the skins enough time to brown off. Next to the shallots came a triad of dressed onions which were also lifted from the allotments eight weeks beforehand allowing their skins to turn brown too, and these uniform onions were likewise bedecked by a dried-up tethering of raffia that was knotted to perfection. Again, Tom grinned slightly as he claimed first prize in those two particular classes. He also won with a bunch of three pulled onions that were the size of footballs, and he claimed first place in the heaviest onion section with a colossal onion that weighed in at just under fourteen pounds. Approaching pairs of tall leeks that were deliberately grown narrow with a blanched bottom showing for over eighteen inches in length, Tom blew relief as he had secured first in that particular category; he had also won the giant intermediate leeks with a duo of gigantic leeks that had a whiteness blanched to eight inches up to a first button with white bottoms bloated to over twenty inches in girth.

"Wow!" exhaled Pat, gaping almost open-mouthed at the leeks. "You would put Percy Thrower to shame, you would," her comment bringing a huge grin from Tom. She continued, "I've never seen anything like this in all my life."

Inching further they came to a stop at the main stall of the show where more than fifty pairs of leeks were on parade, and to Tom's delight he won the best in show with a pair of almost identical leeks that exhibited healthy green flags and blemish free bottoms that were blanched pure white and extended up to a first button that was positioned at just under the limitation of six inches, with one leek having a base circumference of seventeen inches, and the other showing just over seventeen and a half. Pat smiled, saying, "Well, you certainly know your stuff, I'll give you that." She planted a quick kiss on his lips, purring, "I'm ever so proud of you, my love."

"Thank you," he responded with a slight blush just as Hoss, Margret, and Joe joined them.

"Well done," said Hoss, shaking Tom by the hand, "best pair of leeks I've ever seen in my whole life them are, marra, lovely deep green foliage on them."

"Cheers, Hoss."

"Aye... ya Dad would have been... ever so proud of ya, son," agreed Joe, shaking Tom's hand. Inspecting an impressive Robert Gilroy memorial cup which Jack had claimed for another year for the best leek in show, the old man smiled widely, complimenting, "Cracking pair of leeks they are, bonnie lad... worthy winners of any show so they are!"

"Cheers!" Tom grinned.

"What happened to... ya tatties though?" asked Joe, lighting up a Woodbine.

"Buggered the compost up, didn't a'!" sighed Tom. "A's gan'n back to my normal formula next year though."

"Well done!" Margret beamed, hugging Tom.

"Thanks, love." Tom turned to Pat, whispering, "With all the prizemoney a've won I'll get ya a proper engagement ring now."

"You will do no such thing, Thomas Gilroy!" she snapped, taken aback. Fidgeting the ring around her finger, she defended, "I love this ring!" Irene, Jack and Lucy entered the hall. Pat nudged Tom slightly as she drew his attention to them. "Here's ya Mum, Jack, and Lucy just come in, Tom."

"Or aye." Lighting up a cigarette, he waved over welcomely.

"Lucy is so beautiful, isn't she?" whispered Pat before sighing. "She's so elegant."

"Here! She's ne different to you!"

"Of course she is, look at her." Pat's eyes drifted downwards to the floor. "I'm not in the same class as her."

Tom leaned forward; gently lifting her chin with his finger, he planted a soft kiss, whispering, "Well you are in my eyes, love; besides, a' didn't know there was a contest on between you two."

"There's not." She half smiled, "I'm just being silly, wrong time of the month and that."

Tom grinned understandably, then after a considerable pause he faced Pat with a lost frown, asking, "Wrong time of the month and that... for what, like?"

It was mid-September, and a typical autumnal morning greeted Easington Colliery, menacing rain clouds loomed threatening, as rows of thicket had begun to sluff their greenery, with towering trees also shedding the odd leaf or two. Donning winter coats, Jack and the lads took shelter amidst a couple of canvas-covered garages that were located above a grassy ridge known as Parkin's Quarry, which stood directly adjacent a large Liptons store and a multitude of smaller shops running along Seaside Lane. Flicking away a cigarette butt, Oddy loitered in a lit-up doorway of Sparks' Bakeries; after checking up the main road, he waved frantically, capturing the lads' attention. Jack looked around the group, asking, "Right they're coming, are yas ready then?"

"Aye," nodded Hoss.

"Which w-w-way are we r-r-running!?" voiced Billy.

"Down towards Bede Street," instructed Tom, "then we'll split up there." Loading small ball bearings into catapult pouches, they waited until a procession of three police vans came into view. Stretching their arms, they tensioned the catapults, then took aim before releasing their grip, slinging the miniature pellets through the air to shatter out the side windows of the first two vehicles, causing the convoy to screech to an abrupt stop. "How'y then, let's gan!" shouted Tom ahead of them scampering down a squelchy gradient to follow a muddy trail which guided them behind the back of the Methodist chapel, Doctor Brown's surgery, and a couple of wooden garages that stood end-to-end opposite the rear of a sizable Walter Wilsons store. Approaching Bede Street, they slowed to a walk ahead of them parting their ways, with Billy strolling off via Fairsey's fish shop prior to him turning left to disappear down Bolam Street. Hoss strode Beaty Street in the direction of the Leathercap club, while Tom and Jack backtracked to rejoin the main road with Tom bearing right to head off down Ascot Street in the direction of the pit, while Jack turned a sharp left to strut up Seaside Lane where he approached the stationary police convoy just as agitated police officers scrambled up a steep embankment in the direction of Parkin's Quarry.

Passing one of the vans, Jack stumbled upon Wickson who was sat next to Halvey at a window; instantly he banged heavily onto the glass, startling the two before he gave a specific hand gesture while mouthing, 'Fucking wankers,' and Wickson's comeback was to laugh in an exaggerated fashion while Halvey grinned widely, brandishing the old two fingers. Clasping his truncheon, a burly SPG sergeant barged Jack with his shield, ordering him to move on, and Jack responded by raising his hands before smirking widely as he slowly backed off to walk away. Sauntering up the main street, he came to an opening where he turned at the side of a gable end prior to him backpedalling down the rear of the shops to eventually join his brother who had blended in with fellow pickets at the pit gates. Lighting up a cigarette, Jack smiled contentedly as he offered Tom the packet, saying, "Well, that went all to plan for a change."

"Sure did!" Tom grinned widely as he lit up. "We must have done a canny bit damage 'coss there's no sign of them yet."

"A' hope so, a' tell ya what though, young'n, I'd give a gowld pig for five minutes up a dark alley with that fucking Wickson and Halvey, a' hate the cunts with a passion."

"Don't we all!" Tom drew deeply on his cigarette, asking, "Anyway where does that Wickson actually come from?"

"I'm not too sure, somewhere up Coxhoe way a' think, or is it Bowburn." Jack inhaled on his cigarette. "It's somewhere round there, he's a proper woolyback like."

After a good twenty minutes had passed, Oddy joined the picket line, and grinning widely he approached the two brothers, enthusing, "There's a copper being stretchered away from one of those cop vans, he's got blood pissing out of a headwound and everything."

"Champion!" gushed Jack before jesting, "It wasn't that Dryden gadjy by any chance, was it?"

"No such luck, Jack, but it was one of them SPG bastards though."

"Good!" Tom laughed. "At least the twat won't be on duty the day caving men's skulls in."

Oddy chuckled, "He certainly won't." Looking to Jack, he raised a smile. "Lend is a tab, young'n?"

After handing over a cigarette, Jack offered a flame, suggesting, "Give it a couple of weeks and we'll find another spot to ambush them again."

"A' dinit nar about that," voiced Tom, "they'll not leave themselves open like that again."

"Too right they'll not," agreed Oddy, inhaling deeply on his cigarette, "that was a one off that was I'm afraid."

"Are, why," sighed Jack, "we'll work something else out to hit them with." Three police vehicles limped past the pickets to be greeted by the usual chants of 'Scabs! Scabs! Scabs!' before the convoy came to a stop, allowing Wickson and Halvey to be escorted deeper into the pit yard as up in the sky a squadron of raucous geese drew attention as they winged their way southbound in their usual V-formation. Jack pulled his hoody over his coat, covering up his head, "It's getting carder by the day now."

"Aye is it," agreed Tom.

"I'll have to gan, lads." Oddy smiled. Facing Jack, he added, "A' only popped down to let ya nar football training's on tonight at seven."

"A thowt it was the morn night?"

"It was but it's being fetched forward a day, the hall was double booked, the Scouts had booked it for their annual committee meeting or something."

"Why I'll not be there," raised Jack, "I'm gan'n out for a meal with Lucy the night, it's her birthday."

"Very nice an'll." Oddy smiled before asking, "Where yas gan'n te, like?"

"A'm not too sure, some Italian restaurant down Sunderland a' think, but wherever it is a' hope they serve chips, 'coss a' divant think I'll be ower keen on that spaghetti shite."

"Have ya tried proper spaghetti afore, our Jack?" asked Oddy.

"Have a' heckers, like! But if its owt like that hoop stuff ya get from out the tins ya can keep it."

"It's nowt like spaghetti hoops, man, cuz! Just give it a bash, ya'll love it." He turned to walk away, uttering, "Anyhow's I'll catch yas the morn, say hello to me Aunt Irene when ya see her."

Tom beamed friendly, saying, "Aye a' will do, see ya the morn."

"See ya later, cuz." Jack beamed before turning to his brother, suggesting, "How'y let's fuck off ourselves, catch Ma afore she gans to the kitchen, a' could kill a couple of bacon butties."

"How'y then." Tom smiled. Walking away, Tom nudged his brother, saying, "How the hell diss our David nar what spaghetti tastes like?"

"Exactly!" sniggered Jack. "He's never set foot inside an Italian restaurant in his whole life." Talking non-stop the brothers left the pit gates and were inching along the top of East estate when Jack's face suddenly dropped to that of uneasiness, as from the other direction a feeble looking elderly man with a head of thick, silvery hair, limped towards them clutching a walking stick and clothed in a black suit that enhanced the whiteness of his dog collar. And though this man's Spencer Tracy appearance may have given an impression of frailty, the old saying, never judge a book by its cover came into effect as he was none other than Father O'Conner, who down the decades had imposed the most stringent of religious beliefs upon generation after generation of Easington's Catholic youth. Jack gulped, whispering, "Orr nor, that's all a' need, a right ballick'n from himself."

Tom jokingly teased, "You might be in for a tongue-lashing, but a's not, a' was with Ma at first mass last Sunday."

"Dear God!" huffed Jack. "Look at him! He's gone all purple faced already and he hasn't even started yit!"

"Chill out, man," side mouthed Tom, "he's just a weak old man these days."

Jack blew endlessly, uttering, "Weak old man my arse! A' can remember all the clips around the back of me lug a' received from him when a was a young'n, and I'm sure at one point he threatened to perform some kind of half-hearted exorcism on is."

Tom chuckled, "That was after we let all of them sheep into church during Sunday mass when we were pumping that ard organ from outside, wasn't it?"

"Aye, it was, come to think of it!" Jack removed his cigarettes. Forcing a nervous smile he presented the packet to the nearing priest, politely asking, "Cigarette... Father?"

"Tanks, son," said the clergyman in a soft Irish accent. Smiling widely, he lit up. "So tell me, young Jack Gilroy, what have you been doing wit ya bit self dese past few months den?"

"Why tha nars, Father, picketing and that."

"Oh, picketing and dat, and tince when have you started picketing on Sundays?"

"I haven't!"

"I tort, so how come you never attend mass wit your poor mother, anymore den?"

"I've just been a bit busy, that's all, Father, what with the way things are standing and that."

"Bit busy, eh?" The old priest turned to smile warmly at Tom. "Young Thomas here seems to find de time to attend mass, and I'm sure he's just as busy as what t'you are." Focusing back to Jack, he drew deeply on his cigarette, frowning. "I've heard tru da grapevine dat you have found yourself a nice young lady friend?"

"I have, she's called Lucy."

"And does dis Lucy possess a second name by any chance, does she?"

"Of course she does, it's Arkinson, Lucy Arkinson."

"And is de girl of our faith?"

"A' think she is, Father," said Jack, unknowingly blinking doubt.

"Don't tink, lad, ask, and it's about time you did ask, before tings become too serious between de two of yas." He looked Jack direct in the eye, adding, "You know, for a former altar boy you can disappoint at times, Jack Gilroy." Once again inhaling smoke, his eyes drifted from brother-to-brother, ordering, "Keep out of trouble, you two, stop selling dat coal, and keep well away from dose electric cables too." He wagged his finger accusingly. "Take heed, easy money is de work of de devil himself to be sure... and... I'll look forward to seeing yas at mass diss Sunday. Will bote of yas be there?"

"We'll be there, Father," said Jack in a convincing tone.

"Good, may God be wit you's."

"And also with you, Father," said Tom just a tad sheepish.

Looking on as the priest limped away, Jack blew relieved, then turning to his brother, he snapped, "Have you been spouting off in that confession box again!?"

"Have a' heckers like!"

"Why how come he nars about the coal and us nicking that cable then?"

Tom shook his head. "A' haven't the foggiest! It's beyond me!"

"It'll be frigging Hoss again!" moaned Jack all irritable. "It's every time he steps foot in that confession box his gob gallops away with him! Thick as a canteen cup he can be at times!"

Tom's eyed rolled to Jack, and with a half-smile he asked, "So, will ya be coming to mass this Sunday with us then?"

"Don't talk so baldy headed!" he retorted with a slight hint of contempt.

"Jack?" stumbled from Tom, indicating a further question was imminent.

"What!?"

"Do ya think Lucy's really is a Catholic, or were ya just bullshitting?"

"Well, what do you think!? Having said that like, she wears a crucifix round her neck all the time." He smiled mischievously, raising, "Talking about electric cables though, we—"

"Don't even think about it!" interrupted Tom. "Never again!"

"Pity, 'coss a' nar where there's a one lying very handy, not so far to drag the thing neither."

Not a single word was spoken between the brothers as they walked on further to turn into Cuba Street. Opening a gate at number two, Tom side eyed his brother, asking, "So where abouts is this cable at then?" and Jack's response to his brother's words was to grin impishly.

At Sunderland seafront, Roker lighthouse flashed a shaft of light that slowly revolved in a clockwise direction, and on each and every rotation its penetrating beam would briefly illuminate a darkened harbour, revealing an assortment of multicoloured fishing boats that were moored to a quayside by salty ropes. At the centre of a lengthy promenade, Jack and Lucy sat at a corner table inside a packed Italian restaurant that was adorned in traditional Mediterranean fixtures and fittings. A gastronomic aroma of garlic was strong, yet pleasant, as black and white clad waiters and waitresses smiled friendly while rushing from table to table serving customers with a diversity of drinks and mouthwatering meals.

Lucy looked exquisite; her lengthy black hair settled onto a bottle green dress, which hung from off her bare shoulders to flow elegantly before ending at soft khaki sandals. Jack was at his most handsome too, clothed in modern, sky-blue slacks, and a flashy green coloured Pringle jumper that displayed a blue diamond design down its frontage.

Everything in the restaurant hinted romance, from fronting windows offering picturesque views of the lighthouse and harbour, to the dim illumination of the room which went hand in hand with Luciano Pavarotti caressing 'O Sole Mio' ever so softly as background music, even the individual table candles appeared to cast amorous flickers across oldie walls. Jack looked from the window, saying, "It's canny in here, mind, nice and cosy, isn't it?"

"It is that." Lucy smiled, scanning the room, "all the furnishings are genuine antiques which they had shipped over from Naples years ago."

"Get away!? What, all of them?"

"Yeah, I believe so."

"So do you come here often, then?"

"Not recently, my parents still visit on the odd occasion, but when I was a young girl, well, we used to be regulars, we would dine here as a family almost every weekend." She broke into a grin, baiting, "So, tell me, Jack Gilroy, where did you used to wine and dine all your former girlfriends at then?"

"Me!" raised Jack, pointing at his own chest. "Newhere, I've never took a girl out to a restaurant in the whole of my life, in fact I've never set foot in one mesell, why, apart from the Half Moon at Easington village that is."

"You are joking!?"

He shook his head. "I'm not tha nars, restaurants have never been my scene." Half smiling, he added, "I'm more of a Fairsey's fish shop man mesell." Picking up a menu he slowly checked it over, uttering, "Seeing as you're the expert in Italian cuisine, what's your recommendation then?"

"My favourite is Penny Al Forno."

"Penny Al what?" he asked, frowning up and down the menu list.

"Penny Al Forno, it's tubes of pasta cooked in a Bolognese type sauce that has sprinklings of finely chopped ham and diced boiled eggs added to it, it's so yummy."

Jack grinned, joking, "Ham and eggs eh!? I might try that myself then. Will they do is some chips to go with it?"

"Of course they will!"

Jack took Lucy by the hand, muttering, "Will you please let me pay, love? A' feel horrible that you are footing the bill."

"Well, there's no need for you to feel awful, you are on strike and it's my treat, we'll come back next year though, and you can pay for everything then."

Jack almost pleaded, "Please let me pay, Lucy, it's not right, it's your birthday, for heaven's sake."

"No!" she said all determined. "There'll be other birthdays, Jack, just leave it, please!"

"Well, I've got a bit of a surprise for ya anyhow." He took out a heart shaped Rina box; breaking into a smile he passed it over the table, whispering, "There you go, hope you like it, it matches your eyes, and believe you me I'm not as skint as you think I am, me Dad left us standing alright moneywise after he died."

She opened up the box to uncover an expensive engagement ring that boasted a huge sapphire stone that was surrounded by clusters of miniature diamonds. "Is this what I think it is?" she asked, flashing a slight frown.

"Of course, it is, a' dinit gan round buying rings willy-nilly tha nars!"

"So, I take it you have sort of proposed to me somewhere in there, have you?"

"Why aye!"

Stern faced, she handed the box back, and without any hint of emotion, she said, "I'm ever so sorry, Jack but I carn't accept this."

Jack's stomach sank to a churn, his cheeks flushed red at her rejection. "What do you mean you carn't accept it!?"

Firm faced she said, "I just carn't accept it, not like this I carn't." Her eyes directed Jack's attention towards the floor. "But..." she broke into a wicked smirk, "...if you try and propose to me properly instead of some pathetic, half-hearted shambles which that was, well, who knows what the outcome would be, I may even have a sudden change of heart."

"You want me to go, like down on one knee like... don't ya!?"

She mocked, "Yes, that's exactly what I want you to do," then with a put-on voice she mimicked, "like down on one knee like!" By this time everyone in the room was looking on in anticipation of the outcome. Widening her eyes, she once again nodded in the direction of the floor. "Go on then, Gilroy! Get yourself down there!"

Sighing lengthily, he went to one knee, cupping his hands around the opened box he presenting the ring, saying, "Lucy Arkinson, love of my life, it would be a great honour, and indeed a privilege for me, if you would accept this very expensive ring as a proposal of marriage and a token of my undying love and affection for you?"

Not impressed one iota, she shook her head. "Is that it like!? Come on, you can do better than that, Jack!"

"Ehh!"

Wearing an ambiguous grimace she stalled for a few seconds before beaming, "Get up, you silly sod, of course I'll marry you!" Smiling at the room, Jack nodded her acceptance to the audience before he stood to carefully slide the ring onto her finger, then, taking her in his arms their lips touched gently at first before they kissed a truelove kiss as jocund customers applauded ecstatic. Returning to their seats, Lucy gloated over her ring for what seemed like an eternity. Rising from her chair, she parked herself upon his knee, purring, "It's the most gorgeous ring I've ever seen, thank you, my love." Gently wrapping her arms around his neck, they once again kissed, then breaking from the embrace she nibbled his earlobe, whispering, "I love you so much, Jack Gilroy."

"And so ya should! That thing cost me an arm and a leg, so it did!" Joking aside, Jack looked directly into her eyes, whispering,

"Can I ask you something, Lucy?"

"You can ask me anything you want to, my darling."

He puffed his cheeks, hesitated, then asked, "Are you like... Catholic?"

"Yes, I am actually," she replied, slightly confused. "Why do you ask?"

He huffed relieved, muttering, "Nowt really... nowt."

"I know why," she chuckled, gently poking his chest, "it's to do with Ma's religion, and that funny old priest, isn't it?"

"Aye sort of, but it makes no difference to me what religion you are."

"The same goes for me, Jack, I'll marry you in any old church that takes your fancy; to be perfectly honest I would marry you this instant in one of those register offices, or we could even elope to Gretna Green, if you fancied that."

"Gretna Green eh!" he said, widening his eyes. "Now that might not be such a bad idea that."

A young Italian waitress approached the table, smiling friendly she pulled out a pad and pencil from her apron. "Are you readies to orders?" she asked in a broken English accent that the old Jack would have found sexy enough to try his luck at pulling her.

"Yes, we are thanks," said Lucy, grinning affably as she returned to her seat, "could we have two Penny Al Fornos, a ten-inch garlic bread and a side serving of fries please."

"Is that one's side servings of fries or two's?"

Lucy pondered. "Mmm... go on then, make that two portions please."

"And can a' have my chips cooked dead, dead crispy please?" Jack smiled.

"Off courses you cans, sirs," she returned with a slightly flirty grin as she jotted down the order. Retrieving the menus, she leant over the table beaming friendly at Lucy. "I am glads you said yess to this handsome man's proposals of... Mmm...hows do you pronounces it... marriages! For my friend was goings to send myself overs to asks him if she could marriages him if you did not wants to have marriages with him."

"The cheeky mare!" bleated Lucy, smirking over her shoulder at a girl before swivelling back to exchange friendly grimaces with the waitress.

A soft September morning greeted Easington with spectacular tints of orangeness as falling leaves swathed allotment alleyways with a crisp carpet of brown and gold. Perched at the top of a barbed wire fence, a plump robin swayed to balance as he expressed his glee by chirping high-pitched cheeps while in the sky flights of dotted pigeons circled above individual lofts. Hoss and his father had finished cleaning out their loft and were sat smoking on a veranda. Rocking contentedly in his chair, Joe drew on a tipless cigarette, saying, "Don't forget... Tom wants a couple a' bags... of bird muck taking round for his onion bed... after we've finished up here like."

"A' nar, anyhows, he said if he had the time, he was ganna tack them around his sell."

"Are why that's... even better still... saves you carting the stinking stuff off all... ower the place." Joe looked to the sky, whispering, "Ya nar, son... next to a... loving smile from a sweetheart... there's not a finer sight ganning than... a man's pigeons on the wing."

Smiling slightly, Hoss glanced up at the circling birds. "Aye, ya not far wrang there, but it's not exactly my cup of tea, Da."

"I know it's not, son." Joe coughed endlessly. "And speaking of sweethearts... what plans have ya got..." breathing deeply he searched for his breath, "... for you and Margret after... the strike's all finished with then?"

"A' don't really know yet," said Hoss, "a' was hoping we'd probablys end up getting married and that."

"Why get the lass asked... she's a right good'n... so she is." Clutching at his chest, Joe twisted his face due to a discomforting pain.

"Are you alright, Da?"

"Aye, it's just a bit of heartburn son... that's all."

"Ya getting them pains far too regular for my liking, ask the doctor to check them out when ya gan and see him the safta?"

"A' will."

"Do ya want me to come with ya?"

"Why nar... I'll be fine."

"Are ya sure?"

"Aye a's positive... thanks."

"Are, why don't forget to mention them chest pains to him."

"A' won't. Will ya remind Margret... to get some more tins of that... pea and ham soup the... next time... she gans up the street?"

"A' will, we need a couple of loafs of bread an'll and some different kinds of soups for ya."

"A' nar we do, son... but a' like that pea and ham... the best," he said before once again rattling out a string of bottomless coughs.

Jack pulled down a sun visor from the top of his windscreen in an attempt to shield his eyes as he steered his truck down a gravelled track to pass by a bright yellow sign indicating Steve Arkinson Drilling Company Ltd, in bold red letters. Parking in front of a prefab office, he glanced to one side of the compound as a vicious looking rottweiler drew his attention by barking frothy mouthed while pacing back and forth within a caged enclosure that housed a metal lockup along with a fleet of drilling rigs, a pickup truck, and a trio of identical trailers. At the opposite side of the penned impound, hundreds of lengthy pipes and clamping joints were stacked aside a host of drill bits, drilling rods, and an amalgamation of different sized soil sampling chambers, while to the rear of the stockade an old Land Rover stood isolated minus its wheels and engine. Jack smiled his way into a trendy office to be greeted by walls painted in a light shade of grey that just about coordinated with a trio of metal filing cabinets. Strip light fittings were strategically placed throughout a polystyrene-tiled ceiling while underfoot a charcoal carpet ran wall to wall, setting off a small kitchen area and a trio of contemporary desks that were finished in walnut veneer. Lucy sat at a reception desk typing on a keyboard that was attached by a short cable to a recently installed Sinclair Spectrum, the most modern, up to date office computer that was currently on the market. Leaning over, he pecked a tender kiss onto her cheek whispering, "Morning, love?"

"Morning, my darling," she replied. Feathering the side of his face with the back of her hand, she asked, "And what do I have the pleasure of your company for this morning?"

"I've brought ya Da some coal." Once again, he pecked her cheek, asking, "Where's he at anyways?"

"He's just popped up to the shop to get some dog food for Bruno and a jar of coffee and biscuits for me." Fiddling her engagement ring, she sighed, "Jack, I think this ring may need resizing, it's quite loose and I don't want it slipping from my finger."

"Why we'll take it back to the jewellers on Saturday, if you want?"

"We carn't, you and your Tom's working for my father this weekend."

"We'll do it the weekend after then." Crossing the room, he switched on a kettle before glancing over his shoulder, asking, "Orr if ya that uncomfortable with it, ya could take it back ya sell, only if ya fancied though?"

"Do you know I may just do that, have you got the receipt handy?"

"Aye it's in the truck somewhere, a' think it might still be in the glove compartment actually."

CHAPTER FIVE

The sound of tyres scrunching gravel once again set Bruno away barking ahead of the office door creaking as Steve Arkinson stepped into the office clutching a carrier bag. Steve was aged in his late forties; he was quite tall, standing just over six two and was slender looking, yet still he carried a bit of a pot belly; his hair was dark, matching a handsome moustache that crept with a tinge of grey at the edges, and his eyes were penetrating blue. Steve was dressed casually in fawn chinos, a pale blue shirt, and a tie that was strewn in comical, cartoon styled golfers swinging their clubs. "Alright, Jack?" he asked, smiling friendly.

"Aye canit grumble, Steve, and you?"

"Same, son, same." Resting a carrier, he removed a jar of coffee, asking, "Is the kettle on?"

"Yeah," answered Jack. "So, have you decided which site are we drilling at, at the weekend then?"

"Yeah, the one up near Berwick," he answered just as the kettle boiled to a click. "Jim will be with yas on Saturday, but I'll have to pull him off first thing Sunday morning, will yas be alright on your own?"

"Why aye, it's not exactly rocket science."

"Good, there's thirty holes to sink, it's already staked out where you need to drill."

"It's still fifteen feet you want us to drill down to though, isn't it?"

"Yes, and take two strata samples from each hole, one at eight feet, the other at thirteen. I've booked you and your Tom into a couple of rooms for the weekend at a local pub, it's bed and breakfast, and there's an evening meal included, plus they'll provide yas with sandwiches to take out to eat on the job."

"Champion." Jack smiled. "What's the name of this pub then, Steve?"

"The Three Barrels, it's actually half decent, I've stopped there once or twice myself in the past, the food's lovely and they serve a nice pint too." He winked slyly at Jack before teasing his daughter, "And there's a rather tasty young barmaid working behind the bar, apparently she's very hospitable if you catch me drift, she–"

"Dad!" broke in Lucy with a twisted face. "That's not even funny so don't go there!"

He chuckled, "Why it is a little bit, love."

"No, it's not! So, stop it, or I'm telling you now, Jack won't be going anywhere at the weekend."

"I'm only winding ya up, sweetheart!" came back in an apologetic tone. Spooning coffee, he laughed to himself before blowing, "Besides, Jack's not that way inclined." Noticing his daughter's disenchanted expression, he hastily changed the subject. "How's the new computer coping, love?"

"It's brilliant, it's twice as fast as the old one, I've finished all those spreadsheets you asked for."

"What, all of them?" he asked between tearing open a packet of bourbon biscuits with his teeth.

"Yes, all of them, and I've done the entire shift rotas right up to the end of next month too."

"Well done, love." Filling three cups he faced Jack, asking, "Did you manage to get any coal or not, Jack?"

"Yeah, there's twenty bags in the back of the truck for ya."

"Good lad, you carn't get hold of the stuff for love nor money, coal's like hens' teeth around here now, so how much do I owe you then?"

"The same as the last time... nowt."

Steve passed around the drinks before peeling notes from a thick wad. "Here's a fifty quid donation for your mother's kitchen fund then."

"Cheers! Ya don't have to ya know."

"I know I don't, but I want to."

Lucy scowled over her shoulder, ordering, "You better keep well away from that barmaid up there at the weekend, I'm telling you, mind, Jack."

Jack frowned in bewilderment. "What have I said!? It wasn't me, it was ya Dad!"

"I know who it was, I'm just warning you, that's all." Rapidly manoeuvring the tips of her fingers around the keyboard she shuffled her backside into the back of chair, and with an irate glare aimed at her father, she snapped, "Pass the bourbons over... mischief-maker!"

FRIDAY MORNING

At the Colliery Club, pans of boiling vegetables went unchecked, sending swirling steam to mist a ceiling as music sounded from a radio. Irene stood peeling potatoes alongside Debbie, whilst on a separate worktop Tracy and Bev were busy prepping other vegetables. At an additional cooker, Sue stood tapping her foot along to the beat of the music as she leant forward to inspect a huge pot simmering with rich onion gravy. Tracy caught a glimpse of the bubbling vegetables. "Bloody hell!" she whooped, quickly removing the pans to a draining board. "The veg was about to boil dry there!"

"Is it okay!?" asked Sue from over her shoulder.

"Aye!" answered Tracy, prodding a fork. "Just about though!" A soft knocking at a fire exit door drew her attention; knife in hand, Irene opened up to face a trio of strangers who were stood holding boxes brimming with groceries.

"Hi, I'm Catherine Ainsley..." said the youngest of the three who stopped midsentence whilst casting a deep frown at the sight of Irene stood clutching a huge knife, but she resumed, "... and these are my parents, Shelagh and Billy Ainsley. We have come with food parcels. To be honest I don't even know if this is the right place or not, we are looking for a certain Irene Gilroy, a nice man from the picket line gave us directions and we're hoping this is the right..." once again the knife took up her attentiveness, "... place, like."

Within the blink of an eye Irene took to these strangers, "Hello, I am Irene Gilroy," she greeted with a warm grimace, "and yes you are at the right place, come on in... come on." Brandishing the blade, she joshed, "Please excuse the knife, we've got a couple of scabs tied up in a backroom, only joking, there's four of them really..." Her smile stretched to border mischief. "... Actually I'm on peeling tatties, hate the job mind you, but I'm afraid it has to be done." Irene ushered them into the hall, and though they were total strangers she could tell at just one glance that these people were a happy, close-knit family.

Shelagh looked Irene in the eye. "I'll give you a hand to peel them tatties if you want, Irene?"

"Why nar, it's okay, love, but thanks all the same though."

Aged in his late fifties, Billy stood around five foot six and had lost most of his hair with just a little grey showing at the rear of his head; he possessed a rather jolly face that blended perfectly with an impish smile, his shoulders were strong tallying leathery hands that were proud workingmen's hands. Shelagh was a little older than Billy and was rather petite, standing no taller than five feet in her stocking feet, her hair was tinted auburn and styled to just above her shoulders and she boasted a warm, friendly face that was graceful, yet filled with determination. Swanking lengthy blonde hair, Catherine was aged somewhere in the region of her late twenties, or perhaps early thirties, her facial features emulated her mother's gracefulness, yet still she bubbled a certain air of brazenness that was most certainly inherited down from her father; height wise, she once again resembled her mother as she too was petite, standing no more than five feet two.

After introducing these friendly strangers around the lasses, Irene quickly guided them into a separate stockroom. She instructed, "Just put them on that bench there and grab a seat," and the packages were rested down to slight sighs before all sat onto wobbly chairs placed around a tarnished round topped table.

"There's quite a few more boxes still back at the car," said Shelagh, bringing about a huge grin from Irene.

Irene shouted through, "Bev! Tracy! Come in here a minute, flowerpots!?" and the instant the girls entered the room she instructed, "If yas don't mind could yas go to these good people's car and fetch some boxes of groceries back here please?"

"We can get them if you want," put in Catherine, "it's no-bother."

"No, it's okay, we'll manage," said Tracy as the two strangers exchanged jovial smiles.

"Which car is it?" asked Bev.

Handing over a set of keys, Catherine grinned, saying, "It's the light blue Escort in the corner of the carpark, his name is Dave, he has a black vinyl roof, there's quite a bit stuff, mind you."

"That's no problem," said Bev with a grin.

Watching the sisters exit the room, Billy looked to Irene, asking, "Will they be able to manage alright, Irene, they're quite heavy?"

"Why aye they'll manage! They're fit young lasses, man, Billy!" Facing Shelagh, Irene beamed warmly. "So tell me, where have yas come from then, Shelagh?"

"Fairholme, Newcastle," she answered.

"Canny travel then, and by the way, your generosity its much obliged, believe you me it is, things are becoming a bit desperate around here lately."

Catherine queried, "How many meals do you dish out each day, like?"

"We average over eight hundred now, love, but some days we can feed well over a thousand."

"My... good... Lord!" stretched Catherine. "Is it that many!?"

"I'm afraid it is."

"We'll try and get back with more stuff then," promised Billy, "hopefully lots more."

Irene's face once again lit up. "That would be a great help, Billy, every bit helps, it's a pity there's not more folk like you three out there. So, who has been helping you collect all this lot then, your local Labour Party members?"

"Why nor, we did it off our own backs." Shelagh smiled. "With a few friends helping us out like."

Casting a stare satiated in admiration, Catherine eyed her father, chuckling, "One Saturday night Dad even got dressed up as a baby and we pushed him through Fairholme Club in a wheelbarrow with him wearing nothing but a white towel as a nappy and a huge baby bottle stuck in his mouth, great night that was, everyone was in hysterics at the sight of him, and we managed to fill the collection buckets right up."

Laughing aloud, Irene gazed at Billy, saying, "A' bet ya enjoyed it an'll, did ya, Billy!?"

"But of course!" he replied, grinning like a cat in a cream factory.

"He's not called Billy the kidder for nothing, you know, Irene!" tittered Shelagh, bringing about a giggle of laughter from everyone.

Jack came to the doorway, asking, "Can a' have a word?"

"Two ticks, love," returned Irene.

Jack smiled around before turning to walk away leaving Catherine sat wide eyed and open mouthed. "Wow! Who's th... that!?" she mumbled.

"That's Jack."

"He's a dish," fell off her tongue.

"Catherine!" broke in Shelagh. "Stop it! And stop breathing so hard!"

"It's all right, Shelagh, he gets this type of response from the girls all the time, personally a' don't see what all the fuss is about."

"You don't!" exhaled Catherine. "Really!?"

Laughing sharply, Irene replied, "Yes, really, love, but maybe that's because the daft bugger's me son." Beaming around the three, Irene stood, asking, "Tea? Coffee?" The parents' choice was tea, while the daughter, with thoughts still lost elsewhere, decided upon a cup of coffee.

FOLLOWING EVENING

A boisterous rooster grumbled in the end of day. After rattling a partly filled bucket of corn, Joe had finally enticed the last of his pigeons back into his loft before locking the place up for the evening. Walking towards the allotment gate it spit on to rain and instinctively he raised his eyes to a darkening sky, knowing for certain a storm was brewing. Pausing in his stride, he took out a handkerchief to wipe perspiration away from his face and around the back of his neck when from out of the nowhere his face distorted as excruciating pains shot from his chest up through his left arm and into his neck and jawline; eventually these painful spasms eased off, allowing Joe to regain his composure. A flash of lightning lit the sky, closely followed by a clap of thunder before the heavens opened to a downpour of torrential rain. Gritting his teeth, he raised his collar to the wind to set off on his short trek home, but he hadn't stepped a few paces into his journey when he once again clutched at his chest but this time his legs gave way and Joe was dead before even reaching the ground.

The Catholic church teemed as the whole of the village had turned out to pay their last respects to Joe, giving him a sendoff that he truly deserved. A dull tolling from a church bell resonated as Hoss, Tom, Jack and Billy shouldered his casket both into, then out of the church before they followed Father O'Conner through the village cemetery to lay Joe at his eternal resting place. Standing at the graveside, for the first time in his adult life Hoss openly sobbed while he was comforted by soft words from Margret on one arm and Irene on the other. After Father O'Conner had finished a brief graveside ceremony, handfuls of dirt were scattered onto the lowered coffin ahead of the gathering of mourners slowly dispersing in separate groups with a few of them lighting up cigarettes. Heading towards the cemetery gates, Hoss suddenly stopped in his stride to face Irene. "I'm an orphan now, Ma," he muffled whilst drying his eyes.

Irene tightened her clasp on his arm ever so slightly. "Hoss, love, as long as I've got a single breath left in my body you will never be an orphan."

ONE WEEK LATER

Inside a smoke-filled union office, Jack and Tom were sat at a desk, enjoying a cigarette with hands cupped around steamy mugs, while Alan sat opposite, resting his chin over his own hot drink. Fumbling through a top drawer, a smirk tugged at Alan's face as he pulled out a package to reveal an old-fashioned hooked shaped tobacco pipe which boast an oversized bowl that was crafted in shiny briar wood, and much to the brothers' amusement he stuffed the contraption with pipe tobacco then stoked it up by means of deep sucking sounds combined with a thumb constantly flicking across a Zippo lighter. Jack laughed out loud, mocking, "Elementary, my dear Watson! Elementary!"

"Tack the piss all ya want, Jack!" he retorted, puffing merrily away. "But I'm telling ya now this thing is pure class, so it is."

Tom joked, "Tha does look a' bit like that Basil Rathbone mind, Alan, and I'm telling ya now, the first hint of ya pulling out a violin, or the sound of a howling hound in the background and I'm out of here quicker than shit off a stick."

Humming along all content, Alan puffed out clouds of whiffy smoke that soon filled the room. "Yas can laugh all ya want, but this is the new me this is, I'm all sophisticated."

"Ya sophisticated all right!?" Tom frowned. "Does me Ma nar ya've took to a pipe?"

"Nar nor yet, to be honest it's the first time I've ever used it, I'm ganning all Tony Benn and Harold Wilson, like."

"Why a' wadn't count on her letting ya smoke that thing in the house," said Tom, drawing on his cigarette, "especially in front of the telly, it'll interfere with her Coronation Street that thing will!"

Jack teased, "We'll have to get ya one of those deerstalker hats and a tweed cape for Christmas, Alan."

"Keep on gan'n, Jack, but I'm telling ya now, they reckon smoking one of these things isn't half as bad for ya health as what smoking those cigarettes is."

"Who reckons that like?" sniggered Tom.

"Why, everybody!"

Jack broke in, "How'y then! Everybody like who?"

Once again smacking his lips on the pipe, Alan paused in thought then gabbled, "Why, the likes of doctors... and health experts, and the likes of top university professors, and government scientists and that."

Unconvinced, Tom shook his head. "Ballicks government scientists! Ya're just macking it up as ya gan'n along, man!"

"It does smell canny nice like," chortled Jack, "giss a puff!" Alan handed over the pipe and Jack inhaled deeply into his lungs; coughing and spluttering, he managed to mumble, "Fucking...

hell!" as he tried to catch his breath. Quickly handing back the pipe, he babbled, "That thing's fucking mad... me eyes are wattering like hell here!"

Alan shook his head, explaining, "Ya not supposed to tack it right back inta ya lungs, ya daft bugger! Ya supposed to let it mellow in ya mouth then slowly exhale, man."

Jack turned to his brother. "Have a gan of that, young'n, it'll put hairs on ya chist!"

"Like shite a' will! I'd rather wear a Newcastle hat than put that thing anywhere near me gob."

"Have a little gan, man!" encouraged Alan, presenting Tom with the pipe. "Ya never nar, ya might enjoy it."

"A' might shite an'all!" retorted Tom. "It smells fucking rank!"

"Are why..." sniggered Alan. His words hadn't long left his mouth when the phone sounded, interrupting the conversation, "...Hello, Easington NUM, Alan Cunnings speaking..." Within an instant, Alan's light-hearted expression transformed into a concerned scowl. "Who are they like?... Say that again, Trevor, a' didn't quite catch ya there?... Thanks, marra... nor, it's frigging never ending, isn't it." Hanging up the phone Alan eased himself back into his chair with his face drained of colour. Looking at the brothers he sighed endlessly, saying, "There's another two scabs gan'n back into work the morn."

"We gathered that, who!?" asked Tom.

"Norman Kennety," sighed Alan, "and that Kevin Chirlton of all the fucking people!"

Jack snapped, "What, the same Kevin Chirlton who ya had to fight tooth and nail for to keep him his job after the twat was sacked for siphoning men's petrol from their cars. Him?"

"Aye, the very same."

"Do ya nar," groaned Tom, "there was a lot of men dead set against the union for fighting to keep that cunt his job, and that included me."

"Aye, me too an'all!" concurred Jack.

"A' nar that, and a' wished to God I'd listened to yas now."

Jack barked, "He was a twat back then, and he's an even bigger twat now!"

"Isn't that Norman Kennety a north pit winder man?" queried Tom.

"Aye," sighed Alanm "he's in the engineman's union not ours."

Jack sighed lengthily saying, "Poor Don Tapping, he'll gan absolutely berserk when he finds out."

"Too right he will!" agreed Alan. "Cracking union secretary young Don is, straight as a die, and as honest as the day's long so he is." Picking up the phone Alan shushed the brothers then dialled, "... Hello Joe, Joe it's Alan here, get ya sell down to the office as quickly as you can, mate, I'm calling an emergency meeting... nor it's not about that... it's not about that neither... there's two more scabs gan'n back to work tomorrow... I'll tell ya who they are when ya get here, or do is a favour, marra, will ya pop around Gumpy's and let him nar? ... Cheers ... aye best let Alan Ingram nar as well, marra, thanks a lot." Alan hung up, scratching the back of his head he eyed Jack, gasping, "Jack, giss a tab, young'n?"

NEXT DAY

Although the skies were crystal clear over Easington Colliery, an autumnal crispness filled the air, trees leant askew due to a strong wind blowing direct from off the North Sea. At one side of the pit gates, Jack, Tom, and Billy stood amongst a large congregation of pickets who had arrived at the colliery in dribs and drabs with most trekking across open fields after they were turned away at police cordons that blocked off all routes in and out of the village. The whole of Office Street was also crammed with pickets standing toe to toe with row upon row of battle clad Welsh and Lincolnshire police officers who were supported by a heavy reinforcement of SPG officers and detachments of dog handlers with some struggling to hold onto overzealous canines. A timbre of diesel engines broke the morning ahead of a convoy of police vehicles inching Office Street prior to edging towards the pit gates to be met by heavy chants of *'Scabs! Scabs! Scabs!'* Heated outbursts broke out everywhere, truncheons did their now customary role of hammering down on heads, as a routine of angry fists were thrown back in retaliation. *'Here we go! Here we go! Here we go!'* sounded prior to a weighty surge from the pickets smashing through a wall of shields, trampling over injured police officers who were left lifeless where they fell. Wielding his truncheon, Dryden used his short shield to pin a young picket to the floor as he repeatedly beat the screaming kid around his face and head until his high-pitched shrieks ceased, with blood bubbling from the young lad's mouth and nose. Scanning the scene, Dryden grinned fiendishly as he picked out yet another victim, he then proceeded to lash him repeatedly over the back of his head and the picket went to ground with blood streaming from head injuries. Another petrified picket rolled on razor sharp chippings, kicking out and screaming as a dog handler smirked wryly while inciting his dog to attack, wagging its tail enthusiastically, the snarling canine went into a frenzy ripping the man's bloodstained trousers to shreds as it repeatedly sank its teeth into the flesh on his thigh. A burly SPG officer wielded his truncheon as he joined in the assault, lashing the hapless picket around his head and body, leaving him drifting in and out of consciousness with blood seeping from gaping head injuries and deep puncture wounds on his upper leg.

Running battles were taking place everywhere, violent skirmishes were ongoing across the whole of the picket line. Billy had squared up to a cop when he was clobbered from behind by another constable and he slumped to the ground to be dragged away and bundled headfirst into the back of a van. Jack jostled with an SPG sergeant; after trading blows, he managed to rip away the officer's helmet before forcing him down to the gravel floor, standing back a pace he stamped on the officer's face, sending him rolling in agony. Another SPG cop approached with his baton raised. "Fuck you!" snarled Jack, kicking the officer in his balls with so much force that he dropped to his knees like a felled deer.

From out the corner of his eye Tom caught a glimpse of Dryden as he pulverized yet another young picket. Weaving his way through the mayhem, Tom seized Dryden from behind, flinging him to the ground; as he was scrambling back to his feet he once again sent him tumbling, then, squatting over him, he ripped away his helmet, and with one hand gripped tight around Dryden's throat he pounded him repeatedly around his face with heavy blows until his eyes swelled to slits and his head flopped limp to one side with blood trickling from out the side of his mouth. Battered and bruised pickets sat dazed on the floor before most of them were once again truncheoned senseless prior to being carted away to be manhandled into the back of vehicles. The heavy police presence eventually regained control, scattering fleeing pickets off in all directions. Deep inside the pit yard, the backdoors of stationary police vehicles swung open before an escort of SPG offices shepherded a quartet of scabs in the direction of the time office.

Up at the Colliery Club the smell of cooking vegetables drifted from the kitchen into the main hall as the lasses were setting up shop for the day. Stretching out a white cover over a couple of serving tables, Sue looked at Margret, asking, "How's Hoss keeping, Margret?"

"He's okay a' suppose, having said that he's still a bit down in the dumps like, why a canny bit down actually."

"He will be, flowerpots; it takes time to get over the death of a loved one."

Unfolding another sheet, Margret beamed. "He's asked is to move in with him, ya know, Sue."

"Has he!? Well, good for you, girl, ya'll tack ne harm with Hoss, and neither will the littlun neither."

Margret beamed. "A' nar that, the bairn absolutely adores him, and so do I."

"A' nar you do, love, it's as plain as the nose on ya face that you do." Sue smiled beyond Margret, eying Irene as she struggled across the floor clutching a heavy Tupperware container that rattled cutlery with each step she took. "Do ya need a hand, Irene?"

"No, tar, Sue but remind is on to take that beef out the oven, it needs another twenty minutes, and ya nar me, I'm sure to forget about it."

"What ya like?" Sue smiled just as Liz and Jean entered into the hall where they started to assemble more tables. Sue looked to Liz, saying, "What time's ya doctor's appointment, Liz?"

"Half three," she answered with a smile.

"Is Brian going with ya?"

"Nor, he's away picketing for the week down Lancashire."

"Do ya want me to come with ya?" asked Irene.

"No thanks, Irene, I'll be fine." Once again she smiled all appreciative. "But thanks all the same for the offer though."

"Ya showing proper now, mind, Liz." Sue grinned.

"A' nar that," she replied, stretching her smock to tightness over her stomach to unveil an outline of a sizable bump. Looking over her shoulder, she commented, "And I've got a grit arse on is like the back end of a bus."

"That carn't be helped." Sue giggled. "It's all part and parcel of being pregnant a fat arse is."

"Tell is about it!"

"How far ya on now, like?" enquired Irene.

"Just over five months. Eeh sorry, I'm nearing six months now, my good God time flies!"

Smiling broadly, Irene looked Liz up and down. "It's definitely a baby girl ya carrying."

"Fingers crossed, Irene," sighed Liz as John and Micky waltzed into the hall with each carrying huge boxes and Micky flashing his usual grin that overflowed brazenness.

"Compliments of the Co-op, ladies!" whooped John, carefully resting his load onto a tabletop. "And there's boatloads more where that's came from."

"Any chance of a coffee, Sue?" asked Micky as he too lowered his box. "I've got a throat on is like Gandhi's flip-flops, here!"

"Aye but ya'll have to mack it ya sell, we're running right behind."

"Ne bother." He beamed, and with a spring in his step he made his way into the kitchen to join a huddle of other volunteers.

"Mack me one an'all, marra!" shouted John just as a tall, middle-aged man with dark, handsome features, entered the hall all dressed sharp in an expensive looking camel overcoat that matched up with a muffler and a plaid flat cap woven to brown and green checks.

"Can I help ya?" asked Irene, her tone suspiciously blunt as she presumed that this stranger's presence was that of a snooping reporter who was simply up to no good.

"Yes, if you could, we were directed here to liaison with a certain Sue Temple, or an Irene... Gilroy. Tommy Callin from Redhills sent us here."

"I'm Irene Gilroy." She frowned, puzzled.

"And I am Sue Temple," put in Sue, wide eyed and curious.

The stranger grinned friendly, saying, "We have a load of food parcels outside." He held up a large, padded envelope. "And there's some cash in here that we managed to collect before we set off." He handed Irene the envelope. "There's over a grand in there."

To say Irene was overwhelmed would have been a huge understatement. She shouted the girls through from the kitchen, then presenting the cash she whooped, "Girls... look what this lovely man here has just donated..." The girls applauded as Irene looked at him teary-eyed. "...Thank you so, so much... what's your name by the way?"

"James." He offered Irene his hand. "James–"

"Bond," broke in Liz, who just couldn't stop herself, "sorry!"

He smiled. "It's James Taylor actually."

"So where have you travelled from, James Taylor?" enquired Irene, showing him a seat.

"London."

"What like in the capital London?" broke in Sue.

"Yes," he said, "the very place. We are representees from the NUJ–"

"NUJ?" cut in Liz with a frown.

"National Union of Journalists, and we thought it only fitting that we expressed what us genuine journalists truly think of the miners and their struggle, and not the garbage views from the likes of Murdoch's Sun and other inappropriate tabloids."

"Well, that's nice of you." Irene smiled. "Who'd have thought it, friends down in Fleet Street, eh!" She looked to Jean, saying, "Don't just stand there like one a' clock half struck, Jean, make this fine-looking gentleman here a nice cup of coffee?"

"How many sugars, James?" asked Jean straightening herself to presentable.

He smiled. "Just the one please, no milk."

Jean gushed, "Is there any more just like you outside, is there?"

"There is, actually, there are six of us all together."

"Six!?" voiced Sue. "What, have you travelled up in a blinking train?"

He grinned. "No, we drove up in two vans actually, and both are filled to the brim with food parcels."

"Two vans!?" gulped Sue., "Filled to the brim with food parcels!?" She sat all dumbfounded before mumbling, "Ya'd better mack that six coffees and a double brandy for me, Jean, love."

FOLOWING WEEK

The heavens opened over the windswept heaths at Tow Law scattering sheep the length of an open field to take up refuge behind a dry-stone-wall. At the main site entrance into Banksy's opencast mine, Jack and the lads also took up shelter by a wall while opposite, a couple of police vans were parked at a roadside with the occupants sat enjoying steamy drinks within the warmth and comfort of their vehicles. Clasping his coat lapels together, Jack shook his head as he looked over at the huddling sheep. He yawned deeply, mumbling, "A' divant nar wee's the daftest, us or them frigging things?"

"Probably's us," sighed Hoss. Scanning the surroundings, he added, "There's nowt up here but fields of frigging sheep, and a' dinit like the look of them buggers, they're right ugly looking things so they are."

Tom lit up a cigarette, jesting, "A' dinit nar about that like, Hoss, they'd look canny covered in mint sauce."

"Too right they wad," agreed Jack, "there's nowt tastes better than a shoulder of lamb covered in Ma's mint sauce."

"A' like m-m-mutton chops the best me, like," said Billy as he too lit up, "a' love the f-f-fat on them, especially if they're cooked n-n-nice and crispy."

Licking his lips, Hoss drooled, "Mmm ya canit beat the ard mutton chops, the fat tastes better than what the meat diss."

Gazing across the fields, Jack sighed elongated, moaning, "Do ya nar something, if somebody had told me before this strike had started that I'd be standing for over six hours in the pissing down rain in the middle of newhere for a measly fower quid, I'd have thowt that they were off their rockers!" After a quick check of his watch, he raised, "And what's keeping Alan, he's late again for the umpteenth time this week."

"What time's it, like?" asked Tom.

Once again Jack checked his watch, snapping, "Twenty past frigging two!"

"He is canny late like," groaned Tom, "a' wonder what's keeping him?"

Hoss looked to the sky. "A' divant nar but he wants to mack sharp, I'm frigging frozen here."

"It's always t-t-two coats carder up here, H-H-Hoss," said Billy, drawing on his cig.

"Tell is about it!" moaned the big man. "It snaws in the frigging summer up this shithole!"

Billy gazed beyond the lads as in the distance, a mountain of a man dressed in a waxy cowboy-styled coat and a Stetson hat approached whilst sat upon an enormous Shire-type horse. Billy drew attention, gasping, "Who the h-h-hell's this!" As the elderly cowboy drew nearer, his ruffled appearance became apparent, his face was all pockmarked and weather-beaten with a prominent nose that was slightly upturned while a white goatee beard dangled a good ten inches from under his chin to match snowy hair that was lengthy and tousled. Open mouthed, Billy pointed, saying, "Look! It's Wild B-B-Bill Hickock!"

"He looks more like Buffalo Bill to me!" Jack laughed.

With a cheeky grin, Hoss attempted a rather pathetic impersonation of John Wayne, saying, "The hell it is! That there, sitting up on that horsey, is none other than Rooster Coburn himself!" Instantly all broke out giggling.

As the cowboy was passing, he tipped his hat politely, saying, "Afternoon, gentlemen."

"Good afternoon," said Tom open mouthed.

"Good luck with the strike, lads," beamed the stranger all friendly.

"Thanks," was returned in unison.

The stranger sent his horse to trot with Jack shouting, "Watch out for them Apaches, marra! They're just around the newk there," and the man raised a hand in response.

Another ten minutes of standing in the rain had passed before Alan's vehicle pulled up at the entrance of the site, with Alan winding down his window. At once Tom shook his head, moaning, "Where the fuck ya been!? We're soaked ta the skin here!"

"Sorry, a' had ta change a tyre."

A couple of police officers quickly exited a vehicle, one rather plump cop stood next to the wing of the car as the other leant into the driver's side window, instructing, "Move your car now or you will be arrested!"

"Two ticks, I'm just picking the lads up." Alan smiled sharp and false.

The cop ordered, "Never mind two ticks, now!"

"All right, keep ya hair on, man!" Alan shouted the lads over. "Get ya arses in here now!"

As they were climbing into the car, Jack side eyed the plump policeman as he scraped a coin across the car wing, scratching the paintwork. "Huw thuw!" bellowed Jack. Then, quickly approaching the cop, he growled, "What do ya think ya playing at!?"

Other officers quickly exited the vans surrounding Jack.

"I don't know what you are talking about, sir," smirked the officer.

"Aye ya do!" Jack pointed out the fresh scraping on the paintwork. "Ya've just scratched along the side of the car, a' stood and watched ya do it, ya fucking tool!"

"Who are you calling a fucking tool?" raised the cop through gritted teeth.

"I'm calling you a fucking tool, ya grit bag a' shite! And don't stand there gritting ya teeth at me neither, or a' might just knock a couple of the fuckers out."

"Are you threatening me?"

Alan leant his head from out of the side window, intervening, "No he's not threatening ya, officer." Looking at Jack, he almost pleaded, "Leave it, Jack, please get in the car, it's not worth it!"

"Listen to what your comrade says, you scruffy cunt," came sarcastically from the constable as he stepped nose to nose with Jack.

Jack narrowed his eyes, and for a brief moment his instincts cried out for him to snap a headbutt at this officer, but instead he smirked slightly, snarling, "Fuck you!" before stepping into the car ahead of them driving off.

Tom shuffled to comfort in the backseats, saying, "A' thowt for a split-second ya was ganna nut that fucker there, mind, young'n."

"For a split-second a' was," breathed Jack sitting fidgety aside his brother, "a' was so tempted to twat him one."

Alan eyed Jack through his rearview mirror, muttering, "I'm glad ya didn't, son, 'coss that's exactly what they wanted ya to do, they haven't got a single ounce of integrity between the lot of them... bastards they are, fucking bastards!"

Jack lit up a cigarette, saying, "It might have been worth it though, Alan." Inhaling deeply, he continued, "Just to see the look on his face after I'd levelled the fat get."

"It would have been funny, like," laughed Hoss.

"Aye w-w-wad it," agreed Billy.

"It would have been canny funny like," sniggered Tom, lighting up, "but I'm glad ya kept ya head, young'n, well done."

OCTOBER "SHE'S G-G-GONE!"

Although September had given way to October, climate wise the days were similar, mainly dull, wet, and windy with the only notable changes being that the wind was now blowing just that little bit colder, and with each passing day the shadows of night drew in a tad earlier. To the dismay of the Easington miners, another five of their fellow colleagues had broken the strike, taking the total returned back to work now standing at nine, and for the first time since the strike had started, an actual genuine scab bus was laid on to shepherd these strike-breakers through the picket line. Earlier that week, an emergency union meeting had taken place at the Welfare Hall at the request of a few discontented members who sought a vote recommending that the lodge pressed the National Executive for an immediate national ballot, but after a show of hands their proposal was unanimously rejected.

Upping the stakes, the government had endorsed new tactics of nightly raids on so-called activists' houses, resulting in men being hauled disorientated from the comfort of their homes and loved ones to be firstly interrogated prior to them being dragged up before the courts, who then administrated unwarranted court orders preventing them from picketing at any of British Coal's properties for the remainder of the strike.

Emerald-coloured curtains marked the end of day at number two Cuba Street. Mick was happy enough to perch himself asleep upon Irene's lap as she sat knitting; occasionally she would break into a grin as she side eyed Tom, chuckling away whilst lost in a side-splitting episode of 'Only Fools and Horses'. Irene sat pondering, and for the first time since the strike had started, she found herself having doubts regarding its outcome; although still keen to do her bit, she knew deep down that the men stood little, if any chance of winning this dispute, for the signs were everywhere, huge mountains of coal stood stockpiled all over the country and selfish hauliers were more than willing to grab the thirty pieces of silver on offer to move it to wherever required. There was more than a trickle of men returning back to work throughout the various coalfields, and there was very little aid from the TUC, let alone the Labour Party, as Kinnock, for some unknown reason, had turned his back totally on Scargill and the strikers. Thatcher was tapping the law courts into bringing in discriminating new acts including the unjust freezing of all the NUM's monies and assets, yes, the cunning vixen was well and truly outfoxing the foxes with tactical policies that had managed to turn miner against miner a long way back; but now, to the media's delight, the strike was turning brother against brother, and in some communities father against son. Putting all this aside, Irene, like her two sons, was committed to seeing out this dispute to the very end whatever the outcome was going to be. Irene watched Tom cleaning wax from inside his ear using one of her metal hairclips. Frowning deeply, she asked, "What ya doing!?"

Tom side eyed his mother. "Eeh!"

"What ya doing with that hairclip?"

"Cleaning me lug out, it's itchy."

"Why will ya give ower, I'll be using that in the morning; besides ya shouldn't put nowt in ya ear except ya elbow."

Tom chuckled, "That's what me nanna keeps saying."

"Aye and she's right, poking ya ear can cause all sorts of problems, and rinse that clip out in a cup of boiling water when ya gan in the kitchen."

"A' will, a' always does," he replied, throwing the clip onto the mantelpiece top.

Irene yawned lengthily, asking, "When's Billy and Hoss back from picketing, son?"

"They should have returned the safta," he answered, lighting up a cigarette.

"They were somewhere up Scotland, weren't they?"

"Aye," he sighed, "at Bilston Glen again."

"Whereabouts is this Bilston Glen at, Tom; I've heard so much about the place and I've often wondered where it is."

"It's just afore ya get ta Musselburgh and Edinburgh, Ma, but they'll be stopping at Prestonpans like we did."

"A' like the Jocks," she said from over the top of her knitting, "they're nice and friendly."

"They are that... they spoilt us rotten when me and Jack was up there."

"A' know yas said they did, wasn't it an elderly lady who was looking after yas?"

"Aye, she was called Mary, her son was the NUM lodge secretary at Bilston Glen Colliery, she was lovely, cracking cook an'll mind ya."

"I'll have to get Alan to dig out her address so a' can write her a nice little letter thanking her for all her hospitality... wasn't it a young Scottish lass who was keep phoning up here day after day asking for our Jack? Or was it a bit lass from somewhere down in Lancashire who was phoning?"

"It was both," exhaled Tom, "there was one from up Prestonpans way, and one from down Agecroft Colliery."

"Agecroft Colliery?" Irene frowned.

"It's near Manchester, Ma."

Casting a line on her knitting, she breathed, "Poor things, fancy phoning all that way and he wadn't even answer their calls, still, it was for the best a' suppose, with Lucy coming along and that." A knocking at the door set Mick away barking as he jumped from Irene's lap, his yapping soon transformed into tail wagging as he greeted Billy into the room. "Speak of the devil," said Irene, resting her knitting. Noticing Billy's subdued grimace, she asked, "Are ya alright, Billy?"

"Nor, not r-r-really, Mrs Gilroy," he said, sitting alongside Tom, "she's g-g-gone!"

"She's gone, who's gone?" Irene frowned.

"M-M-Marie, sh-sh-she's took the b-b-bairns and left is. All the f-f-furniture's gone too, the beds, wardrobes, c-c-couch, chairs, everything, she's even t-t-took the dog and the t-t-telly and video, b-b-but for some unknown reason she's left the telly r-r-remote control behind and an ard chair from the kids r-r-room. There's a note too, basically s-s-saying she doesn't l-l-love is anymore."

"A' bet a pound to a pinch of salt it'll have something to do with your Tony," broke in Tom.

"You don't know that!" snapped Irene, lighting up a cigarette. "So keep ya thoughts to yourself, lad!"

"I'm afraid T-T-Tom's right, Mrs Gilroy," breathed Billy as he too lit up, "she's put in the letter saying that she l-l-loves him."

Irene moaned, "Why pity about her! He's just a bit kid!"

"She's been besotted with him for yonks!" raised Tom. "The pair of them's not worth a tab end between them, ya better off without her, young'n."

"Well, you can stop here for as long as ya want, son, our Jack's stopping at Lucy's so there's a bed ganning spare for tonight, and there's a couch there for as long as you need it."

"Thanks, M-M-Mrs Gilroy," he said, managing a smile before drawing deep on his cigarette.

Irene stood, asking, "Are ya hungry?" He shook his head in answer. "I'm sure you can manage a bacon butty," she uttered, grinning her way from out of the room.

Tom shouted through, "Mack me a' one an'll, Ma, please!" Checking his mother was out of hearing distance, he looked at Billy, whispering, "Let the fucker gan, Billy, she's ne good for nowt, she's a complete waste of space, she's been sneaking your Tony into your bed every time ya gan away picketing."

"How d-d-do you nar that, like!?"

"Because Hoss caught them at it a while back, but he didn't want to say out to ya 'coss he didn't want ta hurt ya feelings."

With an air of disappointment, Billy snapped, "Some friend he is! He should h-h-have said something s-s-straight away!"

"It's not Hoss' fault, Billy."

"A' nar it's n-n-not, but–"

Tom broke in, "But nowt, Billy, she's no good, she's turned into a right ard slapper, there's even rumours ganning about that your Tony wasn't even the first kid she's been shagging, apparently she was humping the young milkman years ago when you were at the pit on back shift."

"Who, Nitch?"

"Aye, that's him, he was anly a bit kid an'll, in fact a' think he'd just left school at the time."

"A' d-d-don't believe that f-f-for one second."

Tom sighed sharply. "Neither did I, not 'till these recent events cropped up, but now well, a' don't know, was she?"

"A' canit s-s-see Nitch gan'n behind me b-b-back, Tom."

"Here if it's laid out on a plate for him he's ganna tack it, young'n, there's no meat tastes sweeter than easy meat."

"But what a-a-about the bairns though?"

"You can sort things like that out through the courts, marra."

"A nar a' can, a-a-and a' will if and w-w-when that time c-c-comes, but that's the last thing on me m-m-mind at the moment, we've been together ever since we w-w-were kids at school, man!"

"A nar yas have, but she's changed, that twat of a nephew of yours has changed her, and he's a good for nowt piece of shit too, the pock-faced get." Tom lit up. "Anyway, ya can do a lot better than her, have ya seen that grit conk on her?"

Billy gulped. "Ya carn't h-h-help who ya fall in lo...'" when from nowhere Tom's words dawned on him, and he stopped midsentence asking, "...what's wrong w-w-with her nose?"

"Have ya not noticed it?" chuckled Tom. "It's as bent as a coat hanger; ya can hang a donkey jacket on that thing!"

"It's not that b-b-bad," sighed Billy, removing his coat.

Irene popped her head around the door. "I've put some sausages in the pan an'all, Billy."

"Thanks, M-M-Mrs Gilroy," he replied, mustering up a half-hearted smile, "a' hope I'm not b-b-burdening ya?"

"Don't talk so daft! A' might as well do ya an egg and a few chips too," she uttered, retreating back into her kitchen.

Flicking cigarette ash into the fire, Tom whispered, "Our Jack's ganna kill him when he finds out."

"A' don't w-w-want that happening, Tom." Billy drew nervously on his cigarette, "It'll not h-h-help one iota, it'll hurt our poor Ralph so much if Jack beats him up, besides that, I'll never get her b-b-back then."

"Do ya really want her back after all this shit, like!?"

"A' don't know... a' think a' do though."

"I'd better tell him not to do owt then, mind you he might not tack any notice, tha nars what he's like."

"Please don't let him d-d-do owt, Tom?"

"I'll not."

"P-P-Promise?"

"A' promise."

Irene re-entered the room holding a round chocolate tin that was decorated in Christmas scenery and filled to the brim with an assortment of biscuits. Sitting, she faced Billy with a grin, saying, "Tea won't be long, son, I've buttered ya three slices of bread too." Removing the lid, she presented the container, enthusing, "Would ya like a nice Wagon Wheel 'till ya supper's ready, Billy?"

"No, t-t-tar, thanks."

NEXT DAY

Although it was a bright sunny morning, a strong wind blew in from the North plummeting Easington into a cold spell. Smoking cigarettes, the lads were clothed in winter attire, including thick coats, woolly hats and mufflers as they stood warming their hands around a glowing fire at the pit gates. With his tail wagging nonstop, Mick sniffed his way along the foot of a wall before approaching a couple of police vehicles where he cocked his leg to mark his territory up the side of one of the wheels prior to him returning to sit at heel by Jack's feet. It was almost noon and Hoss was all on edge for today was once again, one, of every other but one, Thursdays in the month meaning roast beef and Yorkshire pudding was on the menu up at the Club kitchen, and today there was an additional bonus for him too, as Margret just happened to be on serving duty resulting in him becoming even more eager than ever to get up there. Hoss paced back and forth. Squinting at Jack, he asked, "What time's it now, young'n?"

"Two minutes ta twelve, Hoss, one minute after the last time ya asked is."

Gawking up the street the big man moaned, "There's still ne sign of Pinky and Oddy yet, yad think they'd be here by now... wadn't ya!?"

"There's plenty of time!" broke in Tom with a grin. "It's not even twelve a' clock yet, man, young'n."

Hoss looked around the group, moaning, "Why yad think they'd come in a bit earlier for a change, we've early loused them plenty a' times in the past."

"When have we c-c-come in early for them l-l-like, Hoss?" asked Billy, drawing on his cigarette.

Flicking his cigarette butt into the heart of the blazing drum, Hoss stimulated, "Like not last Tuesday but the Tuesday afore!"

Tom voiced, "Aye, that's because they were all ganning to a funeral.""How'y, Hoss, we'll start the truck up," chipped in Jack as he too cast his cig butt into the fire, "and if ya stop all ya whinging a' might even let ya have me Yorkshire pudding when we get up there." Clicking his fingers, Jack encouraged, "How'y, Mick, son!" Hoss grinned widely as they made the short journey to the truck where Jack lifted Mick up into the cab before they shuffled to comfort with Mick content to sit upon Hoss' lap. After a slight pause of silence, Jack twisted the ignition key a couple of times only for the engine to struggle to a rumble then stall, a further twist of the key finally started the thing up and Jack smirked slightly as he put pedal to floor, revving the engine up to a smoky timbre.

Warming his hands over the pyre, Tom looked at Billy. "Are ya comfortable enough on the settee, Billy?"

"Aye, it's n-n-not that bad actually."

"Ya can have my cot at the weekend, I'm off down Pat's."

"Thanks, a' d-d-divant nar what a' would have d-d-done without yas, mind, Tom, especially Ma, she's b-b-been a G-G-Godsend."

"Here, it's nowt," beamed Tom, rubbing his little friend's shoulder, "and like Dionne Warwick says, that's what friends are for, marra... why excluding the marra bit."

"Did ya nar D-D-Dionne Warwick and W-W-Whitney Houston are f-f-first cousins, Tom?"

"Nor a' didn't actually, now there's a thing, great singers must run in their family, eh?"

"Must do; when we get b-b-back to work as ganna give Ma some m-m-money."

Tom laughed, "Think she'd tack it like!? Not a cat in hell's chance wad she, in fact she would be highly annoyed if ya even tried to offer her it."

"A' n-n-nar that."

"Don't worry, Billy, she nars how grateful you are, ya keep telling her plenty of times each day."

Billy gazed into the fire, asking, "Do ya think Ma and Alan will ever g-g-get married, Tom?"

"A' haven't the foggiest, it's never crossed me mind." He paused, scratching the back of his head in thought. "A' should imagine they will do one day though."

"It would be n-n-nice if they d-d-did." Billy smiled. "They mack a c-c-canny couple them two do."

"Speak of the devil," said Tom, nodding in the direction of Alan as he hurried along Office Street towards them. Checking his watch, Tom joked, "And what time do ya call this like, eh?"

"I've been packing me suitcase, Tom, Blackpool the morn."

"Alright for s-s-some an'all," broke in Billy.

"I'm not gan'n there on holiday, tha nars, Billy! I'm gan'n to a TUC conference, it's never ending for me, work, work, work, and more blinking work so it is."

"Fetch is some r-r-rock back for the bairns." Billy smiled.

"A' will do, how ya keeping anyways?"

Billy came back with, "F-F-Fucking s-s-suicidal still!"

"Why dinit be, ya'll get ower it like a' did with Jean."

"Aye b-b-but Jean didn't f-f-fuck off and leave ya with ya nephew though, Alan, she j-j-just went and d-d-died on ya."

Alan shook his head in disbelief, saying, "And with her dying a' suppose that makes it easier, does it? Anyway, dinit you be contemplating harry-carry, ya've got those bit kids to think about... besides that, ya can do a lot better than her, have ya seen that grit beak on her?"

"Where's all this f-f-fascination about the sh-sh- shape of Marie's beak... a' mean n-n-nose coming from!? There's nowt wrong with h-h-her nose!"

"Yeah right! Ya couldn't bend wire the same shape of that thing is, man, Billy!" Alan looked between the two, saying, "Orr by the way, a' want yas down Hartlepool nuclear power station tomorrow instead of picketing on here."

"Why's that for, like?" Tom frowned.

"I'll tell ya why, Tom, we had an agreement with the transport and general union regarding the transport of hydrogen, but there's a certain tanker driver of theirs being a bit of an arse, he's deliberately speeding dangerously past our lads, and yesterday he nearly mowed a couple of them down, it was by pure luck alone that ne-one was badly injured or even killed by the stupid bastard." Alan handed Tom two ten-pound notes. "There's an extra fiver apiece for ya troubles, besides this yas'll still be paid ya usual day's picketing money for here too."

Billy asked, "What time have we g-g-got to be there for, l-l-like?"

"Six in the morning, Billy." Alan handed Tom more cash. "Jere's another tenner for ya petrol money, young'n."

"Cheers!" Tom smiled. "Bit extra petrol for the weekend."

"Are ya off down Pat's again, like?"

"Aye it's her Da's birthday."

Billy raised his eyes to Alan, asking, "Do ya want us to d-d-do owt special down that p-p-power station, l-l-like?"

"Nor, not really, just to remind this twat'n driver that yas are there, that's all." After a quick check of his watch, Alan smiled sharply, saying, "Look, lads, a's running late, tack care for tomorrow 'coss them cops are shit hot down there." Turning, he was walking off in the direction of the union office when he paused in midstride to look over his shoulder, and with a huge smirk he asked, "Billy! If thy Tony hitches up with Marie, that'll mack him his arn uncle, won't it?"

"F-F-Fuck off!" returned Billy just as Pinky and Oddy approached the pit gates alongside Nobby, Bob English and Bobby Wood. Billy tapped his watch, saying, "And w-w-what time do yas c-c-call this, like!?"

At the Colliery club the waft of roast beef was way above mouthwatering. Lucy had taken a day off from work to help out and was stood at the head of a chain serving out helpings of mashed potatoes. She smiled friendly as she served a balding, middle-aged man, a portion of mash; next in line came a young angelic looking boy who was lanky and no older than thirteen, and though his appearance cried out innocence he was well-known as a notorious windup merchant by the regular volunteers. Facing Lucy, he asked, "Is there any chips, missus?"

Lucy glanced all apologetic, saying, "Sorry, son, it's a roast beef dinner today with a serving of these lovely creamed potatoes."

The young lad glared at her with a dissatisfied squint before his eyes lowered to a colossal pot of mash. "A' divant want any of that crap, a' dinit like mashed chetty!" He loitered around for quite some time flitting his eyes back and forth between Lucy and the steamy pan.

Lucy stood wide-eyed before asking, "Do you want some of these potatoes or not!?"

"Have they got butter in them, like?"

"Would you like butter to be in them?"

"Of course!"

"Good!" she returned sharply. "Because we've added lots of butter today."

He huffed, "Gan on then, a' might as well try some." As Lucy was placing a serving onto his plate, he once again eyed daggers before advancing further along the line until he came to a stop in front of Tracy. "Can a' have baked beans instead of peas?"

"Nor, ya carn't!" retorted Tracy rather bluntly. "Where do ya think ya are, ya granny's yacht!?"

The boy scowled, "My granny's what?"

"Stephen... don't start with ya capers today, a' haven't time! It's either mushy peas or nowt, so there ya gan."

He reluctantly presented his plate, sighing, "Gan on then, a' suppose I'll have some."

With a shake of her head, Tracy served a small amount only to face one eyebrow raised, she added a little more but still a disgruntled eyebrow remained lifted. "Here, ya cheeky little sod!" she snapped, heaping his plate until he beamed brazenly before moving on.

Approaching Bev, the young lad's attitude completely changed. He smiled respectfully, asking, "Can a' have lots of carrots please, Bev? A' love carrots me!" and even though she knew better Bev couldn't stop herself from returning a warm grimace of her own. After she spooned his plate he winked brazenly, saying, "Our Geordie's got the hots for you tha nars, Bev, he thinks ya git, like, top totty and that."

Ladling an extra portion, she uttered, "Does he!?" then leaning closer to the youngster she whispered, "Why when ya get back yerm, Stephen, tell that hunk of a brother of yours he's not so bad himself."

"A' will." Inching the line, he grinned ear to ear as he faced Irene. "Afternoon Mrs Gilroy?" he said in the most politeness of tones.

"Good afternoon, Stephen," came back with a hint of scepticism. Placing a slice of beef onto his plate, Irene frowned slightly asking, "How's ya Ma keeping?"

He stretched, "She's fine thanks."

"And what ya not at school for this time?"

"I've been looking after me Da, he's not very well."

"What's wrong with him, like?"

He hesitated in thought before mumbling, "Orr he's got em... tonsillitis, or it might even be... pleurisy or... scarlet fever... anyway it's something like that."

Irene placed an extra slice of beef onto his plate. "Better get that down ya neck then, keep ya strength up so you can look after him properly."

"Thank you, Mrs Gilroy," he said, fluttering his puppy dogs all innocent.

"Tell ya dad I'm asking after him when ya see him?" she said in the midst of resting a couple of puddings onto his plate.

"A' will thanks," he replied prior to facing Margret who proceeded to flood his plate with rich onion gravy. "Thank you very much," he uttered with a grimace teeming on virtuousness.

"You're more than welcome, son," said Margret before she broke into a lengthy heartwarming smile as she watched him toddle off. "Arr! What a lovely young kid he is, fancy taking time from his studies so he can look after his dad, a' could hug him ta death, bless his little cotton socks."

Irene laughed sharply. "He's not taking time off school to look after his dad, the little shit's playing the nick, man!"

"He never is!"

"Believe you me, Margret... he is! He's like that bloody Casper from that film, Kes! A' right little sod so he is, and the little bugger says owt but his prayers, and he whistles them, gift of the gab that one's got, I'm telling ya now he can tark a man's shirt from off his back that one could, and he could buy and sell us two at a corner end too." Irene stood in brief thought before smiling. "Do ya nar who he reminds me a little bit of, Margret, our Jack, 'coss that sod was exactly the same at his age, yad think butter wadn't melt 'till the little bugger bites ya bloody hand off." The lads entered into the room to join the end of a lengthening queue and the instant Hoss eyed Margret standing ladling gravy disappointment shot his face. Irene noticed his expression; facing Margret she coughed slightly, asking, "Swap ower a bit, love, me back's aching." And to Hoss' delight Margret now stood serving slices of roast beef and Yorkshire puddings.

Jack approached Lucy; leaning over he pecked a quick kiss, saying, "Ya even look gorgeous in that ard apron, so ya do, love."

"I bet you've said that to all the girls in here before," she joked as she served out a portion of mash."

"Who me!" he laughed. "Never!"

"Ya've said it to a c-c-canny few of them, m-m-mind, Jack," put in Billy, his words instantly putting an end to Jack and Lucy's joviality.

"Shut up, Billy!" he chuckled, nudging his little friend before he once again faced Lucy. "He's just pulling ya leg, love," Out of sight, Jack rattled Billy's shin with his foot raising, "Aren't ya!?"

"I am." Billy grinned, his words once again creating a smile to ripple Lucy's face. "It was just a j-j-joke, Lucy."

After they were served meals, the lads picked out an empty table and Hoss smirked widely as Jack scraped a Yorkshire pudding onto his already heaped up plate. "Cheers, marra!" said the big man, seasoning his meal. Picking up his cutlery he smiled all around then started his customary humming as he dived into his meal.

"Watch ya f-f-fingers!" joked Billy.

"And don't forget to come up for air," chuckled Tom.

Looking at Billy, Jack asked, "What ya doing later on then, Billy?"

"Ganing round yerm t-t-to check the h-h-house and put a couple of locks o-o-on the coalhouse door afore all me coal g-g-gans missing."

Jack queried, "Have ya got some locks like?"

Tom broke in, "I've given him a couple of ours what we had gan'n spare at the allotment."

Jack cut into his meat. "Do ya want is ta give ya a hand put them on?"

Billy grinned. "Nor, it's okay, Jack, H-H-Hoss is h-h-helping is out with them."

"Champion!" Jack smiled at the table, saying, "I'm gan'n round Lucy's for me supper the night."

"What with her parents and that like," asked Hoss.

"Nor they've gone off on a minibreak for a couple of days, so you can have me bed, Billy." Looking at his brother, Jack asked, "What ya doing the night then, young'n?"

"Nowt much really, a' might gan ower the wall after Top of the Pops, and get some coal."

Jack stretched, "Watch what ya doing, 'coss there's a lot been getting nicked lately."

Tom shook his head at his brother, laughing, "Shut up, man, Jack! Ya starting to sound like me Ma!"

Seasoning his meal, Jack suggested, "Why don't ya leave it till next Monday night and I'll come with ya?"

Hoss lifted his eyes to Tom, munching, "And I'll come Monday too, I'm running a bit short mesell."

Cutting into his pudding, Tom sighed, "Okay then! We'll go Monday night." Facing Billy, he muttered, "'A' might as well give yas a hand to put them locks on then, Billy."

Billy beamed, saying, "Cheers, m-m-marra."

Tom returned a grin, muttering, "It's ne bother."

"Well, it is t-t-to me!"

Plate in hand, Peter Mallison joined them at the table, smiling. "Alright?"

"Alright," greeted Jack, "owt happening?"

"Nor, nowt much," he replied, seasoning his meal, "or sorry, Steve Fergus and Ronny Kenny got lifted last night."

Tom frowned. "Fergy got lifted? Where at like?"

"Outside the Chinkies, Steve had won a domino card up the Welly, and they popped in for a takeaway supper when a van full of pigs pulled up and set about them before thrawing them into the back of a van."

"Bastards!" said Hoss.

Billy voiced, "It's getting w-w-worse, they can just d-d-do what the hell they w-w-want now!"

Jack asked, "Are they out the nick yet then?"

Peter sighed, "Why not likely, they're still in there!"

FOLLOWING MORNING

In constant drizzle, the lads had parked up at the rear of their fellow pickets' vehicles before walking a short distance to join the mass who had gathered on a grass verge not fifty metres up the road from the entrance to Hartlepool nuclear power station. At the front of the gathering, oblong shields protected row after row of battle-clad policemen who had blocked off the entire roadway leading up to the plant. Adjacent the pickets, a fleet of a dozen or so police vans were parked nose to tail, each filled with SPG officers, while further towards the plant another convoy consisting of ten or perhaps twelve vehicles were parked double abreast, all occupied with Welsh and Lincolnshire police reinforcements. To the rear of the pickets, a rickety wooden fence fronted a lengthy, sheep-filled field that stretched to end at a sand dune beach. Forty metres down the road a news camera crew and reporters stood in front of a set of weighty security gates and a heavily armoured gatehouse which was placed to one side of an additional yellow and black stripy barrier that safeguarded a tarmac road leading directly up to the nuclear reactors of the plant.

Road tankers frequently entered and exited here, with most of the drivers having the courtesy of stopping to chat with the pickets while presenting documents confirming what loads they were hauling. Billy scanned the scene, moaning, "A' dinit l-l-like picketing down here," he nodded towards the plant, "ya can catch c-c-cancer and all s-s-sorts of stuff from what's pouring out that f-f-frigging thing."

"Ehh!" Hoss frowned confused before asking, "What do ya mean ya can catch cancer!?"

Once again, Billy bobbed his head in the direction of the plant, explaining, "A' mean all the r-r-radioactive shit that leaks from that thing d-d-day in a-a-and day out, it's c-c-contaminating the atmosphere, and everything e-e-else 'round here." Pointing towards a herd of sheep, he added, "And a' wadn't eat one of them f-f-fuckers for love n-n-nor money."

Tom agreed, "Nor me too, Billy, and that gans for all the fish that's caught around here too, they'll be contaminated ta fuck 'coss that's where they dump all the radioactive shit, strite into the sea."

"Aye," agreed Jack, "apparently all the nuclear waste they've dumped in there ower the years has caused the sea round here to rise up a degree or two."

Billy eyed Jack, saying, "It has, b-b-but a' wadn't advise ya ta gan s-s-swimming in the thing, mind, Jack."

"A' wadn't think of it, Billy!" Jack lit up a cigarette, continuing, "Yad gan in there with a set of nackers swinging and come back out the with three fuckers."

"Or n-n-none," laughed Billy.

"Exactly," sighed Jack.

Jim Robson, a renowned Horden picket who was a tall, stocky built redhead with a heavily freckled bulldog face and little neck, approached the lads. "Alright lads!?

"Alright, Jim," they answered one after another.

Jim double checked over his shoulder, whispering, "Here, Jack, get a' grip a' this." Carefully removing a paper bag from out of an inside coat pocket, he handed Jack a Molotov cocktail. "Keep this hidden 'till we're ready."

"Wuw! Wuw! Wuw! What the fuck's this!?" Jack frowned, puzzled. "And what do ya mean 'till we're ready, 'till we're ready for what!?"

Jim stepped closer, whispering, "Look, lads, Micky Jones is up the road and when that fucking driver who's been trying his best to mow us down all week is approaching, he's ganna give us the nod and we're ganna petrol bomb the cunt–"

Tom broke in with a determined stare. "Don't talk so fucking baldy headed! Our youngn's not doing that." He snatched the bottle away from Jack, forcing it back into Jim's hands. "Get one of your lot to do it, he's not doing it."

"So, ya not ganna do it then, Jack?" asked Jim, disregarding Tom as if he wasn't there.

"I've just told ya he's not fucking doing it!" defended Tom. "So either fuck off now, or I'll mack ya drink the frigging stuff!" They stood eye to eye before Jim slowly slid the bottle back into an inside coat pocket before turning to walk away.

Jack smiled at Tom, saying, "A' don't mind doing it, tha nars! He just caught is a bit off guard, that's all."

Tom sighed. "Well a' mind! And give ya heed a shake 'coss ya not doing it! We'll get involved with the push and that's about it, end of story."

"I'm bloody sure!" agreed Hoss. "Ya talking years in jail if ya was caught doing owt like that, man, Jack, it's bordering terrorism that is, or even attempted bloody murder, man!"

"Listen t-t-to Hoss, Jack, he's right," spoke Billy, "that thing c-c-could easily kill somebody and not j-j-just the d-d-driver."

"Okay!" Jack smiled with a sigh. "A' catch ya drift!"

In the distance, Micky Jones started waving his arms frantically, drawing the men's attention. "Right, lads!" encouraged Jim. "Come on then, let's give these bastards some jip!" The lads joined other pickets as they surged forward in oneness, forcing the police into the middle of the road while in the distance a tanker truck sped towards them. Like an enormous rugby scrummage, pickets and police drove one another back and forth with SPG officers leaping from vans to join in with the tussle. The tanker driver dropped down through his gears to a crawl, further police reinforcements joined in the chaos, and as the police were forcing the pickets back onto the verge from out of nowhere, a domino of three mini explosions sounded, spattering the tanker with a combustion of flames, causing the driver to break to a sudden stop prior to him jumping from his cab. The flames rapidly danced the tanker with yellow and blue flashes as the pickets were driven further back until they were pressured up against a flimsy fence, which soon gave way, sending men and officers tumbling down a small embankment to land in a watery ditch. Skirmishes were everywhere, pickets and officers clashed in open fields with onlooking sheep standing grass mouthed in bemusement.

Jack rolled on sodden grass grappling with a SPG constable before two other policemen lashed him about his head until he weakened. As they were hauling him away, he lashed out kicking and screaming before they eventually managed to manhandle him into the back of a police van with Jack screaming, "Fucking monkey hingers!" as he rattled the vehicle's cage doors in an aggravated rage.

Tom struggled to crawl his way back up a slippery embankment and he had just about reached the peak when a police officer's boot to his face sent him tumbling back overs into the watery dyke where he was pounced upon by a trio of truncheon-wielding SPG officers prior to him being dragged away facing back overs with his face all bloody and swollen. The stench of burning petrol fumes was strong, Hoss had already fought off a couple of SPG constables when he was unexpectantly truncheoned from behind, sending him down onto one knee, and even though a quartet of burly officers struggled, they eventually succeeded in bundling him into the rear of a van. Billy had somehow avoided being arrested and was stood by Tom's vehicle totally bemused, with not the slightest inkling that the others had been apprehended. Eventually, the flames died, with pickets limping away from the madness, and even though the tanker driver had lost the use of his transporter, once again the men were on the wrong side of a hiding. After all the pickets had dispersed, Billy was left standing on his lonesome by Tom's vehicle; not knowing which way to turn, he inched towards where the fence once was, then gingerly leaning forward he looked over the ridge of the embankment, nervously raising, "Tom?... Hoss?... J-J-Jack!?"

At a Blackpool bed and breakfast boarding house located one third of the way up Albert Road, Alan and Benny had settled themselves at a table inside a packed lounge. Directly in front of them a television was mounted halfway up an extensive wall that flaunted plum and gold stripy wallpaper which was way over the top and not so easy on the eye. From out of nowhere an elderly landlady appeared at the lounge doorway holding a TV remote. She looked at Alan directly, asking, "Want evening news on, duck?"

"Aye please," he returned, smiling gratitude. As the television set warmed up, violent scenes that had taken place earlier that day outside Hartlepool nuclear power station were showing on the screen. It didn't sink in at first what Alan and Benny were watching as scenes of a tanker engulfed in flames was transmitted, the penny still hadn't dropped until a camera cut to a close up shot of Jack being hauled away kicking and cursing like a man possessed. Alan faced Benny all open mouthed just as an even clearer shot of Tom surfaced with his face all battered and bloody, the camera then scanned a violent scene showing police and pickets clashing before focusing in on Hoss as he knocked a couple of SPG officers to the ground before once again the broadcast of an engulfed tanker filled the screen.

"Jesus Christ!" blew Benny facing Alan. "'A' wadn't like to be in your shoes when Irene gets her hands on ya."

"What do ya mean?" asked Alan, narrowing his eyes.

"Why it was you who sent them down there to sort that driver out in the first place, wasn't it?"

"Aye but a didn't think for one second that someone was ganna petrol bomb the bugger!"

"Are, why, she'll not see it like that."

At the rear of the room a young union official with hair thickened in gel shook his head tutting condemnation whilst dressed to the nines in an expensive suit, and matching shirt and tie. Laughing falsely, he criticised, "No wonder the rest of us at the TUC won't back them, animals the lot of them are, nothing but bloody animals."

Alan glanced over his shoulder at the stranger, defending, "Here, if you believe that report, you're an idiot, marra."

"Camera never lies, mate," came back without any hint of a working-class accent.

Alan snapped, "Well, it's lied often enough where we come from, believe you me it has."

"Violence has never solved anything, mate," returned the stranger; then breaking into a smug grin, he continued, "it proved that when Margaret Thatcher put you lot in your place at Orgreave after Scargill tried to flex his union's muscle, it doesn't work that way anymore, mate, not in this day and age, society won't allow it to."

Alan defended, "Here, I was at Orgreave so shut half your gob!" He jumped to his feet all flushed and bothered, continuing, "Ya nar nowt, lad! Anyway, Thatcher said there's not such a thing as society... please tell me... what union do you represent?"

"Me, Transport and General union."

"Orr aye, and which branch?"

"Nottingham and Derbyshire."

"That figures!" broke in Benny with more than a hint of sarcasm. "It's the likes of your members who's costing us the strike by running scab coal all-ower the place."

"Here, mate!" sniggered the stranger, "if you carn't get your own members to come out on strike, don't be harassing any of my lads for just doing their jobs."

"He's not your mate," cackled Alan sarcastically. "He's my mate, not yours, and he's been my mate for a lifetime now, so believe you me when a' say he would never have mates like you, not in a million years wad he."

Benny voiced, "It's fundamental knowledge that you should never cross a picket line, bonnie lad."

The man beamed. "Yes, you're exactly right, it is, if it's an official picket line that is, but yours isn't official, is it? Because a certain Mr Scargill wouldn't grant you lot the right of a vote in the first place, dinosaurs you lot are, outdated dinosaurs?"

Alan approached the mouthy stranger. "You lot!" he snapped. "You lot! Who the hell are you calling you lot! Ehh!?" After standing nose to nose, Alan stepped back a pace to eye the stranger up and down. "Any man worth his salt wouldn't cross any picket line, and any union official that stood back and let them isn't worth his salt neither, even if he's dressed in a pathetic... double breasted... blinking yuppie suit like yours!" The pounding of a gong sounding from the foot of the stairs indicated that an evening meal was ready to be served. Once again Alan scrutinised the young man. "Go on then, fuck off in there and enjoy ya meal, but before you do just remember this, back yerm where I come from there will be bits of kids going to bed tonight on empty stomachs, having nowt to eat for their teas never mind their bloody suppers... mate!!" Alan looked on as the stranger and his cohorts left the room before returning to his seat where he lit up a cigarette. Sighing lengthily he mumbled, "Benny, if that's the future of our TUC, let alone our Labour Party, then God help us all."

"Too true, marra," agreed Benny, patting Alan on his shoulder, "too true, but settle ya sell down a bit or ya'll be setting ya palpitations away again."

Alan stood bleating, "Fuck this!" then rushing from the room, he snarled, "I'm not finished with that twat yet!"

Irene sat half in and out of Emmerdale Farm as Tom yawned boredom while brandishing yet another set of freshly formed black eyes. Billy was in deep thought as he sat staring at a print of a lascivious Spanish Lady which hung from the chimney breast alongside a mirror and a huge, wooden framed photograph of his holiness himself. Irene cast her eyes in the direction of the painting, asking, "Do ya like that painting, Billy?"

"Aye, it's c-c-canny nice, like."

"We've had that for years now." She lit up a cigarette. "Our Betty and Jim brought us it back from Spain way back in the sixties, she's quite pretty, isn't she?"

"She's b-b-beautiful," confirmed Billy as he too lit up.

"A' wonder who painted the original?" broke in Tom.

"God knows," answered Irene, shrugging her shoulders. "It's a bit of a mystery a' think."

Billy sat in deep though before slowly coming out with, "I think it m-m-may have been... J.H. Lynch who p-p-painted the original, Tom."

Irene shuffled her chair in deep curiosity. "How do you know that, Billy?"

"I don't know, Mrs G-G-Gilroy, a' just d-d-do."

Tom chuckled. "A' bet tha doesn't nar who the girl in the painting is though?"

Billy drew on his cigarette. "It's... Jean Shrimpton, she w-w-wasn't even Spanish, she w-w-was a popular English m-m-model throughout the s-s-sixties."

"Arr, ya having us on now, mind, Billy!" whooped Irene.

"He's not, Ma," broke in Tom, lighting up a cig, "if he says that's who it is, ya can bet a pound to a pinch of salt it will be."

Irene grinned at Billy, uttering, "You're wasted down that pit you are, son, ya should be a teacher or something."

Billy grinned. "W-W-What with this s-s-stutter," before he once again drew deep on his cigarette.

Suitcases in hand, Alan and Benny wandered through the freezing streets of Blackpool in search of fresh lodgings after they were unfortunately evicted from the previous premises for allegedly using threatening behaviour. Everywhere they searched they were met by neon rejections blinking **No Vacancies** from out of the corners of heavy lattice windows.

"What we ganna de?" asked Benny, passing over a cig. "A'm bloody frozen here!"

Alan yawned, fed-up. "God nars!" After presenting Benny with a flame, he lit up himself before they smoked their way by numerous bed and breakfasts. The hint of cigarette smoke had long waned as they trudged up and down street after street for well over three-quarters of an hour until they finally came across a blue neon light flashing 'Vacancies' without any hint of a No fronting it. "Thank fuck for that, I'm frigging knacked here," said Alan, puffing his cheeks.

"Tell is about it," whinged Benny, blowing a sigh of his own, "me arms have gone numb and me back legs have just about buckled here."

Stepping into the building they were hit by a welcoming warmth of a crimson lobby way. At a far side of this restricted corridor a smile awaited, cast from a beady eyed fat man who had somehow managed to squeeze himself inside a tight cubbyhole that doubled as an office. If a face could tell a story, well, heaven knows what this poor fellow's fable was, as deep-set furrows filled both his face and bald head before stretching over elderly ears to continue around to the back of his neck.

"Any rooms, mate?" spoke Alan, hopeful.

"I'm afraid we only have the one twin room available," answered the man, stretching crinkling lips to form a grin, "you will have to share."

"We're not bothered, we'll tack it," broke in Benny at once. "I'm ower knacked to be traipsing all ower Blackpool all night."

"That'll be eleven pounds a night from each of you." The man presented a guest book, and after they had paid and signed a register, he raised, "The bar is open till one," his face visibly rippled in sequence to a multitude of chins with each word spoken, "and breakfast starts at half past seven, finishes at half nine." Another weathered smirk ran his face as he handed over a key attached to a white tag showing a black number. "Your room is on the third floor... number eighteen, I hope you have a nice stay."

"Thanks a lot, marra." Benny smiled. "It's much appreciated, we've been all ower the place looking for rooms."

The man grinned openly, uttering, "You were very lucky to get this room, we were also fully booked until a last-minute cancellation came in, everywhere is full up in Blackpool, it's TUC conference week."

OVER A WEEK LATER

The lads had just finished a morning stint on picket duty at the pit gates. Breaking from the others, Billy raised his coat collar to stride though wind and rain bypassing numerous streets as he made his way up to his old house to pick up a length of rope that Jack had asked to borrow earlier that day, and while he was there, he thought he may as well check the mail and give the place a quick once over. Entering his backyard, his heart sank as he was greeted with a couple of smashed locks strewn across the yard and a coalhouse door hanging free while just about attached to a single bottom hinge. Inspecting inside the now emptied nook he cursed, "B-B-Bastards!" Sighing elongated, he tugged open an adjoined door to enter into an off shot that, over the years, had been used as a storage room for unwanted household junk, where once it was a whiffy outside lavatory. After sifting through oodles of jumble he eventually tugged out a rope to loop it loose between thumb and elbow prior to tying up the ends. Rising up half a dozen concrete steps he put key to latch; closing his eyes he inhaled endlessly before reluctantly opening up to be greeted by a strong whiff of mustiness. The house wasn't anything like the warmth of a home it once was, as now it was just an empty, cold shell, except for a solitary chair, two remote controls, and a carpet running from room to room.

After checking through heaps of mail, vivid flashbacks of past epochs came flooding back, happier times when this place was indeed a functional, family home. Billy stood slaked in memories, recalling his cheerful girls laughing aloud as they played with their toys shot through his mind. A pensive grin lit his face as echoes of last year's Christmas entered his thoughts, reflections of Alisia huddled in his arms as Kelly rushed the room, whooping, 'He's been! He's been! Santee's been!' with little Alisia unsuccessfully attempting to imitate her big sister's words prior to them ripping away wrapping paper to uncover presents. Another drawn-out exhalation of breath brought Billy back to reality, altering his grin into a pout of despair, then, blowing a bottomless sigh he scanned the empty room thinking how his former life was lost forever, and with him now living an awful, family-less existence, he couldn't perceive any future for himself, not without his girls, as without them there was simply nothing, nothing but an appalling, stomach churning feeling of loneliness. Why bother, he thought, what's the point of carrying on; then within an instant, Billy had somehow lost all rational thoughts, almost trancelike he eyed the top of the archway where a huge brass hook, that once was attached to a bouncy chair, hung inviting from the ceiling, unknowingly, or even not unknowingly, he started unravelling the rope to swiftly whip up an end to form a slip noose with every intention of ending his torment there and then. Dragging the old chair to under the archway, he was on threading the rope through the hook when a heavy pounding on the front window rattled the bare room. Billy glanced over his shoulder, making out it was Jack who was stood cupping his hands at either side of his face with his nose pressed hard against a dust covered pane. "How'y man, Billy!" he yelled. "Stop fucking about, a' haven't got all day tha nars!" and on those simple, typical blunt words spat from out the mouth of his lifelong best friend, Billy was thankfully brought back from the brink of, well, wherever he was heading.

Billy sighed lengthily, whispering, "Time to m-m-move on, Billy, it's time t-t-to move on now."

A friendly photographer, and sympathiser to the miners' cause, was at the club kitchen snapping his camera to produce images that would probably become timeless. Packing up his camera, he faced Sue, saying, "Bye for now, Sue," in a charming well-spoken voice.

"Bye Keith," she replied to delicately push her spectacles back to nose. "Don't forget to giss a butchers at those photos when ya've developed them?"

"I shan't forget," came back with an extended grin. After saying his goodbyes, the shutterbug smiled around friendly before scuffing a little lad's hair on his way out of the hall.

Sue glanced at the girls, encouraging, "One of yas let the second sitting in, first one's about finished now." Tracy unbolted a door, allowing familiar faces entry to form an orderly, plate in hand, queue just as Irene breezed into the room, unbuttoning her overcoat. At once Sue took her to one side, and with a raised eyebrow, she whispered, "Well?"

Irene looked Sue direct in the eye. "Well nowt really, Dr Johnson's booking is in for an appointment to see a consultant."

"Orr dear me," sighed Sue teary eyed.

"Hey, there's no need for tears, flowerpots," reassured Irene with a warm smile, "just because there's a lump there it doesn't mean it's breast cancer, and let's keep it to our sells for now shall we..." Sue nodded as Irene explained, "... a' don't want the boys finding out just yet, let alone Alan, especially after the heartache and anguish he went through with poor Jean's cancer." They exchanged lingering smiles as Irene fidgeted her hair, asking, "Where do ya want is then?"

"Gan on the end, ladling gravy, I'll give Debbie a little smoke break on the tatties."

A FEW DAYS LATER

Even though it was not long past teatime it was already as dark as a hole, due to the clocks falling back an hour. The lads were finding it strenuous pushing a couple of coal laden bicycles down a sodden track which ran at the side of an even soggier ploughed field. Hoss was steering one of the bikes as Billy pushed with both hands clasped around a steel tube where once a saddle had paraded. Leaning against five hefty sacks, Jack struggled to guide the other cycle, while to the rear Tom shouldered his utmost from one side of a back wheel. Entering under the second bridge they found it a lot easier underfoot as they edged a firmer ash path, exiting from the brick arch they came across wasteland where a bunch of kids were sat unfolding ghost stories around a crackling fire just as they had once done when they were adolescent tearaways. The bonfire they were guarding was a pretty impressive one too, at its heart a collection of hoary settees, chairs, and other shards of combustible furniture were heaped together while enclosed within a bushy covering of trees including beech, sycamore, and prickly hawthorn bushes, all recently felled from the top of Station Dene by means of a rusty old bowsaw prior to the kids energetically dragging them back to the bonfire via a drawn-out dirt trail known as the 'Black Path'.

The lads pushed on to advance through Devil's Mouth; after rising its cobbled incline they turned a sharp left to follow the pit wall, taking them by a trio of streets before they turned up into Cuba Street where they rested the bicycles at either side of a green coloured gate showing number two.

It didn't take too long for them to tip the sacks, and with each sack emptied a rattling of coal would fracture the stillness. Jack was on passing around cigarettes when the door creaked wide illuminating up the whole of the backyard while creating a silhouette of Irene standing at the doorway. "Kettle's on!" she whooped.

Tom scratched his Zippo to flame, and lighting up a cig, he asked, "Ma, can ya knock us some bacon sarnies up? We've got to gan back ower the wall to get Hoss' coal yet."

"What's the magic word?"

He smiled, saying, "Sorry... please."

"Aye ne bother, but I'm afraid I'm out of chop brown sauce, it'll be ketchup all 'round." After grunts of displeasure from Jack, Irene turned, and her silhouette was no more.

Hearing a Beatles melody coming from within the house, Billy inhaled deeply on his cigarette. He hummed along to the melody for a little while, then smiling around the rest he raised, "What's ya f-f-favourite song of, like, all t-t-time, like?"

"'Imagine'," came instantly from Jack with Tom voicing agreement at his brother's choosing.

"'Little Red Rooster', by Howlin' Wolf's mine," mooted Hoss, "'coss it was me Da's favourite one too." He looked around with a pensive grimace. "Can ya remember that time up at the Colliery Club when Da got on the stage with the group one Saturday night to sing it?"

"Aye, a' can remember that," chuckled Jack, "he got a standing ovation and everything, great night that was." Jack paused in thought. "What was the name of that group again?"

"Gents!" whooped Hoss. "It was Gents."

"Aye that's them!" enthused Jack. "Canny group an'll mind ya!" He turned to Billy, asking, "How'y then, Billy, what's your favourite song then? And nen of that Mozart or Chopin crap, it's got to be proper music with words and everything."

"Bohemian R-R-Rhapsody," answered Billy without hesitation.

"Great song," nodded Tom, "an all-time classic that is."

"It is an'all," put in Hoss.

"Aye it's canny like," agreed Jack before lowering his voice to a whisper, "but fuck nars what it's all about though, it's mind-blowing."

"A' nar w-w-what it's a-a-about," said Billy.

"How'y then, Billy," chuckled Tom, "spit it out... let's be having it."

"Well, it's j-j-just my opinion, mind, b-b-but I think it's all about a sc-sc-schizophrenic psychopath who kills a m-m-man and then he goes o-o-on trial and is s-s-sentenced to death, and while he's on d-d-death r-r-row awaiting to be e-e-executed he writes a letter home, no sorry h-h-he phones h-h-his Ma telling her he's g-g-ganna get executed ta death."

"D'ya nar something ..." bobbed Jack slowly pondering over Billy's words in his mind, "... a' think ya could be right there, young'n, it explains all the different tempos with him being a stitzo and that."

"A' think he's right too," nodded Hoss.

"A' think ya've hit the nail on the head there an'all, Billy." Tom smiled, bringing about a huge beam on Billy's face.

Jack inhaled deeply on his cigarette, saying, "Having said that like, they still copied off The Beatles' 'A Day in the Life', the way they changed the tempo up and down and that."

"Nor, they didn't," defended Tom.

Jack snapped, "They did, man!"

"Why it w-w-was quite similar, Tom," voiced Billy.

Tom retorted, "Here! I'm defending you here, Billy, it's your all-time greatest song, not mine!"

"I'm just s-s-saying it's s-s-similar."

"Orr here carry on!" moaned Tom.

The door half opened. "The sandwiches are nearly done! Do yas want them inside, or out?"

"Outside!" answered Tom. "We're hacky black!"

TWO DAYS LATER

Irene swished her curtains to be met by a damp, cloudy day. Switching on her TV she faced reports of a bomb attack on a Brighton hotel where all the top brass Tories were staying for a Conservative conference. Fleeting thoughts of 'the boys better not be involved in this' stupidly ran her mind as she watched Thatcher standing handbag in hand while holding an interview in front of a badly damaged building. Irene's grimace dropped to that of disappointment; wondering how the hell this woman had managed to walk out from all that rubble seemingly unscathed. The door sounded to a creak ahead of Tom, Jack, and Billy breezing into the lobby way chanting, *"Maggie! Maggie! Maggie! Boom, Boom, Boom!"* their little ditty sending a huge grin rippling Irene's face.

Jack entered the room. Irene looked up at him, saying, "Thatcher's just been on the telly talking about an assassination attempt, there's not one single scratch on her."

"Why what did ya expect," groaned Jack, eyeing the television, "yad have to drive a grit big wooden stake through her heart and get Father O'Conner to say a prayer or two over her to harm that one, the evil cow."

Tom and Bill waltzed into the room with Tom joining the conversation with, "They reckon there was five minibuses around the back of the hotel shunting all of Leon Brittan's little rent boys away from the prying eyes of the press cameras."

"No, there wasn't," said Irene.

Jack put in, "Nowt sa likely, Ma, they reckon he's a proper nonce like!"

"Who is?"

"That Leon Brittan!"

Frowning all serious she responded, "He's not a nonce at all, Jack, everyone knows he's Jewish." After a lengthy pause she looked at Tom, directly asking, "What is a nonce?"

Tom half smiled, uttering, "It doesn't matter, Ma."

NOVEMBER "WHY AYE!"

Bonfire night had come and gone, dark nights lingered long, daylight not so, as hedgerows and lofty trees swayed leafless to the command of ever-changing winds, while ruddy breasted robins grew from fat to round in preparation for a forthcoming winter.

Solidarity for the strike hadn't waned in the slightest at Easington, even though another strike-breaker, an electrician named John Birry, had returned back to work, taking the number now tallying up into double figures. Irene had attended an eagerly awaited consultant's appointment and was now waiting for a date to have this awkward lump surgically removed, without one single word of her malady passing her lips to either of her boys, or indeed Alan. Jack and Lucy were still lost in love, Tom was planning to spend more time down at Pat's father's farm as Pat had moved back there permanently after passing out as a nurse with flying colours. Billy was still lodging rent-free at the Gilroys' abode, but the good news was he had perked himself up notably after his zany episode at his old house. Hoss and Margret were now living blissfully as a couple after she had agreed to move in with him, with plans of marriage on the horizon as soon as the strike was over, and her decree absolute finalized.

Alan and Irene were sat watching evening television when Irene lit up a cigarette, after a lengthy sigh, then a considerable pause, her stare crossed from chair to settee with her softy raising, "Alan?"

"What, love?"

She fumbled, "We need to talk."

Alan's instincts prepared him for the worst as premonitions that Irene's next sentence would probably be somewhere along the lines of her giving him some specific reason why she was going to end their relationship there and then. His face dropped markedly, and though he didn't really want to speak the next few words, "What about?" was spoken almost as a whisper.

Again, she faltered. "I've got to go into hospital... for an operation... I have a lump in my left breast that needs removing."

Alan's face fell further as he now wished it was just their breakup she had just announced and not this; he opened his mouth to speak but found no words until, "... it's not cancer, is it?" fell out.

"They don't know yet," she said, crossing the room to fold an embrace.

"You're not in any pain, my love, are you?" he whispered, his cheek huddled delicately against hers.

Pulling back slightly, she shook her head with a smile. "There's no pain whatsoever, it's just such an annoyance narn that it's, well, there really."

"How long have ya known?" he asked unawares his bottom lip was trembling slightly.

"A' few weeks now... not long."

His hands shook visibly as he lit up a cigarette. A host of questions ran his mind, of which he chose, "Why didn't you tell me before, Irene?"

"I didn't want ta worry ya." She stroked the side of his face. "Not after what ya went through with poor Jean and that."

He stretched a sigh. "Does the lads know? Have you told them yet?"

Again, Irene shook her head, uttering, "No, not yet, I'm going ta tell them tonight as soon as they return back from getting coal."

"And do you want me here when you tell them?" He drew deeply on his cigarette, not noticing that a single tear ran his cheek.

"Of course, I want you here," she replied with a cordial grimace, "and there's no need for tears, I haven't even been diagnosed with anything yet. The consultant's even said there was a high probability that it was nothing."

Once again, he blew his cheeks. "I divant like probabilities, Irene, I've had enough of those things to last a lifetime, I prefer definitely."

They sat huddled watching television not really knowing what they were viewing, and after a while the front door creaked to sprightly voices sounding in the lobby before the sitting room door opened ahead of Jack, Tom, and Billy grinning their way into the room.

"Did yas manage alright then?" greeted Irene with a huge smile.

"Why aye!" laughed Tom. "There's another ten bags there, should last a bit."

"Owt ta eat, Ma? A's famished!" said Jack, sitting aside Alan and his mother.

"Yeah, there's some tattie-ash on the cooker top," she said as once again a motherly beam was lit.

"Champion!" whooped Jack who was now back to his feet and heading in the direction of the kitchen door. "Did ya mack any stotties?"

"They're in the oven, they should be nice and warm still!"

Now Billy sat himself alongside Alan, saying, "It's f-f-frozen out there." Looking at a waning fire, he asked, "Should a' p-p-put some c-c- coal on the fire, Ma?"

"Why aye!" Irene grinned. "Ya divant have to ask to put coal on the fire, son, just do it," and on those words Billy left the room.

"Alright, Alan?" asked Tom, resting a packet of cigarettes onto the top of the mantelpiece.

"Yeah," came back amidst a rattle of elongated sighs.

Tom instinctively knew there was something amiss; he puckered, "You two all right?"

"Of course, we are, we're fine," reassured Irene, "go and get ya supper, son."

Tom left the room unconvinced at her words.

It took a couple of coalhouse trips for Billy to resurrect the fire back to a blaze before he joined the brothers at the dining table where they sat for a good half hour or so eating, with the main topic of conversation concentrating around Billy himself, at whether or not he was going to ask Bev James out on a date. After finishing their food, they re-entered the sitting room to be met by a familiar melody sounding the start of Brookside on the telly. Tom sat alongside Alan and Irene as the other two comforted themselves into separate chairs. Irene coughed brusquely, dragging their attentions away from the Merseyside soap.

"What's up, Ma?" side eyed Tom. "There's something rang, so don't sit there saying there's not!"

"Well... I've got something to tell yas..." she fumbled on, "... now don't go jumping to any conclusions and that, but I've got to go into hospital to have a lump removed from my left breast."

"When?" wide eyed Tom.

"I don't know, but it shouldn't be long."

He quickly followed up with, "It's not cancerous, is it?"

"They don't know that yet, they will run some tests after they remove it." Irene eyed Jack with a look of concern as he sat dumbstruck and teary-eyed. "They said it's probably's nothing to worry about, Jack."

Wiping his eyes, he jumped to his feet, sniffing, "Aye, and that's the exact thing they said about me Da too, probably's nothing to worry about! And we all nar how that ended... don't we!?" And on those words, he stormed from the room to stomp his way up the stairs ahead of a heavy slamming from a bedroom door, shaking the whole house.

"D-D-Do ya want a cup of t-t-tea, Ma?" asked Billy. She shook her head in reply. "Alan?" came next and he nodded in answer. "T-T-Tom, w-w-what about you?"

"No, tar, thanks," he replied as a teary-eyed Billy stood to drag his way from out of the sitting room.

Hoss was stood brushing his teeth with a towel wrapped around his waist when Margret joined him in the bathroom where she quickly removed her clothes prior to stepping into a bathtub that he had run with add-ins of pleasant-smelling bath salts and other womanly stuff. After rinsing out his mouth he spat into the sink, asking, "Has the bairn gone ower then?"

"Aye, just though, me Mam'll have been stuffing him all day with blinking kets again, a'm sick ta death of telling her about it."

"That's what nannas do, man, Margret," he chuckled as he turned to leave.

She purred, "Don't go just yet, stop and talk a bit!" Glancing over her shoulder she raised an eyebrow. "Ya can wash me back for is if ya want, or better still lose that thing and get ya arse back in here." Hoss didn't need asking twice, removing the towel he stepped into the tub where he carefully positioned himself behind her sending the water rising considerably to just below an outlet hole. Wrapping his huge arms around her shoulders, he tenderly cupped her breasts, sending her to a contented calmness. "Mmm! That's nice," she sighed all relaxed.

OVER A WEEK LATER

Having just finished eating, Hoss and Billy were sat at a table at the Colliery Club enjoying a smoke when Tom rushed into the room to join them saying, "Alright?"

"Aye," said Hoss. "What time's Ma having her operation?"

Tom checked his watch. "Sometime in the next couple hours if all goes to plan. I'm ganna shoot back through there now, a' only came back 'coss she forgot her dressing gown and nighty and she's refusing to wear the hospital ones."

Hoss sighed prolonged. "Give her my love and tell her me and Margret will be in the night to see her."

"A' will." Tom looked to Billy, asking, "Fancy coming through now? Or are ya ganna gan through the night with Hoss and Margret?"

Billy nodded, "N-N-Now if that's alright." Rising from his chair he looked at Hoss, saying, "See ya l-l-later, Hoss."

The big man looked on as the two left the hall. He was sat lost in thoughts when Margret approached the table. "Alright love?" she asked.

"I'm fine," he muttered, trying to force a smile.

Margret leant over, hugging his colossal shoulders, whispering, "Irene will get through this, ya nar, Hoss, she's a lot tougher than what people make her out to be." Pecking faintly onto his cheek, she added, "I've borrowed Dad's car for tonight, and the bairn's stopping over, so there's no worries there."

"Champion."

"Margret!?" shouted Sue, looking over her shoulder. "Mack sharp, hinny!"

Once again, Margret's lips brushed wet against his cheek. "I'll have to go, love, try not to worry too much."

At Ryhope hospital, Alan parked up inside a small carpark surrounded by well-manicured grounds. Clutching an array of flowers that dazzled in mainly pink, he hurried up a half dozen concrete stairs ahead of stepping into an old red bricked building to rush a drawn-out corridor prior to pushing his way through a set of heavy double doors to enter onto a ward where he exchanged silent smiles with Billy, Tom, Jack and Lucy, who were stood at

Irene's bedside with her sat up quite spritely. Leaning over, he feathered a kiss on her brow, asking, "How are ya, love?"

"I'm fine, Alan," she replied, then pointing to her lips she breathed, "ya missed a bit though."

"Sorry." He grinned sharply as he stooped forward to peck her on the mouth. "Are ya sure yar okay?"

"As a' little bit sore, but it's nowt to write home about."

Pulling up a chair, he presented the flowers, whispering, "Any word back yet about when ya can gan yerm?"

"No, not yet, I'm just waiting on the consultant doing his rounds." After a quick smell of the spray, Irene nodded at Lucy, asking, "Will ya put these in some water for me please, love, a' think there's a couple of spare vases at the nurses' station." Flowers in hand, Lucy smiled around before wandering off to push her way through a different set of doors.

Alan asked, "Have you had owt to eat yet?"

"Just a slice of toast and a cup of tea after me opp, tell ya the truth a's not that hungry, love, a' just want ta get off home now."

Tom put in, "Ya'll have to see what the consultant says first when he comes 'round, Ma."

Jack asked, "Do ya want is to get ya some fresh water?"

"Nar, tar." Irene twisted her face slightly. "To tell ya the truth, son, a's not ower fussed on it, it's got a funny taste about it."

Jack half joked, "That's 'coss they put stuff in it to stop people getting horny."

"No, they don't!" contradicted Alan.

"What stuff?" Irene frowned.

"A divant nar what it's called," said Jack.

"B- B-Bromide," put in Billy, "that's what it's c-c-called, they used to put it in the w-w-water during the w-w-wars to stop the soldiers getting h-h-horny."

"Aye but they don't use it in hospitals though, Irene, so don't worry," said Alan with a twist of his face. Scanning the ward, he looked on as a nurse straightened a neighbouring bed before fluffing up pillows to ease an elderly lady back to comfort. Grinning slightly, Alan caught the nurse's eye before he shuffled closer to Irene, whispering, "She looks canny busy?"

Irene raised, "The poor lass never stops, man, Alan, nen of them do, good as gold so they are." Lucy returned with vase in hand to rest the display onto a bedside table. Irene smiled her gratitude, saying, "Thanks, sweetheart, yar a real good'n."

Silence fell upon the ward as a stout faced elderly ward sister, with fat legs and arms teetered alongside a tall consultant whose hair was greying and untidily swept behind furred ears which matched hefty eyebrows that rose and lowered above expensive gold rimmed spectacles. His face was pallid, showing shadowy bags under his eyes and deep wrinkles at either side of his mouth, which somehow fit an overlarge nose bursting in rubicund veins, but despite his old man's appearance, he waltzed the ward from bedside to bedside like a medical Zeus as an entourage of lesser, white coated demigods, trailed one step behind, grasping onto clipboards whilst constantly jotting down each and every word he spoke. Approaching Irene's bedside, he rattled coughs of disapproval as he looked around the visitors. "Sister," he said softly, "you know hospital policy, two visitors per patient only."

"Sorry, Mr Speckman." Her narrowed eyes ran the group, saying, "I'm afraid three of you will have to leave please, you can wait to the smoke room, but you may still give each other mini breaks at the bedside." They looked around one another before deciding it was best if Alan stayed with Ma on his own.

The sister whooshed surrounding bedside curtains to privacy, and after the consultant had examined a surgical wound, he spoke medical terms to his cohorts, and they penned his every word. Looking at Irene, he asked, "And how are you feeling, Mrs Gilroy?"

"Champion," she replied nervously.

"Any discomfort?"

She smiled. "Slightly sore but not much."

"That's to be expected. Well then–" he scratched the back of his head– "we removed the lump and I'm pleased to tell you your operation went all to plan, we've sent tissue samples off to the lab for tests, your doctors should have the results within two to three weeks."

Taking Alan by the hand, Irene went teary, blowing lengthily she uttered, "Thank you very much, Mr Speckman."

"It was my pleasure, you may go home tomorrow, but you need to take it easy for a week or two." He smiled around, turned, and left with a trail of white coats following.

Irene wiped her tears, then looking up at Alan, she smiled. "Go and tell the boys I'm coming home tomorrow." He leant over, pecking a kiss on her lips and Irene's eyes followed him from the ward before she sighed lengthily with deep thoughts of what the outcome of these tests were going to be.

TWO WEEKS LATER

The sky may have been blue and cloudless, but it was bitter cold, as Easington awoke to a lid of thick frost glistening both roads, and rooftops alike. Dressed in winter clothing, Jack and the lads stood warming their hands around a fire drum. Earlier that morning the scab bus had passed through a soft picket line to half-hearted shouts of 'Scabs, Scabs, Scabs'. Cigarette in hand, Alan walked duffle coated down Office Street to join the lads with a face like thunder.

"Alright, Alan?" greeted Tom.

"A'm a' shite alright! A'm frigging livid here!"

"What's happened now?" stretched Jack.

After a deep drag on his cigarette, Alan griped, "Jumbo, Nobby and Marty Turner were beaten up this morning outside Banksy's, and pretty bad too–"

"Fucking coppers!" broke in Jack. "They're getting worse by the day them bastards are!"

"It wasn't coppers, Jack, it was Banksy's own drivers who set about them, apparently there was boatloads of the fuckers and the cops just stood back doing fuck all, in fact by all accounts they were all laughing and joking, egging the bastards on."

Hoss lit up, suggesting, "Put a mass picket on, Alan, and smash the fucking place up."

"Aye, p-p-put a mass p-p-picket on," agreed Billy.

Jack looked around before whispering, "Better still, give us twenty or thirty quid to get some gear and we'll gan up there the night and fuck all their wagons up."

"What do ya mean fuck their wagons up?" asked Alan all ears.

Jack smiled. "You don't need to know that."

"Here there is then." He smiled, handing Jack money. "There's an extra tenner towards diesel, and I'll see yas alright with an extra day's picketing money too, so do ya worst." Walking off in the direction of the office, he shouted over his shoulder, "Catch yas in a bit, lads!"

Jack eyed the others, whispering, "Right, I'll not be long, a's just ganna pop up the shops."

Tom eyed his brother, asking, "What ya up to, Jack? What ya gan'n to the shops for?"

"To get a shitload of sugar."

"Sugar!?" Hoss frowned. "Why?"

Jack grinned mischievously. "To fuck Banksy's wagons' fuel tanks up, that's why."

"G-G-Got ya," put in Billy with a grin, "good idea, J-J-Jack."

Jack lowered his tone, whispering, "And we're ganna cut through all the wagons' brake lines too."

Hoss smiled sharply, asking, "Are ya gan'n to the shops like right now, like, Jack?"

"Aye, why?"

"Like precisely now?"

"Hoss! For crying out loud, what's tha after!?"

"Will ya get is a couple of pies while ya passing Burdess'?"

Wearing an impish grimace, Jack rolled his eyes around the group. "Union money not mine, so does anyone else want pies?" and they nodded in answer ahead of him turning to walk in the direction of his truck.

Hoss scratched at the back of his head, shouting, "Jack! Get me three pies instead of two please!" Acknowledgement to his words was given by Jack raising his arm.

Tom's eyes narrowed as he observed his big friend heartily scratching away at his scalp. "Thuw hasn't got nits has tha, Hoss!?"

Hoss snapped, "Shut up, ya daft bugger! It's Marie's shampoo! It's got me head as itchy as owt, and it frigging stinks!"

"S-S-Stinks of w-w-what?" broke in Billy.

Hoss huffed, "A' divant nar, Lily of the Vally shite or something stupid like that! A's ganna pop to the chemist and get me sell a bottle of Vosene shampoo on me way back yerm, and I'm ganna get a bar of Imperial Leather too, a's sick ta death of that Fuzzy Wuzzy bear shite."

Tom smirked, "Fuzzy Wuzzy bear... what? What the hell's that?"

"It's kids soap shaped like a fucking bear!" snapped Hoss, once again itching at the back of his head. "Apparently, women use it to soften their skin up ..." Tom and Billy stood stern faced for as long as they could before they both burst out giggling. "... How'y, lads, it's not funny, a' wadn't laugh if it was one of you two washing ya sells in Fuzzy Wuzzy bear soap, all the time." Their laughter increased as Hoss broke into a grin of his own, chortling, "Why, a' might laugh a little bit a' suppose."

CHAPTER FIVE

"Thuw's fuzzy wuzzy, ya daft bat," chuckled Tom.

Unbuttoning her overcoat, Irene breezed into the club singing end to join Sue, Debbie, Tracy, Bev and Liz who were sat around a table having a quick smoke break. Slowly removing a headscarf, she grinned widely as she flaunted a soft perm running with blonde highlights. "That looks gorgeous, that does, Irene." Debbie smiled. "It really suits ya."

"Thank you, Debbie," she said, sitting, "do ya not think it's a bit ower the top like?"

"Why nor," broke in Sue, "it suits ya down to the ground."

"It looks great," put in Liz.

Lighting up a cig, Irene noticed Debbie wasn't smoking – she offered her the packet, but Debbie shook her head, saying, "No thanks, I'm not allowed, Irene."

"Why not for?" Irene frowned.

"I'm just not." She slowly broke into a grin, beaming, "'Coss I'm pregnant!" Irene's eyes narrowed as she instinctively totted dates up in her head. "Don't worry, Irene, I'm only twelve weeks gone, it's not your Jack's it's my Peter's."

Irene grinned widely, saying, "Sorry, love a' was way out of order there, congratulations, flowerpots!" They hugged for quite some time with Irene whispering in her ear, "Well done, love, a' bet your Peter's ower the moon, is he?"

"He's ecstatic," she sighed, adding, "all we need now is for this frigging strike to end so we can get back to normality."

Sue looked at Irene, asking, "So, when are ya coming back to join us then, Irene?"

She smiled wide eyed, saying, "Now... this instant! If a spend another day looking at them same four walls, I'm ganna gan absolutely potty... so where do ya want is at then, Sue?"

"You can gan on the dumplings if ya fancy, I'll have ta gan soon to get ready, a's meeting up with the chairman of the

343

County Council today, and the mayor of Peterlee too, apparently they have extra funds available seeing as we're feeding so many mouths each day."

Irene smiled at Sue. "Why just be ya sell, and demand things from them, don't just ask." Turning to face Tracy, she drew deeply on her cigarette, asking, "What's the stockroom standing like, Tracy?"

"It's chocka for now, but you know how sharp it empties, Irene."

Liz smiled. "I think we need to try and put an extra disco on, on a Sunday night to raise the coffers up a bit, I've got a few nurse friends who are willing to put a bus on and come through for a night out, and where there's nurses there's one thing for sure, lads will follow."

Sue encouraged, "Get in contact with them then, Liz, we'll try and put a one on a week come Sunday, if nowt else, all the lads will love it."

"A' think it'll go down a treat," put in Bev, widening her eyes as she gushed, "me and Billy's going out to the pictures this Saturday night."

"What, my Billy!" enquired Irene, delighted. "Like on a proper date and that!?"

"Aye, he asked is out when he walked is home from the disco last Friday night."

"He's lovely Billy is," said Irene.

"He is too," agreed Sue.

Irene raised an eyebrow at Bev. "Don't you be going hurting him, mind, Bev, he's still a canny bit fragile."

"A' wouldn't think about it," sighed Bev.

"Aye ya wad," broke in Tracy.

"No, a' won't, stupid!" she snapped, sending daggers at her sister. "A' really like him, a' nar he can be a bit goofy at times, but he's a gorgeous kisser."

"We don't need to know about that," said Irene, blowing smoke.

"Irene!?" hooted Debbie.

"What, love?"

"Will ya blow some of that smoke ower here? A' could kill a tab, me!"

A midnight drive through the remoteness of the Durham moorlands was eerie for Jack and the lads. Narrow, winding roads hadn't yet the privilege of illuminating road lights except for an occasional embrace of welcoming amber when passing through isolated, stone-built hamlets. After travelling beyond the village of Tow Law, they approached the main entrance to Banksy's compound where Jack slowed his truck to a gentle stop not fifty yards further along the roadside. Turning off the vehicle lights, the night darkness became apparent within an instant, then, exiting from the warmth of the truck they shivered in response to a frosty November chillness.

Jack and Tom clung onto carrier bags weighted with numerous bags of sugar while Hoss and Billy walked, clasping a couple of plastic five-gallon canisters in each hand with Hoss also gripping a large bolt cutter. The lads trod in silence towards a wire fencing where Hoss swiftly cut away a sizable gap, allowing them entry into a vast compound to feel their way up to a fleet of wagons that were parked bumper to bumper two abreast. Jack unscrewed a fuel cap on the first truck to tip in bags of sugar before approaching another where he repeated the procedure; this went on until every wagon in the fleet had their fuel tanks well and truly spiked. Jack whispered to Hoss, "Pass the bolt cutters ower, young'n." After the big man had fumbled over the shears, Jack raised, "The fuel tank must be somewhere back there, Hoss, you and Billy start filling up the containers, there's more empty containers in the back a' tha truck, me and our young'n 'ill sort these brakes out."

With each holding containers, they left the brothers to quickly make their way to a huge fuel tank that was cubicle in shape and constructed out of a dull, greyish coloured metal. Hoss tried to work a nozzle, but to his annoyance he found the thing was secured by a padlock, so turning to Billy he whispered, "Go and get them bolt cutters," and his little friend quickly turned to backtrack his way to rejoin Jack and Tom.

"J-J-Jack, we need the cutters, the t-t-tank's padlocked."

"Mack sharp then," breathed Jack, handing over the shears, "and bring it strite back when ya finished."

Billy rushed the short distance to join Hoss where the big man promptly pinged the lock with ease before he started filling a container to the smell of whiffy diesel. Once again Billy joined Jack, as he was handing over the cutters, Jack whispered, "Billy, go and get the rest of them containers now while Hoss is filling them others up." Opening up the cutters to maximum width, Jack severed a wagon's brake line with a single snip.

Tom looked at Jack, saying, "You can manage here on ya own, young'n, a' might as well give Billy and Hoss a hand shift that fuel."

"Gan on then, but be as quiet as ya can, we dinit want to disturb security." Tom swiftly left, leaving Jack to move onto the next truck where he nipped off another brake hose with ease.

Almost twenty minutes had passed before Hoss had finally finished filling the last of the canisters. Jack tied up the end of the nozzle, keeping the diesel flowing constant on full pressure before he strewed it to the ground with fuel spewing everywhere. He smiled at the lads, saying, "They're ganna get a canny shock in the morn when they wake up to all this shit." His grin extended broadly. "How'y then, let's get the fuck out of here." With each carrying a couple of filled containers, they retreated back through the compound prior to stepping through the cut away to eventually drive off with not only a mission successfully accomplished, but also Jack having an additional windfall of over sixty gallons of free diesel.

ONE WEEK LATER

At Easington allotments, the day was dry, yet a heavy sky lingered threateningly. Outside his father's pigeon loft, Hoss was reminiscing his way through the morning whilst slumped to comfort in his old man's rocky chair. Glancing over his shoulder, he smiled pensively, half expecting his dad to appear at any time at the doorway with a sweeping brush clasped in his hand. Hoss' eyes glazed damp as reality thumped him with the fact that this was never going to happen, not now, not ever again. Togged in a combat jacket, jeans and a flat cap, a small man, aged in his mid-thirties smoked his way along the allotment pathway, his name was Davy Marr, and he was here to buy the loft. "Alright, Hoss lad?" he said politely.

"Aye not three bad, Davy," welcomed Hoss, slowly rising to his feet, "do you want to take a look inside?"

Davy shook his head with a warm grimace, saying, "There's no need for that, marra, I've been inside that loft hundreds of times." He drew on his cigarette, asking, "Are ya sure about the price though? Ya could get a lot more for it tha nars, Hoss."

"A' nar a' could but me Da would want you to have it, Davy, on the condition you kept the thing painted in red and white stripes though." Laughing slightly, Hoss brought attention to the hoary rocky chair. "And that owld thing stays at the exact spot where it's at now."

"A' wadn't dare do any other, ya Da might come back and slap is around the back of me lug if a shifted that owld thing! Are ya happy enough to wait 'till after the strike's finished before a' can like, square ya up and that?"

"Why aye! That's ne bother!" he answered, lighting up a cigarette. "There's fower bags of corn in the loft, and all the garden tools and that are in the cree, there's a brand-new hosepipe there too, it's never even been unravelled yet." Handing over a bunch of keys, Hoss sighed lengthily, mumbling, "Enjoy it, marra, it's a great set up ya've got now." After exchanging smiles, Hoss walked off, pausing at the exact spot where he had come across his father laid dead, he looked back over his shoulder, and with tears filling his eyes he scanned the loft and surrounding sheds for the very last time, then, exiting the allotment, he cast a redolent smile as he carefully dragged a creaky gate to a close behind him.

Even though it was broad daylight, Billy, Jack and Tom took a risk to slink up onto the duff heaps at Easington to sieve out coal as Mick wandered alert with his tail wagging non-stop and a wet nose permanently glued to the ground. Jack vigorously shook a riddle, sifting out nuggets of coal to tip into a sack held open by Billy. After Tom had heaped another shovel into the contraption, Jack once again waggled away powdery duff to leave another reaping of small, shiny nuggets. Looking at his brother, he blew fed-up, saying, "Tack five, Tom, me arms are about ready to drop off here."

"Do ya want me to go on the riddle?" asked Tom.

"Nar, I'm fine, a' just want a smoke." Jack handed around a cigarette packet. Lighting up, he puffed his cheeks, asking, "This is the last bag though, isn't it?"

"Aye," broke in Billy. Glaring beyond the lads, he looked on as in the distance a security van sped across the pit yard. "Security's d-d-doing a shift ch-ch-change, mind."

"A' couldn't give a monkey's toss," said Jack, shivering his shoulders, "as too tired out to be messing around with them fuckers today, if they come ower, they come ower."

"What's the matter with ya, Jack!?" asked his brother.

"A' dinit feel nowt flash, young'n." He drew deeply on his cigarette, moaning, "a' think as coming down with summit."

Billy looked to Jack, saying, "Ya l-l-look nowt flash neither mind, J-J-Jack."

Tom broke in, suggesting, "A' tell ya what, why don't we just fuck off now with what bags we've already got filled, eh!?" The other two agreed and with a cig dangling from the corner of his mouth, Tom held a feeble bicycle steady for Billy to start stacking the thing up with hefty sacks. Once the bicycle was loaded, Jack went to grab the handlebars, but Tom stopped him in his tracks, whispering, "Hang fast, young'n, I'll get this." Billy rearranged the bags to balance, then, off they went forcing the old boneshaker across the black heaps in the direction of the pit yard. Chancing their arm, they decided to take a short cut via the pit gates despite a couple of police vehicles parked up there. Treading further into their journey, Jack leashed Mick, sending him into a doggy huff, then approaching the picket line Tom whispered, "If the cops stop us the coal's for the picket line fire, mind." Glancing at Jack he once again asked, "Are ya alright, young'n?"

Jack moaned, "A'm a' heckers like, a's aching from top ta bottom here."

Billy broke in, "Ya m-m-might have the f-f-flu, tha nars, Jack, it's kicking about."

Tom glanced back, snapping, "Billy! Is thuw pushing back there, or just hinging onta that frigging seat, or what!?"

"I'm p-p-pushing, man!"

"Why push a bit harder! Me back legs are buckling here!" They managed to skirt the police vehicles unchallenged. Rising Office Street, they turned a sharp left to briefly join a main road to go by a metal-topped bus shelter before Tom leant into the sacks to steer another left taking them down a short alleyway; after manoeuvring a tight right-handed bend, they inched along the top of East estate until they rolled into Cuba Street where their journey ended at number two. Much to Mick's delight, Jack unleashed him as they entered the yard prior to Jack stepping into the house, while Tom and Billy started emptying out the sacks into an already half-filled coalhouse. Switching on a kettle, Jack spooned coffee into a couple of cups prior to him picking out a Lemsip sachet from a separate wall cupboard to sprinkle the yellow powder into a chipped mug. Opening a fridge door, he grabbed a half-filled bottle of milk to pour out just the right amount into one of the cups, resting the bottle back to the fridge door he refused the temptation of a chicken drumstick as he waited for the kettle to boil. It didn't take long before a click sounded, and all three cups were filled with a single spoon of sugar added into Billy's whitened coffee. Picking up his own mug, Jack entered into the sitting room where he cupped his hands around the warmth of his drink as he sat facing flames of yellow that danced a palmy fire.

Holding onto their own hot beverages, Tom and Billy joined Jack. Billy handed Tom a cigarette before he leant forward offering a one to Jack, but Jack shook his head in refusal, saying, "Nar thanks, Billy, a' feel as sick as a dog."

Tom looked at his brother. "Get ya sell ta bed for an hour."

"Nar, a' might have a kip on the couch when yas gan up the club for ya dinners."

"Are y-y-ya not coming up, l-l-like?" asked Billy.

Jack shook his head slightly in reply, then facing Tom, he asked, "Will ya run is ower Lucy's later on? A' canit be arsed to be driving all ower the place."

"Why aye, what time?"

"About seven-ish."

"Aye, ne bother." Tom faced Billy, asking, "What are you doing the night then?"

"A' don't know y-y-yet, a' might ask B-B-Bev if she fancies doing owt when we g-g-gan up the club."

"Well, I'm ganna stop in the night and pack some stuff up for the weekend," said Tom, lighting up a cigarette.

"What time ya setting off Saturday, like?" asked Jack, gulping his throat with discomfort.

"About six a' clock."

Jack smiled. "Ya like it down there, don't ya?"

"Aye do a', it's a world apart from all the shit that's gan'n off 'round here."

Jack's grin stretched. "Why if ya've got any sense, yad fuck off down there for good after the strike's finished with."

"Tom wouldn't d-d-do that!" broke in Billy. "W-W-Would ya?"

"Actually, Billy, that's exactly what I'm thinking about doing, and a' might not even wait till the strike's ended neither."

Jack encouraged, "A' dinit blame ya, young'n, you go for it."

Billy sat shaking his head, moaning, "That's n-n-not good, what's Ma g-g-ganna say."

Jack stood to rest his drink onto the mantlepiece. "A' think a' might try a hot bath, it might fetch is 'round a bit." Dragging himself from the room, he moaned to each step he took up the staircase as he lethargically clasped both his hands onto a banister.

Tom drew on his cigarette, saying, "Billy, Ma says when ya gan for the bairns on Sunday, ya have ta bring them back here for their dinners and that."

"A' know, she's already t-t-told is."

"Why when ya pick them up, tack ne shit from that Marie, mind."

"A d-d-dinit, a' just get in and out of there as quickly as a' p-p-possibly can, a' canit s-s-stand looking at her n-n-now."

"And tack ne shit from that little pocked faced twat neither."

"To b-b-be fair he's n-n-never around when a' pick them u-u-up, anyway."

"Tom!? Tom!?" came from an upstairs landing.

Tom raised his eyes bellowing, "What!?"

"Thraw is a towel up, young'n!?"

"Fa fuck's sake, man!" he moaned as he stood to his feet. "It's every time he gans in that frigging bath he's got every fucker in the house running all ower the place after him!"

At Easington club, Margret, Jean, Tracy, Irene, and Debbie formed a chain on serving duty, while in the kitchen Bev stood aside Denice washing and drying a mound of crockery and cutlery. John and little Micky continuously crossed the threshold of the fire exit door while transporting an assortment of boxes from the van. Every now and then they would smile all hopeful as they eyed Jenny Black who was stood isolated at the back of the room welcoming diners with cups of tea and coffee. Tom and Billy entered the hall to join the end of a queue. Spotting them, Irene frowned slightly, thinking where on earth was her youngest at. The lads inched the line until coming to stop in front of her; smiling at the two she mumbled, "Where's our Jack?"

"At yerm," spoke Tom, "he's out a' fettle."

She repeated, "Out a' fettle!?" before asking, "What's wrong with him, like? Our Jack never gets poorly!"

"Why he is now," said Tom.

Billy broke in, "He's g-g-got the flu a' think, Ma."

She exhaled, "Flu!? A' wonder where he's picked that up at then?"

Billy joked, "Probably's from one of them W-W-Welsh cops on the picket l-l-line. Ya never n-n-nar what them buggers get up to when n-n-ne one's around."

Tom eyed his mother, murmuring, "How did the doctors gan, then?"

Leaning over, Irene smiled widely, whispering, "I've getting the all clear, it's benign, no cancerous cells found whatsoever... we'll talk about it later on though when a' get home."

Nudging Billy, Tom grinned from ear-to-ear whispering, "Ma's got the all clear from the doctors, young'n."

"Thank God f-f-for that," he breathed, all relieved. After Irene had served each with a crispy dumpling, they made their way to face Debbie who ladled out a healthy serving of mince.

Hoss rushed the room to pick up a plate prior to him joining the ever-dwindling queue as Tom and Billy tread the floor for quite some time to eventually come across an empty table, and had just sat to season their meals when Hoss joined them, frowning. "Where's Jack?"

"He's back yerm, he's owt of fettle," said Tom.

"Out of fettle?" puckered the big man picking up his cutlery. "A' hope it's nowt serious?"

"It is s-s-serious, he's got the f-f-flu," said Billy.

"I'll pop down and see him after me dinner then."

Tom smiled at his friend, saying, "Just leave it for now, Hoss, he's having a bit of a kip, pop round at teatime though." His grin widened as he continued, "Ma's getting the all clear by the way, she hasn't got cancer."

"Thank fuck for that," blew Hoss all relieved.

Bev crossed the room, politely ordering, "Lift ya plates, lads," and they raised their plates, allowing her to rub a dampened dishcloth over the tabletop. Beaming widely at Billy, she battered her eyes, asking, "What ya doing tonight, Billy?"

"Nothing really, a' w-w-was wondering if ya fancied ganning d-d-down the Trust for a game of p-p-pool?"

"Whatever," she replied before suggesting, "or, if ya fancied, we could just go back to mine to watch a video?"

"Why aye, that would b-b-be nice."

"Right, I'll pick ya up at Irene's at about seven then." Not taking her eyes from his, she grinned widely then slowly turned to walk off.

Hoss watched Bev's every step, leaning across the table, he whispered, "A' still carn't believe you've managed to pull her, like, Billy."

"How's that l-l-like?" queried Billy.

"Aye how's that like, Hoss?" broke in Tom with a huge grin.

"Nowt, nowt," returned the big man.

Billy bleated, "Nar, c-c-come on, s-s-spit it out! But be very careful of ya w-w-words, or I'll be ower this t-t-table at ya."

Hoss blushed all of fluster, saying, "Why, besides the fact she's drop dead gorgeous, she works as a doctors' receptionist and has her own car and everything."

"Do ya nar how bad that sounds?" sighed Tom. "Absolutely pathetic so it is."

"Aye, absolutely p-p-pathetic," agreed Billy.

"Sorry," sighed Hoss, blushing even deeper, "a' was just saying like, a didn't mean nowt bad by it tha nars."

After dropping Jack off at Lucy's house, Tom returned home to park up at the rear of his brother's truck. Entering into the sitting room, he was greeted by a motherly smile as Irene sat with a contented Mick on her lap. "Is our Jack okay?" she asked.

"He's fine," said Tom sitting in front of the telly. "What ya watching?"

"Minder." Irene grinned. "A' like Dennis Waterman, and that George Cole, they're so funny together."

"They are that," he said, handing his mother a cigarette.

"Are ya all packed for the weekend then, love?"

"Yeah, just about." Lighting up his cigarette he blew smoke, asking, "Where's Alan?"

"Ya've just missed him; he's gone to..." she raised her eyes to the ceiling, "...yet another union meeting." After a pause she sighed lengthily saying, "Ya do realize that one of these days ya ganna gan down to visit Pat and ya not ganna come back, don't ya?"

"Don't be daft!"

"Nor, ya will." Irene drew deeply on her cigarette. "And do ya know something, I'll be as pleased as punch if ya did–" again she blew smoke– "but never forget where ya real home is, son."

He grinned. "As if a' ever could do that, Ma."

From out of nowhere, the front door burst open, followed by three battle-clad SPG officers rushing the room with shields in one hand and cudgels drawn in the other. Tom instinctively jumped to his feet as Irene sat, panic-stricken. "On the floor!" screeched one of the officers. "On the floor! Hands behind your heads and on the fecking floor now!" Irene struggled herself to the carpet as Mick growled to attack an officer before a hefty kick to his head ended his snarling and he lay silent on his side with his whole-body twitching.

"Bastard!" yelled Tom with a boot now pressed hard against his back pinning him down helpless. Dryden waltzed into the room; lifting the visor on his hard helmet, he smiled devilish with eyes shifted back and forth between Tom and Irene before a grin stretched into an evil leer as he glared down at Mick laid out lifeless.

"Trouble with a vicious dog I see, lads?" he joked to dark grins from his fellow officers. Looking down at Tom, Dryden grasped him by the hair, and without any emotion in his voice, he beamed, "Help the gentleman up then." At once two of his colleagues dragged Tom to his feet and Dryden stood nose to nose before drawing his truncheon to lodge it hard under Tom's chin. "Where's your fecking brother!?" he snarled, and Tom's answer was to smile defiance. Dryden brought his truncheon down hard onto the top of Tom's head, sending blood streaming. Twisting his face, Dryden screamed, "Where's ya fecking brother? Where's ya fecking brother!?" Spitting in the sergeant's face, Tom grinned boldly, and despite Irene's hysterical pleading for the cop to stop, Dryden went into a total frenzy, lashing her son heavily around his head and body until he folded to the carpet in a semiconscious heap, but the assault didn't stop as the cop kept on thrashing out until a brutal blow to the side of Tom's temple sent his eyes rolling into the back of his head with blood streaming from both ears.

"Please God! Please stop! You're going to kill him!" pleaded Irene in a high-pitched hysteria.

Dryden flicked his head, indicating for his colleagues to leave the room; pressing his foot rigid on Tom's throat he side eyed Irene as he raised his baton with intent. "Do you want me to stop?"

Sobbing openly, she nodded before crying out, "Yes! Please stop! Please! My boy needs an ambulance!"

Smiling fiendishly, he stood in front of Irene, softly saying, "I may stop if you are especially nice to me." His eyes brought Irene's attentions to his trousers where he slowly unzipped his flies.

A fellow officer rushed to the door, raising, "The inspector's here, sarge!"

Dryden gently touched Irene's hair, politely saying, "Until we speak again, my dear," then breaking into a wry grin he blinked unconcerned as he looked down at Tom before turning to leave the house.

FOLLOWING MORNING

Lucy parked the firm's old Land Rover outside Jack's home, and they were sat talking when an elderly neighbour clenched his coat lapels together as he tapped on the vehicle's side window. Jack rolled down the rigid glass to be hit by a sharp waft of coldness. "Jack, there's nobody in, they're down Hartlepool hospital," spoke the man.

"Hospital!?" repeated Jack. "Ma hasn't took poorly again is she, Albert?"

"Nor it's not ya Ma, Jack, it's your young'n, the cops raided the house last night and they haven't half set about him."

Jack frowned, repeating, "Cops... Beat him up!?"

"Aye big style!" The old man cleared his throat. "I've got your Mick at mine, he's took a kicking too but a' think he's ganna be okay."

Jack sighed, "Cheers, Albert, look I'll have ta gan, but I'll pop in yours when a' get back." Facing Lucy, he mumbled, "Do ya mind running is to the hospital, love?"

"Don't be daft," she replied, forcing the vehicle into gear and speeding away.

With emotions way above trepidation, Irene stood at her son's bedside in a trance-like state rubbing her upper arms nervously. Tears ran her face as she looked down at her boy laid comatose while wired up to monitors that constantly bleeped out all sorts of medical information onto several screens. A drip was inserted into the back of his hand, snaking up a stand to where a bag hung half filled with clear liquid. Tom lay eyes closed and motionless, his face had swollen to a yellow and black bruising with a huge fluid lump the size of a fist, ballooning around his left temple. A young nurse entered the side room holding a cardboard tray hosting a couple of needles. Picking up a clip board, she studied the monitors and was jotting down readings when Irene whispered, "Any news about the X-rays yet, Rita?"

Clipping the board back to the foot of the bed she smiled encouragement, saying, "Yes, we have excellent news; Tom's skull has no fractures and there's no sign of any bleeding on the brain."

"So, when will he come around then?"

"When he's ready to," she said amidst injecting Tom with the two syringes. Facing Irene, she suggested, "Irene, why don't you go and get a catnap in the smoke room, and I'll waken you if and when there's any changes."

"No thanks, I'd rather just stay here if ya don't mind, love," she replied, rolling her teeth to chew nervously against her bottom lip.

"It's up to you, Irene, but if you feel the need for a bit of a kip, or even just a smoke please let me know, I'll be on the ward somewhere." Another reassuring beam was cast as the nurse turned to quickly leave the room.

After ten minutes had passed, Jack and Lucy rushed into the room and the instant, they eyed Tom, Lucy wept shocked while Jack stood stunned. Irene sobbed, "Look what they've done to him, Jack." She broke down completely, mumbling, "A' thowt they were ganna kill him, look at his bit face, look at it."

Teary eyed, Jack hugged his mother tight, saying, "He'll pull through, Ma, ya nar how tough he is." Approaching the bed, he sat to take his brother by the hand. Looking over his shoulder, he asked, "What did these coppers look like, Ma? Any distinct features?"

Standing in thought, she wiped her eyes before breathing deeply, mumbling, "Yes, the one who set about him had a funny shaped blob of a nose and the most hideous eyes I've ever seen, lifeless they were, there was no emotion behind them whatsoever."

Jack grit his teeth in anger. "A bet it was that Dryden!" and on those words Tom squeezed Jack's hand ever so slightly. "He can hear us!" beamed Jack. Stroking his brother's hand, he asked, "Was it Dryden who done this to ya, young'n," and once again Jack felt a weak grasp.

"Get him, Jack!" snarled Irene. "You go get him and you hurt him!"

Lucy broke in, "Don't you dare, Jack! Let the police sort this out, I'm sure there's proper procedures to go down, they carn't just get away with actions like this."

"They won't do nothing, they're all the frigging same, man, Lucy!" said Jack, rising to his feet.

"You're not doing anything, Jack," raised Lucy. "I'm telling you now, you're not."

He stood his ground, promising, "Orr but I am though! Have ya seen the state he's left him in!? Look at him, man!"

"Yes, I know, Jack, it's terrible, but if you retaliate where does it end, somebody is either going to be killed, or put in prison for a long time, I'm telling you now, you go after him and it's over between us."

Jack stood shocked; narrowing his eyes, he asked, "Is that right, is it?"

She looked straight into his eyes with determination, muttering, "Yes, it is, it's up to you, Jack, make your choice."

Jack held her stare, and with a hardening tone, he said, "A' think it's best you leave, Alan will give is a lift back yerm when he arrives."

Lucy stood, teary. "Don't do this, Jack! Please don't do this!"

"Just go, Lucy," he said, looking through her, "go on, get ya sell away!"

"Stop it now, you two!" intervened Irene.

"No, I'll not stop, Ma! If that's the way she feels, best it ends now."

Lucy whimpered, "You don't mean that, Jack."

"Yes, I do though, go-on, go."

"Right, if that's how you feel there's nothing else to say." Teary eyed, she turned to drag herself from out of the room.

"Go after her, son," said Irene, "take no notice of what a' said before, she's right."

"Nor, Ma, if she carn't accept the way I am, it's best it ends now, she nars all the shit we're going through."

"You don't mean that, it's plain ta see ya adore the lass, and she adores you too, she's just concerned at what might happen."

"Mother, I'm not running after her, end of! If she doesn't realize that we're fighting for our pure existence here, well, let's just say she's not the girl a' thowt she was."

Tom blinked open his eyes, mumbling, "Don't tark so fond, ya thick heeded bugger!"

TWO WEEKS LATER

A wind bawled strong rattling gates and coalhouse doors throughout the estate of East. At number two Cuba Street, Jack entered the sitting room, handing over a cup to his mother as she sat with Mick dozing on her lap. "Tar, son." She grinned, resting the steamy drink onto a coffee tabletop. Looking him over she couldn't help but notice his lost expression. She sighed, "Things carn't carry on like this, Jack, ya standing there as miserable as sin, ya haven't eaten or slept properly for ages, and ya've hardly stepped through that front door for the last fortnight, not even to gan picketing. Go and see her, son, sort things out with the poor lass." Jack shook his head in reply before she advised, "Ya'll leave it ower late, mind ya, and ya'll loss her forever."

Raising his cup to his mouth he blew away steam, mumbling, "She nars where a' live."

"Aye, and you nar where she lives too, it's the man's prerogative to mack the first move when making up after a fall out, not the women's."

"Just leave it Ma, please."

The stairs thumped ahead of Pat entering the room holding onto a couple of empty bowls. "Tom wants a cuppa, Ma, does either of you two want one?"

No, tar, we're good, love," said Irene, raising her filled cup. "Did he manage his broth okay?"

"Yeah, he polished the whole lot off," she said prior to entering the kitchen.

Irene shouted through, "Get ya sell some more if ya want, flowerpots, there's plenty there to gan at!"

"Thanks, I shall, it was lovely!"

Jack lit up a cigarette. "A' might pop down the club for a pint later on."

"Why, keep out of that singing end, there's nowt in that disco for you."

"Mother, if a' wanted to go in the disco end a' would, but a' don't, a's just ganna pop in the bar to meet up with Pinky, Lukey, and Jarpy."

Irene sighed deeply. "Please ya sell what ya do, Jack."

With a shake of his head he eyed at his mother, sighing, "A' will please me sell, ya've just told is a' need to get out, and now ya saying dinit!" Rising to his feet he left the room adding, "Mack ya mind up!"

She shouted after him, "Jack, by all means gan out! But divant gan galivanting all ower the place!"

"I've got ne intention of galivanting about the place!" was returned ahead of Jack's footstep sounding on the staircase.

Pat re-entered the room, asking, "Has he not come to his senses yet?"

"Why nor, a' don't think he ever will, a really think it's over between them, Pat."

"It's a shame," she said, raising her eyes to the ceiling before, "Ma?" stretched from her lips.

"What, love?"

"I've got to go back down home in the next few days for work commitments, but I'll be back up next weekend, is it okay if I take Tom back down the farm with me for a while? That's if he's fit enough to travel by next week, that is."

"You don't have to ask me things like that, love, you're both grownups, you do what's best for you two."

"Thank you." She hugged Irene, saying, "I love you, Ma."

Irene whispered in her ear, "And a' love you too, flowerpots." A clicking of a kettle interrupted the embrace and Pat left the room. Stroking Mick, Irene pointed a remote and the television lit up to Blankety Blank; once again aiming the device, the volume increased by a trio of green coloured bars showing on the screen.

Jack popped his head around the door, saying, "I'll not be lang, Ma."

"Jack, please keep out of that singing end, son, there's nowt in there but temptation."

He smiled. "I'm not going to the club, I'm just popping down Hoss' for an hour."

She returned a grin. "Good lad, mack sure ya get wrapped up properly, it's card out."

"A' will," he replied before leaving the house just as Billy entered the house.

Irene greeted, "All right, bonnie lad?"

"Yeah, ch-ch-champion."

"There's some broth and dumplings on the cooker top, get what ya want."

TWO DAYS LATER

A spectacular crack of dawn brushed a canvas sky with shades of amber that cast faint shadows around the elevated pit shafts and the surrounding chimney rooftops. Easington beach banks had woken to a slight frost as Jack straddled Mowgli while looking out to sea where he took in a flock of seagulls as they floated beak under wing in the calmness of the water. Inching along an orange glow of the horizon, a huge ferry had set sail from Tyneside and was leisurely heading south-westerly on its customary crossing to the port of Amsterdam, while closer to shore bobbed a couple of brightly coloured cobles with diligent crew members firstly hauling up, then casting out freshly baited crab pots. Twitching his fingers on a left rein, Jack clicked tongue against teeth a couple of times encouraging his black steed to walk on following a narrow pathway. Ambling for over a quarter of a mile they entered into a vast field where Mowgli's ears pricked as Jack sent him firstly to trot, then to a gallop. Jack raced the big horse around the field for a good ten minutes or more sending Mowgli blowing healthy from his flared nostrils. Pulling on the reins he sat upright easing the steed down to a steady canter. As they were travelling alongside a wooden fence, from out of nowhere, Mowgli's head unexpectedly shot up and he let out a loud snort as they stumbled upon a family of touchy rabbits. Jack slowed the horse to a walk as they met another narrow trail leading them down a steep incline to join up with a widened bridlepath that stretched the entirety of Hawthorne Dene.

At the Arkinsons' abode situated on the outskirts of Hawthorn village, Steve walked cup in hand to cross a recently fitted bespoke kitchen where he handed over the steamy drink to Julie, his devoted wife. Julie was aged in her mid-forties and was simply an older version of Lucy, possessing the exact same body shape and facial features, including identical violet-coloured eyes and a head of thick raven hair. "What's she like?" asked Steve with a look of anguish.

"She's just the same," breathed Julie, blowing her cup, "she won't eat nothing, I'm seriously thinking of taking her to the doctors, she was up till all hours this morning vomiting again."

"She's broken-hearted, love," he said, lighting up a cigarette, "a' carn't understand what's gone on between them, she won't tell me a thing."

"She needs to get back to work, Steve, take her mind off things."

"She'll not, I've asked her a million times, do you think I should go over and have a bit of a chat with Jack before I go into work?"

"Why, not likely! That won't resolve anything." Sipping from her cup, she added, "In fact, it may make matters a lot worse, knowing you."

"There must be something I can do, Julie, I carn't just sit back and watch my girl fade away, have you seen all the weight she's lost?"

"I know, but what can we do, she's pining, we carn't exactly force feed her."

He drew deeply on his cigarette, sighing, "Yes we can though, and if that's what we have to do, then so be it." Steve cracked a smile as he looked out of the window, watching Jack ride Mowgli down the driveway. He turned to his wife saying, "Speak of the devil."

Julie joined her husband's gaze, and with a huge beam she whooped, "There's only that daft bugger would have the nerve to come calling on a horse." Swiftly making her way to the door, she opened up with a stern gawk, "Can I help you?"

"Is Lucy in?"

"Yes, but I'm not too sure if I want you seeing her, Jack."

Jack's face descended to a worried frown. "Please, Julie, a' need to speak to her."

"Do you!? Will it be in her best interests if you did though, I don't want to sound too resentful, but you've hurt her so much, Jack."

"I'm not too grand me sell, man, Julie!"

"Jack; you are not going to be a handful for her all her life, are you?"

"Of course I am, but I couldn't imagine going through life without her at my side though, Julie, I love her so much, and I wouldn't, or couldn't, hurt her on purpose."

Julie broke into a smile. "I know you couldn't, what's took you so long coming over, you silly sod?"

"Sorry," he said, batting his puppy dogs all apologetic before asking, "can a' see her then?"

"Of course you can." Her grin stretched as she ushered him into the kitchen. "She's upstairs in her room, the poor soul's never left her bed since you two had your falling out."

Jack raised his eyes to the ceiling, asking, "Is it alright if I–"

Steve broke in, "Go ahead, son, and try and get her to eat something please, Jack, she's hardly eaten anything for almost a fortnight now."

Jack left the kitchen to rise a handsome staircase that curved slightly to the right, after crossing a chandeliered landing that branched either side with five-bedroom doors and a separate bathroom, he entered into Lucy's room to be met by the sound of a tap running from inside an ensuite. Lowering himself onto the edge of a bed, he looked on nervously as Lucy came into the room looking drained. The instant she eyed Jack she smiled dreamily before her legs gave way and she crumbled to the floor. Instantly, Jack rushed the room to lift her into his arms before resting her softly onto the bed. Opening her eyes tears ran her face as she mumbled, "Please don't let this be another dream."

Jack held her close kissing her face. "It's not a dream, my love." Stroking her hair away from her face, he uttered, "I'm so sorry, I should have come straight after ya, I'm just so pig headed."

She breathed deeply. "But you're here now, and that's all that matters. Please promise me, Jack, if we ever fall out again you won't let a single night pass without us making up, promise me now, because if I ever have to go through anything like this again, I will simply just die."

"We won't fall out again, but if we do a' promise not a night will pass." He smiled widely, uttering, "Let's get married after the strike, Lucy."

Widening her eyes, she asked, "Where!? And when do you think the strike will finish!?"

"I don't know when it will finish, but as soon as it does, we'll make plans."

"I'm more than up for that!"

Steve entered the room, asking, "Have you two made up then?"

She nodded, saying, "Yes! We're getting married as soon as the strike's finished, you never know with a bit of luck it may well be over before Christmas."

Steve offered his hand to Jack, saying, "Congratulations, son."

Julie rushed into the room to be met by smiles all around. "What's going on then, are you two an item again?"

Steve whooped, "Orr, they're much more than an item, love!" Hugging his wife, he added, "They're getting married!"

Julie's eyes shifted between the three, and grinning hugely she asked, "When?"

Steve beamed. "I don't know when, but it sounds to me like it may well be a Christmas wedding, just like ours was."

Lucy's face lit up. "That would be lovely if it was." She faced Jack. "What do you think about a Christmas wedding, Jack?"

"Lovely, but a wadn't count ya chickens on the strike being over and done with by Christmas though."

Jack rose to his feet. "Where are you going?" asked Lucy, almost in a panic.

"Taking Mowgli back to his stable."

"Not without me you're not." She quickly rose to her feet. "I'm not allowing you out of my sight, not for one second, not now, not ever!" She skipped the floor to enter back into the ensuite.

"But I'm on the horse, love."

"So, we can walk him back home together," came back slightly echoey.

"Okay, but we're gan'n to the fish shop later on for our dinners, I'm starving."

"Champion," echoed, followed by, "I'm bloody starving too!"

DECEMBER "M-M-MERRY CHRISTMAS!"

December bleezed in depressingly wet and windy at Easington Colliery. British Coal, backed by the Tory government, had placed a huge advertising campaign in almost all of the national tabloids, dangling a tempting carrot in the form of a substantial offer of over a thousand pounds for any miner who was willing to break the strike and return back to work, and throughout the various coalfields quite a few miners had taken up the bribe, but here at Easington Colliery, there was fewer than you could count fingers on one hand who had crumbled, and these treacherous strike breakers were labelled the **BBC** by the local pickets (**B**ack **B**efore **C**hristmas).

Lucy was sat at her desk operating her computer when Steve crossed the room to rest his hands on her shoulders asking, "Have you found it yet, love?"

"Yip, there it is, invoice number one hundred and four-nine, and it's for two thousand and fifty-four pounds plus VAT." She glanced over her shoulder, pointing out, "Dad this invoice is over nine months old, the company hasn't gone into liquidation, has it?"

He snapped, "Have they hell! The bastards just won't pay their bills!"

Jack and Hoss entered the office, with Jack raising, "Coal's there, Steve."

"Champion." He smiled on returning to sit at his desk. "Thank you, another twenty bags, is there?"

"Yeah." Jack grinned.

Steve handed over money, saying, "Give that to the kitchen fund then." Slowly running his eyes over Hoss, he asked, "You two don't fancy a ride down to Whitby on a debt collecting mission, do yas?"

"Dad! They're not!" intervened Lucy, not giving Jack a chance to answer. "You need to go through your solicitors."

Jack grinned impishly, saying, "Sorry, Steve, but I'm afraid the boss has spoken."

"Pity, there was a couple of hundred quid in it to help you on with your journey."

"How much!?" enthused Jack, causing Lucy to widen her eyes at her father.

At the club, the lasses were rushed off their feet serving meals to a lot more destitute faces than they had previously encountered. Debbie relieved Irene from her post, smiling. "Take a break, Irene."

She blew, "Thanks, love," before joining Sue at a small table at the rear of the room. Handing over a cigarette, Irene noticed a look of anxiety running Sue's face. "What's wrong, Sue, love?" she asked, presenting a flame.

Sue drew deeply on the cigarette; blowing a smoke-filled sigh, she moaned, "Take a look around the place, man, Irene, there's families in here just about starving. Do ya know in so many households this is the only meal they will receive all day, people are actually losing weight through lack of food, it's heartbreaking, the poor kids are starting to look so undernourished, and what's Christmas ganna be like for them poor buggers, eh? They're not ganna have a turkey nor nowt to tuck into, let alone a frigging present to unwrap."

Irene comforted her friend with a tight hug. "Maybe it's time to go visit our friends at County Hall again, to seek out extra funding. And I've heard through the grapevine that Jacky Charlton's going to fork out from of his own pocket for every striking miner and their families to have either a chicken or a turkey for Christmas Day."

"Who told you this, like?" asked Sue, wiping her dampened eyes to dryness.

"Alan told me, but keep it shtum, and I think the union are trying to raise money for the kids to open up a bit of a gift for Christmas morning too; it'll not be much, mind, but it'll be something for the poor bairns to open." Scrutinizing Sue, Irene sighed prolonged, suggesting, "Why don't you take a week or so off, flowerpots, give ya sell a bit of a break to recharge ya batteries, you're looking so tired out."

"Why, not likely!" whooped Sue. "Honestly I'm fine, it's just the wrang time of the month, and ya nar how down in the dumps a' get with that!"

"Sue?" stretched from Irene. "Do ya nar that abattoir man from Sunderland who we struck a deal with, with the beef and that?"

"Aye, what about him?"

"Why, do ya think he may have a few turkeys on the go so we can put a bit of a Christmas dinner on?"

"What do ya mean, open this place up on Christmas Day?"

Irene smiled. "Nor not exactly, but we could put a bit of a Christmas meal on, say, Christmas Eve afternoon, I'll get the lads to go around all the allotments collecting sprouts and winter veg and that."

Sue's eyes lit up at Irene's suggestion. Rising to her feet she beamed sharply, whooping, "A' think I've got that abattoir's phone number somewhere in my folder, Irene, a' may as well give him a tinkle now, no time like the present is there?"

NEXT DAY

Word had spread around Easington that a taxi firm from up at Peterlee had been running scabs to a pick-up point where a fleet of scab buses awaited to be escorted by police convoys into various pits. Under a two-storey carpark at Peterlee town centre, a few carloads of balaclava-clad pickets including Jack, Billy and Hoss, pulled up at a taxi rank belonging to J.H.N. taxicabs. Wielding baseball bats, three brawny pickets rushed inside a constructed wooden-clad office where they threatened the terrified staff before totally ransacking the joint, smashing up two-way radios, telephones, office furniture, and a set of cabinets, while the main body of men – including Jack, Billy, and Hoss – upended a couple of taxis before rocking a minibus onto its side ahead of them scampering off to quickly speed away.

FOLLOWING WEEK

A scab bus inched through the pit gates at Easington to faint chants of discontentment before twenty or so disheartened pickets dispatched in separate groups. Hoss, Billy and Jack were stood at the picket line, warming their hands around a fresh, shiny fire drum, when Hoss looked to Jack, saying, "Fancy ganning ower the wall for coal the night, Jack, a' need some money to pay me lecky bill."

"How much do ya owe, like?"

"Fowteen quid," he said, scratching his chin.

"I'll get ya it," said Jack.

"But a' won't be able ta pay ya back for yonks."

"Dinit worry about it, Hoss, did a' say owt about ya paying is back?"

"Are ya sure?"

"Why aye I'm sure, I'll fetch it down the morn for ya."

"Still fancy gan'n for coal though?"

"Nar, not the night, a's ganning into hospital to see Pop, he's getting a cyst, or something cut from out of his head today and they'll be keeping him in overnight."

Hoss smiled gratefully, saying, "Tell him I'm asking after him then, and thanks very much for the money."

"Aye, and t-t-tell him I'm asking after him t-t-too, Jack," put in Billy before asking, "when's Tom c-c-coming back yerm from

Pat's? He's been g-g-gone yonks now."

"A' haven't the foggiest, before Christmas a' hope," answered Jack, just as Norman Halvey approached, trying to exit the premises by means of the pit gates. Jack stretched out his arms, stopping him in his tracks. "Where do ya think thuw's gan'n, scab?"

"To the shops, and what the fuck's it got to do with you, like?"

"Not through these gates ya not, go back in there and get the cops to escort you out the scab door."

"Fuck you!" snarled Halvey.

Jack scuffed him by his coat lapels, and through gritted teeth, he threatened, "I'm not pissing about, scab, fuck off back the other way, you're not passing through our gates."

A burly cop jumped from a van, ordering, "Hey you! Get your hands off him!" But Jack held his grip. "I said remove your hands from him this instant!" repeated the officer, drawing his truncheon.

"Let the scab go, Jack," intervened Hoss, "he's not worth it, young'n." Staring directly into Halvey's eyes, Jack reluctantly released his grip.

Halvey looked around the three, smirking, "The strike's just about finished with ya fucking fools, yas have lost it big style."

Jack warned, "Don't you dare walk through them gates, Halvey, or I'll put ya fucking windows out again."

"So, that was you who did that, was it?"

"You bet ya bottom lip it was me." Jack grinned before baiting, "A' hear your lass is getting humped all ower the place over Horden, and she's telling everybody ya've anly got a little cock."

Rubbing the back of his neck, Halvey looked at the cop, saying, "I want to press charges against this man, he's really hurt my neck." The cop waved over a couple of colleagues and Jack's hands were forced up behind his back to be quickly handcuffed before he was dragged away and manhandled into the back of a police van.

Billy glared Halvey in the eye, growling, "You horrible, h-h-horrible piece of sh-sh-shit, Halvey," and the scab's response was to stand shaking his head with a wry smirk before he walked off in the direction of the pit gates.

Clutching a carrier bag, Jack entered a hospital ward to visit his grandfather when from out of nowhere, a frail old man approached him, asking, "Mister, will ya get me ball for is please?"

"Why aye," beamed Jack, "where's it at, like?"

"Over here." The old man led him to a bed. "It's gone under there somewhere."

Jack hunkered to look under the bed. "Are ya sure it's gone under here, 'coss a' canit see owt, marra?"

"Yeah, it definitely went under there."

Jack slid further under the bed with just his backside sticking up in the air when a nurse drew his attention with a succession of sharp coughs. "Excuse me, sir, what are you doing under there?"

"He's lost his ball," returned Jack, "but it's not under here." He knelt to rise to his feet, adding, "I've looked everywhere." Facing the old man, he sighed, "Sorry, mate, but a' canit see it anywhere."

The nurse tutted, "He hasn't lost his ball." She politely continued, "Alfie's just a bit confused at the moment, aren't you, Alfie?" The man lifted his shoulders with a lost expression as the nurse smiled at Jack, and with a shake of her head, she mumbled, "I've seen it all now," before she linked the old man and they turned to toddle across the ward.

Jack approached his grandfather's bedside, saying, "How are ya, Pop?"

A huge smile lit the old man's wrinkled face. "I'm fine, young'n." He noticed Jack's fresh blackeye. "Been dancing with the cops again, son?"

"Why aye, a' got locked up this morning, I've just got out."

"Why, watch what ya doing, or ya'll end up in jail just like a' was way back in the 1926 general strike."

"How long did ya get jailed for again, Pop?"

"Six months in Durham prison, and it was a proper prison in those days, not like the holiday camp it is today."

"What was it for? Ya sparked someone out, didn't ya?"

"Aye, the chief inspector of Durham police, a right shithouse he was too."

"Didn't ya do time later on in life an'll, when ya was in the Communist Party?"

The old man smiled hugely, reminiscing, "Aye, it was just after the war, we were fighting Oswald Mosley's black shirt fascists in Newcastle, and we knocked the living daylights out the bastards, a' got three months for that, ya Nanna hit the roof, calling the judge a fascist sympathizer." He chuckled aloud. "The owld hen nearly got sent down herself."

Jack tittered, "Bit of a rebel in ya day, weren't ya, Pop!?"

"A' was way more than that, Jack." His eyes twinkled as he continued, "A' wasn't always an ard fart like I am today, tha nars, just a blink of an eye ago a' was just like thuw is, daft as a brush and frightened of bugger all."

"Good old days eh!?" "Believe you me, there was nothing good about those days, bonnie lad, and there's nowt good'll come about the current state of affairs neither, mark my words it won't, yas are heading into a disaster."

"We'll see." Jack smiled. "Anyway, when ya coming yerm?"

"Now! If ya could sneak is out under that coat of thine; I'm bored shitless in here, and ya've got to gan down the corridor to a smoke room for a puff, they'll not even let ya have a drag in bed."

"That's in case ya burn the ward down, man, Pop, there's oxygen lines and all sorts of inflammable shit inside here, tha nars."

"Aye whatever, did ya fetch is owt to eat in, a's bloody starving?"

"Aye." He handed over a carrier bag. "Ma's sent a corned beef and potato pie in for ya."

"Champion!" he said, opening a side drawer to carefully place the package alongside his cigarettes. "I'll have that later on when a' gan for a smoke to watch the telly. Orr, is ya nanna still staying at yours 'till a' come yerm?"

"Aye, she's getting waited on hand and foot."

The old man smiled. "Well good for her, I'm glad some bugger is!"

ONE WEEK LATER

Up on the windswept heights of the Peak District, evening winds howled strongly, scattering snow to form drifts up against drystone walls and isolated buildings. Smoke blew at an angle from a trio of chimney stacks at the Turners' farm as Pat and Tom lay naked under bedsheets with her head snuggled against his pecs. Stretching to a bedside table she passed a glass over to Tom along with a couple of rather large torpedo-shaped tablets. "That's the last of them, love." She smiled. "Your course is all done and dusted with now."

Popping the pills one at a time, he moaned, "Thank God for that, it's like swallowing a pint glass necking them bloody things."

"Have you given anymore thought about what we are doing over the Christmas period, Tom?"

"Yeah, a' would like us to gan back up yerm for Christmas dinner and come back down here for over the New Year."

"Champion, I can show you off at our young farmers' dance on New Year's Eve then!"

"Orr, God," he grumbled, reaching to light up a couple of cigarettes. Handing one over, he continued, "A' couldn't think of nowt worse, drinking bloody cocktails as women tark all posh while kissing each other on the side of their cheeks."

She laughed. "It's not like that, silly, it's just young people enjoying themselves, and believe me it can get a bit rowdy at the end of the night too."

"Or, why that's something to look forward to a' suppose then, there'll not be any coppers there, will tha?"

She smiled. "Why no, just farmers." Drawing on her cigarette she put on a serious face, baiting, "We'll have to get you one of those nice tweed dress suits and a matching shirt and dicky."

Tom looked at her in disbelief, snapping, "Don't tark sa fond! I'd rather gan in me ard pit oweralls and pit boots than to wear one of those wretched things."

Pat frowned. "Tom... you're not going to be this miserable all our life's, are you?"

"A' divant nar, probably's," he said straight faced before they both burst out giggling which led to a lengthy kiss.

"Put some coal on the fire, love?" she whispered, pecking on his earlobe, and Tom jumped naked from the bed to throw half a scuttle of coal onto an already glowing fire before he shivered his way back across a stone-clad floor to join Pat back under the warmth of the bedsheets.

Cigarette in mouth, Pat left the bed. Wrapping herself into a dressing gown, she smiled over her shoulder, saying, "I'm going to have a bath."

"Leave the watter in for is then?" he asked, drawing deeply on his smoke.

"Tom, the bath is humongous, just get in with me." Quickly tiptoeing from the room, she entered into a white tiled ensuite where an oval shaped corner bath rested deep and huge; the instant she turned on a tap steam slowly rose to mist the room.

Tom shouted through, "Pat!?"

"What!"

"Dinit put any of that bubble bath stuff in please, it macks me eyes sting!"

TWO DAYS LATER

A soft picket line was filled with groups of disheartened pickets. Christmas was rapidly approaching and thoughts of families and loved ones overpowered a now almost meaningless sight of a couple of scab buses passing through the gates. Jack, Hoss, and Billy were footing it up Office Street when a police van slowly approached from the other direction with its passenger window wound fully down. Dryden sat smiling as he participated in his usual routine of flashing money at the pickets, but this time Jack snapped – picking up a half brick, he cast it crashing against the side of the vehicle, instantly the van screeched to a halt with Dryden and half a dozen of his colleagues jumping out. Jack grinned at the others before scampering away in the opposite direction to his friends, with the officers hunting him in close pursuit. Turning right at the bottom of Office Street, he sprinted along the side of the pit wall; after glimpsing over his shoulder he entered into Cuba Street, again he glanced over his shoulder before slackening to a stop to slowly pivot, facing his pursuers. Dryden stood to the forefront, baton drawn at the ready, but unknown to the officers Jack had lured them into a trap as to their rear thirty or more pickets blocked off the entire bottom of the street all armed with cricket bats, baseball bats, pickaxe handles and other weapons. Another forty, perhaps even more, pickets appeared at the top of the street, they too were armed to the teeth as they stood menacingly. Jack stepped forward, saying to the cops, "You lot keep out of this! This is between me and that evil twat!" and to Dryden's astonishment the cops lowered their truncheons and backed away. Jack grinned, and through gritted teeth, he snarled, "Come on then, ya cowardly piece of shit! Let's see what ya made of now!" Advancing towards one another, Dryden swung his baton at Jack's head, but he ducked to grab the cop around his midriff; after a struggle he forced Dryden to the ground, straddling him he ripped away his helmet, then clenching his fists to white knuckles he was more than ready to pound him senseless when thoughts of Lucy shot his mind, and he slowly released his grip on the cop to stand back towering over him.

Dryden struggled back up to his feet, seething, "Come on! Come on! Finish what you fecking started, you dirty northern ponce! Come on, finish it!"

Jack smirked carefree saying, "A' just did," before he slowly turned to walk away with his comrades following.

CHRISTMAS DAY

Bing Crosby crooned White Christmas at number two Cuba Street. Red and green paper streamers stretched alongside balloons from all four corners of the sitting room ceiling to meet at a centralised rose bowl. Along the walls, hundreds of Christmas cards ran on strings of wool, while a freshly felled Christmas tree, that Irene's two sons had somehow provided from heaven knows where, took up a whole corner, exhibiting a variety of fairy lights that blinked different colours to twinkle betwixt assortments of baubles, Christmas tree toys, and glittering tinsel of metallic gold and silver. A collection of Santa Claus figurines, puppet type reindeers, and pot snowmen filled a hearth alongside a sprinkling of silver glitter, with an empty sherry glass stood aside a couple of half-eaten carrots. In the dining room steaming vegetables were rested inside metal serving trays and bowls that stretched a sideboard top. The Gilroys' Christmas table was packed. Donning paper hats, Billy, Bev and his two girls were positioned alongside Pat and Tom; across the table sat Jack and Lucy next to Hoss, Margret, and young George. Pop and Ma Garside sat opposite one another, while Irene was seated at one end of the table with Alan facing her from across the other side with Mick sat at his feet.

"Where's all these chairs come from, Ma?" asked Jack.

"The Colliery Club, John and Micky fetched them down for is yesterday, they've been in the outer house all night."

"Who, John and Micky!?" joked Jack, only to be nudged slightly by Lucy.

"Nor, ya daft bat, the chairs!"

Tom looked down at a huge turkey, asking, "Where's the leg a' lamb gone?"

"I gave it to Liz Ord, they needed it more than us, with them having a new addition to their family and that, besides, there's more than enough turkey there for us to gan at." She looked to Alan, asking, "Are ya ganna do the honours, love?" Glancing at the table she encouraged, "Help ya sells to the veg and Yorkshires then, there's plenty more in the kitchen and there's a separate jug of mint gravy in there an'll."

"These sprouts look lovely, Ma," said Lucy, ladling sprouts coated in hot butter and shavings of crispy bacon.

Irene beamed, "Thanks, pet, they were pulled fresh from out the allotment yesterday, and they've had a good frost on them, so they should taste nice and tender."

Pat spooned roast tatties to the plate joining mini heads of cauliflower. "Them roasties look perfect, Ma," she said with a grin.

Irene returned a broad smile of her own. "Thanks, love, they're done in the usual beef dripping, as always."

Margret filled Hoss' and George's plates before starting on her own. Grinning widely she said, "Those tatties do look nice, Irene, nice and crispy."

"Thank you, our Tom grew them especially for Christmas Day."

"And me too, Ma," broke in Jack.

"Me too, my arse," chuffed Tom.

"Language! There's bairns at the table," ordered Irene, widening her eyes at her eldest.

Alan placed a huge serving tray into the middle of the table, saying, "Some turkey there, help ya sells."

After all the plates were filled, they tucked into their Christmas dinner, with Billy commenting, "That s-s-stuffing's absolutely lovely, Ma."

"Aye is it," agreed Bev, "best I've ever tasted that is, Irene."

Once again Irene cracked a smile, saying, "Thank you." Looking around the children, she enthused, "Are you enjoying it, kids!?" and they all replied with hamster cheek nods. Irene then looked on at Hoss with a concerned frown. "Everything okay, Hoss?"

He beamed, "Yeah, everything's champion, Ma, thanks."

Unconvinced, she blinked, "Is ya dinner all right?"

He grinned. "It's lovely."

"So why are ya not humming for then?" she asked, slightly alarmed.

"A' don't do that anymore, Ma." He grinned. "but the dinner is lovely, and I'll be having seconds straight after I've finished this one."

"How'y then it's time for ya Christmas toast, Ma," encouraged Jack, but Irene shook her head in a blushed silence.

"No, come on," said Tom. Clapping to a rhythm he encouraged the whole table to chant, *"Speech! Speech! Speech! Speech! Speech!"*

Irene raised her glass, and after puffing her cheeks, she toasted, "Well... who would have thought that sitting here this time last year, we would have had to encounter the turbulent atrocities like what we are currently going through this year, and though there has been so much heartache and despair everywhere, this strike has brought fresh faces to our table, special, lovely faces, and there is new found love around the table too." She beamed widely. "There's Hoss and Margret," her face lit up saying, "and there is Billy and lovely Bev here–" her smile stretched even further– "then there's our Jack and Lucy, and our Tom and Pat, but there's also another love here, and that is my love for each and every one of you sat around this table, and that includes this wonderful man here," she cast an affectionate beam across table at Alan, purring, "who I love so, so much."

"Me too, love," he said, returning a devoted grimace.

"But we shouldn't forget loved ones we've lost neither." Raising her glass she looked directly at Hoss, toasting, "To loved ones lost." They all joined glasses raised to missing loved ones when Irene upraised her glass further, whooping, "Merry Christmas everybody!"

Merry Christmas was returned in unison, except that is for Billy, who trailed just a tad flash with his own... "M-M-Merry... Christmas!" ....

EPILOGUE

After the Christmas of '84 had past, despite the most ardent of the strike's supporters holding out steadfast, everyone knew deep down that the outcome was inevitably going to end in defeat, yet still the dispute dragged on into the March of '85. Over the weeks and months, once lively picket lines had diluted to an almost pathetic, half-hearted few, as men feared not only for their own safety, but also for an additional threat that they would be instantly dismissed if they found themselves arrested in or around any of British coal sites, as government-backed police forces intensified their heavy-handedness by arresting as many men as they possibly could.

The girls at the kitchen carried on with their voluntary duties, relentlessly feeding the masses right up to the last day of the strike, and after the strike had finished, they became more politically minded than what they had ever done before, with lots of female councillors elected in forthcoming elections on both Parish and County councils.

Out of two thousand six hundred men who worked at Easington Colliery fewer than fifty broke the strike, and out of these fifty strike-breakers, thirty-four were actual NUM members with the other sixteen belonging to other unions. Some men chose not to return back to the mines after the strike, and that included Jack and Tom Gilroy, with Jack deciding to work alongside his future father-in-law at his drilling company, while Tom left the village to reside in the Peak District as he too joined his future in-laws; and after time spent studying firstly at college, then university, he excelled in his pursuit at becoming a first-rate farmer.

The atmosphere at Easington pit was never the same after the strike, animosity between the miners and management was high, and at times bitter, as scabs were protected to the point that a man could lose his job for just having the slightest of arguments with them; yet still, most of the scabs took early redundancies to leave the pit and indeed the village for good.

The final nail in the coffin for Easington Colliery came when the pit, despite it making a huge profit, closed for good in the April of 1993, propelling the village into the depths of despair and hardship, which to this day it has never really recovered from. For the instant the mine had closed, all the banks and building societies uprooted and deserted the place, once thriving shops closed down to be left boarded up, while most of the pubs and clubs shut down and were either completely demolished or vandalized beyond repair, leaving the village and its community, physically, and mentally scarred.

SPECIAL ACKNOWLEDGEMENTS

This book, though only a novel, is dedicated to all those striking miners, both dead and alive, who stayed out steadfast throughout the turbulence of a year-long struggle. May God bless you all. And to all the woman volunteers who worked tirelessly at feeding the miners and their families throughout numerous kitchens spread across our once proud coalfields, a special thank you goes out to all of you for all your hard work and tremendous commitment that you had shown throughout the entirety of the dispute, as without your selfless actions the men would have been starved back to work within the strike's infancy. A special thank you goes out to Karen Thomson for your wonderful artwork on my book cover, and my heart held appreciation goes out to Robert Huitson, Alan Cummings, and Pat Mccarthy for taking up their precious time in helping me along with my book. And we should never forget, lads and lasses, that, "Ding Dong! the Wicked Witch is Dead!" ... Now you all take care.

Printed in Great Britain
by Amazon